THE MURDER TRAIL

THE MURDER TRAIL

A DC IZZY WILDE CRIME THRILLER
BOOK 1

DG PENNY

RIVERTREE PRINT

20231207.001.1

MAY 2023

THE FOREST OF BOWLAND, LANCASHIRE

ONE

When Rosie Wilson saw the stranger emerge from behind the shed in the yard, her stomach turned over. Caxton Farm was a quarter mile from the road, at the end of single-track lane. They didn't get casual visitors. Th barely got visitors at all. Rosie would have liked more, Mike didn't hold with strangers.

Rosie stood at the window of her daug bedroom, watching the man look around; as if ch whether he was alone.

Stop it! He's lost, that's all. Nothing mor follow the footpath then come down our lane b

Rosie gripped the handle of the vacur tighter, as if she could use it as a weapon. Sh the cot, where Grace lay on her back, a spread as if she was doing a free-fall parac' was asleep. The soft humming of the vacu its magic, after all the rocking and cooin'

The man had moved when Rosie

she stayed rooted to the spot, wishing the dogs were still around. They'd have been barking their heads off by now.

She knew she should run downstairs and check the doors. Mike usually locked them if he knew he'd be out all day, but sometimes he forgot. The farmhouse sat in rural Lancashire, but it had the latest technology. CCTV cameras, and trackers on all the equipment. It might be off the beaten track, but not entirely off the grid – just some of it.

Rosie wondered where the man had come from. The nearest footpath was a distance from the farmhouse. It crossed the top eighty acres where a copse of oak and ash stood, but you couldn't see the house from there. The occasional rambler came down the farm lane despite the PRIVATE sign at the top gate. Sometimes they found their way to the house. If Mike was here, he'd send them packing. Rosie was more understanding. But not today.

The man turned away, spoke to a girl who came from behind the shed to join him. She appeared to be eight or nine years old, dressed in a blue waterproof coat, jeans and boots. He held a rucksack in one hand, the other out for the girl to take, and she smiled. When the man turned back to the farmhouse he was also smiling. The simple presence of the girl eased Rosie's concerns. She looked beyond the river to the top of the slope where the footpath lay. They must have taken that way, or she would have seen them descend the track to the house. Mike's tractor crawled along the slope. Behind it, a spreader threw pellets to either side. The slope was too steep for growing crops, but ideal for sheep. The sound of the

tractor came and went on the breeze. She expected Mike to return for lunch soon, because he had forgotten to take the tin box Rosie had left on the kitchen table for him. The thought of his return comforted her. Except soon, suddenly seemed a long time.

A knock came at the side door Rosie and dropped the vacuum hose, the clatter on the floor making her jump. Her heart beat fast as she descended the stairs.

The knock came again, more insistent.

Rosie glanced at the dresser in the hallway where keys lay tangled together in a bowl. Over a score, some rusted, others more recent. She didn't see a key in the front door, which meant Mike had locked it from the other side when he left. She hoped he had done the same with the other doors. Then she scolded herself. *They're lost, that's all. And the man has his daughter with him.* Rosie started forward, setting her face into a smile, which faded as the door of the boot room opened.

The man was ordinary-looking, with brown hair grown a little long. She would probably walk right past him without a second glance on the street. His daughter was different. Long red hair that curled like some pre-Raphaelite painting, bright green eyes and a sweet face.

"What were you doing in my shed?" It just came out. Rosie meant to say, 'Do you want something?' Instead, *that* came out.

He smiled. "I'm sorry to intrude. We were walking along the footpath and ran out of water. I was looking for a tap."

"Well, we don't have one behind the shed. It's at the

back of the house." Rosie wondered if she was telling him too much, but it was only a tap.

"Could I trouble you for a glass of water for my daughter? And then we'll be on our way."

Rosie wanted to slam the door in his face, but she was more afraid of appearing impolite than she was of him. He wasn't much taller than her, slimly built and a little pasty-faced. His voice was nondescript, lacking any accent. Not local, then. He didn't look like the footpath type, but it took all sorts. She glanced down at his daughter, who offered a shy smile. Rosie stepped aside, so they could enter the house.

"What's your name, sweetheart?" she asked.

"Cally," said the girl. She glanced at her father, then said nothing more.

"The kitchen's through here, on the other side of the hall."

"We'd better slip our boots off," said the man. "They're a bit muddy."

Rosie almost told him not to bother, then changed her mind. She had washed the stone slabs of the hall only an hour since, so waited while they untied their muddy boots and walked through the wide hall in their socks.

She glanced at the boots then, because it was her nature, picked them up and set them neatly with the others before following them through the hall. It was not quite up to manor house standards, but nice all the same. The staircase rose to a turn and then doubled back, its dark wooden railing smooth from the touch of many hands over the years. She and Mike had lived here since his father retired and passed it on. Wilson after Wilson doing the same for over a century. Good Lancashire farming stock. Or so Mike claimed. Rosie's family had taken to it more recently. She'd met Mike when she went to a dance in Clitheroe, organised by the local Young Farmers branch. Rosie hadn't fancied him that first night, even though she'd let him kiss her. She'd have let him go further if he'd wanted, but he hadn't. Not on that first date, anyway. Sometimes it takes time for love to spark. Rosie was unsure if it had yet. But her life on the farm was good, and Mike gave her space for outside interests.

She went to the kitchen doorway. The girl sat on the edge of the big sofa, hands in her lap. The man stood at the sink, two glasses in his hands, the rucksack at his feet with the top open. He put the glasses down, then sprinkled something into one of them. When he turned and saw her watching, he held the glass up.

"Isotonic," he said. "It'll perk Cally up in no time. We're very grateful for your kindness."

"You're welcome," Rosie said. "Is water all right, or would you prefer a cup of tea? Or coffee? I might have some cake, too." She closed her mouth with a snap, aware she was trying too hard.

"Tea would be lovely," said the man.

He reached into his jacket, and for a second Rosie's heart pattered in her chest. But all he pulled out was a mobile phone. He stared at the screen before putting it on the kitchen counter.

"Sorry, we don't get any signal down here," said Rosie apologetically, as if it was her fault.

"We're used to that when we follow these trails."

"Do you do a lot of walking?" Rosie filled the kettle and set it on the Aga, then put three tea bags into the pot. She took two mugs from their hooks and set them on the counter.

"Every chance we get. We've done a few further south, Offa's Dyke and the Cotswold Way. I'd like to walk the Pennine Way, but that had best wait until Cally's older."

"How far have you come today?" The kettle started to whistle and Rosie poured hot water into the teapot, swirled it and replaced the top. She snugged a knitted cosy over it.

"Only five miles. We're heading to Beacon Fell Country Park, then hoping to get a taxi to Preston. Home tomorrow."

"It's a fair walk to the country park, and steep. Where is home?" Rosie felt more relaxed now. The man seemed harmless, and his daughter was sweet. Perhaps five miles had been too much for her, because she seemed to have fallen asleep on the couch, slumped into a corner. Rosie wanted to lie her down more comfortably, but stopped herself. Not my daughter. Not my responsibility.

"London," said the man. His voice sounded different, harsher than before, and Rosie moved away from him.

"I'll just tell my husband we have visitors." Rosie went into the hallway and reached for the walkie-talkie they used, instead of mobile phones, when Mike was working.

"Fuck that."

Not the same harmless man who had stood in the kitchen. Rosie moved faster, but before she could reach the walkie-talkie a hand grasped her shoulder, and something slammed into her side. When she looked down, there was blood dripping onto the floor she had so recently cleaned.

She swung around, aiming a punch at the man, but he blocked it easily. Rosie saw what he had struck her with. It was an old, rusted hand scythe. The pain in her side spiked at the thought of the curved blade slicing into her.

"What do–" It was all she got out before the man swung again.

Rosie's last thought was of her daughter asleep upstairs. Grace would wake soon and expect her snack and a story. She tried to roll over, making some effort to protect herself, but darkness swirled around her as she felt the man tugging at her clothes.

"No..." she tried to say, but nothing came.

As the last of her consciousness faded, she heard a sharp cry from the baby monitor and tried to say the word again, but everything was too much effort, and she gave in to the relentless darkness that awaited for her.

* * *

The man stood beside the cot and looked down at the wailing infant. The crying disturbed him for reasons that came only slowly. Just as most thoughts came slowly to him. When the reason surfaced from the sluggish swamp of his mind, he realised the crying reminded him of his estranged children. Both girls, like this one. Both of whom had cried, like this one. He knew it was why he had taken Cally when he found her. She had cried a lot at first, but that had faded. She was better now, but also starting to ask questions. The kind he couldn't, or didn't want to, answer.

For a long time, he did nothing as he tried to work out exactly what it was he should do, unaware of the blood that dripped from his fingers onto the pale pink carpet.

The girl looked so young, so innocent, so pretty. He thought of Cally downstairs, recalling how he had found her. It hadn't been the first time he had killed, but it had been the first time the voice spoke to him. The first time anyone offered him a purpose in a life that had drifted for too long. Taking the child had been almost accidental, but that too had changed his life.

That house had been nothing like this one. A semi in Brighton, built in the 60s, with small rooms. The couple who lived there had done their best. Garden borders filled with flowers, and a small shed out back. The lawn had been recently cut. He had smelled the grass through the open back door. The estate sat north of the city, hard against the Downs. There had been no girl with him that day, so the woman who opened the door had been more suspicious. As he stepped forward, she tried to punch him in the face, but there was no strength to the blow. Looking back, everything had been too fast. And then he'd heard a cry, just as he heard a cry today. He didn't know what the girl's name was, but he called her Cally because he liked the way it sounded. Now she knew nothing of where she came from. But there were those questions all the same. The kind he couldn't answer. He had taken her with him when he'd killed before. Five times. Six now. Each time, Cally slept through the slaughter. It was never his choice. Just as the victims were never his choice. The voice picked them. Told him where to go, and what to do. That voice would tell him what to do now, if only he could get a signal on his phone.

As he carried the child downstairs he glanced at the dead woman sprawled naked across the floor, and turned the infant so she wouldn't see the sight. He rocked her, made cooing noises, and slowly she settled until only tiny sobs emerged.

He went into the kitchen, unsure what to do about Cally. If he left her sleeping, the police would find her when they came. Did she know too much about him? He was still trying to decide, when the sound of a tractor pulling up in the yard made it for him. He looked at the front door, looked at Cally, then turned and ran. Out through the side door. Not enough time to pull his boots on and lace them up, so he slid his feet into wellingtons two sizes too big, and rushed out just as the engine of the tractor stuttered into silence.

He ran, the infant bouncing in his arms.

He stopped behind the barn until he heard a shout of anguish, then started to run again.

Splashing across the shallow river. Running up the hill and into a wood. Running for his life.

TWO

It was Detective Constable Izzy Wilde's first day off in two weeks. She had planned to sleep late, but dreams of her dead sister woke her a little after dawn. She lay in her double bed, a place that had never seen another person lie beside her, and watched as the coming of daylight creep across the ceiling. It arrived early at this time of year.

Izzy tried not to think of Gabi but, as always, failed. Memories of the final time they were together, laughing at the prank they were about to play. Memories of how everything had turned to disaster. Izzy pushed the swirling thoughts away with an effort of will.

Finally, the chaos in her mind receded, and she slipped into a deeper sleep. When she rose a few hours later, she went for a run, pushing herself hard to drive out the last of the memories. She ran narrow side-roads that reached out from Goosnargh, revelling in the landscape that lay around her. Her mind stilled, until all she knew was the rhythm of her feet on the road, the kiss of the breeze against her skin, the sound of birds and the occasional passing car. She waved when someone waved at her. Izzy knew many of the locals, but was close to none.

She was in the shower when her mobile rang. Izzy reached out, answered it and listened.

"When was this?" she asked.

She listened some more, stepped out of the shower, and thumbed the screen of her phone to open a map.

"It says twenty minutes, but I can do better than that."

She waited, then nodded and hung up. She dressed in the clothes she had discarded the night before, and was in her car within sixty seconds. She was on the Inglewhite Road five seconds after that.

She knew the farm. There had been a quad bike stolen a few months before, and Izzy had been sent because this was considered her patch. She had taken a report and filed it, sure the quad bike would be long gone. This time, it was something she couldn't file and forget.

A man had called 999 at 10:17 that morning, the 13th of May, and asked for an ambulance. The dispatcher had done her job and managed to get what she could from him. A woman on the floor, covered in blood. Blood everywhere. The man said it was his wife, Rosie. He was Mike Wilson. Caxton Farm.

Izzy braked hard as a tractor emerged from a field. She leaned on the horn and went around it, her wheels throwing up mud. The tractor driver gave her the finger. She offered two in return.

Fifteen minutes after leaving her house, she saw a sign for the farm and skidded into a narrow driveway. Tarmac at the top, but it soon turned to dirt. She had to stop to open a gate. Left it open, so those coming behind wouldn't have to do it.

She glanced at the farmhouse nestled in the valley. It looked peaceful, but she knew different.

The front door was open when she stopped in the yard behind a tall blue tractor with a piece of machinery hooked up to it. She opened the boot of her car where her forensic suit lay, but as she did so a man emerged from the house. She recognised him from her previous visit. He was tall, broad across the shoulders, and covered in blood. On his hands. On his clothes and face. Izzy held her hands up to make him stop.

"Please remain where you are, Mr Wilson. Can you tell me what happened here?"

He stared at her for half an minute, his eyes tracking her as if he couldn't believe they had sent a woman. A young woman at that, slight of build, with dark hair normally tied in a plait behind her head, but which now hung loose across her shoulders. Izzy knew men found her attractive, but ignored the fact. Ignored the men, except now she could not. She had a job to do.

"Please, Mr Wilson," she said.

"She's in here. Rosie's in here." He turned and went inside.

Izzy followed, stopped in the open doorway and peered into the wide hallway. She realised she had forgotten to clip her body-cam on, but it was too late.

13

What she saw made her swallow and take a deep breath. Mike Wilson held his wife in his arms. Her head lolled, displaying a deep gash across her throat. There were other wounds, but only the one at her throat, and another on her side, looked deep. She was naked, her clothes folded neatly beside her as if she had removed them and was ready for bed. They were covered in blood.

"Mr Wilson, I need you to let her go now and step away, please."

Izzy stayed on the flagstone doorstep. She toggled her radio, but got only static. When she checked her phone, she saw it had no signal either. She wondered how out in the sticks she had to be for neither to work. But there had to be a landline somewhere because the man had called this in.

This. Mike Wilson. His wife. He was still cradling her. A domestic; or something else?

"Where is your telephone, Mr Wilson?"

He looked at Izzy as if seeing her for the first time, his eyes bright with pain.

"What have I done?" He looked around at the blood. "What have I done?"

"The telephone, sir?" Izzy almost added, 'It's only blood,' but stopped herself in time. Not what he would want to hear at that moment.

"Over there, on the dresser." His voice was dull, emotionless.

Izzy had to step inside, but set her feet delicately, trying to avoid the blood. She saw other footprints where someone hadn't been so careful. They might be Mike

Wilson's, but they could also belong to the perpetrator. She told herself to make no assumptions. Izzy silently cursed. Evidence was already compromised. This was a fuck up. She knew they should have sent someone more experienced, but she had been the closest. She was only eighteen months out of uniform, but knew how to do her job.

She saw the telephone on the far side of the hallway and circled around to it, stepping high, watching where she set each foot. She lifted the receiver, and dialled the number for Preston police station, knowing it would be quicker than going through despatch. It was the first time she'd had to use a house phone to report in, but the lack of a mobile or radio signal meant it was her only means of contact.

"I'm at the scene," she said when she was put through to Detective Inspector Harry Gray. "How long until an ambulance and reinforcements arrive?"

"Your guess is as good as mine, Izzy. You know how it is, but they'll know to prioritise. What's it like there?"

"Fucked, boss. The woman's dead, and I can't get her husband to let her go. There's blood everywhere, up the stairs, through into a big kitchen. He keeps saying it's his fault, and he's not wrong. He's walked it all over the house. I'm trying not to touch anything, but I need CSI here now."

"On their way. The whole team's on its way, but it'll take them a good half hour at least. Can you manage until then?"

"Looks like I'll have to."

"Leave your radio open so we can hear you," said the DI.

"There's no signal, boss. Pass that on to the others. Look, I have to go. I may have to compromise the scene. I can't see any other way of doing it. I'll step away once the cavalry arrives, but I must find out what happened here first."

"It's a tough call, Izzy, but you're doing good. Keep it up."

She put the receiver down, but left it off the hook. For a second, she stood listening but heard no sirens. She was on her own.

Do it, she told herself.

She got as close to Mike Wilson as possible, and shook his shoulder.

"Mr Wilson, this is doing no good. I need to talk to you."

He turned and looked up at her, his eyes wild, madness and anger in them. She didn't know the man well, but the anger worried her most. He might lash out if she tried to make him move. Izzy knew she could take care of herself. Two years in uniform had taught her that, but getting into a fight in the hallway would only make a bad situation worse.

"Help is on its way," she said. "I need you to move away from your wife, please." Her hand was still on his shoulder, and she felt his tension.

"When did you find her, Mr Wilson? Did you call emergency services straight away?"

"Checked on her first," he said. At least he was talking

now. "Did CPR, then..." His voice trailed off. "We learned it in Young Farmers. Lots of accidents on farms. But..." He shook his head.

Now he had started to talk, she wanted to keep him going. Find out as much as she could, while everything was fresh in his mind.

"Did you see anyone else when you returned to the house?"

He shook his head again. "Came back for my snap. Rosie always puts it ready for me, but today I forgot." He wiped a hand across his eyes to clear tears. It left more blood on his face. "I'd've been out until five or six otherwise. There's a lot of work to do on a farm. It never stops."

He straightened up, and Izzy increased the pressure on his shoulder, relieved when he grunted and stood. He stared down at the body of his wife.

"She's gone, ain't she?"

"We need to wait for the paramedics, Mr Wilson." Rosie knew the procedure was to check for a pulse, but she didn't want to do that in front of him. Besides, he was right. Rosie Wilson was dead.

Now Izzy heard the sirens. Distant, but on their way. Sound travelled strangely in these hills, and the roads twisted and turned. But on their way.

"Where's Grace?" he said. "Have you found her?"

"Who's Grace?"

"My daughter." He looked around, his gaze jumping from place to place. "Where is she? I went upstairs, but she weren't there. Where is she?"

He pulled away from Izzy. She grabbed at him, but he was already hammering up the stairs. That was why there were bloody footprints on them. But how many sets? Had he killed his wife, and this was all for show? But the daughter? Grace?

Given the opportunity, Izzy leaned over and placed two fingers on the woman's throat. She waited, but felt no pulse. She straightened up and went into the big kitchen, stepping carefully to avoid the blood. She was looking for something to lay down, to make a safe path. Bin bags. Plastic sheets. Anything. What she found instead, was a girl lying on the couch.

She tiptoed back into the hallway and called up the stairs, "Mr Wilson, your daughter's down here in the kitchen."

He came down fast, three treads at a time, almost knocking her over as he went past. Izzy turned to see him standing over the sleeping girl.

"See, she's all right. Must have slept through everything."

He glanced at her with a scowl, and Izzy stepped back.

"That ain't my daughter. Grace is only eleven months old. That ain't her!"

THREE

The kid began to cry as the man entered the wood at the top of the bank, and he questioned whether it was a mistake to take the infant. Except Cally was growing up and becoming curious. This morning, she had mentioned her distaste for walking. Not so long ago, she would never question his decisions. Based on the news reports when he stole her away, he knew she would soon turn nine. She'd start asking for lipstick and short skirts. In a few years, she'd be attending high school and looking at boys differently. For a long time, the two of them had remained inconspicuous. He had changed his alias twice, but kept Cally's name. How could he explain it to her if he hadn't? He knew he should have been less lenient before fleeing the farmhouse, but he couldn't kill her. Watching her grow up reminded him too much of his own girls. Despite being married to Tracy for five years, he remained clueless about the perceived wrongdoings that had led to their separation. Self-reflection wasn't his strong suit. For him, life was a monotonous grind, at least until he discovered the voice. Things became simpler after that, except for moments like this.

He set the wailing infant down on a pile of dry leaves and pulled out his phone, then cursed. No signal. Not even a single bar. He held it up and moved his hand around. The wails of the kid were starting to annoy him. He could feel them buzzing into his skull like an electric saw.

He turned away and walked further uphill. The woodland was well managed, with occasional piles of logs cut from felled trees. He wondered if it belonged to the farm. Wondered if the woman ever came up here. He also wondered what she had done that meant she had to die, what she had done to anger the voice at the end of a cheap burner phone. He never questioned the voice, nor gave any thought to why he was asked to kill. There were no explanations; no justification. Just a package in the post. Everything explained. The details, the method itself, were left up to him. The only instruction was not to bring a weapon. Not to buy anything that could be traced. So he made do with whatever objects he could find. And he liked to walk, so he approached every location on foot.

He stopped abruptly, so lost in his fantasy he'd almost walked out onto the road. A car blared its horn as it rushed past, and he moved backwards until he couldn't be seen. This time, when he waved the phone around, he got a signal. Only two bars and 3G, but it would do. He tagged the eight pictures he had taken. One of the woman when she came out of the kitchen the first time. The others showed her on the floor, the first with her fully dressed but bleeding. Later, she was naked. There were two close-ups of the wounds. The original one had flakes of rust around it. Then the others. He hoped eight would be enough.

He waited as the phone tried to send the images, but it kept timing out. He had to try again, then again, sending one at a time. It took over twelve minutes, and he cursed these out-of-the-way places. He could still hear the distant wails of the kid. He wondered if it was hungry. He patted his pockets but found nothing. Not anything it could eat, anyway. He pulled out a gold wedding ring and stared at it. It was warm to the touch, and he pretended it was the residual warmth of the woman, rather than his own. Shafts of sunlight caught the ring, turning it to fire. He moved it backwards and forwards, fascinated. When he returned to himself, the kid had stopped crying, and he wondered if it was dead. He tried to decide if he wanted it to be dead or not. Cally had been excellent camouflage for him on his little outings. The kid could be the same, but this time he determined he would get rid of it sooner. He should have done that with Cally, but she'd softened him. He thought it might have started the first time she called him daddy. And when she was younger, she reminded him of his own lost girls. Now, Cally was on the cusp of becoming a woman, and he knew what that meant. Trouble.

When he descended the slope, he discovered the kid wasn't dead, only sleeping. The crunch of his feet on leaves woke it, and it started to sob. He picked it up, but the noises were softer now, easier to ignore. The baby scent of it brought memories flooding back, and he kissed the top of its head.

Back at the road, he glanced at the sky, looked at where moss grew on one side of the trees, and turned right. It was too far to walk to Preston, but with luck, there might be a bus before long.

Each time he heard a car approach, he sank back into the woods, and when the trees ended, there were hedgerows. He climbed a wooden gate and walked on the far side of the hedge, ducking down each time a car passed. At one point, he heard sirens, which grew rapidly louder until their wailing filled his head. Three identical cars swept past at speed. He smiled. *Too late, my friends,* he thought. *Too fucking late.*

After fifteen minutes, he saw a sign for a bus stop. He climbed the next gate and walked back to it. The kid had gone to sleep again, and snot and tears streaked its face. He pulled a handkerchief from his pocket and wiped it away, careful not to wake it again.

Ten minutes passed. A few cars went by, but there were no more sirens. Even if there had been, he knew he could stay where he was. Just one more dad with his daughter, waiting for a bus into Preston. He started to spin a story, a reason for the journey. Created a name for himself, in case anyone asked.

Her mum's in hospital, and we're going to visit. No, nothing too serious. Silly accident. Slipped and fell on a rusty knife in the yard.

Ten more minutes went by, and he began to grow nervous. Standing around didn't suit him. There were police nearby, and more would be on the way. He turned and started to walk. The kid woke again and bellowed as loud as it could. He put it against his shoulder and jiggled it up and down, but it only cried harder. The noise was starting to get to him. He wondered what would happen if he grabbed its legs and swung its head against a fence post. He smiled at the thought, still smiling when a car pulled up. An old Volvo estate, mud-spattered, black smoke burbling from the exhaust. A window came down. The old kind that required a human hand to lower it.

"Are you lost?" The question came from a woman of close to eighty.

He peered past her at the driver, presumably her husband. He was the same age.

"I was waiting for a bus, but nothing came."

"You're out of luck," the man said. "Four buses a day out here, two in, two out. The last one's gone an hour since. Where are you heading?"

"Preston. We're going to see my wife. She's in the hospital."

"Sorry to hear that. It'll be the Royal you want, I expect. Here, hop in back, we can drop you off there."

He was grateful there had been no need to state which hospital his wife was in, because he didn't know Preston, other than the train station where he and Cally had arrived two days before. He tried the back door of the car, but it was locked.

"Bugger," said the man. "Kiddie locks. Never could

work out how to turn them off." The man reached back, unencumbered by any seat belt, and opened the door from the inside. So not child locks. Perhaps the doors locked automatically to stop random strangers from getting in the back. Maybe someone who was up to no good. Someone who might have murder on their mind.

He smiled, slipped inside, and pulled the door shut. When the driver started off, there came the loud blast of a horn as another car came past.

"Speed arse," said the man, and laughed.

"Sorry about all the noise my daughter's making. I think she's worried about her mum. Hungry too, I expect, but I forgot to bring anything with me."

The woman half-turned, a slow move that took several seconds. "We stopped for petrol, and I bought some biscuits. They're in that bag beside you. Help yourself, my love."

He peered into the bag and pulled out a pack of Jaffa cakes. He held an edge to the kid and then pushed it into her mouth. She instantly stopped crying and sucked the topping off the biscuit.

"She's a sweet little thing, isn't she?" said the woman, still looking back.

"Takes after her mum."

"What's her name?"

For a moment, he thought she meant the dead woman's name, then realised she wanted to know the kid's.

"Cally," he said, the first thing that came to him.

"A sweet name for a sweet babby. What's her mother's name?"

"Um. Jenny."

"Another sweet name. I'm Beth. Beth Martin. This old inebriate is George. Nice to meet you." She held her hand out.

He reached out and shook it, noticing blood on his hand. He thought how easy it would be to pull the old woman closer, and slide a knife into her throat. If he had a knife. Shame.

She held on to his hand and continued to stare at him. He realised she was waiting for him to offer a name.

"Pleasure to meet you, Beth and George. I'm Peter Jones."

"You ain't from round 'ere," said the man. He, too, half-turned, and the car drifted to catch a front wheel on the grass verge. He jerked the wheel hard, too far the other way, and they swayed down the road until he regained some semblance of control.

He said nothing, in the hope the minor crisis might distract the man from his question.

They entered Preston from the east after crossing the M6, and were immediately entangled in heavy traffic. Despite his protests to drop him off anywhere, the couple insisted on going through the city to the hospital. He was relieved they didn't offer to come inside with him.

Once they drove away, he returned to the road and crossed it, considering himself fortunate when he saw a sign for the railway station. He still had two return tickets, and Cally's would work just as well for the new kid.

As the train pulled away from the platform, he took his phone out. He wanted to look at the pictures again, but knew he couldn't. He would keep hold of the phone until he got home and download them to his laptop. They would be better there. Bigger screen. Then he'd destroy the SIM, reset the phone, and dump it. Leave it in a coffee shop for someone to find.

FOUR

"Outside, now," commanded Barbara Jessup, the principal Scene of Crime Officer.

Izzy's thoughts snapped back to the present. Shock, she thought. Everything happening too fast.

"What?" she said.

"I don't want you contaminating the scene, any more than you already have. Leave now. Wait outside. I'll talk to you shortly." Barbara turned away to organise her team. Another CSI, unfamiliar to Izzy, was laying down metal plates to walk on.

Outside, a constable stopped her to record her movements. He seemed to know her. "Sorry, Izzy, I need your details." He opened the access log. "What time did you arrive?"

"Twelve-nineteen," she replied.

"Pretty accurate, that."

"I checked my watch." She regretted her sharpness at

once. It wasn't his fault she was stressed. He was doing his job, just like everyone else.

"Of course. You're one of the good ones. Have you been in or out since?"

"First time outside...?" She left a question hanging. His face was familiar but from where she couldn't recall.

"Griff," he said. "Griff Owen." He sounded disappointed at her lack of recognition. "We met at that course on evidence three months ago. What's it like in there?"

"Bad." Izzy hesitated, wondering if she should have been so candid. She could do with a coffee. Strong coffee.

When an ambulance entered the yard, Izzy was grateful for an opportunity to escape. She went to her car, shut the open boot, and then perched on the passenger seat, her legs outside. She half wished she smoked.

As two paramedics entered the house, Izzy's gaze went to the tractor Mike Wilson must have driven into the yard. She considered his earlier comment about forgetting his snap. She didn't recognise the word, but after a moment realised he must have meant lunch.

When Barbara Jessup approached, Izzy stood. Barbara quickly swabbed Izzy's hands, and collected nail scrapings. "Tell me what you touched."

"I tried to minimise contact, but I had to touch him, and her. I checked for a pulse, but she was gone. Mike Wilson wouldn't release his wife. I went into the kitchen to find something to put down on the floor. It was only me. I was on my own."

Barbara sighed. "The forensics will be challenging,

but when aren't they. Don't sweat it, Izzy. I know this is a shit show, but you were first-responder."

"What do you think?" Izzy asked. "Is he in the frame for it? He said something weird to me. 'It's all my fault.' But he might've been talking about coming back too late to stop what happened."

"Judgment isn't my responsibility. It's yours and your team's."

"I assume someone will be calling the MIT."

"They will." Barbara looked back at the house. "There's a lot of trace in there, and we'll work it as hard as possible. Prints. DNA. Bloods. And then there's the girl. You said she's not his?"

"That's what he said. His daughter's only eleven months old. Grace."

"That girl can't be her then. One of the paramedics is taking a look, but can't wake her. We'll need to bag her clothes for analysis once she wakes. My guess is she's been given something."

"I thought you weren't meant to speculate," Izzy said.

"Fuck you," said Barbara with a smile. "Try not to screw up another of my crime scenes. Okay?"

Both women turned as a car came fast into the yard. It was filling up rapidly, and there would be more to come. Detective Sergeant Jack Ward climbed from the back seat and approached them. Jack, with his dark hair and good looks that he seemed unaware of, had been assigned to mentor Izzy when she arrived in the detective squad. He was reserved, a trait Izzy had come to appreciate. She'd recently discovered he wasn't interested in women, a revelation she hadn't seen coming.

"You were first on the scene?" As he spoke, his eyes continued to scan the surroundings. The house, the barn, and the tractor standing in the yard with ten vehicles around it.

"I was. I'm sorry I didn't follow–"

"You should know better," said Jack. "I expect Babs has already pointed that out. But you did all right. It's a hard lesson being first-responder, and I hear you handled yourself well."

Izzy wondered who he had told him that.

"Once Babs has finished with you, suit up and find me. I need you to walk me through everything you saw."

FIVE

Izzy belatedly donned her white protective suit, squirmed her feet into plastic booties, then pulled on neoprene gloves. She left the hood of the suit down as she started to write up her notes, but looked up as Jack approached from the house, suited up as she was.

"I thought I told you to find me when Babs finished with you."

Izzy tried to suppress a flare of anger before realising Jack must be as tense as she was.

"I wanted to write record some notes while things are still fresh in my mind."

"Sorry, you're right. Have you finished?"

"Not quite, but I've got the main bits down, if you need me."

"Come walk me through it, Iz. It'll jog your memory as well. You can finish your notes once we're done. After that, I think you should head home. Isn't it meant to be your day off?"

Izzy laughed. "Some day off, Jack. I don't want to go home. I want to be part of this."

"Not up to me. We both know when MIT take over, they'll be calling the shots." Jack's voice was calm, as always. Izzy appreciated his steadiness, which in turn steadied her. "Tell me what you saw and where you went," he continued. "There's a deceased woman and a husband to question about what he witnessed. Not to mention that poor girl unconscious in the kitchen."

Around them, the farmyard was controlled chaos. Two ambulances, four police cars, two CSI Transits, and a black van parked away from the others waiting to take the body to the morgue. A perimeter was set up manned by four constables. Tape marked off the tractor, the barn, a shed and the house. Another line of tape ran across a field adjacent to the barn, where two CSIs leant over, examining the ground close to the house. A barrier sat before the open doorway, but could be moved for access.

Izzy followed Jack to the house, pulling their hoods up so only their eyes showed. She hesitated, recalling the scene inside. As the first-responder, she knew she should have performed better.

Stepping plates were positioned, and she took care to use them. Rosie Wilson remained undisturbed, awaiting the Scene of Crime Officers to finish their work. There was no dignity in death, even less in the case of murder. Yellow numbered crime scene markers had been placed, each indicating potential evidence. Izzy knew from past experience that this apparent disorder concealed a highly professional operation. Videos and photographs were being taken, sketches made, and evidence collected, tagged and recorded.

"Babs has done a thorough job," Izzy said. "Where's Mike Wilson?"

"Sarah's got him in the back of her car. We needed him out of the way to prevent further contamination." Jack paused at the kitchen entrance. Two paramedics were still attending to the still-unconscious girl. "Give me your thoughts on the dead woman, Iz."

She glanced at Rosie Wilson, then made herself look harder. When she entered the hallway, chaos had engulfed her. Now she had more time.

"It looks too ... calm," she said, searching for the right word. "Too organised. Wouldn't you expect a naked woman to be more violated?"

"And the clothes, neatly folded that way? I want you to see the scene. Tell me what you think it means."

"He was interrupted before he could do anything to her?"

"That's a possibility. Anything else?"

"He wanted to demean her." As she spoke the words, Izzy was sure she was right. "He wanted her naked for all the world to see. He folded her clothes to tell us he had no designs on her body. She was dead. His work was done."

"What about the husband? Could he have done this to her?"

Izzy reflected on her arrival.

"He seemed genuinely upset."

"Or a skilled actor?"

"He's a farmer, Jack."

The corners of his eyes creased as he smiled. "Young Farmers' clubs do Am-Dram all the time."

Izzy laughed. "He might have committed the crime, but I'd say he was broken. Sometimes, you get a gut feeling about these things." She paused as Jack prepared to speak. "Yes, I know, assume nothing. But if he is the culprit, where's his daughter? He was beside himself when he didn't find her in the cot. And who's the girl over there?"

"All good questions, Iz. We'll try to find the answers soon. For now, avoid making premature judgements."

"He said something peculiar, but it might be due to panic or guilt, for not being here. None of this might have occurred if he had been."

"Survivor guilt, Iz. We've all seen it. What did he say?"

"'What have I done.'"

Jack stared at her. "You can't think he meant he was late for lunch."

Izzy tried to work out if that had been a criticism, which would be out of character for Jack. She was aware he was trying to mentor her. To make her think for herself. It was what she liked about their relationship. Jack was a skilled investigator, but never attempted to take over. He always asked Izzy for her thoughts. Guided her in the right direction.

"I don't know. He was distraught. Would he be that way if he had killed her?"

"I want to know what you think, Iz."

"My gut feeling or something else?"

"It's too soon for something else. When we get more data, we can analyse it. For now, your gut is all we have."

Izzy closed her eyes a moment to recall the scene. "He came to the door when he heard me arrive, then returned inside and knelt beside his wife. He wouldn't let her go. I thought he might lose his temper, so I put my hand on his shoulder, and eventually he stood. Why would he fold the clothes, Jack? Men don't do that."

"I do."

"Why am I not surprised?"

"Did you see a weapon?"

"Nothing near the body. There are knives in the block in the kitchen, but they're all still in place. CSI has tagged them so they'll check for blood, but they look clean."

"What about the blood on him?"

Izzy closed her eyes again. The tall man with brown hair. Blood on his hands, his arms, his face. Blood down his sweatshirt, which showed faded letters from some feed manufacturer.

"I think it was all hers. I saw no wound on him."

"He hasn't been swabbed yet, but Sarah took a good look and says he doesn't seem to be injured."

"I assume she looked for scratch marks?"

Jack smiled. "She did, and found nothing fresh. He's got marks on the backs of his hands. and one on his face. She asked him about them, and he said he's a farmer, it goes with the job. She did say they were at least a week old."

"When I saw the girl on the couch, I thought she was his daughter."

"There's an empty cot in the room next to their bedroom," said Jack. "Bloody footprints beside it. The assumption is Mike Wilson left them there when he checked on his daughter, but they could also be from the killer. Again, we'll know more when CSI finish."

"Do you think she's been killed as well?" Izzy asked, then nodded when she saw his eyes narrow. Collect and collate. Only speculate after they had gathered all the evidence.

Izzy glanced at the girl on the couch. "What the hell happened to her? I see no wounds."

"They reckon she's been drugged. There's a baggie on the worktop. It's empty, but forensics will tell us what was in it."

Izzy glanced at the evidence marker.

"Sorry, I missed that."

"You had a distraught husband to take care of. You did good work, and it's not as if this is a clean crime scene. Did he say anything else to you?"

"Only what I told you. Then he mentioned trying CPR, which might account for the blood on him. Said he learned it in Young Farmers. I asked if he'd seen anyone, but he rambled again about his daughter. Which is understandable."

"That's my assessment, too. There's blood on the kitchen floor, but not much."

"Wilson didn't come into the kitchen until I called him down. He told me the girl isn't his daughter. Said she's too old."

"Anything else?"

"I didn't check any other doors. Are they all locked?"

"Three entrance points. There's a key still in the front door, which is assumed to be how Mike Wilson entered. Which means it was most likely locked earlier. We can ask him to confirm that. There's a door at the back beyond a corridor from the kitchen, which is also locked. Another at the side of the house in the boot room, which is not locked, and no key in it. Whether that's the way someone left, we don't know, but CSI is looking for prints in there. You did excellent work here, Iz. It's not a clear-cut crime scene. It's a mess. It will take time to make deductions, but we're used to that."

"What about CCTV?" Izzy asked. "Given my experience with local farmers, they often install security systems due to frequent theft."

"Good point. I'll have someone check, we might strike lucky. You seem to know a lot about farms."

"Living out this way, I get sent to most of the reports of theft. Farm equipment can fetch a tidy price, though most of the time it's bundled into a container in Liverpool and shipped abroad, where fewer questions are asked. It's also worth checking the tractor. These days, a lot of them have tracking systems installed."

"It's a bugger there's no radio or mobile signal down here," said Jack. "I left an officer on the top road so he can pass information on. I'll radio him once we're outside and get him to ask. Then we'll see how Sarah's getting on. Care to join me?"

"Do you think my presence might upset him?"

"It could be beneficial if you do. Let's find out."

As they started towards the hallway, one of the paramedics halted them.

"We need to transport the girl to the hospital. She's stable, but remains unconscious."

"You'll require an officer to accompany you," said Jack. "Wait a moment and I'll find someone."

Izzy watched him depart, slightly irritated to be left behind.

"Someone's on the way," said Jack to the paramedic when he returned. "Okay, Iz, let's go."

Izzy thought Jack sounded stressed, and she could appreciate why. He was the Senior Investigating Officer, until MIT took the case over, with many responsibilities resting on his shoulders. But she couldn't think of better shoulders for them to rest on.

SIX

Mike Wilson sat in the back of an unmarked police Sierra. He wore a white forensic suit with the hood pulled down. It wasn't to protect him but because his own clothes had been removed and bagged for analysis. The suit looked a size too small for his broad frame. Sarah Anderson, the senior Family Liaison Officer, sat in the front but was turned to face him. She glanced up as Izzy and Jack approached, then got out and leaned back into the vehicle.

"I need to speak with my colleagues for a moment, Mr Wilson. Please stay where you are."

"Mike," he said, his voice dull. "Nobody ever calls me Mister."

"How is he?" asked Jack, stepping away so they could speak without being overheard.

"The paramedics gave him something to calm him down, so he's a bit out of it, but at least he's lucid now." She glanced at Izzy. "I hear you found him."

Izzy nodded.

"Tough call," said Sarah. "How was he?"

"As you'd expect. Upset. Angry. Looking to lash out at someone. Anyone."

"You did well to handle him."

"I did what I had to, but I think I fucked up the scene."

"Sometimes there's no choice. Don't sweat it."

"Have you got anything out of him?" asked Jack, returning the conversation to the crime.

"He keeps asking about his daughter. Is there any progress on that?"

"We're looking. There are traces of blood on a door handle in what seems to be a boot room on the side facing the barn. More trace on the floor and outside, but it's gravel, so hard to identify. What we do have are footprints going across the field. Babs is having them checked now, making casts, trying to get some idea of whether they're male or female, and how heavy they are. We might've missed them altogether, but the ground's soft from a leaking gutter on the barn."

"I heard about the footprints," said Sarah. "I asked him if he went into the boot room, and he says no."

"Like he'd admit it if he killed her," said Jack, causing Sarah's lips to thin in annoyance.

"What happened to not jumping to conclusions?" she asked. "You don't have enough evidence yet and won't do for at least a day. There's a lot of trace scattered around. Outside as well as in."

A constable Izzy didn't recognise approached. As he did so, his eyes were on the seated man.

"What?" said Jack, his voice sharp.

"The tractor's got one of those fancy GPS things installed, sir. We've sent for an expert. A company in Preston supplies them, and their stickers are on the bottom of this one. They say it'll tell us where it was and when it arrived back here."

"Good work," said Jack. "Sorry I snapped at you. And don't call me sir."

"Okay, s–" The constable closed his mouth, then gathered himself. "I'll try to remember, sarge."

"It's all on my computer," said Mike Wilson from the back of the car, where he'd lowered the window. His eyes were glazed from whatever the paramedics had given him, but he'd overheard the conversation. He started to open the door. "I can log on and show you if you want. It's all on the internet these days. Got fuck all mobile signal down here, but great internet."

Jack crossed to him. "No need for that, sir. The experts will do it for us. Better you don't touch anything just yet."

Mike Wilson stared at him, then sat back as if in slow motion. Jack closed the door and stepped away.

"What do you want me to do with him, Jack?" asked Sarah. "He can't stay here, and a cell's hardly the right place for him in his state. And we can't use anything he might say while the sedative remains in his system."

"I take it the techs swabbed him when they took his clothes?" Jack waited until Sarah nodded. "Good. I also want another examination once we get him away from here. The clothes he was wearing should have been bagged and tagged by now. I'll get a constable to fetch him something from the house. He can take them with him or change here now he's isolated from the scene." Jack looked around the yard. "Though we don't know what might be significant, so best wait until you get him somewhere else." He glanced at the constable, who stood as if waiting to be dismissed. "You, go ask for some of this man's clothes to be brought out. Ask Barbara Jessup what can be released, then bring them here. Can you do that?"

"I can, sir."

Once the constable had gone, Jack said, "I have no idea what his name is. He must be new."

"Peter Robinson," said Sarah, who seemed to know everyone, from a first-day starter to the Chief Constable. "This is his first week on the job."

"Maybe I should have sent someone with more experience," said Jack.

"It'll do him good," said Sarah. "What do you want to do with Mr Wilson once he's changed? And a good call on getting him out of the forensic suit. We've used the Travelodge before, and I'll call through and see if we can take him in through a fire exit. People will wonder what's going on if they see him dressed this way. I'll call as soon as I get a signal and see what they've got free, then take him over there. I'll stay with him until you need him for interview."

"I don't want you going with him on your own," said Jack.

"Of course not. I'll get a big, strong male constable to come with me. Or maybe Peter." Sarah smiled. "It'll be more on-the-job training for him." She glanced at the house. "Is the body still in there?"

"We're waiting for the pathologist. He needs to finish up a post-mortem before he can come over. Stay with Wilson until Peter returns, then take him with you and make that call. I want to take a closer look around inside. You okay with that, Sar?"

She nodded.

Izzy and Jack returned to the hallway, then along a short corridor into what had to be the boot room Sara had mentioned. Izzy was grateful Jack had taken command at the car. It had given her a chance to gather herself, and she felt better for it.

"Did you come in here?" he asked.

She shook her head. "Didn't get the chance." She looked around. Coats on a rack screwed to the wall. A Belfast sink. Boots and wellingtons lined up beneath the coats. Two sizes. His and hers. All apart from two pairs which stood out. They weren't lined up with the others, and their sizes differed. Izzy pointed to them.

"Has anyone tagged those, Jack?"

He looked at where she was pointing. Shook his head. "What am I meant to be seeing?"

She went closer before going to one knee. Pointed again, careful not to touch anything. "If I had to guess – and yes, I know I can't do that – these two pairs have fresh mud on them, and look smaller than Mike Wilson's. This pair belongs to a child of about eight or nine. Like

43

the one in the kitchen." She pointed to the line of welling-tons where there was a gap. "And I'd say a pair of these are missing."

"Fuck, Iz, why hasn't anyone else seen that before?"

"Someone would have noticed."

From the yard, both heard the arrival of another vehicle.

"With luck, that's the pathologist," said Jack. "Come with me in case he wants to ask you anything. We'll tell Babs about the boots in here on our way out."

Except when they saw the new arrival, it was an almost new Range Rover with all the bells and whistles, worth 150K at least. Too rich for the pathologist, even if he had wanted to be so bling. A constable stood at the driver's window, asking who they were and what they were doing there.

"Find out what they're after," said Jack to Izzy. "Looks like it might be some local landowner come to have a nosey around. He should have been stopped by the constable at the top gate. I need to talk with Sarah again about the girl, before she disappears with Mike Wilson."

SEVEN

The driver of the Range Rover buzzed his window down as Izzy approached. His face seemed familiar. She suspected she had seen him somewhere before, but couldn't recall where.

He looked her up and down before saying, "You're not in charge here, are you?" The man was in his forties, tall, his head almost touching the roof of the vehicle. His dark hair was neatly cut and she could smell some kind of oil on it. No doubt the kind that cost a small fortune for a tiny bottle. He was county set – tweed jacket, checked shirt and red trousers. She couldn't see his shoes, but knew they would be highly polished brogues.

"I'm Detective Constable Wilde, sir. I need to know who you are and why you are here. This is a crime scene, and only authorised personnel are allowed. Can I have your name?" Izzy's words were clipped.

"I'd rather speak to Jack Ward. I saw him when you came out of the house."

"If you tell me why you are here, sir, I will consider it. Until then, please remain in the car." Izzy glanced past him at the man in the passenger seat. Younger, good-looking, dressed in a cream linen shirt and blue jeans. His expression was apologetic. "I will need both of your names," she said. "And again, your purpose."

The driver stared at her with bright blue eyes. His good looks were spoiled by an arrogant expression. A man used to getting his own way. Izzy met his stare with her own and, after a moment, saw something change in his.

"All right, but I'm telling you now, you're making a big fucking mistake, Ms Wilde." He deliberately neglected her rank. No doubt he considered a constable beneath his attention. He took a breath and said, "My name is Haddon Cain, and my companion is Rob Peters. He's the chief technician at my company, and someone phoned to tell us this farm uses a piece of our kit. They want us to analyse the data." His gaze remained cool. "Is that enough for you, miss?"

Izzy was used to ignoring insults tossed her way. They went with the job.

"Thank you, Mr Cain. Yes, it is. I need to ask you to confine yourselves to the tractor only." Izzy waved a hand to Griff Owen to come and record the names of the two men. While he was doing so, she ran back towards the house and peered inside without entering. "Babs, has anyone swabbed the tractor yet?"

Barbara Jessup looked up from where she knelt close

to a bloodstain on the lowest tread of the stairs. "We have. Do you need to move it?"

"Got some arsehole here to take a look at the tracking unit."

Barbara smiled. "Does his name happen to be Haddon Cain?"

"How did you know?"

"As soon as you called him an arsehole. But rumour has it he knows his stuff. Or at least employs people who do."

After Barbara returned to her work Izzy went outside, aware she still wore the white bodysuit but unable to take it off because she wore only underwear beneath. Her own clothes had been bagged and tagged. At least outside, she could pull the hood down. Griff had finished recording the details of both men in the log, and passed her on his way to the entrance door.

"Make sure neither of them tries to get inside the house, Griff," Izzy said, and he offered a nod. Izzy suspected she may have underestimated him earlier.

At the car, she said, "The tractor's there. Please don't touch anything else."

Haddon Cain nodded at his companion. "Go check it out, Rob. Make sure you copy all the data to a couple of USB drives, just in case." He glanced at Izzy. "All right if I smoke?"

"As long as you remain inside the car, sir. And don't throw any cigarette butts out of the window."

Cain smiled as if he had achieved a small victory. He pulled a flat, silver case from inside his jacket and removed a small cigar. He lit it with a gold lighter, waving the flame until the tip glowed bright.

"I know Mike and Rosie," he said, through a cloud of smoke, relaxed now. "They're good people. What happened here? I assume not an accident, if this many police are present."

"I'm afraid I cannot say at the moment, but we are grateful you came out so promptly."

Izzie glanced to where Rob Peters knelt in the cab. She was pleased to see he had pulled on neoprene gloves, so at least he wouldn't add to any fingerprints. He had taken a panel off the dash and held a tangle of wires in his palm. A small laptop sat on the seat, and she watched him plug a lead from it into something she couldn't see. He glanced back and met her eyes, offered a smile. Izzy was used to the reaction, but didn't smile back. He might only be feigning a friendly attitude to make up for his boss.

Izzy wanted to leave but felt obligated to stay with the new arrivals. She had a suspicion that left to his own devices, Cain might ignore her request to remain in the car and start nosing around to find out what had happened. Fortunately, Rob Peters' work took less time than she expected. He came back with the laptop open in one hand.

"How long will it take for you to analyse the data?" Izzy asked him.

"I can give you what you want now." He tilted the screen so she could see it, but whatever it was meant to tell her was a mystery.

"Does it show what time Mr Wilson returned to the house?" She was aware of Haddon Cain watching and listening, but short of sending him away, which she couldn't do, there was no other option. She pulled her notebook out and opened it, making sure neither man could see what was written there.

"I can tell you when the tractor returned. It'll take me a little longer to check the CCTV to see if Mike was in it, but it would make sense he was. The tractor left the yard at 7:15 this morning. It went to the top forty, and then returned to the yard at 11:15. I can give you the seconds and show you its exact movements if you want."

"No need, but we'll need access to the data as soon as possible."

"I'll put it in the cloud and send a link. Haddon can also drop a USB stick off at … where are you based, Hutton?"

"This team has come from Preston, but yes, Force HQ at Hutton will be best. They'll no doubt be picking up the case." As soon as she spoke and saw Cain's expression, Izzy realised she had made a mistake.

"I assume that means they're assigning the Murder Team to this," said Cain. "Which means someone's been killed. Is it Mike or Rosie? God forbid it's their little girl."

"I can say nothing, sir, and would recommend you make no speculation regarding events."

"Well, this isn't a theft, I can tell that much. You've got people everywhere. All these vehicles. Someone's got to be dead, and if you want to know where Mike was, I assume it's Rosie." Cain shook his head. "She was lovely.

Such a sweet nature. Not to mention a looker. I'll have to break it to Carol. They were good friends."

"There will be a press release when we are ready to inform the public, Mr Cain. In the meantime, I must request you keep any speculation to yourself." Izzy knew whatever she said, Haddon Cain was unlikely to be the kind of man to follow instructions.

Rob Peters had gone to sit inside the car. The small laptop was open on his knees as his fingers flew across the keyboard.

"I think you may be finished here, Mr Cain," Izzy said. "Once again, our thanks for such a prompt response."

Rob Peters closed the laptop and leaned across towards the open window.

"Mike's got CCTV set up all over if you want me to check it while I'm here. We installed a state-of-the-art system a year ago. Everything's streamed to the cloud. No point of failure." Rob Peters laughed. "Somebody threw a bunch of money at the Forest of Bowland to lay fibre everywhere. There might not be any mobile signal down here, but there is superfast internet. But I'll need to get inside to access it. Everything's hard-wired for security. No wi-fi that might get hacked."

"I don't think I can allow you into the house, Mr Peters," Izzy said.

"No problem, I can do it all from our office when we return. I offered as a courtesy, in case you wanted to see it now."

Izzy was about to make a response when another vehicle arrived. This time, it was a mud-spattered Toyota

Rav-4, which she knew belonged to Benton Philips, the pathologist. She said something meaningless to the pair in the Range Rover and walked across to it.

"Sorry we're late," said Gwynn Buckley as he climbed from the driver's side. "Benton had a PM for a drowning to finish up, and didn't want me to come alone."

"I heard. Besides, your patient isn't going anywhere. Not yet, in any case."

Gwynn leaned back into the car. "Do you want me to confirm death and we can get..." –he glanced back at Izzie– "...her?"

She nodded.

"Get her back to the morgue in Preston?"

"Go ahead, I'll wait here for you."

If he wasn't going inside, Izzy wondered why Benton Philips had bothered to accompany Gwynn Buckley and not send him on his own. A seniority thing, perhaps.

Gwynn opened the rear door and donned his own white suit and booties, then walked beside Izzy towards the house. He said nothing, but she was sure he would like to. His boss was in his sixties now, and lacked the urgency and application he once had. Even so, he rarely allowed Gwynn Buckley the chance to work without supervision. Izzy had heard talk about easing Benton out, and letting Gwynn move up, but as with all such things, there would be the right time and place.

Gwynn and Izzy signed in and then stepped inside. The scene was less frantic now but still active. It would remain so for the rest of the day and probably into the next.

Gwynn stood over the naked body of Rosie Wilson, and shook his head.

"Bit of a formality, Izzy. She's dead." He looked across at her. "Is that black van in the yard the transport?"

Izzy nodded.

"I'd better go through the motions, then." Gwynn went to one knee, carefully using one of the metal plates, then checked for pulse and breathing before standing. "She's starting to cool already. Probably these stone slabs – they suck the heat from a body." He glanced at his watch. "I'll record time of death as 14:47. Okay, let's get her out of here. I can tell you more once I've finished the post-mortem." Gwynn looked at Izzy. "Are you all right? You look knackered."

"I'm fine. Early start, long day, that's all." Izzy suspected she looked worse than she felt. Either that, or she was fooling herself.

"Take it easy. Looks like your day might get longer yet."

As Izzy walked back outside, she almost ran into Jack.

"Ah, I was looking for you. Things are settling down around here now. I think it's time we spoke to Mike Wilson, and I want you with me. Are you okay with that?"

When she nodded, Jack said, "I came with the others, so we'd best take your car. I promise you can go home after, but I need to know if he claims anything different since you found him. He's had some time to think things over since then."

EIGHT

"What's the situation with the MIT?" Izzy asked as she turned onto the B road and headed west. It seemed like days rather than hours since she had come this way.

"They're setting up an incident room at Hutton HQ, they've got everything they need there." Jack smiled. "Word is they trust us to do the grunt work without them looking over our shoulder all the time."

Izzy snorted a laugh. "That's generous of them."

"They're all heart."

"Where are we going to talk to Mike Wilson? At the nick?"

"I called Sarah and asked how he was doing. She said not so good. He keeps asking about his daughter, and we've nothing to give him. She thinks it better we talk at the hotel in the first instance. At the moment, he's a witness rather than a suspect."

"According to the tractor tech people, he arrived back

at the farmhouse at 11:15am. I got a call ten minutes later but don't remember when he dialled treble-nine."

"11:21," said Jack. "So six minutes from getting out of the tractor to calling us."

Izzy glanced across briefly. "Six minutes? He finds his wife dead, and it takes him six minutes to call the police?"

"That could be the shock," said Jack. "And didn't you say he tried CPR? Was that before or after his call?"

"I didn't ask," Izzy said. "It would make sense after he made the call, but we can check when we see him."

"The call handler recording shows he asked for an ambulance first. She questioned him, found out what had happened and called us as well." Jack twisted in his seat to ease some stiffness. He looked too big inside the car. Izzy could see him trying not to notice the empty fast-food boxes half-filling the footwell. "I suppose he could have killed her within six minutes, but it's unlikely. Apart from which, why then dial treble-nine? I don't consider him a suspect. What others think, I'll leave up to them. What about you, Iz? You were first on the scene."

"I told you – he was upset. Genuinely upset. You get a bit of a feeling for these things after a while."

"Is this is your first murder?" Jack asked.

"Since I came out of uniform," Izzy said. "But I attended two domestics where you just know the husband or boyfriend did it. Another was an argument between neighbours that got out of hand. Living out here, almost everyone's got at least one shotgun. You

54

worked with me on that one, Jack, when you were a DC. It was clear to us that the neighbour was guilty as sin."

"I remember. So we go easy on Mike Wilson. It would help us to find out where his daughter is, one way or another."

"If she's dead, I'd say it was done outside the house. It looked like the only trace of blood in her bedroom was tracked upstairs. That's not to say she wasn't killed outside, but I saw the troops working their way up the hill. If there's anything to find, they'll find it."

"God, I hope she's still alive. What if the poor bugger lost his wife and kid in one day. It doesn't bear thinking about."

"But it happens, Jack. We both know it does."

"Yeah, I know."

"Any chance we can stop for a couple of minutes at my place, so I can get out of this fucking suit?"

"So long as you promise to put some clothes on after you do."

Izzy laughed. "I've got nothing of interest to you, Jack." She flung the car into a sharp bend.

Jack grabbed at his door handle. "Any chance you can go a bit slower? My nerves aren't up to you driving like Stirling Moss."

"Who?"

Sarah Anderson came out of the hotel room to meet them.

"How's he doing?" Jack asked.

"A bit better now. The paramedics gave him another shot to calm him down. We could probably manage him between me and Peter, but he's a big fella. Strong. I take it you want to talk to him?"

Jack nodded.

"You realise you can't use anything he says in evidence," said Sarah. "Not with him being drugged up."

"All we want to find out is the train of events from his point of view." Jack glanced at Izzy. "I'd like you to take the lead on this. He already knows you, and to be honest, you're probably better at questioning suspects than me."

"Except he isn't one yet, is he."

"Sorry," said Jack. "Habit." He looked at Sarah. "Has he said anything to you that might make us think differently?"

"He's said very little. Watched TV most of the time. One of those house-buying programs where people have more money than sense. I take it you want me to sit in?"

"Unless you have to get away."

"I called Carl to let him know he's cooking tonight, so I expect it'll be beans on toast. The kids can find their own way home. I texted Harry and asked him to wait for Mel, so they can walk back together."

The room was the same as ten thousand other chain hotels. A big bed filled most of the space, a too-large TV bolted to the wall across from it. Mike Wilson sat on a chair, staring at the screen, where someone was complaining the property didn't have enough land to erect yurts on. His gaze strayed to the three of them, then returned to the TV. Peter Robinson sat in the only other chair, also watching the TV. He nodded to Izzy and Jack as they came in.

Sarah sat on the bed.

"Can my colleagues talk to you, Mike?" she asked, keeping her voice soft.

"If you want." His eyes didn't stray from the screen.

Izzy waited, saying nothing, knowing silence was their friend.

Eventually, he turned his head and looked at her.

Izzy saw the confusion in his eyes, a redness around them, and she wondered if he'd been crying. His hair stuck out in all directions, as if he'd run his fingers through it repeatedly.

"We are sorry for your loss," she said, the words a cliché, but she had to use them.

"Have you found Grace?"

"Not yet, Mr Wilson, but we're looking. We have men and dogs searching the hillsides."

"Her's dead, I expect."

"We don't know that. There's always hope."

"Until you find 'er."

Izzy perched on the edge of the bed so she wasn't looming over him. Jack leaned against the wall next to the door and crossed his arms, then uncrossed them.

"If you can, I'd like you to tell me if you saw anyone when you returned to the house."

"No one. Weren't looking, mind, but I'd've seen if anyone were on my land."

"Was the front door closed when you arrived?"

Izzy watched his gaze turn distant, and knew he was reliving his arrival in the yard, unaware anything was wrong. She saw the moment he recalled seeing his wife's mutilated body. Saw a tear track from one eye.

"T'was shut and locked," he said. "Had to go back to the tractor for my key."

"Do you always lock it when you leave the house?"

"Course we do. We might live in the middle of nowhere, but thieves don't care."

"What did you do when you entered the house?"

Mike Wilson tensed, and Izzy did the same in case he lunged at her, but the moment passed. Whatever the paramedics had given him was working.

"I went to 'er, o'course. Down on me knees. Took her hand. It were warm." Another tear came, this time in the other eye. "I thought it were a good sign. That she was still alive. So I went to the phone and called for an ambulance."

"Not the police?"

"She did that, the woman at t'other end. Asked me a bunch of questions, and said I'd need both. Asked me if Rosie were still breathing, told me to start CPR. But we're a long ways out from Preston, so if Rosie were alive, she was gone by the time anyone got to us." His gaze met Izzy's again. "It were you first there, weren't it?"

Izzy nodded. "I live near Goosnargh and drove as fast as I could." She was aware her vowels had broadened. She could never match Mike Wilson's, but she sounded more like a local now. "You'd been upstairs by then, hadn't you?"

"Had to look for Grace, didn't I? But her was gone. You sure you haven't found her and're just keeping bad news from me?"

"We wouldn't do that, Mr Wilson."

"Mike," he said. "Nobody ever calls me Mr Wilson."

"What did you do after you called?"

"Went back to Rosie, o'course. Held her hand and spoke to her in case she could still hear me. Stayed there till you came in and found me." He shook his head. "You told me Grace were asleep in the kitchen. Took me in there, but it weren't Grace. Who was it?"

"We don't know yet, Mr Wilson, but we will find out. We—"

Jack's phone sounded. He pulled it out and glanced at the screen.

"I need to take this," he said, before leaving the room.

"I expect they've found her," said Mike Wilson. "They found Grace, ain't they?"

"We don't know that, Mike." It was Sarah who spoke, her voice like the touch of velvet. "You must have hope."

"Can't have no hope with Rosie gone, can I?"

"You need to be strong for your daughter."

Izzy let Sarah take over. There was more they needed to know, but she doubted much of it would come from Mike Wilson. He had found his wife lying dead in a pool of her own blood. His daughter had disappeared, and a strange girl lay asleep in his kitchen. He had seen nothing. All he had done was tramp over any evidence, but Izzy couldn't blame him.

"We need to go." Jack stood at the door. He raised his phone to indicate the call was important.

"They found her?" Mike Wilson rose to his feet. "They found Grace?" He started forward, but Sarah moved fast to stand in front of him, her hands on his chest.

"Please, Mike, sit down. If they had found your daughter, Detective Sergeant Ward would have told you."

"You okay if we go?" asked Jack.

Sarah nodded.

"They're sending someone to bring him in," said Jack. "They'll be here any minute. But we can stay if you want."

"You're not going to be trouble, are you, Mike?"

He shook his head. "Never any trouble, me."

NINE

"What is it?" Izzy asked once they were outside.

"DI Gray has received information about the Wilsons. Their marriage might be rocky."

"In what way?"

Jack shook his head. "Don't know yet, only that they've heard something, and need us back at headquarters. Harry Gray says he wants Wilson questioned under caution, as soon as he's fit to do so."

"He didn't kill her," Izzy said. She blipped the car doors and got behind the wheel, half-turned to Jack when he got in the other side.

"We never make assumptions, Iz," said Jack.

"I know, sorry. Whatever it is must be significant enough to call us back. Still no news about the girl, I assume?"

"Didn't say anything one way or the other, but they'll be doing a fingertip search so it could take some time."

Izzy pulled out into heavy traffic. She had to stop

almost at once to wait for the lights when they turned onto Lancaster Road.

"It might be quicker to walk," said Jack with a smile.

Izzy saw a police van coming towards them. She checked her mirror and saw it turn in the direction of the Travelodge, no doubt on its way to pick up Mike Wilson.

Parking at headquarters was jammed, so she left the car in a space on the street and walked back along the road with Jack. DI Gray had left instructions for them to come directly to his office. As they walked along the second-floor corridor, Izzy glanced to her left to see a whiteboard had been set up with the name of the farm, together with Mike, Rosie and Grace, but nothing more. Everyone knew that now the Murder Investigation Team were taking over, things would be moved to headquarters in Hutton.

"How did he seem?" asked DI Gray, the question for Jack. He hadn't told them to sit so both Jack and Izzy remained standing.

"Shook up, but pretty good considering. Keeps asking about his daughter. Any news, boss?"

"They're still searching. Found some footprints and a few threads from a woollen blanket caught on brambles. They say they'll reach the road before dark."

"Does that mean our perpetrator took the girl?" Jack asked.

"If they did, they went to the top road. With luck, we might find someone who saw them."

"It sounds like from what you say, boss," Izzy said,

"that Mike Wilson isn't a suspect. What's this about their marriage?"

"You met Haddon Cain, didn't you, Izzy? Did he say anything to you about them?"

"Not much," Izzy said. "Only that he knew and liked them. He said Rosie was a sweet girl."

Gray stared at Izzy for a moment, then glanced down at the papers in front of him.

"That's not quite what he told me when he came to the station. He brought a copy of the data from the tractor, and asked to see me. We play golf together, so maybe he felt more comfortable talking to me than a detective constable."

"So what did he say?" asked Jack.

"That they'd been having a few problems. Marital problems."

"Was Mike Wilson playing away?"

Gray shook his head. "No, Rosie was. At least that's what he hinted at. Though I'd be surprised if she had the time. Young kid and all that. Haddon didn't make an outright accusation, but I can read between the lines as well as the next man. He wondered if Mike Wilson might have found out what was going on, and lost it. You can see how it might go. He comes home and they argue. He loses his rag and ... well, we all know sometimes it doesn't take much, does it? No doubt sorry after the event, but too late then."

Izzy wanted to say, 'I don't believe it', but knew she couldn't. She glanced at Jack, who took up the challenge.

"Except we currently believe someone else took their

daughter, boss. The timeline doesn't fit with that explanation."

Izzy saw Gray control himself and take a breath before speaking.

"I'm not saying anyone's changing their mind, or taking their eye off the ball, but if they had problems in their marriage, it might be significant. We can't dismiss anything at this point."

"The data from the tractor shows Mike Wilson arriving in the yard six minutes before he dialled treble-nine," Izzy said. "Hardly enough time to argue badly enough for murder, boss."

"Haddon told me it was impossible to cheat the tracking unit. If Wilson turned it off, there'd be a gap in the data showing he'd done so. But he also said the tech in these machines these days is so good, Wilson could have left the tractor running and come down the hill half an hour before he claims."

"He said none of this to me," Izzy said.

"No, well..."

Izzy waited for more, but nothing came.

"You said this Cain dropped the data off for us. Who's checking it out?"

"I sent it down to Clem. He's looking at it now, but says it might take a while."

Izzy expected Clem McDermott had. The man had once been at the cutting edge of advances in technology and computing, but that time lay twenty years in the past. Izzy hoped Clem was aware of the same and passed the data on to Priya Devi. Young, beautiful and clever,

Priya had joined the police as a civilian worker, to support the force's IT infrastructure, but her responsibilities had expanded, and she was now the go-to person for anything to do with modern technology.

"What do we do now, boss?" asked Jack. "Do MIT want to talk to us?"

"I expect so. Go to Hutton and introduce yourselves, see what they say. Keep your ears open and report back to me."

As Izzy walked beside Jack towards the stairs, she said, "Can you manage without me for a while? I don't expect they're sitting around waiting for us, are they?"

Jack slowed and turned to her. "MIT will want to speak to you, Iz, as first-responder. They're going to need your input. Why do you want to leave now?"

"I'll only be a couple of minutes. I want to check on this data Cain brought over. You know what Clem's like. I'd prefer it if Priya analysed it. Go grab a coffee or something. I expect you've not eaten lunch either, have you?"

"When have I had a chance? Same as you." Jack stared at Izzy for a moment before nodding. "Okay, but don't be too long. And try not to rub Clem up the wrong way. He might not be as sharp as he used to be, but he has his uses, and his experience is invaluable."

TEN

Clem McDermott liked to call the space where he worked the data suite. In reality, it was a small, cluttered room in the basement of the Lancaster Street building. Four desks, backed against three walls, barely allowed space for the door to open. Most of the light came from the array of screens, but a few desk lamps added a little extra illumination where needed. The overhead fluorescents were rarely used because their light was too harsh, and they could interfere with the monitors. When Izzy entered, Clem was leaning close to one of them, his hand on a mouse. He was the only occupant of the room, which was not unusual. Since lockdown, when Clem had insisted on coming in, his assistant had continued to work from home on a secure connection.

"Where's Priya?" Izzy asked.

"Went home with a copy of the data." Clem glanced at the corner of his screen. "It has gone seven."

Clem was an anachronism. A lecturer in the local

college, he had been asked to offer advice and assistance to the police twenty years ago, and subsequently employed as a consultant. As computers became more central to police work he'd been offered a permanent position. Priya had arrived only two years ago, and hadn't been Clem's choice. He claimed she was appointed as a box-ticking exercise.

"Have you got anything from the data yet? I take it you're working on the memory stick Haddon Cain handed over."

Clem tapped the side of his laptop. "Looking at it now."

"Anything useful?"

"Too early to tell. There's a ton of data. It's going to take me hours just to filter what's relevant from the noise."

"If you find anything, I'll be with MIT in Hutton. You know my number."

"*If* I find anything I'll send it directly to the correct authority there."

Once she returned from the basement and regained a signal, Izzy took out her phone and called Priya.

"What do you want, Iz? I'm busy with something new here."

"Which is why I'm calling. I just spoke with Clem about the memory stick Haddon Cain handed over. He's taking his own sweet time with the data. You know how stubborn he can be. His way is always the right way."

"I would never dare say that, Iz, but I'm having fun

here. This data is wild. I can run through some of the highlights if you come over."

"I need to go to Hutton with Jack. And are you allowed to take evidence out of the building?"

"I've still got all my permission from lockdown. They even provided me with secure kit, which I still have. I guess the permission still applies. Nobody's told me otherwise. Besides, I work better here."

"I'll see if I can come over when MIT are done with me, unless it's too late."

"Come as late as you like. You can stay over in the spare room. I promise not to bite." Priya hung up. No goodbye.

Izzy stared at the screen. She never quite knew what to make of their relationship. Professional, yes, but there was always a tension between them. Izzy knew Priya liked girls, but was unsure if she included her in that list or not. Whichever it was, they worked well together, and for Izzy that was more than enough.

ELEVEN

Izzy glanced through the open door into the meeting room where the Murder Investigation Team had set up their Incident room. None of them would get much sleep tonight. The first hours of any investigation were the most critical.

She saw six people, including Jack, in the room. Izzy recognised Detective Superintendent Ed Harrison. He had worked at Lancaster Street a few years ago, before being recruited to head up MIT-1, located in force HQ in Hutton. He did good work and let anyone who didn't do the same know it. His head turned as Izzy entered the room, and he offered a brief nod before returning to the whiteboard, where the heading read OPERATION PORT-LAND. Someone in admin would have issued the name at random from a master list. Rosie and Mike Wilson's names, together with Grace's, were listed down one side. Photographs were stuck on with magnetic pins. Rosie lying naked on the floor, her lifeblood spread around her.

Another of Rosie when she was alive, and Izzy studied it as she listened to the updates. The image had been taken at some celebration; a wedding or a dinner party. She wore a light summer dress, and she was laughing. Izzy glanced between the two pictures, a sense of sadness and waste seeping into her. She was startled when her name was spoken – and from the tone, not for the first time.

"Yes, boss?"

"You look shattered, Izzy," said Harrington. "I'll send you home once I've heard your impressions as first-responder. I'd like to hear them now while they're still fresh." He held a hand up. "And yes, Jack told me you'd already been through all this, but I want to hear it for myself." Harrington looked across to the others. "Have we heard anything about the girl yet?"

"Which one, boss?" asked a female detective Izzy didn't know. "The baby or the older one?" Her voice carried a soft Scottish accent.

"Both, but the older one first, because she might be able to tell us what she was doing there and even give us a name. Any word from the hospital?"

"Nobody's contacted us, but I'll chase it up," said the woman.

"Do that, Ailsa. The rest of you know the drill. Follow up on forensics. Who's at the post-mortem?"

"Garry," said a short female detective with dark hair. "He called in and said he'll be another hour."

"Anything from CSI yet, Carys?"

"It's too soon for DNA, but fingerprints are in. I'm

running them through the system now but haven't got a hit yet."

"How many different prints were at the scene?"

The woman consulted a notebook and pulled a face. "Too many, boss. I've got thirteen different sets listed. When I remove the dead woman and her husband, that still leaves a lot."

Harrington glanced at Izzy. "Did you touch anything when you went in, or were you gloved?"

"Gloved, boss, but not suited. It was chaos, and I needed to act fast."

"Jack, I want you to brief the team on everything you know about the scene," said Harrington. "Izzy, I want you to do the same once we've talked." He led the way to an office set in one corner, leaving the door open. As soon as he sat, the others returned to their work. "Take a seat. Do you need anything? Coffee, water?"

"I'm fine, boss."

"Are you?"

Izzy met his firm gaze. "Tired, but we both know that goes with the territory." She liked DCI Harrington. He was sharp and treated those on his team well.

"We've got Mike Wilson sitting in an interview room downstairs with Sarah Anderson. Word from Preston is you're a good interviewer, but I'd rather someone else take his statement. You're too close to him right now. Tell me your impression of him when you arrived."

"Do you suspect him?"

"It's sensible not to rule him out yet. Particularly with

this new information that their marriage might have been rocky."

"He seemed genuinely upset when I got there. In a panic. Covered in blood. I was worried he might try to attack me. You know how some people get."

"Could it have been an act?"

Izzy closed her eyes for a moment and went back to those first moments. Then she opened them and shook her head. "If it was, he's a bloody good actor, boss. I'd say not, but I might be wrong. Like you say, it's too early."

"I remember you from when I was a DI in Preston," said Harrington. "You were in uniform then. I also remember when you applied for detective and got it. You made an impression."

"That was just before you got your promotion," Izzy said.

"It was. Do you think you might look for advancement in a few years?"

Izzy shook her head. "I don't want the paperwork. Nor all the other stuff that goes with it."

Harrington offered a smile. "I can't say I blame you. Sometimes, my own days of being a DC appear rosy in hindsight. You have no ambition to rise to the heights of your father, then?"

Izzy glanced away. Why did he have to mention the man? She hadn't spoken with him in over three years. After she left home, he contacted her most weeks, but when she refused to pick up, he slowly accepted she wanted nothing to do with him. Why was as much of a mystery to Izzy as to her father.

"I met him at a conference a month ago," said Harrington, failing to pick up on Izzy's reluctance. "He asked how you were getting on, and I told him you're doing a good job." Harrington laughed. "He said he would expect nothing less."

"I didn't ask him to pull any strings," Izzy said, her voice flat.

"Nobody ever thought you did. I remember interviewing you, and you never even mentioned policing ran in the family. I just thought with him being a Chief Superintendent now, you might want to follow his example. But I get it – you'd prefer not to talk about him. I'll make sure not to mention it to anyone here." Harrington sat up a little straighter and returned the subject to the case. "So, you don't think Wilson killed his wife?"

"I don't. He was in complete shock when I got there. He was sure it was his fault she'd been killed. It was all I could do to get him away from her body, and try to preserve whatever evidence wasn't already messed up. I saw his reaction when I showed him the girl on the couch in the kitchen. I'd swear he'd never seen her before." Izzy watched Harrington scribble some notes. "There was hope on his face when I told him she was there, then deflation when he realised she wasn't his daughter. Is there any news on her?"

"The searchers have finished on the slope where the footprints led them. They found a couple of pieces of evidence that someone went that way, and had a young girl with them, but nothing to identify who our suspect is. What do you think the older girl was doing in the kitchen?"

"I've no idea. It's bizarre. Is she still out cold?"

Harrington called into the room. "Ailsa, have you called the hospital yet?"

"Done, boss. The girl's starting to come around."

Harrington turned his attention back to Izzy. "I want you to go with Sarah to the Royal and speak to the girl."

"Why me?"

"Because this is as much your and Jack's case as mine right now. I don't want to swan in and start treading on toes. The Forest of Bowland is your patch, and local knowledge is going to be invaluable. We're based in HQ at the moment, but MIT spreads itself across the entire force area. This means I want both of you as part of my team for the duration. I've already cleared it with DI Gray. You're seconded until we find out who killed Rosie Wilson."

"Thank you, sir. You said there were rumours about their marriage. I heard Haddon Cain told DI Gray about them, but he didn't say who the man might be."

"I heard you met Cain and weren't a fan."

Izzy kept her expression neutral. "I'm sure it was a disappointment to him. But he was quick to send the data in, and that will be invaluable."

"He's also offered access to all the CCTV from the farm. It's backed up on their servers in the cloud. The memory stick that's currently with Clem is a subset of that data. DI Gray says he knows Cain and that he knows the Wilsons socially. They're farmers, and farmers are his biggest customers. He's the kind of man who makes sure he buys everyone a drink now and again, sends flowers and chocolates on birthdays and anniversaries."

Izzy almost said, 'You don't like him, do you?' Then she pursed her lips together. Liking someone was irrelevant to the investigation. Instead, she said, "What did you hear about their marriage?"

"Bear in mind this is hearsay and will need confirming. But it seems Rosie Wilson was on her third, or maybe her fifth, affair since they married."

"Her third?"

"Cain didn't say as much, but I think he believes the kid isn't Mike Wilson's. I guess we'll find that out soon enough. Barbara told me they have enough from her cot and clothes to get a DNA analysis."

"Did Cain tell you who Rosie was seeing?"

Harrington shook his head. "I asked, and he wouldn't say. I suspect he knows, of course, and we might need another conversation with him. But if it is true, it changes things. If Mike Wilson found out she was playing away, he doesn't seem like the kind of man to take it lying down."

"I'd expect him to have a go at whoever was screwing his wife, not kill her. And like I said, boss, I don't think he did it."

"We'll see." Harrington put his hands flat on the table. "All right. Go brief the team, and then you and Sarah go talk to the girl if the doctors think she's up to being questioned. We need to know who she is and what she was doing asleep in that house. She's no Goldilocks, that's for sure." Harrington rose and walked out to speak with one of the others.

Izzy stayed where she was, thinking about what she'd been told. If Rosie Wilson was having an affair, DCI Harrington was right. It changed everything. It opened up a whole new raft of suspects. They would have to question Cain, and push him to reveal what he knew. They needed names. Harrington said Rosie could have had several affairs. Over how long, Izzy wondered. Had she always had a roving eye, or was it something new? Come morning, they might have a whole new stack of actions to follow. Izzy wiped a hand across her face, aware of how tired and grubby she felt. She was tempted to go home, shower and catch a few hours of sleep, but knew she couldn't. Now was the time to push, to find out all they could.

She rose, intending to go outside to breathe some fresh air, when Jack approached her.

"The girl's awake, and the doc says you can talk to her. Sarah's waiting for you downstairs. Come back when you're done. We'll all still be here." Jack cocked his head and studied her. "How did it go with Harrington?"

"Not too bad. He's good, isn't he?"

"He always has been."

"I assume he asked you to join the team until this is solved, same as he did me?"

Jack nodded.

"It didn't sound like we had a choice," Izzy said.

"Of course not. And it makes sense. East of Preston is our patch. We know the ground, the people."

"At least this is a nicer building than Lancaster Street," Izzy said. "And you get to see trees and fields through the windows."

"Don't get too used to it. I hear they sometimes decamp to locations closer to the scene. Old police stations, and village halls." Jack smiled. "All of which have a surfeit of cobwebs and damp."

TWELVE

Izzy drove back into Preston, found a parking space at the hospital, and used her phone to pay. She knew she ought to reclaim it on expenses, but considered the time spent on admin not worthwhile.

Something must have shown on her face, because Sarah offered a smile as they walked towards reception. "You've had a long day, Iz. Try to chill."

"Sure, sometime next month with any luck. Did you get any more out of Mike Wilson?"

"Nothing, but I didn't want to push him too hard. They took him into an interview room against my advice."

"Did you hear about their marriage? It seems Rosie was having an affair. Or maybe that should be affairs, plural."

Sarah slowed. "No, I didn't. Someone should have told me. Not that I'd want to confront Mike with the information without a lot of preparation. It changes things."

"Complicates the case all to hell, yes. We'll have to trace any men she's been screwing and question them. But maybe this girl can tell us what happened at the farmhouse. She was there. She might have seen or heard something."

"God, I hope not," said Sarah. "And don't go in too heavy. She's a minor and needs treating with sensitivity, which isn't your strong point."

Izzy laughed. "I'll leave the talking to you, then."

They informed the desk who they were, and while they waited, Izzy saw Sarah check the body cam strapped to her chest. She would need to wear it while they spoke with the girl, so they had a record of both what they said and her responses.

They were taken into a side room where the girl sat on a bed, dressed in a hospital gown. A nurse sat in a chair at the side of the bed, but rose when Izzy and Sarah were shown in. Sarah switched her body camera on and checked the recording light.

Izzy stood back, knowing Sarah was better at dealing with kids than she was.

"Is she well enough for us to ask some questions?" Sarah's voice took on a new tone, one that oozed calm and sympathy.

"Yes, you can talk to her. Doctor Matthews wants a word before you leave, so I'll tell him you're here. Do you know how long you might be? He goes off shift soon."

"Not too long, I hope," said Sarah.

When the nurse had gone, she sat on the edge of the bed and reached for the girl's hand. Izzy studied her. She wasn't into kids, never intended to have any, and didn't understand them, but it was clear that Sarah had a connection. It was as natural to her as breathing.

"Hey, sweetheart, how are you feeling?"

"My head's all fuzzy, but I'm all right, thank you. I was sick when I woke up, but I'm better now. I had some juice and ice cream." The girl's voice was soft and carried a faint southern accent. Not full-on London, but by the time she reached sixteen, it probably would be. "Do you know where Daddy is?"

"I don't, sweetie. Can you tell me your name?"

"Cally. I'm eight and a half."

"You're very grown up for someone who's eight and a half," said Sarah. "What is your daddy's name?"

"Frank, but I never call him that."

"And his last name?"

The girl stared at Sarah. It was clear from her expression she wanted to help, equally clear she didn't have an answer.

"I always call him Daddy," she said eventually.

"That's all right, sweetie. Do you know where you live?"

"London."

"Do you know the address?"

The girl shook her head. "Number 7, that's all I know. Daddy told me I could have my own key when I'm old enough for big school."

"Which school do you go to now?"

"Daddy teaches me at home. He says when I'm eleven, I can go to a big school, but I don't know its name. We might have moved by then, anyway. Daddy moves all the time."

"Can you remember the names of any of the streets where you lived?"

The girl stared into space for a long time before shaking her head. "Only one. West Road. Something West Road."

"Great West Road?" Izzy asked.

The girl looked at her and nodded. "Yes, I think that's it." She smiled. "You're very pretty."

"Thank you, Cally. But I'm not as pretty as you."

The girl's smile widened, making Izzy's statement true. Cally had a sweet face that would soon become beautiful, and her honey-red hair hung in long curls to frame her face.

"Can you tell me why you were at the farmhouse, Cally?" asked Sarah.

"We were walking, and I got thirsty. Daddy brought water, but we'd drunk it all, so we went to the house to ask. There was a nice lady there. She was very pretty. She got me water, and I sat on a big sofa to drink it." Cally's eyes widened. "She had the biggest, bestest kitchen I have ever seen. I think it might have been bigger than our whole house!"

"And then you went to sleep?"

"I do that sometimes. Daddy says there's a name for it, but I can never remember it. He says not to worry because I always wake up."

"You said you were walking. Walking where?"

"We follow footpaths and long-distance trails." She smiled to show pride in remembering the correct name. "Daddy likes to follow long-distance trails. We've been all over the country, to loads of different places."

"Do you like walking, Cally?"

"Not as much as Daddy, but it's all right. I get more tired than Daddy, and sometimes he forgets I'm only eight. We stayed in a nice house last night, right by the path. The lady there was kind to me."

Sarah leaned forward. "Where was that, sweetie?" Her voice remained soft, as if any answer was unimportant.

Cally shook her head. "I don't know. It was nowhere, all on its own. Looking outside, I could only see one other light, far off. A nice lady was there on her own. It was called Bed and Breakfast." Cally smiled. "I had sausage, bacon and egg for my breakfast. And toast, of course, with jam. Daddy had the same, but more. And then we brushed our teeth, and started to walk."

"Did you pass through anywhere else while you walked?" asked Sarah.

"Not really. We saw a few houses, but they were a long way away."

"Did you see any names for these houses?"

Cally shook her head. "Sorry, no. I should have tried harder."

"It doesn't matter, sweetie. I don't suppose you expected anyone to ask. You're doing so well."

"When can I see Daddy? Is he in the hospital, too?"

"I'm sorry, he's not. We're trying to find him, so anything you remember will help us. Have you ever fallen asleep like this before, when you and your daddy have been out walking?"

"I think so, but I can't remember when, or how many times. Five or six, I expect. It's that long name daddy told me that I've forgotten."

"So it could have been more than six?" Izzy said, wondering if the man they sought always used Cally as cover. Did it mean he had killed before, at least five or six times? Izzy was about to ask more when she caught Sarah's expression. This wasn't the time to pile in on the girl. Later, perhaps, but not now. Izzy sat back and gave a nod to Sarah. Go on; I'll shut up.

"Did your daddy ever take you to a doctor about this falling asleep?"

Cally shook her head. "He told me it was nothing to worry about, so I don't. Most of the time, it doesn't happen. Only when we go walking. I expect I must get tireder than I think, and just go to sleep when we stop."

"Do you have a mummy?"

Cally shook her head. "It's only me and Daddy." She gave a shy smile. "Sometimes Daddy says I'm the only girl he likes. He tells me women cause trouble and heartache. But he likes children. He says they're innocent."

Sarah glanced at Izzy to ensure she had noted what Cally said just as the door opened and the nurse returned.

"Doctor Matthews says he need to leave before they

find him another job to do. If you want to talk to him, you need to do it now."

"We have to go now, Cally," said Sarah, still perched on the side of the bed. "But we'll come and see you again soon." She leaned in and squeezed the girl's hand, before releasing it and standing.

Izzy followed Sarah out, wanting to tell her she didn't think they had finished with Cally. Even as the thought came to her she knew it was inappropriate. Cally wasn't a suspect. But she would know more than she had told them so far. A tall, slim man stood in the corridor waiting for them. He was dressed in biker's leathers, and held a helmet in his hand.

"Doctor Matthews?" Izzy asked, getting a nod in return. "You wanted a word with us. I assume it's about Cally."

"I ran some tests because I was concerned about her state of catatonia. MRI, CT-scan and bloods. Someone gave her a hefty dose of Gamma-butyrolactone." He smiled. "Better known as GLB."

"When you say a hefty dose, doctor, how much?"

"It took her eight hours before she started to come around, so I'd say two or three times what might be prescribed for insomnia. Not that it's used for that in this country anymore. Whoever gave it to her can't have been aware of how dangerous a dose that high might be."

"How dangerous?"

"Potentially fatal. In sufficient dosage, it can lead to respiratory depression and death. In fact, it and GHB are the second most used drugs for suicide in the UK. That's one lucky little girl in there." He started to turn away.

"Can you send your results to our pathologist?" Izzy asked.

"Already done. I emailed them to Gwynn Buckley. He pinged me back and said he's passed them on to your team." This time, he managed to get away.

Sarah nudged Izzy in the side and grinned. "I would. How about you?"

"I guess he's all right," Izzy said, knowing she ought to play along with the banter, and they both laughed. "I thought you were a happily married woman."

"I'd never do anything, of course, but we've been married twenty years and sometimes a woman's eye wanders." Sarah winked at Izzy. "But you're a single girl, Iz. You can do more than look."

"He wore a wedding band."

Sarah sighed theatrically. "There are times I worry about you."

Join the club, Izzy thought.

As they left the building, she said, "Cally's a sweet girl, but we might have to question her harder if we want to find out who this man is."

"She has to be an innocent party in all this," said Sarah. "She doesn't need you giving her the third degree. Apart from which Social Services have been in touch. They want me to let them know when Cally can be released to them. They're looking for somewhere to place her temporarily until we get the DNA results back. It might tell us who she really is."

"She can hardly return to her 'Daddy', can she."

"That's an interesting point," said Sarah. "If she is his daughter, then she's going to spend a lot of time in care. What kind of parent could do that to their child?"

"You know the answer better than me," Izzy said. "I'm glad I don't do your job. Some of the things you deal with are too much for the rest of us."

"But they *do* need dealing with," said Sarah. "And there are pluses as well as negatives."

"Which is this? Izzy asked.

"Too soon to tell. Could be either."

As they reached Izzy's car, Sarah's phone rang. She answered, said 'yes' several times, then broke the call.

"That was Social Services. They've got a temporary foster carer for Cally, and want her released into their care. I need to brief her case worker, but I already know Flis Roberts, and she's good at her job. Young and dedicated enough not to be burnt out yet. I'm going to have to leave you, Iz. Good luck." Sarah came close, hugged Izzy and kissed her cheek.

Izzy opened her notebook and wrote down what Doctor Matthews had told them. GLB. She thought of the high dose, and wondered if Cally had been meant to never wake again.

THIRTEEN

Once Sarah had gone, Izzy sat in her car staring into space. All she wanted to do was drive out of the city to her small cottage on the outskirts of Goosnargh, take a long shower, and curl up with a book. But she knew she couldn't. Not yet. She started the engine, and drove through the city, traffic quieter now as the exodus from work tailed off.

Priya Devi answered the door to her dockside apartment almost as soon as Izzy knocked, and led her inside.

"You took your time," Priya threw back over her shoulder.

"I've been busy with a murder," Izzy said. "Or haven't you heard?"

"Ha-ha," said Priya. "Come and let me show you what I've got."

Izzy had been in the elegant apartment several times before, but despite a view across the marina and spacious rooms, she had no aspiration to live in the city herself.

Priya had made the place her own, with oriental rugs on the floor and Indian wraps on the walls. There were two sofas in the main room, but Priya went to her desk and patted the chair at her side.

Izzy sat and leaned closer to the screen. "Show me what there is, then."

"All the tracking information for the tractor Wilson was driving. I called Rob Peters and asked him if it could be programmed to self-drive. He said in theory, yes, but in practice Wilson would never do it. He even had the feature disabled."

"Can you confirm what time he returned to the house?"

"Rob said he told you that already. Eleven-fifteen. Six minutes before Wilson dialled treble-nine. I checked the scene photos, and no way is six minutes long enough to do what was done to her. I reckon he's in the clear."

"Have you passed this across to MIT?" Izzy knew that all extra information, even if it was duplicated, would be useful. One touch might be good; six touches better.

"Not yet. I'm still working through what else is on the memory stick and in the cloud. The CCTV from this morning, the same going back a couple of weeks." Priya moved her mouse and clicked the screen, which changed to a colour image frozen in time. "This is him arriving outside the house." Priya tapped the screen where Mike Wilson was half out of the tractor cab. She tapped again. "And here's the time. Eleven-fifteen and seventeen seconds."

A thrill ran through Izzy. "And earlier?"

"If you're asking if I have an image of the killer, then no. Let's assume Rosie Wilson was killed no more than an hour before her husband returned — and the post-mortem will provide a better timeline. I've gone back that far and there's nothing. Nothing at all."

"Show me." Izzy half expected Priya to offer an objection, but she scrolled and clicked, and the timestamp in the top corner changed to 10:05 and the tractor disappeared as if by magic.

"This is a great system," said Priya. "High definition. Shame there's no sound." She hit play.

Priya switched between several cameras. They showed the front of the farmhouse, the interior of the barn, and the track leading to the yard.

"It's like this the whole time until he turns up," said Priya. "A few birds flying past. A rat crosses the yard at 10:42 and goes into the barn. At 10:47 there's a slight movement in one of the upstairs windows." Priya advanced the playback and then slowed it to normal. "Here." She pointed.

Izzy saw the movement of a curtain, then a hand drawing it back, but nothing else.

"Rosie Wilson?" she said.

"Looking at someone approaching the house, perhaps," said Priya.

"If so, where are they? The camera is pointing right at the front door, which is shut. When I got there it was open, and the key was on it."

"I saw him use it. He had to go back to the tractor for the key, but that was mere seconds. It's possible whoever killed her knew about the cameras, and approached from a direction they don't cover. That's the only thing that makes sense."

Izzy stared through the big window, to where people walked their dogs on the far side of the Marina.

"If you're correct, it means the killer knew the farm, and knew Mike and Rosie. That would imply someone local. I need to go back there and walk the scene. Look at the angles, work out if someone could approach the house without being seen."

"It's too late tonight," said Priya. "I'll come with you tomorrow if you like. I can hook up to the cameras and see if you can avoid them."

"I don't want to drag you out there. It's, you know, really rural, and you're a city girl. Besides, if you have this kind of access, you can watch me from here. I'll go with Jack. Now, show me what else you've got. I'm curious if the killer scoped the place out before he struck. Is there any way to fast forward through the dull bits?"

"Even better, I can program it to only show significant movement. Give me a second, and I'll set it up. Be a babe and go bring us two coffees. There's a place along the quayside. Are you hungry?"

Izzy thought about it and decided she was. She'd skipped breakfast, and didn't recall eating anything all day.

"Starving."

"I'll order. Indian? Chinese? Something else? But please, not burgers."

"Indian. You choose."

As Izzy walked along the quayside, where a sharp wind slapped water against the stone blocks, she thought about Priya. The two of them were close, maybe even friends. Izzy knew she needed one. But whatever their relationship, they worked well together.

Priya was a civilian in the Lancashire force, as were most of the technical and administrative staff. She was meant to be based at Lancaster Street Police Station, where she would be expected to share the small basement room with Clem. But lockdown had changed all that. Priya had been provided with a fast gigabit connection and secure equipment. Somehow, nobody expected her to cross the city to work from the basement anymore, though she did have to report when required. It was an arrangement that suited both her and Clem.

A few times when she and Izzy had drunk the best part of two bottles of wine, Priya had told her she was estranged from her family, who had turned their backs on her when she came out. Now she was in touch with only one of her sisters, who had told her their father still lived in the hope of arranging a suitable marriage with a nice boy. Preferably a cousin. Izzy never spoke of her own family or what lay in her past, and knew she never would.

Izzy took eight minutes to find the coffee shop, order and return. Priya wasn't at her desk, but appeared when she heard the door.

"I've put plates to warm. Now, let's see what else we can find out."

They sat side by side in companionable silence while

the screen jumped and jumped again, stopping each time Priya's program recognised significant movement.

"I've gone back as far as the data I was given," she said. "Which is about four weeks." She grinned. "You ought to go out for a drink with that Rob Peters, he's a bit of all right."

Izzy laughed. "Says you."

"I might prefer my own sex, but my eyes work just fine, thank you."

They sat and watched a mixture of tractors, each fitted with different attachments, drive in and out of the yard. They watched Mike Wilson cross and re-cross it. Watched Rosie Wilson walk to her car, a small Fiat, with her daughter in her arms.

"Can you pause that?" Izzy said. "Now go back a bit. Can you slow it right down?"

"I can do anything you want."

Priya went back until Rosie Wilson appeared, then set the display to click forward at a reduction of ten times.

"Stop it there," Izzy said, after a minute. "Can you zoom in and print that? Rosie Wilson and her daughter. We might need a good shot of them together."

"Of course." Priya did as asked. She sent the raw image to the printer before cropping it, so only Grace Wilson was shown, almost full face. The image was a little grainy, so Priya ran it through software until it was sharper. "I'll email this to the MIT, but I expect they already have plenty of pictures of her from the house and their phones." Priya started the stuttering scenes running again.

understand. Dogs get old or sick, have accidents, get run over. They die. But both together?"

"Maybe they both ran out and got under a tractor," said Priya.

"Or maybe someone poisoned them because they didn't want the dogs around when they came to the house."

"That smacks of premeditation rather than just coming across the house randomly."

"It's another pointer the killer might be local. At the least, it implies a degree of planning." Izzy glanced at the time on her phone. "Someone needs to ask Mike Wilson about the dogs. He was going to be interviewed when I left to come here. It's usually me they call on for that in Preston, but MIT will have their own people. With luck, he's still sitting in a room waiting. I need to get back to Hutton. Can you continue looking through the rest and make notes on anything suspicious?"

"Of course. What about your food?" Priya checked her phone. "It's ten minutes away."

"Sorry, I need to go. I'll grab something on the way."

Priya grinned and rubbed her flat belly. "All the more for me."

Izzy drove south through light traffic before picking up the A59 and following the signs for Southport. She parked outside the Lancashire Force HQ, and as she walked inside she almost ran into Jack.

"Where have you been?" His voice was short, expressing an unusual annoyance.

"With Priya, studying the CCTV data from the farm.

Someone needs to talk with Mike Wilson about his dogs."

"That might have to wait a while. He's been rushed to the Royal Hospital with a suspected heart attack. I tried to call you."

Izzy fished her phone out of the back pocket of her jeans. She'd had it on silent while they worked, and not checked. Now she saw three missed calls, all from Jack.

"Sorry."

It seemed to mollify him a little. "What's this about dogs?"

She told him, then said, "I've also got a list of plates from cars that turned up at the house over the last four weeks. There might be more. Priya's checking the recording now."

"How come Priya's doing it? I went to see Clem, and he said the data could take days, if not weeks, to analyse."

"Clem might have been a technical god in his day, but that day was a long time ago. Priya has access to the same data from her apartment and has much better software than Clem."

"In her apartment?" said Jack, his expression stern. "Not here at HQ, or in Preston?"

"She still has authority from lockdown, when she worked from home. She requested permission to continue to work that way, and it was granted."

"Okay. You'd better update MIT on what you've learned. I'm being sent to conduct a couple of interviews. I expect I won't see you again until morning, but good work today, Iz."

Jack turned and strode away.

FOURTEEN

There were fifteen number plates on the list Izzy and Priya had made, and now she handed them to Carys Morgan to identify the owners. Carys would feed them into HOLMES, and cross-check names returned for any history. Izzy expected it to be a dead end, but one that had to be followed up. Most of them would belong to local farmers or, like Haddon Cain, those who supplied goods and services to farmers. The incident room was quiet, the members of the MIT bolstered by three officers from Preston, plus Izzy and Jack.

She went to stand in front of the incident board and scanned the notes, names, locations, and photographs. As she had suspected, there were three excellent images of young Grace Wilson pinned there. When Izzy sensed someone approaching she turned to find Superintendent Harrington coming to join her.

"Jack told me he tried to get hold of you and couldn't," he said. "I think everyone assumed you'd clocked off and gone home. If you had, nobody would have blamed you."

"I wouldn't have done that without telling someone, boss. I was with Priya Devi looking at the CCTV from the farm. We identified several visitors in the last four weeks, which is as far as the data Priya has access to. I've handed the list of car plates to Carys for cross-checking and elimination. We also discovered a couple of things that might — and I mean only might — point at a local suspect."

"What things?"

"There are two sheepdogs on the CCTV, but they disappeared two weeks ago. Also, we checked the hours before Rosie was killed, and saw no one approach the house until Mike returned."

"Does that place the husband in the frame?" asked Harrington. "Wouldn't be the first time or the last."

"I don't like Mike Wilson for it, but I think it's worth pursuing the local aspect."

"We're already collating information on anyone in the area with a record that might indicate they could be in the running."

"How many?" Izzy asked.

"No more than a dozen within six miles. We'll spread the area out if we think we need to, but those dozen will be questioned tomorrow, for elimination, or to be looked at further. That's where Jack's on his way to now. I told him to take one of the Preston officers with him."

"Jack told me Mike Wilson's been rushed to the Royal."

"Ailsa called to check on him just before you walked

in. It was an anxiety attack, not his heart. No great surprise after the day he's had. They say they'll send him back here within an hour. I spoke with your DI, and he says you're a good interviewer so you'll get a chance to ask your questions. I was planning to send Ailsa in with you, but do you think two women might be too much for him?"

Izzy was surprised Harrington had asked, but also pleased.

"It's possible, but I think it could work. It'll give us a chance to see how he reacts. Do you want us to do it when he gets back?"

"Best as soon as," said Harrington. "What is it you want to ask him about? I take it you found something?"

"The usual stuff, boss. Had he fallen out with anyone lately, crossed anyone. And I want to know what the party was about, and what happened to the sheepdogs."

"You think it might be important?"

"I don't know, but if they were deliberately killed, it could show pre-meditation. Maybe the killer didn't want those dogs around when they came for Rosie Wilson. Someone should go to the farm to find out where they're buried and dig them up. If they were poisoned, it's more evidence of pre-meditation."

"I'll arrange it, but only after you've interviewed Wilson. You can ask him where he buried them rather than us having to search."

Izzy nodded, then looked at the image of the dead woman on the incident board, another of her taken at some event where she was wearing a red dress. So vibrant in life. An empty shell in death. "Any news on the daughter?"

"The entire hill and woods in the direction of the footprints have been searched now. We also sent dogs in after they had a good sniff of Grace Wilson's blanket. They caught her scent and tracked it to the roadway, then nothing."

Izzy considered the new information, but it was still too sparse to make sense of, something Harrington would also know better than her. She was acutely aware she was an incomer to the team, only here because of her local knowledge. It was a chance to learn more. To prove herself.

"How do you want us to approach Mike Wilson?" she asked. "As a suspect or a witness?"

"Witness, I'd say, but remember he might still have done it. What we found on the hillside could be nothing but a courting couple indulging themselves in the woods, though the dogs indicated the girl had been there. There's a bus stop close by on the road."

Izzy suppressed a smile. "Out that way, boss, someone would be lucky to get more than one bus a day."

"We're checking on it, but the admin department at the bus station is closed until eight in the morning. We'll try to get the names of drivers out that way, and ask if they picked anyone up. There's a lot to do yet, Izzy, but it's always like this at the start."

"I'd like to thank you for this opportunity."

"Make sure you learn from it."

Harrington had been a good DI at Gaol Street, and the

word was he was a good leader of MIT-1, but he always seemed as if he came from an earlier generation than someone his age. He dressed in a manner that reinforced the impression. Always a tie and a V-neck sweater. Today, he wore a brown tweed jacket, the middle button done up, and brown brogues on his feet.

"Has anything come back on the rumours of Rosie Wilson having an affair, boss?"

"I spoke with Haddon Cain, but he says he doesn't know names, only the rumour."

"So who did he hear it from?"

"Says he can't remember. In the pub, he thinks, and he might have had a few by then."

"Which pub?"

Haddon looked at Izzy. "He thinks it was the Hodder Arms near Clitheroe, out your way."

"A bit further east, but yes, I know it. Nice pub, good restaurant."

"That will make someone's job easier when they're sent out to make enquiries, then," said Harrington. "The landlord might know something if the rumours have been around a while. Did you ever meet Rosie Wilson?"

"Not when she was alive, boss." Izzy saw Harrington wince, and knew she could have put it better.

"Cain said she was a looker. Had something about her. Men were attracted to her. He said she responded as if she might be attracted to them in return. Some women are like that."

"Are they?" Izzy couldn't help herself. The casual sexism of his remark annoyed her. *Some women!*

Harrington ignored her. "Go talk strategy for the interview with Ailsa."

"Good cop, bad cop, boss?"

"Good cop, better cop," he said. "The man's broken, you'll see that. He lost his wife only ten hours ago, but we need to find out what he knows tonight. Whether or not we can rule him out. Come find me after, both you and Ailsa."

"It might be late, boss."

"I'm not going anywhere."

FIFTEEN

Izzy sat with Ailsa in the canteen. It was closed, but a machine in one corner dispensed a dark brown liquid. There was a rumour it might resemble coffee, and she needed the caffeine. Ailsa was unfamiliar to her, and she the same in return. They needed to build a rapport, and fast, before they talked to Mike Wilson.

Ailsa was a couple of inches shorter than Izzy, and a couple of years older, she guessed. They sat side by side, staring through a window across the A59 where cars still moved north and south, their headlights flashing bright. Izzy studied Ailsa's reflection in the window. Hair a mix between red and blonde, and bright blue eyes that hinted at a possible Scandinavian gene pool somewhere in the past.

"You've heard the rumours about the wife?" asked Ailsa. Her Highland accent remained strong; soft and calming.

"We're going to have to tiptoe around it," Izzy said.

"Maybe ask about their marriage and see how he reacts. Do you want to lead on this?" Izzy was aware Ailsa was a DS to her DC, and this was her nick.

"The boss said he wanted you to." Ailsa showed no indication she minded. "He also said you had something about dogs. That's new."

"They were on the CCTV ten days ago, but no sign of them now. I wondered, that's all. I'll ask him about them if you want. And about anyone he or she has fallen out with recently. If there was any bad blood between them and a neighbour."

Ailsa offered a smile. "I come from a rural area, Isabella. I know all about feuds." She pronounced Izzy's name correctly, the double-l closer to a soft Y.

"Izzy, not Isabella. Most people just call me Iz."

"Then that's what I'll do."

"You're from the Highlands, aren't you? Do you speak any Gaelic?"

"Aye, I do, but there's not much use for it down here."

Izzy knew the conversation was irrelevant to their task, other than they needed to build rapport fast.

"We could sit here and make notes for half an hour, or play it by ear."

"I hear he's downstairs now, so let's go."

Izzy nodded and set her mostly un-drunk coffee on the table with relief.

When Mike Wilson was led into the room, his hair stuck out at all angles, and his cheeks were flushed. Fortunately, he had been given no more tranquillisers, so anything they learned could be logged as evidence.

Mike looked at Izzy, at Ailsa, ignoring the female constable who had led him in.

"Thanks, Angie," said Ailsa. "We'll call you back when we finish."

PC Angela Pugh closed the door as she left.

Izzy knew that depending on his answers, Mike might be released and offered a hotel room until the CSIs had finished with his house.

"Please, take a seat, Mr Wilson," she said.

"Mike. I told you before. Or is this going to be more formal?"

"No, not formal, Mike," Izzy said. "Would you like something? Tea, coffee, water?"

"I'm up to my eyeballs in coffee." He stared at the two chairs on the far side of the table but remained on his feet for the moment. "Do I need a solicitor?"

"You can ask for one if you wish, but this conversation is to record what you recall about today's events. You are not a suspect." Izzy made sure not to say at this moment in time, even if that was what they all knew.

"Any news on Grace?" His voice was sharper, the tranquillisers out of his system.

"Not as yet, but we will, of course, tell you as soon as we hear anything. It's a good sign we have found nothing so far." Izzy didn't need to explain why. She hoped Mike would work it out for himself. No news meant no body. Izzy had her own theory about what had happened to Grace Wilson, but kept it to herself for the moment. "Please, sit." She smiled. "We can't start until you do."

He looked at them both, but Izzy wondered if he actually saw them. She studied him, looking for any slight tell. They were both young women, both attractive. She searched his face, his eyes, but there was nothing there. She wondered what the real Mike Wilson was like. She had met him only once before, when she was sent to record the theft of a quad bike. Then, he had been business-like. Theft of such equipment was common in the farming community. He needed a police report so he could claim the insurance. Izzy hadn't met his wife that day.

Finally, Mike sat. Izzy and Ailsa did the same, slightly offset, so neither was directly opposite him.

He glanced at the tape machine, then back at Izzy.

"Are you going to record this?"

"Like I said, this is for information only."

"I thought I'd told everyone what happened already."

"Our enquiries have raised a few questions, and we'd like to run through them with you if you don't mind."

He shook his head, but said nothing. Waiting. Exhausted. Grieving. No doubt still in shock.

"We've been studying the CCTV from your farm, so I know to the second what time you arrived back in the yard. I've also read your account. And I was first there, of course."

"I remember you. I..."

Izzy waited, but nothing else came.

"This might sound irrelevant, Mike, but I saw something on the CCTV that confused me. Two sheepdogs. Can you tell me where they are?"

"Dead. Buried round back of the yard, both of 'em."

Izzy made a note of the location to pass on to Harrington.

"Can you tell me what happened?"

He stared into Izzy's eyes, a barely contained anger in his.

"Poison, had to be. Some bastard poisoned my dogs."

"Are you saying it was done deliberately?"

"Might've been an accident, I s'pose, but I'm careful about things like that. There're some farmers put poison down for buzzards. Blame 'em for killing lambs, but not me. I like seeing 'em hangin' up there over the hillside like they could fly forever. Carrion they eat, not living things. But others still put poison down."

"It's illegal," Izzy said.

Mike grunted. "So's driving too fast, but we all do it. Some farmers believe themselves above the law. Can do what they like on *their* land. But we're only looking after it for the next generation, is what I believe."

Izzy saw his expression change when he realised what he had said. His next generation was missing.

"Do you think Grace will take on the farm one day?" asked Ailsa, sensing an opportunity, deliberately using the present tense. She smiled. "I know my dad wanted me to."

"Your Pa's a farmer?"

"Cattle and sheep in the Highlands."

"Hard living, that," said Mike.

"Aye, a hard living, but he wouldn't want it any other way. You too, I think, yes?"

"Yes, me too."

"Did your wife know farming before you married?"

There was silence. Mike looked down at his hands, red from work, the nails bitten to the quick.

"Aye, Rosie came from farming stock," he said eventually. "She knows the life."

"Your farm does well," said Ailsa. "Nice house. A lot of land."

"A bit over fourteen hundred acres," said Mike. "Some better than others. Down along the river's the best. I keep sheep on the higher slopes, so I had the dogs."

"Was your wife upset when they died?" asked Ailsa.

"'Course she was. They were more like pets than working dogs, truth to tell. We even had 'em sleep in the house. Downstairs, o'course, not on the beds. Some neighbours thought we were daft, but we couldn't help it. They were good dogs. Right good dogs." The anger showed in him again, just beneath the surface, simmering, ready to burst free.

"Do you think any of your neighbours might have poisoned them?" asked Ailsa.

"They'd have to answer to me if they did, so no. Not the ones nearby, in any case."

"You got on all right with them?"

Izzy saw where Ailsa was going with her questioning.

"Pretty good, sure. Farmers work together most of the time. It can be a hard job. You must know that. Good neighbours count for something."

"And your wife, Rosie, she got on with them too?"

"Sure."

A tiny frown line formed between Mike Wilson's eyes.

"The wives got on?"

A nod. "They did. Cake bakes and stuff. You know, to raffle for Young Farmers." He almost smiled. "Not that most of us are young anymore, but it don't seem to matter."

"Is that where you met Rosie, at Young Farmers?"

"At a dance in Longridge." Almost a smile. "They do good'uns there." This time, the smile broke the surface for a moment. "Used to be some good fights too, when I was a lad. Always the way in the country. Lads pushing their luck. Trying it on with someone else's girlfriend. Never meant 'owt, though. All pals again the next day."

"Did any ever try it on with Rosie?" asked Ailsa, now Mike had given her an opening.

"Not twice. I saw to that."

"It sounds like you had a good marriage."

She's better than me at the soft stuff, Izzy thought.

"Good enough. Ups and downs, like every other marriage, but more ups than downs."

"Did Rosie ever get bored, being in the house alone all day?"

Mike seemed to consider the question as if it had never occurred to him.

"P'raps, sure. But there was always summat to do. Feeding the hens, gathering the eggs. Looking after Grace these last eleven months. And I never expected her to stay home and stare at the walls. She has her own car. Little Fiat. Blue thing. Slow as fu– well, slow, you know what I mean. She takes herself off anytime she likes."

"Visiting friends, I expect," said Ailsa.

"And shopping, o'course. Into Preston if she can stand the traffic. Liverpool sometimes, on the train mostly. Been takin' Grace with her lately. Mums and Tots group, though Rosie tells me it's Dads and Tots too these days. Different world now, ain't it? Not like my dad's time. Men did the work. Women raised the young'uns. No, not like that anymore."

"Where were these Mums and Tots groups?" asked Ailsa.

"Church hall in Whitechapel most of the time. Sometimes, they had away days as far as Clitheroe and Blackburn. Went to Carlisle once on the train."

"You never wondered where she was?"

Tread carefully now, Izzy thought, but she trusted Ailsa.

"She always told me where she was going. 'Course she did."

"You're not the jealous kind these days, are you, Mike." Ailsa smiled, the expression enough to melt a glacier.

"Rosie never gave me cause. We're solid. The three of..." His voice trailed off, and his eyes filled with unshed tears. "Her's dead now though, ain't she." His eyes met Izzy's, moved on to Ailsa's as the more compassionate of them. "When can I bury her? Nobody's said."

"We need to complete our investigation first, Mike,"

Izzy knew there wasn't much more to get out of Mike Wilson, and now was not the best time to push him. Give it a day or two and try again. See if they couldn't push harder next time. Maybe get Ailsa to press the questions and suggest an affair.

It occurred to Izzy they'd heard about Rosie having an affair, but what about Mike? He was a good-looking man. Well-off by the look of his farm. She had seen husbands go off the rails when a kid arrived. When their wives spent all their time on the new one and none on them anymore. It was something worth checking out. But not tonight. He was upset, and Izzy could feel the buzz of exhaustion flowing through her. She glanced at Ailsa, and raised an eyebrow in a question. *Are we done?*

"Thank you for your cooperation, Mike," said Ailsa. "We will need to talk to you again, but we are finished for tonight."

"Can I go home?"

"Not yet. I'll talk with the Scene of Crime officers and find out when they will release the scene. You may have to find a hotel for a few days. We can help arrange that if you like."

"I got a mate who rents a cottage to visitors. I'll give him a call and see if it's empty."

"You can leave the address with PC Pugh once you know. I'll contact you as soon as you can go home. We will, of course, deep clean the house for you."

"We got a cleaner."

"I'm sure you do, but this is standard practice."

When Angie came to lead Mike out, Izzie and Ailsa stayed in the interview room. It was quiet, and they could talk without being overheard. Izzy made notes, and saw Ailsa doing the same. It would have been better to take them during the interview, but it might have irritated Mike Wilson. They both worked for ten minutes, then checked their notes against each other's.

Izzy turned her chair so she was facing Ailsa. "Tell me what you think."

"He referred to her throughout as if she was still alive. You'll have noticed it as well. It tells me he's not come to terms with it yet."

"It's going to take a few days, if not longer. But does that mean he's innocent? What's your gut feeling?"

"Can we trust our instincts, Izzy?"

"Possibly not, but you've got one, haven't you? Same as I have."

Ailsa smiled. "Tell me yours, and I'll tell you mine."

"I don't think he did it," Izzy said. "I'll tell you my reasons when you've told me what you think."

"I agree. He's angry and confused. The drugs they gave him don't help because he's coming down from them, and his mood is bouncing backwards and forwards. Apart from which, his wife's dead and his daughter's missing. No wonder his head's fucked up." The expletive, coming in Ailsa's soft accent seemed out of place, but Izzy didn't really know her well enough to know whether she swore like a Scots Guard or not. "Tell me what else you've got."

"I was the first on scene, you know that. I saw him in those initial seconds and minutes. He was all over the place. If it was an act, it's the best I've ever seen. So no, someone else killed Rosie Wilson. And that someone else abducted little Grace."

"Why the girl?"

"My guess is it's to do with the girl on the sofa in the kitchen. She's eight or nine now. Growing up. Asking questions. Sarah and I went across to the hospital to talk to her." Izzy smiled. "I was just finding my feet at that age. I could be a little bugger. Were you like that, Ailsa?"

The smile was returned. "I was worse. I was a tearaway. Boys half the time. Lost my virginity at fourteen, and got a taste for the illicit."

Izzy laughed, partly because Ailsa gave the impression of being so innocent.

"It must've been hard finding suitable candidates in the Highlands," she said.

"Oh – I learned to walk real fast. And I had a bike. Then a motorbike. Dad had a couple of quad bikes, and I took one of those when he let me. Didn't tell him what I was up to, mind."

"Of course not."

They were getting away from the point, Izzy knew, but it was so easy to talk with this pretty woman. She wanted to ask her more. Was she married? Did she have kids? What did she want from life? But they had a murder to solve.

"This is all conjecture, so bear with me," Izzy said. "What I'm thinking might be bollocks, so... Anyway. It's the girl, Cally. I think she was there as cover."

Ailsa frowned but said nothing, waiting for Izzy to go on.

"The farm is isolated. A strange man arrives alone,

Rosie Wilson would be unlikely to let him in. She'd lock all the doors and call Mike. He'd be there in a minute."

"Someone told me they had a landline, but no mobile signal."

"There was one of those walkie-talkie units on the sideboard. No doubt he has one with him when he's away doing whatever he does. Rosie would've used it if she was worried. Whoever arrived had the girl in tow. When we spoke with her in the hospital, she called him daddy. That changes the situation, doesn't it? A man and his daughter. Maybe she wants a glass of water. Rosie lets them in, and he kills her."

"In front of his daughter?"

"I don't know if she's his daughter or not. It would take a hard-hearted man to take his own daughter with him when he intended to kill. But seeing what he's done, he will be hard-hearted. I think he took little Grace Wilson and discarded Cally."

"Which is why people are checking CCTV on local buses and Preston station."

"I think Harrington more than half believes Grace Wilson is dead and buried."

"He's not said that yet."

"No, he's not." Izzy washed a hand across her face. "I need to shower and get some sleep, but not yet. Maybe not until tomorrow night."

"The first twenty-four hours," said Ailsa.

"You'll know all about that. How long have you been with MIT?"

"Three years. I was a PC in Southport before I applied."

"What do you do between incidents?" Izzy asked.

"Same as you, I expect. Boring shit."

"Do you live in Southport?" Izzy didn't know why she asked, except she liked Ailsa, liked the sound she made when she spoke.

"Churchtown," said Ailsa. "Which means yes, I suppose, but the residents there think they're something better. My husband – Garry – works in the town centre. He has nothing to do with the police. He fixes cars. I like the drive to Hutton once I get out of Southport. It's not far, and I like to look at the scenery. Weirdly, all that marshland reminds me of home. Stark, unforgiving."

"Not quite the Highlands though, is it?"

Ailsa smiled. "Not all of Scotland's mountains. Besides, that's the attraction. The mountains and moors can make you feel awful small." Ailsa leaned across and patted Izzy on the leg. "Now, let's go tell the Super what we think. There's going to be a whole lot of new actions coming down the line, and I bet I know who gets to handle half of them."

"I want to help if they'll let me," Izzy said.

"I heard the boss seconded you and Jack to the team for the duration, so yes, you can help."

After Ailsa had gone, Izzy thought about herself. Single. Averse to getting close to anyone. She had never invited a man back to her small cottage. Why, she didn't know. Except something lay inside her she deliberately ignored in case turning the stone over revealed a truth she didn't want to acknowledge. She knew what it was. Nothing surprising. Nothing new. It was what happened to her sister, and how her father had dealt with it. DCS Vick Blackwood now, according to Harrington, and on his way to Chief Constable if he had anything to do with it. She could imagine his disappointment if he heard she was content to remain a detective constable.

She sighed and rose. Time to face the Super. It might distract her from her memories. From the pain that still lurked, ready to emerge.

SIXTEEN

Ed Harrington looked even tireder than Izzy felt as she approached him. Ailsa stood at his side, and hopefully had already updated him on what they had learned from Mike Wilson. Both glanced at Izzy.

"This thing about the dogs," said Harrington. "I'll try to get someone out to the farm, but is it significant? And can you stop finding new actions for us to deal with?"

"I'm only doing my job, boss." Izzy offered what she hoped was an apologetic smile, but wasn't sure it worked.

"I know you are. Sorry, Izzy, but we have so many lines of enquiry now it feels like this could take weeks, not days. Ailsa tells me you both think Wilson is in the clear."

"At the moment, but it depends on what turns up."

"And their marriage?"

"He believes it was sound. No hint he suspected his wife was having an affair."

"Affairs," said Harrington.

"Do we trust this Haddon Cain?" Izzy asked. She saw Harrington's face stiffen, and knew she'd made a mistake.

"It seems to me he's the only person doing anything useful around here. He supplied the CCTV, the tracking data from the tractor, and he's only provided us with the information he thinks might apply to our investigation. He's a civilian doing our job for us. We need to pull our fingers out." Harrington stared at Izzy, making her aware she was an outsider. Here, at force headquarters, she was a guest. Then Harrington softened his tone. "We're kicking our heels right now. We've got people to talk to, but the DNA results won't come back until tomorrow at the earliest. Barbara Jessup put the highest priority on it, but science takes its own sweet time. Go home, Izzy. You've been on this all day, and you look shattered."

"Call me if anything crops up, boss."

"I will. Now go. I'll see you tomorrow. Bright and early, mind." Harrington turned to Ailsa. "You too. Go see your husband and daughter, but the same goes for you. Bright and early. Tomorrow's another day."

As the two left, Izzy said to Ailsa, "When he worked in Preston, he could always be relied on for a good cliché. I see he hasn't changed."

"Everyone has their quirks," said Ailsa. "Even me and you, I expect, but he's a good boss. You'll see that."

Izzy watched Ailsa walk off to a dark grey Ford. She turned to wave before getting in. Izzy walked to her own car and drove through light traffic before turning north-east and speeding up. She wanted to get home. Wanted another shower and something to eat, and then she had more work to do. It was only an idea at the moment, but one she could dismiss – or not – in a few hours.

Izzy sat at her small dining table and spread an Ordnance Survey Explorer map of the Forest of Bowland out. The smell of frozen lasagne cooking in the oven scented the air, and made her stomach rumble. She had showered and dressed in a long towelling robe, her dark hair still wet. She found Caxton Farm after a few minutes, then realised she needed the map that joined to the west to see the entire picture. She rose and went to the cupboard she had taken the first map from, searched through several others, checking the back to see the areas covered. She knew Priya would be appalled she still used paper maps, but she preferred them. Trying to view them on a phone screen just wasn't the same. Finally, she found the one she wanted. She dropped the closed map on the table and took the lasagne out of the oven. She didn't bother with a plate but set the plastic container on a placemat and grabbed a fork. While she waited for it to cool enough to eat, she spread the new map, folded it and found the B road she had raced along. Despite it being only that morning, it seemed a week ago.

Izzy marked the farmhouse with a highlighter. Then she stared at the roads and footpaths that ran nearby. There was only one road, so she concentrated on the paths. There had been mud-stained boots left behind. Size nine and a kid's size four. Larger footprints led away because the killer had worn Mike Wilson's wellingtons. Izzy assumed he had been carrying Grace Wilson.

She stared at the map without seeing it, wondering if Grace was still alive. The searchers and dogs hadn't found a body, which was a good sign. It meant there was still hope. This wasn't the first murder Izzy had worked on, but it was certainly the most confusing. The others had been domestics, and there had been witnesses. Here, there was nothing. All the evidence they had was circum-stantial or thirdhand. Izzy had hoped talking with Cally might have helped, and it had, but only to rule out several lines of enquiry. She might still prove useful, though. And Izzy knew the next time they talked with Mike Wilson, they would be harder on him.

Izzy returned to the map, her finger tracing the foot-paths. The biggest one around the region was the Ribble Way, but it didn't go anywhere near Caxton Farm. Instead, she started at the farm itself, and searched for smaller footpaths. Several ran close to the farm, but none through it. Only one ran for any distance. It followed the river Brock as it meandered southwest, ducking beneath the M6, and then fading out at the village that shared a name with the river. Brock made sense. Easy to reach from Preston station. Close enough to Caxton Farm. She opened a map on her phone and searched for hotels and B&Bs. There was a Travelodge to the south of Brock, which served motorway traffic. It didn't feel right, but she made a note to check.

The lasagne was cool enough now, and she ate it while continuing to study the map and making notes. She wrote actions for herself, actions that could be allocated to members of the team if Superintendent Harrington thought them relevant.

After eating enough, she took the remaining food and tossed it in the bin, then poured herself a large glass of red wine and returned to the table and turned on a light.

It made no sense for the killer to have spent days walking a footpath if he intended to kill Rosie Wilson. Logic said he would go directly to the house. Most likely sit and scope it out before approaching. Did the footpath mean she wasn't his intended prey, but nothing more than an unfortunate accident? In the right place at the wrong time. Or the other way around. Cally said they spent the night at a B&B, but in which direction? Izzy retraced the footpath, looking for places that might fit her meagre description. There were several possibilities, and Izzy wrote the names down. More actions. More work. She knew it was often the way of an investigation. Dull and diligent was the way forward. Everything had to be checked out, but she didn't have to do it all herself. Izzy knew she had a habit of doing that. Of not trusting others, only herself. Except she trusted Jack and Priya. She thought she might trust Ailsa. She would have to make herself trust the other members of MIT. Even then, there were more lines of enquiry than even they could action, so they would have to trust the officers who would be sent out. It was possible a few might even be stationed along the route or live nearby, and their local knowledge would be invaluable.

She needed to talk with Harrington in the morning about her footpath theory. She thought about calling him now, aware he would still be in the incident room, but she was too tired.

She poured another glass of wine and went up the narrow stairs to her bedroom. She attempted to still her mind as she picked up the book she was reading. Tomorrow would be soon enough.

Outside, an owl hooted, and another replied. A moment later, something screamed. Nature, red in tooth and claw. Just like humanity, sometimes.

It was that last image before a fitful sleep took Izzy that, she later believed, brought the memories crashing through her sleep to bring her awake, drenched in a cold sweat. Outside, dense darkness still held sway, but Izzy's mind saw sunshine. It had returned to a place a long way south, to Herefordshire, where she was raised before everything bad happened. Her wide eyes saw sunshine ... and blood ... her sister's blood, even though she had never witnessed it. Her father had made sure of that.

There was pain in the visions that danced in the dark. Pain and guilt, even though she was not the guilty one.

SEVENTEEN

JUNE 2015

It had been Gabi's idea.

These schemes were always Gabi's idea, but this one was wilder than any before. Izzy and Gabi were twins – identical twins – otherwise the plan could never have been hatched. Seventeen years old, about to be eighteen. Same height, same face, same body, same hair colour and eyes. Different personalities. Izzy was quiet, studious, shy. Gabi was ... well, Gabi was just Gabi. A force of nature. If Izzy's personality favoured their mother, then Gabi's favoured their father. Charismatic, brash, born leaders, givers of orders. And still, somehow, it was Izzy who had a boyfriend. Gabi didn't, not at that moment. And those she did get never lasted long. Izzy suspected Gabi's personality scared boys off. She was too much to handle. Fun for a while, then not.

"You seeing Ricky this weekend?" Gabi had asked. They sat on Izzy's bed, which was neatly made. The only pictures decorating the walls were one of the snow-capped peaks of the Sierra Nevada mountains east of Granada in Spain, the other of a river running crystal-clear through a woodland's dappled shade.

"Maybe," Izzy said.

"Do you do ... you know..." Gabi slid a finger through her circled thumb and forefinger.

"Of course not!" Izzy wasn't as shocked as she made out, and she knew Gabi had lost her virginity more than a year ago.

Gabi laughed. "I bet Ricky wants to, though, doesn't he? Has he tried it on?"

"No." It was a lie, but Izzy wasn't going to tell the truth to her sister. Not to anyone.

Gabi was quiet for a moment, and then she made the proposal. A joke on Ricky. On everyone.

"It won't work," Izzy said.

"I can pretend to be you for a bit, I'm sure. Or do you want to do the dirty with him Saturday night?"

"We're going to see a movie in Hereford."

"And after?"

"After, he'll drive me home."

"But stop on the way.

"Maybe."

Gabi grinned. "I bet he feels you up, doesn't he?"

"No." Another lie.

Gabi wore her down, as she always did. Just as their father wore people down until they agreed to his terms. As a Detective Chief Inspector in the West Mercia Force, spanning three counties, it was a valuable skill.

In the end, Izzy agreed to Abi's terms. They swapped

phones in case someone texted or called, and Gabi wore Izzy's clothes, even down to her underwear.

"In case he finds his courage and manages to get that far," Gabi said with a wink.

The knock on the door came at three on Sunday morning. It woke Izzy, who sat up in bed. As she did so, the knock came again. Firm. Official. How she knew that, she couldn't tell, but a coldness filled her chest. Her first thought was her father. She knew he was working on an investigation into organised crime groups in the force area. People who dealt drugs, and used guns and knives like others used their fists. Ricky kept a knife under the seat of his car. Just in case, he claimed.

When the knock came a third time, she heard her mother's bedroom door open, and then a shuffle as she descended the stairs. Izzy slipped from her own bed, went out and crouched on the landing.

Her mother opened the door to reveal two uniformed police officers, one male, one female.

"Mrs Blackwood?"

She nodded. "Has something happened?"

"Is there anyone else with you?"

"My daughters are upstairs in bed. My husband is out."

"We tried to contact DCI Blackwood, but he was off-grid. We are here about your daughter, Isabella, Mrs Blackwood."

Her mother took a step back. "No, they're upstairs asleep. Do you want me to call them down?"

"Can we come inside for a moment?" The male

constable glanced at his companion and offered a nod. A team.

"What is this about? I can't believe Izzy has done anything illegal."

"I'm afraid we have some bad news for you, Mrs Blackwood. We would rather not discuss it on your doorstep. And you might want to call your other daughter downstairs."

"Other..." Izzy's mother raised a hand to her face. "No ... dear God, no."

And with that she collapsed, keening, to the floorboards.

Izzy ran down the stairs and knelt beside her.

"Are you Gabriella?" the female constable asked.

Izzy looked up. They both seemed so tall.

"No, I'm Izzy."

A frown crossed both constable's faces.

"Are you sure?"

"I think I know my own name." Beside her, her mother tried to stand, without success.

The female constable knelt beside Izzy and offered assistance as they helped her mother to her feet, before leading her into the kitchen. Which is where they told her the horrific news.

"I am afraid your daughter was found beside the B4532. She was airlifted to Hereford hospital, but I regret to have to tell you that she died before they reached there. We are sorry for your loss, Mrs Blackwood." He glanced at Izzy. "For both your loss. We need to ask you some questions, and best if we can do it now if possible."

Izzy's mother's face was stiff with shock. She stared into space but saw nothing.

"Ask me." Izzy drew on her mantle of competence. The one she wore when she wanted to appear fearless.

The female constable looked between Izzy and her mother, then came back to Izzy.

"Do you know where Iz – sorry, Gabriella, was going last night?"

"Out with my boyfriend."

"Your boyfriend?"

"It was a joke. We're identical twins. Gabi thought it would be funny."

"I see. What is your boyfriend's name?"

"Ricky. Richard Hamer. He works in a warehouse in Hereford. Admin." Too much information, Izzy thought, as she closed her mouth.

"What age is he?"

"Nineteen."

The male police officer looked at Izzy. "And you are?"

"Izzy is almost eighteen, officer," said her mother. It seemed to placate the man for the moment.

"Does this Richard Hamer drive a grey Ford Fiesta?" He recited the number plate.

"He does. Has he been injured as well?"

"We won't know until we find him. His car was found badly damaged in a field on the Builth road. Your daughter was in the passenger seat. She had no seat belt on, which accounts for her injury. The surrounding area was searched, but it appears the driver fled. Can you tell me what you know about Richard Hamer?"

Izzy did. Not that she believed Ricky could ever be in an accident or would abandon an injured Gabi if he was. She often berated him for driving too slowly. Except, according to the police officers, there was evidence. And as the weeks and months passed, the evidence grew, until Ricky confessed that he and Gabi had argued when he discovered the trick she had played on him. When asked if he had been racing another car, he said no. Izzy, watching from the balcony, caught the tell on his face. The judge didn't, neither did the jury.

Death by dangerous driving. Manslaughter. Because the law had no word for womanslaughter. Much as it should.

Ricky was sentenced to six years. Out in three with good behaviour. Had Gabi been the daughter of anyone other than DCI Vick Darkwood, he might have got away with less. It was an accident, after all, and accidents happen.

When Izzy requested a visit, Ricky refused, and kept refusing the entire time he was in Worcester prison. But he couldn't ignore her once he was released.

Izzy heard Ricky had returned to work, so headed to the giant warehouse north of Hereford. She sat in her car and waited.

Ricky came out just after four in the afternoon, and stood beyond the tall, wide entrance. He pulled a pack of cigarettes from his pocket and lit one. Something new, a habit acquired in prison. He was thinner than the boy she remembered, his face sallow, his expression harder.

Izzy got out of the car and approached him.

He saw her too late, started to turn, and then stopped. Ricky knew what Izzy was like. She would keep coming. Best get it over with now.

Izzy slapped him hard across the face, sending his cigarette spiralling away to land in a shower of sparks.

"Tell me why you lied," she said.

"I never lied, Iz."

She got closer. "How long did we go out together, Rick? Three months? Do you think I'm stupid? I know you. You could never drive fast. Did you know it wasn't me?"

"Straight off, Iz. Pretty fucking obvious it weren't you. She was hungry for it."

Izzy stared at him. She wanted to slap him again, but instead said, "You fucked her."

"She wanted me to. She was wild, Iz. I barely had any say in it. Then we argued. She told me she wasn't you, as if I didn't already know."

"I watched you in court, Ricky. There was another car, wasn't there? You were racing."

He said nothing for a moment, his eyes refusing to meet hers.

"It was an accident, that's all. Must've taken my eyes off the road for a moment. It was dark, and raining. I didn't mean to hurt her." Ricky's body language screamed he wanted to be somewhere else. "It happened just like I told it in court. I deserved to be punished, Iz. Did my time and want to get on with the rest of my life now."

"You're lying. Tell me what happened."

"That *is* what happened, Iz. That's exactly how–" Ricky broke off as a car pulled into the yard. His gaze went to it, eyes widening. He turned abruptly and walked away.

When Izzy heard a car door shut, she turned to see her father walking towards her. Tall, broad-chested, with thick, dark hair and a permanent shadow on his cheeks and chin. A force of nature.

Izzy loved him and feared him in equal parts. Gabi had worshipped their father, and he had worshipped her in return. But since her death, he had shown nothing.

"What are you doing talking to Ricky?"

"Did you help him get his job back?" she asked.

"Not me. He made a mistake and served his time. Seems the manager of this place believes in second chances."

"But not you." Izzy clenched her fists. "What are you doing here, Papa? Watching him?"

Her father stared into her eyes. Izzy knew he was trying to intimidate her, but it no longer worked. She could be hard, too.

"I can't tell you why I'm interested in Ricky, but know it's got nothing to do with what happened to Gabi."

"You're investigating him?"

"I told you, I can't say. Now go home. Don't contact Ricky again, he's bad news."

"I'll go home, but then I'm leaving. Now I've finished Uni, I've applied to join the police. But not here. Up north, where you won't be able to help me out."

She thought he'd tell her not to be so stupid, but he

said nothing. Only turned and walked to his car. He didn't even look in her direction when he drove off. After she left home he called her every day for a fortnight. Then every week. It took six months before he stopped altogether, but it seemed he still kept an interest in how his daughter was doing. Three years after leaving home, she received a letter from her mother which told her she was divorcing her father. It said she could never have found the courage to do so, if Izzy hadn't already turned her back on him. It went into no detail why, but didn't need to.

In her own bed, in her own house, Izzy eventually found sleep again, but it was fitful and filled with nightmares which dragged her again and again to the surface. When the sun finally rose to end her torment, she got up and prepared herself for work.

EIGHTEEN

Izzy showered, then spent the best part of an hour recording what she had gleaned from the maps. She had been tempted to do it the night before, but knew she was too tired. In light of her nightmares, she wished she had. Now she concentrated hard on the task, to help erase the remnant of the dream. A few additional thoughts occurred to her and she added them. She wanted herself and Jack to visit the accommodation possibilities she had identified. She trusted Jack more than anyone else. They worked well together. There were times it seemed they knew each other's thoughts almost before they did themselves. Whether Harrington would approve her request was another matter. Which is why it surprised her when, at seven-fifteen that morning, he looked up after reading her two pages of notes and smiled.

"This is good work, Izzy. I'll get these entered and actioned." He tapped the second sheet. "You're asking here that you and Jack visit these hotels."

"Hotels is too posh a name for most of them, boss, but yes. Jack's good with people. They like him."

"But you're not? Preston told me you were one of their best interviewers."

Izzy shrugged. "I do all right, but you know it can be an act, put the fear of God into someone, but Jack has a talent I don't possess. I want to be more like him. Calmer. Better with people."

Harrington stared at her until she felt uncomfortable. Eventually, he said, "I don't see that in you, Izzy. Don't be too hard on yourself. I'll sign off on your request. We'll be waiting all day for DNA results from the girl found at the farmhouse. The same for the Wilson's little girl. I'd like to know if she's Mike Wilson's daughter. If not, we might have to spread our search wider and put out a call for DNA samples. We can tell people it's for elimination."

"Men only?" Izzy asked. "Might be an idea to ask for both, then we just don't bother analysing anything from women."

Harrington hesitated again, before nodding. "Okay, a good suggestion. I'll authorise that. It'll mean taking more swabs, but I like the idea of not pinning down what we want the samples for yet." He rose. "All right, I'll get these items actioned. Find Jack and tell him what you're doing. Report back before the end of the day. I'll probably try to sleep in my own bed tonight, so try not to leave it any later than 10 p.m."

Izzy found Jack standing beside Carys Morgan, who was in her usual place in front of a keyboard. Both glanced at her as she reached them. Both smiled.

"Are we getting anywhere?"

"You've not worked with MIT before," said Carys. "But you need to know it takes time. We don't do short-cuts here, and don't know what's relevant at the start. Did you want me?"

"I want Jack. We've got work to do."

Carys looked a bit disappointed, but returned to her keyboard almost at once, her fingers flying so fast Izzy could barely follow them.

"What work?" asked Jack.

———

Jack drove. He said it made him feel safer.

Izzy sat with her arms crossed, trying not to let her impatience show.

"Which one do we start with?" asked Jack.

"The furthest from the farm, then work our way closer. The girl said they stayed in a B&B the previous night, so it should be fairly close to Caxton Farm. I traced a possible route Cally and Frank may have taken, and made a note of small hotels as well, just in case. There are also a few pubs out that way that do rooms. She can't have walked more than ... I don't know. Five Miles? Ten?"

"I'd have said five would be a push. You might be able to manage ten miles in less than two hours when you're running, but she's just a kid. If we don't get a hit, we'll have to go further out."

Izzy nodded, getting used to his driving, not so annoyed by it.

"Yes."

The first place was still serving breakfast for five guests when they arrived.

"A man and his daughter?" said a red-faced woman after she returned from taking a plate of sausage, bacon, eggs and beans to a man who looked as if he didn't need it and shouldn't be eating it. "No, nobody like that, dear."

The next place was the same. They passed beneath the M6, heading east, and tried a few others, but didn't find what they were looking for until they knocked on the door of a stone-walled house with roses growing around the porch.

A young woman opened the door. She was handsome rather than pretty, dressed well in a light sweater and canvas jeans, her auburn hair piled on top of her head, held there with a clip.

"Yes," she said in answer to Izzy's question. "Two nights since. The 12th. The girl seemed tired, and I was worried about her, but come morning she was fine again." She looked at them both. "Do you want to come in? Cup of tea or coffee?"

"Coffee, please," said Jack.

"A glass of water if I could," Izzy said.

She looked around the small dining room the woman led them into. Everything had been cleared away, and there was a sharp scent in the air where she had cleaned the tables. She poured coffee for Jack from a carafe on the side, then poured water for Izzy before sitting. She was young, and when Izzy checked her left hand, she saw no ring.

"Do you live here alone?" she asked.

"Me and my guests, but yes, most of the time between ten in the morning and three or four in the afternoon, it's only me. I like it that way. What about the man and his daughter? Are they in trouble?"

"We're just making enquiries," said Jack. "No trouble yet, but we're trying to track down anyone who might have passed a specific location yesterday."

"Is this about what happened at Caxton Farm?" asked the woman. "It was on the news last night. Terrible goings on, and not so far from here either. You don't expect it on your doorstep, do you?"

"Did you know either Mike Wilson or his wife?" Izzy asked. The farmhouse was only a few miles from where they sat.

The woman shook her head. "Driven past the sign for it, but no, as far as I know I never met them."

"How did the man pay for their room?"

"Cash. I take cards, but cash is always welcome. It saves me the card issuer fee, see. Fifty pounds, it was."

Izzy didn't know if that was expensive or not, but less than most of the hotels around Preston that anyone would want to stay in.

"Did he book in advance?"

The woman smiled. "It was a walk-in. People follow the paths into the Forest of Bowland, thinking they'll get through it in a day." She laughed. "They're too used to cars whisking them past all the scenery, and don't realise it's different on foot. They get more tired than they think and look for somewhere to stay. I get walk-ins sometimes and am happy to oblige if I have space. As it was, the night before last I was empty."

If there had been no booking, it was another avenue of investigation closed off. Whoever the man was, he was careful.

"At what time did they leave yesterday morning?"

The woman looked up into a corner as she thought back.

"About eight-fifteen, eight-thirty."

"Did the girl seem reluctant?"

She had another moment of thought before she shook her head.

"She seemed keen enough, but like I said, a bit tired."

"And the man?"

A shrug. "He was ready to leave. Seemed impatient to get on their way."

"I meant, what was he like?"

"Oh, ordinary."

"Can you describe him?" asked Jack.

She took a moment to gather her thoughts, then said, "Average, like I said. Average height, brown hair cut a little long, and I think his eyes were brown. There was nothing to make him memorable.

Izzy wanted to ask if she had felt anything about him. Instinct. Just as she could tell if someone could be trusted or not. Might be a danger or not. She believed most women had the ability. Most men had no idea they did.

But she knew she couldn't ask. It would be a leading question, and inadmissible.

Instead, she said, "I take it you cleaned the room after they left?"

"Of course."

"Would it be possible to take a look at it?" asked Jack.

"I'll just get the key."

Once she left the room, Jack said, "I don't suppose we'll get anything from the room, but Ed Harrington will ask if we looked. It's them, isn't it, Iz? The man and the girl."

"I'd say so, but let's see what forensics show. And it's close enough to the farm as well. If they left here at 08:30, how long would it take to walk there? What is it, four miles to the turnoff down to the farm?"

"Along the road, but—" Jack broke off as the woman returned, a plastic fob in one hand with a key dangling from it.

They rose and followed her up the narrow stairs. At the top, she turned right and walked to the end of a short corridor, where she unlocked a door.

The room was small but had two single beds, and a window that looked across rolling green fields and woodland. In the distance, the rolling peaks of the Forest of Bowland could be made out.

"Would you mind if we looked around here on our own?" asked Jack.

"Of course not. I'll be in the kitchen. Just call me when you're done."

Izzy opened a door into a bathroom. Wash basin,

toilet, small shower. It gleamed, and she knew they would be unlikely to get anything from it, but CSI might be able to fish hair from the plug to confirm the man and girl were here. When she went back into the room, Jack was on his knees, looking under the bed.

"Not a speck of dust. She keeps this place cleaner than my house."

"Definitely cleaner than mine," Izzy said. "We might get something here, so Harrington will want to send CSI to see what they can find."

Jack nodded. "Agreed." He turned to look through the window. "Not a bad view."

"Faces east," Izzy said. "Which is the right direction, but no view of Caxton Farm." She glanced at Jack. "I want to walk the footpath I believe they took. See what they saw. You don't have to come with me."

"I thought you might want to, so I brought my boots."

"Did you find anything to help you?" asked the owner when they returned downstairs.

"You keep everything spick and span," said Jack, which made her smile. "However, I need to ask you to leave the room untouched, and I'd like you to lock the door. We'll be sending out a forensics team to check the room. I take it you have wi-fi here for guests?"

"I do, and it's free."

"Did he ask for the password?"

The woman had to think. "I'm sorry, I should know, but I can't remember. Mind, most people don't. It's written on a card in every room, so there's no need to ask."

"You said they were the only guests that night?"

She nodded. "That's right."

"When the forensic team comes, they'll bring a tech expert with them. They'll want access to your router but shouldn't need to take it away."

The woman looked worried, but nodded as if it was all becoming a little too much.

"They only stayed the one night," she said.

"You said the man paid cash for the room," said Jack, "but you'll have taken his name and details, won't you?"

"Of course, it's the law. I'll fetch my book."

Jack glanced at Izzy. "He'll have given a false name and address. He paid cash, so she had no record of any card, and there's no requirement for any form of ID. Particularly in a place like this."

"She seems good at her job," Izzy said.

The woman returned with a book and opened it to the most recent page. "It's the third to last entry." She pointed.

Izzy leaned closer and noted the details, even though she knew they would be false.

"I'm going to need to take this as evidence."

The woman frowned. "Is that allowed under data protection? I know I must keep all this for twelve months, but..."

"I'm sorry, but we are the police," Izzy said. "I'll need you to sign for it, and it will be returned to you as soon as possible. I take it you have another book you can use?"

"I do, but..."

Izzy saw the moment she accepted the fact. Jack must

have seen it, too, because he went to the car for a receipt pad.

"Would it be all right to leave our car in your drive-way?" Izzy asked, once the book had been bagged up and the receipt handed across. "We want to walk a little on the footpath they took."

The woman offered an apologetic smile. "Normally, I'd say yes, but I have an early arrival today and need the drive clear. There's a lay-by a hundred yards along the road, though. Your car will be perfectly safe there. We get no crime out this way."

Neither Izzy nor Jack pointed out that was no longer the case.

Once they were outside, Izzy called the number the man had given in the guest book. She was unsurprised when it showed as 'number not known'.

NINETEEN

A few hundred yards from where they parked the car, a green sign in the hedgerow read FOOTPATH. Arrows pointed in two directions, but only one would take them towards Caxton Farm. Izzy and Jack climbed a stile and followed a clear path through woodland to the river Brock. Izzy knew from the map the footpath would shadow it most of the way to their destination.

"Do you ever go walking?" Jack asked Izzy.

"I've been known to, but rarely."

He grinned. "But you have the boots."

She looked down at her feet. "These? Timberland. I bought them because I thought they looked cool. I think this is the first time I've worn them off-road."

As they left the woods, Izzy took her phone out and checked the signal. It was low, and only 3G. It might be sufficient for a conversation, but not much else.

"I'm hoping he used the wi-fi at the B&B," Izzy said.

"The mobile signal's too poor out here to surf the web. It's a shame we don't have the phone, or Priya could have tracked his entire journey. She might still be able to do something with the data from the masts."

"She's good, isn't she." Jack's breath grew short as the ground rose. The Brock splashed and fell across rocks as it made its way west. Hills showed ahead through gaps in the foliage.

"Priya's the best," Izzy said. "I'm hoping she'll stay around long enough to replace Clem. He must have enough years by now to take retirement." Izzy rechecked her phone. The signal had improved, but still only 3G.

"Clem will hang on to the bitter end," said Jack. "And I suspect Preston's too much of a backwater for Priya. She'll be off to the bright lights as soon as she can."

Twenty minutes later, they passed through a longer stretch of woodland, and emerged to continue climbing towards where Caxton Farm lay somewhere ahead. The slopes to either side of the river rose more steeply, and Izzy could see the road she had driven along hugging the hillside. When she checked, her phone had lost any remnant of signal.

"Why do you keep checking your phone?" asked Jack. "Are you expecting a call?"

"I thought he might have been doing the same. There's an OS app he could have used rather than a paper map. I'm just curious, is all. Wondering if he made any calls, looked anything up."

"Such as?"

"Why did he pick Caxton Farm, Jack? Was it random, or did he choose it?"

"If he chose the farm, that implies Rosie Wilson was his target, right? And those poisoned dogs also imply pre-meditation."

"I agree. You know me, I have to worry at every loose thread."

Jack smiled. "Not a bad habit for a police officer."

It felt good to Izzy, the two of them walking side by side, their feet tramping across fallen leaves and hard-packed ground. The silence was broken only by the soughing of wind through the treetops, and the chuckle of water running over rocks. The landscape of hills and valleys rose and fell all around them. Their killer had walked this way, and Izzy wanted to get inside his head, to work out why he came here when he did. Was the date significant? Was the location? What had brought him to this specific place?

And why had he brought Cally?

There was an even bigger question – why had he abandoned her and taken Grace Wilson?

And one more: Had he killed before? And if so, would he kill again?

Izzy knew that MIT didn't like to think they were dealing with a serial killer, but the idea couldn't be ignored. Except there was no evidence this was anything other than a one off event. A victim found along the way.

It was half an hour before they came to a stone bridge where the road crossed the river. On the far side, they glimpsed Caxton Farm, nestled between the surrounding hills. Izzy glanced along the narrow C road she had sped along. Saw where she had almost run into the tractor, and the track that led to the farmhouse. The footpath continued beside the river on the far side of the bridge, and Izzy led the way until they could look across to the house. Tree cover hid them from it, as it would have hidden the killer.

When she stopped, Jack turned and looked at her. "What is it, Iz?"

"He stood here and watched the farmhouse." She smacked her forehead. "I've been thinking he watched from the road, but this makes more sense if he walked the trail. I bet he had binoculars and watched the farm. Probably watched Mike Wilson's tractor move backwards and forwards." She pointed. "He was on that slope on the other side of the river."

"How did he get to the house without being seen?"

"He went along the side of the woodland, over there. It almost reaches the farmyard. That's how he did it."

Izzy thought of the man approaching the house from the woods. Had Rosie Wilson seen him? Would she have been afraid, or would the presence of a young girl have eased her fears? She thought of the CCTV playback, which showed fingers against an upstairs curtain. Yes, Rosie Wilson would have been apprehensive. But how had the man felt? Excited, nervous? She wanted to know what thoughts had gone through his mind as he stood where she did now. Walking the track had been an attempt to get inside his head, but it had only partly succeeded.

"We go the same way," she said, turning aside and re-entering the woods. She didn't wait for Jack, hoping he would follow.

The woods felt redolent with meaning now because she was sure the killer's feet had trodden where her own boots did. She scanned the ground as she walked, half expecting to see footprints, but there were none. The leaf cover shifted in the breeze and would soon cover any trace.

They came out less than a hundred paces from the door that had stood open when Izzy arrived. Blue and white police tape ran all the way around the house and barn, which lay on their left. A small shed sat to their right which, if the man had gone to it, would have hidden him from someone inside the house. There was no sign of anyone working inside the house, which meant CSI must have completed their tasks.

Izzy tried the door of the shed, surprised when it opened, then saw why it wasn't locked when she stepped inside. Old farming and gardening tools hung on pegs. An ancient table held pots and a bucket of compost. A metal sweet tin was home for packets of seed.

Izzy ran her fingers across the tools, each hanging from a nail embedded in a wooden bar. The tools swayed from her touch until she reached and took down a small, curved blade. She knew there would be a name for it, but didn't know what it was.

"He came in here and took something." She pointed. There were two nails where nothing hung, but one of them may have held the same implement she held in her hand. "I think he took whatever was hanging there. Why this and not bring a weapon with him, I don't know."

"That's too much speculation," said Jack.

She turned to look at him. "Is it?"

"If he did, where is it? We'd have found the weapon by now. Every inch on both sides of the river has been fingertip searched."

"What if he took it with him? Put it in his rucksack. The woman at the B&B said he had one. A medium-sized rucksack holding their clothes. Big enough to hide something in."

"Wouldn't he want to toss it the first chance he got?"

"He seems to be forensically aware, so wouldn't want to do that close to the scene. He probably still has it. A trophy, perhaps. It will have Rosie Wilson's blood on it. And that blood will be on the clothes in the rucksack. Find him, find the sack, and we have all the evidence needed."

Jack pulled a face. "If we had the faintest idea who we're looking for, you could be right. But we don't, Iz. He's still a cypher."

"We have the girl. She has to know more than she's told us so far."

"You can't question her hard."

"I know that, Jack, of course I do. But Sarah was fantastic with her. I'm sure with time, we can get more out of her."

Izzy pointed to the hillside beyond the farm."He would have climbed to the road, but not on the farm track. I think he would return to the woods here and follow them along the riverbank to the road. Then he walked. Or took a bus, though I don't think they run much around here. Maybe someone took pity and offered him a lift. We need to put something out on the local news tonight and ask if anyone saw a man walking along that road."

"Carys said the press office was preparing something along those lines. As well as more about the case, and a request for witnesses."

Izzy returned to the shed and put the tool back on its hook. She took a picture of the row of tools on her phone, and then walked out. From where they stood, the door of the boot room was less than twenty paces away. She glanced left and right, then looked up at the barn.

"What is it?" asked Jack.

"Priya and I studied the CCTV footage from the barn and saw no movement, but the cameras don't face this way. Did he know that? He could cross to the door of the boot room without being observed. I wonder if it was unlocked, or did Rosie Wilson let him in?"

"A stranger?"

"A stranger with a cute kid in tow. Most people would let them in. It's why their boots were there, because he took them off. They both did. We need to get back and tell the team what we've discovered."

"Which is what, Iz? You've spun a theory out of thin air. I can see it's possible, but there's no hard evidence."

"Then we look for evidence."

"Good luck trying to convince Harrington. You'll need to make a pretty strong case for it." Jack held his hands up in front of him. "And I'm not telling him."

Izzy walked away fast, almost breaking into a run.

TWENTY

"You took your own sweet time, didn't you?" Superintendent Harrington stood behind his desk, glaring at Izzy and Jack.

Izzy bit down on an answer. Harrington had approved their trip to attempt to discover where their killer stayed. Did he expect it to take five minutes?

"Sorry, boss," said Jack, always the steadying hand. "But we found where they stayed the night before the attack. A place called Magpie Cottage. A B&B on the road between Brock and Caxton Farm. The owner showed us what the man wrote in her book, but it will be bollocks."

"Maybe not," said Harrington. "Perhaps he's not the sharpest tool in the box."

"We can hope," Izzy said. "We brought the book back in any case. I'll get it checked out. Jack's right, he'll have made the name up, but it might tell us something. Hand-writing can, can't it?"

Harrington didn't look convinced. "I don't want to

call in a profiler to tell me he touches himself with his left hand, even though he's right-handed. What took so long?"

"We walked the path I believe he took from the B&B to Caxton Farm," Izzy said. "I think I know how he got there without being seen on the CCTV. I also think I know where he got the murder weapon. From the garden shed. I took a photo, and I'll copy it across to Carys."

"Except we don't have a murder weapon," said Harrington, but he sounded more accepting now. "Uniforms have searched the entire area for half a mile out, and found nothing we don't already have. I've called them off for now. Waste of resource."

"Anything new?" asked Jack.

"Not a lot more than you already know." Harrington's frustration showed in his voice. "We're in that need-to-know, but know-fuck-all window, waiting for results. Waiting to find out more. I've got people going through the CCTV from Preston station on the assumption he might have arrived there and left the same way. I'm also sending a team to the farm to search for the dogs. If they were poisoned, it might show someone had it in for the couple. Did this woman at the B&B give you a description of the man?"

"She said he was someone you'd ignore if he passed him in the street. Even if he sat down across from you in a coffee shop."

"I'll send someone out to see if she can describe him well enough for a sketch. It'll be a start."

Izzy reached into her pocket and put a small card on

Harrington's desk. "Those are her details. Phone number, email and postcode. You might want to send CSI out as well, to see if they can get anything that will confirm it's the same man and girl."

Harrington glanced at it and nodded before going on. "Barbara is still pushing the DNA people hard and says we might get something this evening. The way our luck is going right now, he'll be an unknown, together with the girl. But I'll ask if she thinks it's worth going to the B&B." He looked at Izzy. "I'm wondering who this girl is. She calls him daddy, but is she really his daughter?"

"What does Sarah say, boss?" Izzy knew the FLO Sarah Anderson would have more to say about it than anyone.

"She told me calling him daddy might mean she is. The kid's only eight or nine. If he is her father, would he abandon her like he did?"

"Maybe because she *is* eight or nine," Izzy said. "She's starting to grow up. To ask questions he doesn't want to answer. I think he did her a favour by abandoning her. He's had her locked up tight with him her entire life. God knows what that must have been like."

"She's in the system now," said Harrington. "Social Services have placed her with a temporary foster on their rota. Do you honestly believe her life's going to be any better?"

Izzy shrugged. "Don't know, boss. What do you want us to do next?"

"You can see if Priya has found anything on the station CCTV. She's down in the basement with Clem at the moment. She returned to save his blushes because he struggled with the data Haddon Cain gave us. Jack, find out who we've got to put a sketch together. I think they appointed someone new from the college last year. Both of you check the situation board before you leave." Harrington turned away, dismissing them as his gaze turned to his screen.

"Boss?" said Izzy.

Harrington continued typing.

Izzy waited until he glanced up.

"Are you still here?"

"Jack told me the press office is working on something for the papers and TV. It might be worth asking for witnesses who saw a man and infant on the road from the farm towards Preston. I checked, and there are only two buses a day along that road until you get closer to Brock, and he'd have missed both. It's possible someone stopped and gave them a lift. A man with a baby in his arms, people would show sympathy."

"Assuming he had the kid with him."

"On his own then." Izzy stared at Harrington, refusing to back down. She saw the moment he decided to give in instead of fighting her. No doubt he would have thought of the action himself soon enough.

"All right. I'll get Ailsa to write something and ensure it reaches the press office in time. Tell her what you want to include, but keep it short."

Izzy turned away to brief Ailsa, then went downstairs to find Priya. She was in the basement, but there was no sign of Clem.

"Where is he?" Izzy asked as she slipped into the chair next to Priya.

"Gone home."

"Why?"

"He started getting weird as I was working. I think he finds a lot of the new tech baffling. Give him some code to analyse, or physical data he can cross reference, and he's like a pig in shit. But he's afraid of how fast I work."

"Clem's not all bad," Izzy said. "I've been told he's done brilliant work in the past. And there's still a place for old-school grunt work. Not everybody can be a genius like you."

"Or as pretty," said Priya with a grin. "One day, you'll weaken and fall for my charms."

"Dream on." Izzy knew Priya meant nothing. She might prefer her own sex to men, but they both knew their relationship was strictly platonic. "I'm surprised Clem left, though. He's usually more dedicated than that."

"I think we might have argued a bit," said Priya. "He blew his top and told me I had no right to access the data from my apartment. I showed him my authority, but it didn't change anything. Then I'm afraid I told him to go fuck himself."

"You did what?"

"It's been a long time coming." Priya laughed, but there was an edge to it. "I think I shocked him. He didn't expect language like that from a nice Indian girl."

"Then he doesn't know you well."

"Too fucking right."

159

"Don't let Clem get to you. Everyone knows what he's like. Have you found anything relevant on the CCTV from Preston station?"

"Too much feed, as usual, and the quality is shit. It would help if I had a time window to search in. I've gone back ten days, and am up to five days ago now."

"I might be able to help you with that. Me and Jack just got back from the B&B we think he stayed in with the girl. He was there the night before the killing, making it the twelfth of May." Izzy leaned closer to Priya. "If you came to commit murder, how long would you hang around before doing the act?"

"We both know somebody killed Mike Wilson's dogs ten days before," said Priya.

"He wouldn't want to hang around that long. If it was him who killed them, then he came out here, did it, and went back to London."

"London?"

"The girl told us that's where they live. In a flat in London close to the A40, but she doesn't know the address, and can't describe it well enough to give us a chance of tracking him down. Besides, we don't need to know when he arrived, though that would be corroboration. He killed Rosie Wilson before noon yesterday. I reckon he caught the first train he could out of Preston back to where he came from."

Priya grinned and opened a fresh window on one of the three monitors, and pointed.

"There are a bunch of options. When should I start looking?"

"I got to the farm just before noon. We also know Mike Wilson called treble-nine at 11:21. The killer would be gone by then. Ten or fifteen minutes tops on foot to the C road. The best-case scenario is he found a lift almost immediately, and reached Preston in half an hour. Start at 12:30 and check the trains to London."

"He might have been cleverer than that, and gone someplace else," said Priya. "Caught a bus down to somewhere like Liverpool, Ormskirk, Southport, and then London from there. Or across to Manchester and down."

"All right, but unless he did take a bus – and I'm afraid to tell you they have CCTV on most of those too – he'd still have to use Preston station to get to those places, and we both know it's not Kings Cross. Let's start at 12:30, and see what we find."

"We?"

"I pissed Harrington off," Izzy said. "It might be best if I stay down here with you for a while."

"Then I'll give you the shit job and set you up with a feed from the bus station on Clem's computer. Just make sure you wipe the mouse first. He had a tuna baguette for lunch, and he's not the neatest eater."

They found a strong possibility just before the direct train to London left Preston at 15:18. A man of medium height walked onto platform four. He carried a young child in his arms, wore a rucksack on his back, and a peaked cap pulled low so his face was obscured. Priya nudged Izzy, who turned away from her own screen with relief.

"Freeze it there for me." Izzy leaned closer to the screen. The image was in colour, but grainy. The girl he carried was an infant with wispy red-blonde hair, her face clearly visible.

"Print that."

She waited, then went to the printer. She hoped the image would be good enough for Mike Wilson to recognise his daughter. They had better pictures of Grace from the house, so this one wasn't needed for identification, but it would prove her presence if Mike confirmed it was Grace.

"Move on," Izzy said as she retook her seat, ignoring the feed from the bus station. They had their man now.

"He's a clever bastard, isn't he?" said Priya.

"Too clever, which doesn't tie up with what Cally told us about him. When we were at the farm, I worked out how he got to the house without showing on the cameras. They don't cover the side of the house and the shed."

It was as if the man knew where every camera was, ensuring there was no clear view of his face. But now they knew what he was wearing. Izzy had already noted the Wellington boots on his feet. The way he moved showed they were a size or two too big as he shuffled along. She stood up.

"Where are you going? I thought you were trying to avoid Harrington, and we haven't finished here yet."

"I have. I'm going to the station to see if anyone

recognises the guy and remembers selling him a ticket. He might've had to buy one there and then, unless he had an open return. Finish watching, then go back to, say the 11th and 12th, and see if you can find him coming in."

"Fuck, that's a lot of trains, Iz."

"Not so many. Besides, I trust your skill. You know my number if you find anything."

Izzy went upstairs to update the team and ask if she could be assigned to check out the train station. She avoided Harrington, and after Carys had uploaded the picture of Grace Wilson, she tapped at her keyboard and told Izzy to go. The traffic was heavy, so it took her a while to reach the station, but the trip was a waste of time. She showed the image of the man and child to the staff, but nobody remembered them. She asked for, and got, a list of staff on duty that afternoon, together with their addresses. There were twenty-seven names. Izzy knew Harrington would curse her because it meant another twenty-seven actions. Another twenty-seven people who had to be interviewed. But it was the nature of the work. Always had been, always would be. Even with advances in technology and surveillance, in the end, it still came down to standing in front of people and asking questions. The slow, steady accumulation of information.

TWENTY-ONE

Harrington was unhappy when Izzy brought the stack of new information. She saw the stress on his face, but he told her she had done the right thing, and set people to allocate the interviews. When the actions were assigned, Izzy was asked to carry out six of them herself as a tainted reward. Before she left, Harrington called everyone together and went to stand at the whiteboard.

"Okay, listen up. We just got the final results of the PM back. Nothing is surprising regarding Rosie Wilson's injuries. The initial blow pierced her liver. Even if there had been no others, she would have bled out in five or ten minutes. According to– " He consulted a sheet of paper in his hand, "– Gwynn Buckley, who carried out the examination, Rosie Wilson was stabbed five times with a curved blade." Harrington glanced briefly at Izzy before going on. "There were flakes of rust in the wounds, tiny but obvious." This time, his eyes returned to Izzy and stayed there. "DC Wilde took a photo of the shed at

Caxton Farm. It shows a gap in the line of tools, and current thinking is whoever carried out the attack took something from there to use as a weapon." He gave a brief nod of acknowledgement. "So we have new info to work on."

Harrington looked around the room. "Gwynn said he thinks Rosie's wedding ring is missing. She had a pale circle on the third finger of her left hand where it had been. Does anyone know if it's been found?"

"Nobody's mentioned it, said Ailsa.

"All right. Flag it up to ask Mike Wilson when he's next interviewed. Find out if she removed it frequently or not. The PM also threw us another curveball. Rosie Wilson was pregnant. About three months, according to Buckley. He took samples of the foetus for DNA analysis."

"Are you saying the kid might not have been Mike Wilson's?" asked Ailsa.

"Let's wait for the results, but we should consider the possibility because of the rumours about Rosie Wilson having affairs."

"What are you suggesting, boss?" asked DS Ryan Wade. "That whoever knocked her up might've killed her? Or her husband did when he found out?"

"I'm suggesting nothing, Ryan, and I'd prefer nobody speculates. I'm simply informing you of what we know so far. It might feel like we're spinning our wheels, but this is only day two of the enquiry, and as you are all aware, the data will start to come in thick and fast now. Okay, we all have work to do, let's get on with it."

The light had faded from the sky by the time Izzy

returned from interviewing her final potential witness. It had been a waste of time, none claimed to have seen the man or girl. Izzy looked forward to a few hours of reading and a glass of wine. As she left the building, she almost walked into Priya.

"I was about to call you," said Priya.

"Can it wait? I'm shattered and off home."

"I need to show you something."

Izzy stared at her. "I'm not in the mood."

"I found something on the CCTV from the farm. But not here. Come to my place. You can–"

"I'm going home after," Izzy said. "Come on, get in my car, so I don't have to come back here."

At Priya's apartment, she sat beside her where she had the day before. Priya's MacBook woke up fast, and she brought a still image up.

Izzy let her breath go.

"When was this?"

Priya tapped the top of the screen. "April 24th, 17:24 hours."

"Fuck."

"Yes. Fuck."

"Have you sent this to MIT?"

"I wanted to show it you first. You know Mike Wilson the better than the rest of us."

The still image showed Rosie Wilson on her knees in the yard outside the barn. Mike Wilson stood over her, his face dark with anger. There was no sign of Grace, which was fortunate.

Priya clicked and swiped, and the image jerked and

ran. There was nothing but an empty yard shown on the screen.

"He arrives in his Land Rover in thirty seconds," Priya said. "Rosie comes out to greet him. But you'll see all that for yourself."

Izzy watched as a dark grey Discovery came into the yard too fast, gravel spraying as it skidded to a halt. Mike Wilson got out and strode towards the door just as Rosie appeared.

He stopped, arms at his side.

Words were exchanged.

Mike Wilson lifted a fist, and Rosie took a step back.

He followed her, then slapped her hard on the side of the face. Hard enough to send her to her knees, and bring a pink bloom to her cheek.

He stood over her, fists bunched, then pushed past her and went into the house.

A minute passed before Rosie Wilson got to her feet and went after him. The door closed. Rosie had been crying when she followed her husband.

"We might try a lip reader," Izzy said, "to see if they can work out what was said, but it's a long shot. You can't see enough of Mike's face, and Rosie has hers down most of the time. Is there anything else?"

"I've been through everything I've got and no, nothing else. I thought you'd better see this as soon as possible. What was the argument about, do you think? Her having an affair?"

"According to Haddon Cain, it was affairs, plural."

"Do you think her husband knew about the affairs, and the pregnancy?"

"It's possible. Or maybe that was her telling him. If it was, he might know the kid isn't his. This looks like it could be his reaction to finding out. How come we haven't seen this before?"

"I called Rob Peters and asked if he'd sent me everything," said Priya. "I flirted a bit because he thinks he might be in with a chance. I let him keep on believing it because he can be useful. They have the best tech in Lancashire."

"Why didn't he send this stuff over with the rest?"

"Told me he only found it today. Mike reported a fault in the camera, so Rob assumed there was nothing on that feed. This morning, he logged on to see what the fault was and discovered there wasn't one. He searched through backups and found what I've just shown you."

"Bit late to find this out," Izzy said. "He should've checked all this yesterday."

"I didn't say as much to him because he's one of the good guys. Maybe you ought to give him a try, Iz. He's not my type, but even I admit he's pretty hot. For a man, of course."

Izzy ignored the obvious attempt to match her up, even though the same thought had occurred to her. Rob Peters was indeed hot. He was also a good guy – or gave the appearance of being one. Izzy knew time was passing. She was still young, but couldn't turn her back on relationships forever, or one day she'd wake up an old maid, regretting everything she never did.

"Maybe I ought to talk to him and find out how much he knows."

Priya grinned. "Yeah. Do that."

Izzy pulled a face at her. "Did he say the camera was faulty or not?"

"Told me someone had turned it off."

"Turned it off?"

"That's what he says."

"Is that even possible?"

"They run on electricity, Iz, so of course it is. He said maybe Mike accidentally knocked a switch or something."

"Or it was deliberate, if he knew what the camera might show, and didn't want it on file. He might have thought he could delete stuff himself."

"According to Rob, he couldn't do that. Everything's streamed to the cloud in real-time. Even if he switched the camera off, and even if he knew how to access the data – which Rob says Mike doesn't – it will always be there. They keep the last three months of data on their own servers, the rest is archived in the cloud."

"I'll have to call Harrington and tell him what you found. You can send him the clip. This case is turning into a bucket of eels. He's sent people to a few local pubs closest to Caxton Farm to chat with the locals. They'll ask about Mike and Rosie. Hopefully, they might get something useful. It's a long shot, mind."

"I'll call Rob now and ask him to confirm everything he told me." Priya reached for her phone and pulled up his contact details. She put the phone on speaker so that

Izzy could hear. The phone rang a long time before going to voicemail, and Priya hung up.

"I'll try him again later. Are you staying?"

Izzy shook her head. "Going home. But first, I need to tell Harrington what you've got. Can you send a link to his work email and copy me in?"

"It'll be there by the time you get to Hutton. Faster than a speeding bullet."

By the time she arrived back at Lancashire HQ and the incident room, Ed Harrington had gone home. Only the rump of the MIT remained. Ailsa Grainger was writing notes on the whiteboard as she received reports from the interviews of railway staff. Carys Morgan was in her usual place in front of the HOLMES keyboard, and Izzy wondered if she ever went home.

"I want to show you both something," Izzy said. "It might be important."

"What have you got?" Ailsa came across to where Izzy pulled a chair out and sat.

"I want to show you, not tell."

Izzy found Priya's email and clicked the link, grateful she had set it to the exact moment on the ten days of recordings from the farm cameras. She waited until Carys joined them before hitting play, then waited.

"Oh shit," said Ailsa when it was done.

"This could change everything," said Carys.

"Will it? What would the boss do if we asked him to come back in?"

"Tear you a new one," said Carys. "This is important, but Mike Wilson isn't going to do a runner. It can wait until morning. But you need to be here early, Izzy. You have to be the one to tell him."

"I'm not sure I'm in his good books."

Carys laughed. "Ed puts on an impressive angry face, but he knows who the good guys are, and who aren't. He thinks you're one of the good ones, Izzy. You and Jack both. He told me he wants to invite you to join us at Hutton."

"Fat chance of that."

"Think about it," said Ailsa. "We need good people, and you might find it more interesting here."

"I like it where I am," Izzy said, ending the conversation, realising as she did so she was once more turning her back on change.

It was full dark by the time she got home, and only as she opened the door did she remember she had meant to stop for a bottle of wine. She went to her knees and opened a cupboard. Far back sat a bottle of bourbon from Christmas, and she pulled it out. Just the one. Maybe two. She felt she deserved it. When her phone pinged, she glanced at the screen to see Priya had sent her Rob Peters phone number, and ten kissing emojis. Izzy laughed. Her thumb came out to delete the message, then stopped. It wouldn't do any harm to keep it for now. She copied the number and added it to her contacts.

Upstairs, she set the glass on her bedside table, undressed and slipped under the quilt. She opened her book and sipped the fiery liquor until she felt sleep creeping up on her. She fought it for a moment, fearing a repeat of her nightmare, but in the end, she could fight it no longer. She set an alarm on her phone, and turned out the light.

As she drifted, she thought about relationships. Marriages. Couples. She'd only ever had one boyfriend, and that hadn't turned out well. Never wanted one since. For most of her adult life, Izzy had believed she didn't need anyone. She knew it was because of what had happened to Gabi, but time erodes pain eventually. Now, she was no longer sure what she wanted. The job, yes. She liked working in rural policing, and liked the people she met. But did she want more? Was it time to start acting like a regular person?

She thought of Rob Peters. Maybe Priya was right. Then she smiled as sleep stole over her, amused she thought she might stand a chance with him.

By the time the owls hooted, she was fast asleep.

TWENTY-TWO

Beth Martin didn't sleep as well as she used to, so she sat downstairs watching the late news after George went up to bed. She could hear him stamping around. He'd likely be asleep before she went up, but would rise at least three times in the night. One of the joys of an old man's prostate, he claimed. She smiled at memories of their youth. They hadn't been old then. And the sixties were a wild time, particularly out here in the backwaters of Lancashire. Close enough to Liverpool and Manchester to be the haunt of rock stars and actors. Easy to reach London if necessary, but far enough away from the big cities that few people recognised them. And those that did tended to ignore fame. Beth was about to turn the television off, and go to the kitchen to make herself a cup of warm milk with a dash of brandy, when a news item came on.

"Police are seeking witnesses in an ongoing case. They ask anyone who might have seen or offered a lift to a man with a small child on the road from Brock Mill towards Brock on Saturday, the 13th of May, to contact them. If anyone has any information..."

Beth didn't hear the rest. She went upstairs as fast as her knees allowed.

"George, come downstairs now."

He looked up from the book he was reading. "Used to be it was upstairs you wanted me to come. What's up, old girl?"

"Something on the news. A man and a child. Like the ones we gave a lift to."

"What about them? Are they all right?"

"Police are looking for them. Come downstairs now, instead of asking all these questions." Beth turned and descended the stairs.

The news had finished, and a weather presenter told them tomorrow would bring more rain, with temperatures below average for May, at twelve degrees. Beth had no idea if that was warm or not. She still thought in Fahrenheit. Despite that, she knew how the TV remote worked and pressed the green button. After a moment, the local news played again, and she fast-forwarded to the clip she had seen and pressed pause, pleased with herself.

She heard George coming down the stairs, a clump-shuffle as he descended one step at a time. They were both getting old, she knew, but still slept upstairs. For how long, she wasn't sure, but didn't want to admit defeat just yet. Their son and daughter had already been on at them that the house was no longer suitable.

Wouldn't a nice retirement apartment in Ormskirk or Formby suit them better? It had made Beth look up how much their stone cottage was worth. When she found out, she knew why the kids wanted them to move.

"What is it?" George asked as he dropped into his armchair.

Beth pressed play and remained standing as the item ran again. When the telephone number was read out, she paused and rewound. She fetched their notepad and pen, and the next time it played, she wrote the number down.

"Do you think that's who they're looking for?" asked George. "He seemed such a nice man, and the girl was a poppet."

"It only says they want to talk to him. Perhaps he's a witness or something. It is him, isn't it?"

"Don't know, old girl. There must be a lot of families with babbies around these parts. Some of them might even take them for a walk."

"Walking along the road like he was? Shall I ring the number?"

"At this time of night? Everyone will be in their beds, like we should be."

"It's the police," said Beth. "They don't sleep. Well, they do, but not all of them at the same time."

She went into the hall and dialled the number. It rang so long she suspected George was right, but hung on so she wouldn't give him the satisfaction of it. Then someone picked up, and she told them what they had witnessed.

TWENTY-THREE

Izzy was deep asleep when her phone woke her to the sound of Taylor Swift. She reached out and answered.

"Grumpy today, aren't you?" There was amusement in Jacks voice.

"Am I late or something?" Izzy checked her screen to see it was 6:35.

"Giving you a heads-up is all. We got a call last night from a couple out your way who said they gave a lift to a man and a young child on the afternoon of the murder. Harrington's sending the sketch artist out to you. When he gets there, go with him and interview them while he tries to get a likeness."

Izzy replayed what Jack had said.

"How long?"

"Don't know. He lives in Chorley, and left there a few minutes ago, so how far is it from your place?"

"He should be here in twenty or thirty minutes. I need to shower."

Izzy cut Jack off and rolled out of bed and into the bathroom. By the time a knock came on the door, she was dressed and only slightly damp. She opened the door to reveal a young man. If pushed, she'd have put his age at sixteen or seventeen. His brown hair was long and pulled back in a ponytail. He was tall and slim, wearing cargo pants and a college sweatshirt under a leather jacket.

"Are you Isabella Wilde?" His voice was deep, belying his teenage looks.

"I am. And you are?"

"Jeff Harding."

He offered his hand, and she gave it a perfunctory touch before looking past him in search of a car.

"How did you get here?"

"Motorbike," he said. "Honda 400. But there's rain forecast so we can take your car if you prefer."

Izzy glanced at the sky. Low clouds, but dry so far.

"I'll ride pillion if you've got another helmet. I take it you wore one?"

"Coming to meet a police officer?"

Izzy decided she liked him. He wasn't wary of her like some men. She also liked how he hadn't checked her figure out, keeping his eyes on her hairline.

"Let me get a waterproof jacket just in case."

Three minutes later, Izzy was perched on the pillion seat as Jeff Harding took the B road north-west. She leaned forward and shouted.

"I assume you know where you're going?"

He nodded instead of trying to answer.

Izzy relaxed, enjoying the sense of motion, and the

lack of a car body surrounding her. She'd never ridden a motorcycle herself, but sitting behind Jeff, she got an idea it might be fun.

Ten minutes later, he turned off the B road before passing the single-track lane, which led to Caxton Farm. He didn't so much as glance at the entrance, and Izzy wondered if he knew what had happened there three days earlier. She turned in the saddle to look down, but saw nothing through the trees.

The old couple lived in a large cottage, set into a hill-side with a terraced garden at the back that gave onto a sheep-dotted hillside. An elderly woman with white permed hair opened the door.

"You must be the police," she said to Jeff Harding.

Izzy suppressed a smile, knowing what she must be thinking. Policemen look younger all the time.

"I'm Detective Constable Isabella Wilde, Mrs Martin." She showed her warrant card. "And this is Jeff Harding. He's here to sketch the man you said you offered a lift to. May we come in?"

"Oh, yes, of course. Where are my manners? Tea? Biscuits? I have some nice ginger cake as well."

"Tea would be lovely," Izzy said.

The woman led them into a living room, where anti-macassars guarded the wooden arms and backs of the furniture. A man sat in one of the chairs, a copy of the Daily Mail shouting a lurid headline about immigration in his lap. He started to rise, but Izzy waved him back down.

"Mr Martin?" she asked.

"George," he said. "Please, call me George." He smiled. "And I expect Beth is making you tea, isn't she?"

"I missed the chance of a cup before leaving," Izzy said. "I'll wait until she brings it before we talk about what happened the other day, if you don't mind."

"What did he do?" asked George Martin, not waiting for his wife to return.

"I'm afraid I can't say anything about a current investigation, Mr Martin, but likely nothing. We are enquiring about any men and children travelling into Preston on Monday."

"We dropped him at the hospital. Didn't look sick to me, nor the babby, but we didn't like to ask. Said it was his wife they were visiting, mind, so t'wouldn't be them was sick, would it."

Izzy was eager to learn more, relieved when Beth Martin returned with a tray.

When tea was poured, biscuits put out, cake cut and everyone seated, Izzy said, "Do you mind if Jeff asks you what he looked like first?"

"Twas Beth saw him better'n me," said George. "You had a right good look, didn't you, pet?"

"Stared right at him," said Beth. "What is it you want to know?"

"As much as you can recall," said Jeff. "Let's start with hair colour."

"Black, I think, but he had a cap on. One of those the young 'uns wear, you know, with a long bit at the front."

"Eye colour?"

"Brown, I remember that."

"Did he wear glasses?"

Beth had to think a moment before shaking her head. "No glasses."

"Moustache, beard?"

"Clean shaved, but a bit stubbly like he'd not bothered that morning."

"I take it he was white?"

"He was."

"Clothes?"

"One of those walking jackets. Blue one, I think. Didn't see his trousers nor his boots." Then, "Ah, yes, I did. He was wearing wellies. They looked too big for him. He walked awkwardly when we dropped him off at the Preston Royal. I thought at the time he must have come out of the house too fast and picked the wrong pair."

"Do you think we can go into the kitchen so I can try to sketch him?" said Jeff.

Izzy was impressed at his skill in managing the old woman. His deep voice was soothing, and she saw how Beth wanted to mother him. To please him. But she noted he had asked only about appearance, and missed a vital question.

"Before you go, Mrs Martin, what age would you say the man was?"

"Oh..." She drew the sound out as her gaze searched the ceiling. "It's hard when you get old. Everyone looks so young, but maybe forty, perhaps a bit older."

"Thank you." Izzy made a note as Jeff stood.

"Let's take our tea and cake," he said, "and I'll do the best job I can."

When they were gone, George Martin said, "Is this about the murder of Rosie Wilson, miss?"

"I'm afraid I can't–"

"I suppose it is, then. Was it that man who killed her?" He raised a hand. "I know, you can't say. Didn't look like a killer mind. And he had the babby. A killer wouldn't be carrying a babby around with him, would he?"

"Did you talk to him?"

"Beth did. I need to concentrate on my driving these days." And then, as he realised what he had said, "Not that I have trouble or nothing, but the roads are busier than they used to be, aren't they?"

"Indeed they are, sir," Izzy said. "I expect you listened though, didn't you? Did he say what they were doing on the road at that time of day?"

"Going to Preston Royal to see his wife. She was in there for something, but he didn't say what. Said her name was Joan. No, Jenny. Jenny Jones."

"Did he offer his name?"

"Peter Jones."

It differed from the name used at the B&B, and Izzy suspected both had been made up on the spot.

"Do you agree with your wife about his age?"

George took a moment. "I didn't see as much of him as she did, but I'd say she was close enough."

"What was your impression of him?"

"I thought he sounded a bit edgy. Worried about his wife, I thought at the time."

"Edgy how?" Izzy made no notes, not wanting to distract the man from his story. She could write them up later. Maybe compare them with whatever Jeff found out from Beth Martin.

"Not sure I could put my finger on anything specific. It might have been nothing more than the babby crying. She bawled her head off when they got in the car, but he gave her one of Beth's biscuits. Jaffa Cake." He smiled. "Shut her up right off, it did."

Izzy wasn't sure an eleven-month-old was meant to eat Jaffa Cakes, but she supposed if the man were their killer, he wouldn't much care. Except he had taken Grace for a reason. A reason Izzy was getting a feel for. Getting a feel for him, even if everything was still fuzzy. He was bold. Or stupid.

"Did he say what the girl's name was?"

"Cally. Pretty little thing, all blonde hair and blue eyes, but all babbies have blue eyes, don't they?"

Not eleven-month-old ones, but Izzy kept the thought to herself.

One thing George Martin's recollection confirmed was that the man he gave a lift to was a person of interest in the case. The girl in the hospital said her name was Cally. In the heat of the moment, it would have been the first thing that came to the man.

Half an hour later, Izzy patted Jeff on the shoulder and pointed to a field gate.

"I've been here before," said Jeff when he removed his

helmet. "To the B& just along this road a few miles, to make a sketch of the same man."

"Are the two sketches similar?"

"Yesterday's isn't as good as today's, which I believe is much closer to what he looks like. Beth Martin admitted to having cataracts, but told me she still sees well enough, and her description of him was excellent."

Izzy climbed from the pillion seat and stretched her legs, aware Jeff was watching her. She played it up a bit, amused. He was young, but at least he wasn't on the job. He was good-looking, and that voice was amazing. She imagined he wasn't short of admirers at the University. Her thoughts were unusual enough for Izzy to wonder where they had come from before dismissing them. She had sat close behind him while he rode his motorbike through the narrow lanes, both of them leaning in unison on the corners. That's probably all it was.

"Do you have both sketches with you?" she asked, distracting herself.

"In the top box." Jeff put the machine on its stand and opened it with a key. He pulled out a sketch pad and turned to the last completed page, then showed it to Izzy.

"This is the one you just did?"

He nodded.

"It's good. You have talent."

"So I've been told, but this doesn't require talent as much as accuracy."

Izzy turned the page to look at the previous sketch. There was a resemblance between them, but they could also be of two different men. The hair colour was the same, but in the first, the eyes were grey, and in the second, brown.

"Beth's description was much better," said Jeff. "She told me she was staring straight at him once they started off. Got a good old look, she said." He smiled. "Is he the man who killed Rosie Wilson?"

Izzy tried to decide whether or not she could tell him. He wasn't job, but he was seconded to it for now.

"Maybe," she said.

"I've never sketched a killer before. This is only my third job with the police. I did a man who beat someone up in Miller Park, another who exposed himself down by the cycle track alongside the Ribble."

"I assume you sketched his face, not..." Izzy pointed down, and Jeff laughed.

"Yes, only his face. They caught him, too. Caught both of them. So maybe I'm not too bad."

"No, maybe you're not. How did you get the gig?"

Jeff smiled. "When I finished my degree, I discovered the college offered a Forensic Artist course. I liked the idea, so took it. I expected I'd have to move away to find work, but someone from the Lancashire force contacted my tutor to say they had a vacancy, and was there anyone he could recommend. He sent me for an interview, and I got the job. It's only as and when, but the extra money's welcome."

"Your tutor must have thought you were good enough," Izzy said.

Jeff shrugged. "I won't pretend. I was the best student in the Art course, and I've always had a side hustle sketching people. Men, women, kids, dogs." He smiled. "About three-quarters of the class were girls, more into fantasy and fashion. And the other guys were, well, not as good as me. The police warned me it might mean looking at things some people would rather not see. Or learn about things, anyway. Like this, I suppose."

"You mentioned Rosie Wilson," Izzy said. "Did you know her?"

"Not really. Met her a few times. My parents are farmers living out this way, and it's a small group even around here. The ones who make money, anyway. They're good for getting work through. Seems they like a picture of the missus on the wall." He smiled. "Sometimes not even wearing much, though I reckon they put those in a bedroom, rather than downstairs where anyone can see them."

"You said your parents are farmers." She decided not to respond to what he said about the nude drawing.

Jeff nodded.

"But you didn't fancy it?"

He shook his head. "Dad thinks I'm nesh. Mum wants me to do what I enjoy. I've got two older brothers who work the farm, so I'm somewhat surplus to requirements."

Izzy knew they had drifted away from her purpose, but she was interested. It was a pleasant distraction from the case, though she was aware of time passing. Also of dark clouds gathering from the coast, curtains of rain hanging beneath them.

"You don't look old enough to have a degree."

He laughed. "I still have to show ID every time I buy a bottle of wine in the supermarket, or order a pint in a pub. Twenty years from now, I'll be grateful for it."

"Why did you take the police job?"

"Being an artist is a hard slog, and only about one per cent ever make a living at it. This pays the bills, and lets me save for a place of my own. And I still draw portraits in my spare time. That's what I'm best at. It's not fashionable, and it's not sexy, but I enjoy trying to capture the souls of people." He glanced down shyly. "I'd like to sketch you if you'd let me."

"Why?"

"You have an interesting face."

Izzy laughed because it was most likely the truth. She knew she was attractive, and that's what most men saw. But she thought what Jeff Harding saw was her interesting side. Or maybe interesting was the wrong word. Complicated might be better.

"I wouldn't make a good subject," she said, closing the conversation.

Jeff shrugged. "Up to you. But I think you would." He swung his leg back over the bike.

"Not yet," Izzy said. "I need to gather my thoughts and record some notes before we go. Can you wait five minutes?"

"Of course."

Izzy opened her notebook and sat on the grassy bank beside the road. She closed her eyes and thought about her talk with George Martin. She noted to ask Jeff if he knew anything she didn't. When she was done, she closed the book, stood and stretched. She saw Jeff had his sketchpad open. When she approached, he closed it, trying to make the movement casual, but she took it from him. When she opened it, she saw her image on the page, her head down, a frown between her eyebrows. She stared at the sketch because it had captured a side of her she hadn't been aware of. She glanced up at Jeff.

"Sorry. It was an invasion of privacy."

Izzy smiled. "It's fine. Can I keep it?"

"Of course. But don't tear it out until I drop you at your place, or it might crease."

"I'm not going home," Izzy said. "Can you take me to force HQ in Hutton, if it's not too far out of your way? I need to report in."

She held him tightly as they rode through the countryside, and then weaved through the city traffic on the Honda. After Jeff dropped her off, Izzy watched him ride away, thinking how it might be if she could soften herself enough to and have a boyfriend. She almost laughed, because the word sounded so old-fashioned in her head.

TWENTY-FOUR

There was a buzz in the incident room when Izzy entered. All members of MIT-1 plus Jack stood at the whiteboard, where Ed Harrington was writing information up. New information, Izzy hoped. It felt as if progress had stalled. It was time they got a break. She hoped the sketch Jeff had made might be one.

Jack glanced at Izzy as she approached, and used his hand to tell her to stand beside him. Harrington also saw her, and turned from what he was doing.

"Good, we're all here. I want to go through what we know so far and what we've found out this morning. We're only waiting for Barbara Jessup, who should be here any minute. Did you find anything out from the old couple, Izzy?"

She reached into the stiff envelope Jeff had given her, and pulled out the two sheets of drawing paper showing the likenesses he had produced. She left the sketch he had made of her inside.

"Jeff Harding has produced two sketches of our suspect, boss. The first at the B&B, and a better one from the couple who called in last night. The old woman reckons it's a pretty good likeness."

She handed both sketches to Harrington, who studied them for a moment before passing them to Carys Owen. "Scan these into the system, in case they throws up a match, then send copies of the better one to everyone on the team." He turned to the others. "All of you take a good look. Memorise the face. I'll decide when to tell the press about it." He glanced at Izzy. "Good work, by the way."

"Not me, boss. Jeff Harding made the sketches. But I did get some good intel from Mr and Mrs Martin. I'll enter it once we finish here."

"Anything we need to know right now?"

"The main thing is that from Beth Martin's description, and what she said about the man they gave a lift to, he is almost certainly our suspect. He had a young girl with him and wore wellingtons too big for his feet, carried a rucksack and spoke with a southern accent."

"All good stuff." Harrington turned his attention to the others. "I want us to double-check the CCTV at the Preston train station again, now we know who we're looking for. Priya tells me he was careful on the way out, but he may have been less so on the way in. I'll email her the image and ask her to check against it. She won't like it, but it has to be done."

"We know he was in Preston, boss," said Carys Morgan. "How critical is it we know when he arrived?"

"We won't know that until we know the rest,

Carys," said Harrington. "If he was here two weeks ago, it could indicate premeditation. It might even be he who poisoned the Wilson's dogs. The longer he was around, the more people will have seen him. If he came later, it also tells us something: he came for a reason. Rosie Wilson wasn't some random. If that's the case, we need to know why her. Did he know her? Did she know him? Or her husband?" Harrington pushed a hand through his short hair. "Okay, let's go through it again and see if anything jumps out at us. Time's passing, and the more it does, the less chance we have of catching this bastard. Carys, what does HOLMES give us this morning?"

"I put those names in we got last night, after Simon and Ailsa went on a pub crawl of the area around the farm. No pings on them other than the odd speeding ticket, so we might be able to give credence to what they say."

"Some people get all the cushy jobs," said DS Ryan Wade.

"You were all here when I asked for volunteers. As I recall, you had some music thing at your son's school, Ryan."

"Aye. And in retrospect, I'd've jumped at the chance to miss seventeen recorder recitals, boss."

Harrington and a few of the others laughed.

"We've all been there. Anyway, we now have the names of three men to interview, and hints that the number could even double. Rosie Wilson looked as if butter wouldn't melt, but underneath, rumour has it, she was always ready for a new liaison. Did you hear anything about Mike Wilson?"

"Nothing," said Ryan. "Everyone told us he worked his bollocks off day and night. Too tired for anything else."

"I hope you made clear you were police. Otherwise, anything you discovered would be inadmissible in court."

"We did, boss. Ailsa was a star. We visited nine pubs and got a bit from each of them."

"Do you agree, Ailsa?" asked Harrington.

She nodded. "I do. And from the way a lot of the men acted, I don't think Rosie Wilson was the only one putting it about. They seemed a touchy-feely crowd. The men, that is." Ailsa grinned. "Though Josh got a couple of propositions, so it's lucky Ryan couldn't come, with him being a married man and all."

"Chance'd be a fine thing," said Ryan.

"All right, back to the case," said Harrington. "Let's draw up a list of names to interview. Assign them to Izzy and Jack, as they live locally, and it's their patch. Ailsa, can you summarise what we have so far?"

She passed between Izzy and Jack to stand at the board before glancing down at the tablet in her hand.

"Do you want the works, or just the highlights?"

"Best do both in case anyone has missed anything."

"All right. So, the deceased is Rosie Wilson, age twenty-nine. She married Mike Wilson in twenty-twelve when she was eighteen. Just eighteen. The wedding was three days after her birthday. One daughter, Grace, eleven months old, is missing.

"CSI has identified nineteen separate prints at the farmhouse with an additional five others on the tractors and another four in a Land Rover. Rosie Wilson drove a tiny Fiat, and we've got another five prints from that. One set is Rosie's, another her husband's. The other three are unknown at this point, but they could well be from a garage service. Semen stains were found on the passenger seat. They've gone off for DNA analysis. We've identified several people from the number plates of the cars at the party at Caxton Farm, and through other contacts. Actions have been raised for officers to call on them, and ask a few standard questions, which I have put together, and to ask if they are willing to provide a DNA swab. Purely voluntary, of course, but a couple of coppers on the doorstep can make it hard to say no.

"We now have what Izzy says is an image that looks like our suspect. From the information provided by the girl, who is now in the care of Social Services, we believe our man comes from West London, close to the A40. Priya and Clem are double-checking CCTV at the train and bus stations, looking for any sign of him arriving. We believe we have him on the way out, and the clothing matches what he was wearing when he left the B&B that morning. If he was on that train, it gives us a timeframe to look at Euston's CCTV. Maybe even the underground, which would give us a location nearer where he lives. According to the notes Sarah and Izzy took when they spoke with the girl, our suspect's first name is Frank, but we don't have a surname. No point running that through the system."

Ailsa took a moment to catch her breath, and Harrington said, "Are we sure the girl doesn't know her surname? How can that happen?"

"I thought the same thing, boss," said Sarah. "So I got permission from the Social to have another chat, and she truly doesn't. She's been home-schooled, but doesn't know a lot of what you'd expect for someone her age. My guess is he kept her in the dark about a lot of things."

"Does the fact he used GLB on her lead us anywhere?" asked Jack.

"Unlikely," said Sarah. "You can pick it up at twenty places in Preston, hundreds if he comes from London. Barbara said it's impossible to match it to any other sample, so there's nothing there other than he used it. And used it on the girl. Barbara is cross-referencing the DNA from the scene. If we get lucky, he'll have left some trace. If so, we cross-reference it to the girl to see if there is a relationship.

"Thanks to Izzy and Jack," said Harrington, "we are fairly certain we know the footpath they took from the B&B to Caxton Farm. Local police are contacting ramblers' associations, to see if anyone saw anything along the route. Apparently, from what we've learned so far, it's a popular path, so we might get lucky. And we now have three names for lovers of Rosie Wilson, thanks to Ailsa and Simon. Those conversations are actioned for today. Barbara is promising DNA results by the close of play tonight. And–"

The door opened, and the senior CSI just mentioned

strode into the room. From her expression, she had something for them.

"What have you got?" asked Harrington. "Give me something we can use."

"I think this might fit the bill, boss. I got a DNA analysis for the girl at 11:20 today and fed it into the national database of missing persons. I got a hit. And you might not like what I'm about to say."

"Tell us anyway, Babs."

"Her name is, or maybe I should say was, Abigail McFadden." Barbara held a hand up as Harrington started to say something. "Let me finish before anyone speaks, because this is the meat of it. Seven years and five months ago, Jessica McFadden, living in Brighton, wife to Charles McFadden, was found dead. A single knife wound to the chest, which entered her heart. There is no indication of sexual activity either pre- or post-mortem, but whoever did it left a trace behind. Hair and skin flakes. The DNA was analysed, but there was no match in the system then. What has come back now are hits from several other subsequent murders, including our case. We have a match for the offender, and also for the girl we should now be calling Abigail McFadden. Hers were found at four of the murder sites. Jessica McFadden was found by her husband, when he came home from work. He was an initial suspect, but ruled out early on. Their daughter, Abigail, had been abducted from the house. The conclusion reached at that time was she had been killed away from the house, and her body was never found." Barbara frowned, as if she was trying to think if she had forgotten anything, then gave a slight shake of her head. "Okay, that's it for now."

"Fuck," said Harrington. "Are you telling me whoever killed Rosie Wilson has done it before?"

"There's a DNA trace for him, yes, and it's the same girl. The MO is different. No footpath noted nearby in Brighton, but that might have been his first time."

Harrington looked at each of them. "Are we looking at a serial offender?"

Barbara shrugged. "Not for me to say, but the science appears to point that way."

"Tell me about the other – what, murders?"

"Yes, boss. Murders.

"One just over five years ago, a second two years later, and another eighteen months back. Almost identical MO in all cases, except no kid was taken. No kid in the house. A woman dead on the floor when her husband comes home. DNA trace on the living room sofa in two instances matches the one we got back for Abigail McFadden – who we've been calling Cally until now."

"She was there and asleep," said Izzy. "It's his cover. Turns up with a young girl in tow. Talks his way inside. Asks for a glass of water and drugs her so she sees nothing. Then he goes to work."

"When we spoke with her, she told us she often falls asleep," Sarah said. "Her father – or the man she believes is her father – told her it was nothing to worry about. He's a monster."

"No argument from me on that," said Harrington. He took a breath. "Okay. We're going to have to tell the

National Crime Agency there may be a serial out there. Ailsa, get on to them, and tell them what we have. Ask if they have anything else that matches. In the meantime, the rest of you get on with what's planned for the day. You know what your actions are, so do them."

TWENTY-FIVE

"Do you think we have a serial offender, Iz?" asked Jack. Rain streaked the windscreen as he drove over the M6 and took the A59 east.

They were on their way to interview the three men rumoured to be lovers of Rosie Wilson. Izzy looked down at her phone for the first address, deep in the Forest of Bowland, near the village of Chipping. She pinned it and closed the phone.

"Maybe. And if we're right, the NCA might or might not take it off us. Depends whether they believe the same thing Harrington does."

"Four previous cases, if Babs is right."

"Four we know of. Babs didn't give us the dates, did she?"

"Not exact ones, no. The girl was taken seven and a half years ago when her mother was killed. Then she was put at the scene of another killing five years ago, more since. Those are long gaps between the first and second case if we're looking at a serial."

"Those are the ones we know about," Izzy said. "Now the link's been made, someone will start looking for more connections. Sarah's a wizard with HOLMES. If there's anything out there, she'll dig it up. I bet she finds more killings, or maybe attempted killings." Izzy pointed ahead. "Keep on this road at the junction. It'll be quicker to Kiln Farm if we go this way."

"You live around here, don't you?" asked Jack, as they passed the 30-limit sign on leaving Goosnargh.

Izzy pointed at the small semi-detached brick cottage she had left a little more than two hours before.

"That one," she said.

Jack took a glance. "Nice and quiet. Unless your neighbours are the rowdy kind."

"Old lady who was born there, and said she's going to die there too if they let her. I go around a couple of times a week to check on her. She makes me tea and feeds me cake. Good cake, too. She's old school."

"Do you want to take the lead when we do the interviews?"

"If that's okay with you. I want you to watch them for any tells and to see how they react to a woman asking the questions."

"We're already pretty sure who killed Rosie, so this could be a waste of time."

"I don't think so," Izzy said. "It'll give us a feel for what she was like. How much she might've slept around."

"Not much sleeping involved by the sound of it," said Jack, and Izzy laughed before cutting herself off. She wondered if the job had eroded some of her humanity. She knew between themselves, they often forgot there were actual people involved.

"If she was as prolific as we've heard, might it be another of her lovers who killed her?"

"I suppose it's possible," said Jack, "but it pushes the limit of believability. He lives in London and has a kid in tow. We might be able to make a better evaluation when we've spoken with these three men today."

Izzy opened her phone as they passed a sign for the Beacon Fell Country Park.

"There's a sharp right bend in about a mile. Take the single-track road straight on; then we go up towards Blindhurt Fell, as far as the road takes us. At the top, there's a track that runs off on the left. Kiln Farm's at the end of it."

Jack changed down to third gear as they climbed the steep slope, then down again to take the turn. From the ridge, they could see west to the coast and Blackpool Tower, but not for long. The cloud cover was creeping slowly down the hillside, and would soon blanket them in damp fog.

Kiln Farm sat in a slight depression where it would be sheltered from the worst of the wind.

"He knows we're coming, doesn't he?" said Jack.

"Sarah rang all three. We've got forty-five minutes for each interview. She worked out the travel time between each location. The last one's up near Clitheroe, so she left that to last."

"What do we know about – what's his name?"

"Ethan Walton. Twenty-nine years of age, so near the same as Rosie Wilson. Farms with his father, mother and brother. He's got six penalty points on his licence for speeding, one in Preston, the other on the M6. Nothing else. The second guy is over twenty years older than Rosie. The last somewhere in between."

"How many lovers do you reckon she might've had?"

"Lovers? They sound more like distractions. She doesn't seem to have stayed with any of them long, and everyone says she'd never leave Mike. I expect we'll know more by the time we finish today."

Ethan Walton was waiting in front of the house for them. A stout woman at his side would be his mother. No doubt he and his family had seen their car descending the track. The farmhouse was smaller, and less well-maintained than Caxton Farm. Beyond it, on the slopes, sheep grazed.

"Mr Walton," Izzy said, "I'm Detective Constable Wilde. My colleague is Detective Sergeant Ward. We would like to ask you a few questions about your relationship with Mrs Rosie Wilson."

"Best come in," said the woman. "We can talk in the snug."

"We need to speak with your son alone, Mrs Walton," said Jack.

"I know what he's like, so you can't shock me. Can't keep it in his pants. He's always been the same."

"We still need to speak with him on his own."

For a moment, Izzy thought the woman might offer a stronger objection, but then she shrugged.

"I'll put the kettle on. Need a brew on a day like this."

"That would be lovely," said Jack, getting a smile in return.

Izzy suppressed her own smile. Jack could charm anyone.

They sat on two sofas facing each other. Izzy and Jack on one, Ethan Walton on the other. He was tall, with a thatch of blonde hair, and piercing blue eyes. Izzy could see how he might attract women. As well as being good-looking, he had a presence about him.

"I take it you know the reason for our visit, Mr Walton?"

"Call me Ethan, please. Did you come all the way out from Preston?"

"We did."

"I've seen you before somewhere," he said to Izzy, already trying it on. "In a pub?"

"Possibly the Seven Stars, or in Preston. I assume you go into the city sometimes?"

"Most weekends." He leaned forward, his eyes locked on Izzy's, and she felt the attraction of him. "What is it you want to know about Rosie?"

"Do you admit you and she had a relationship, Ethan?"

"No point pretending otherwise. Do you know who killed her? There's plenty around here who would like to see him strung up by his balls."

Izzy noticed Jack making notes, but was aware they hadn't yet started. "How long did your relationship go on for?"

"A couple of months. Ended it over a year ago," said Ethan. "That was the way with Rosie. We had a fling at school, too, even shorter. A week, that was. But God, she was hot back then. Still is, of course." His expression changed, and he said, "Was."

"These relationships were relatively short, then?"

"Like I told you. Rosie knocked your socks off, and then moved on."

"Was it always Rosie who ended the relationship?"

"Yeah, both times. She can never stay with one bloke for long. Apart from Mike, that is. Seems he has something the rest of us can't give her. Money, most like. Or status. Mike's one of the richest farmers around here. Even when she was playing the field, Rosie always went back to him. P'raps she saw him as a haven from the madness of her sexuality."

"Are you saying she had several relationships with men?"

"Several?" Ethan laughed. "More like seventy. A dozen or more I knew about before she left school. Not just men either, according to gossip." He looked hard at Izzy, perhaps searching for some sign of shock, but she showed nothing. "I saw a photofit on the news last night. If you have a suspect, why are you talking to me?"

"Because we need to know whether Rosie Wilson might have made any enemies. Or her husband had."

"Mike's a big softy. He knew Rosie put it about, but

always took her back. Not that she ever left him or noth-ing. It was an itch she had to scratch, was all. She liked sex, I suppose. More than most folks, I'd say, men or women."

Izzy was frustrated at the man's calmness. A woman he had slept with was dead, but he gave no indication Rosie's death affected him.

"Do you know the names of any of her other lovers, Ethan? Recent ones would be useful to us. The more recent, the better."

"Knock on twenty doors in the Forest, and you'll probably find at least one guy she's had a fling with. But I can give you a few names. There was–" He broke off as his mother came in with cups, a teapot, and a plate of fruit cake already sliced and buttered. She set them on the table and remained standing beside it.

"Thank you, Mrs Walton," Izzy said, staring at her until she turned and left. When she had gone, Izzy rose and closed the door, which had been left ajar.

"Now then, these names," she said. "And then, if you are willing, I would like you to provide a DNA sample."

"Christ, there's too much work in that list of names for the two of us," said Jack as they drove back to the narrow C road.

"We don't need to interview all of them ourselves," Izzy said. "Let's see what else we get from today, and then Harrington can decide."

"Tell me something, Iz. Was Rosie Wilson an outlier?"

"Do you mean the sex? Turn left at the bottom and take the sign to Chipping. The next place is halfway between there and Clitheroe. And yes, I'd say Rosie was an outlier." She waited, trying not to smile because she knew Jack wanted to ask her more. When he said nothing by the time they reached the B road, she said, "What's your experience, Jack? You're not bad-looking. Have you ever been with someone you couldn't handle?"

He laughed. "Pretty much every single time, but it's no good asking me about women, Iz. You know I'm no expert on them."

"Did you believe him when he said Rosie had been with both women and men?"

"What, am I supposed to be an expert on lesbians because I'm gay? You need to ask Priya about that, but it wouldn't surprise me, if Rosie were as sexually voracious as Walton claimed."

"Have you got someone in your life at the moment?" Izzy asked.

Jack glanced at her briefly. "What is this, Iz? We don't have these conversations. Be careful, or I'll start asking back. You're a looker. I've seen the way men look at you. But I've never heard you talk about anyone."

"Nothing to tell, Jack. I don't do relationships. But I suspect you'd like to."

Jack was silent.

Eventually, as they passed through Chipping, he said, "Yes, I would, but it's hard to find someone who wants the same things I do, particularly around here. You know what it's like. I might prefer my own sex, but I'm not into that mad scene of one-night stands. I need someone to come home to on a cold night. Someone to share things with. As for ... well, the sex ... maybe I'm like you, and it's not important. It's like the Wild West out there if you go searching on the web. I expect I'll find someone eventually. Just as I you will."

Izzy shook her head. "Yes, you will. You're a handsome man with a gentle charisma. As for me ... I don't think so."

She almost told him the reason why, then baulked at opening up to him as much as it would require. Apart from which, she didn't know the answer herself.

TWENTY-SIX

Their second call beyond Chipping provided little extra information, other than confirming Rosie Wilson's voracious appetite for sex. Dylan Baines was an older man, who seemed grateful Rosie had been his lover, if only for a few brief weeks the year before. He spoke in a soft voice in his living room because his wife was in the kitchen preparing their lunch. He told them she knew nothing of his fling with Rosie. It had been a foolish one-off thing he deeply regretted.

"Who instigated it?" Izzy asked.

"She did, of course. I've never chased after anybody. Never intend to. She wouldn't take no for an answer. Why she picked me is a mystery."

Izzy thought she knew the answer. Dylan Baines was old school. Tweed jacket, corduroy trousers, a Range Rover for him, a Discovery for his wife. He ran an entertainment business and a wedding venue. Old Lancashire family. He knew everyone, and everyone knew him. Rosie would have picked him out as much for his contacts as his looks, which were ordinary. He offered them lunch before they left, but they refused. It would have been awkward eating in their kitchen and making small talk with his wife. She would wonder why the police wanted to speak with her husband. Jack had told her only that her husband was a witness to an incident in Preston.

"He's right about one thing," Izzy said. "He's never going to stray again."

"They were a pleasant enough couple. Moneyed, and with influence. Not at all like Ethan Walton."

"Influence and sex. Rosie sought both, but I suspect when push came to shove, she would always choose sex over influence. But yes, I liked them both."

"This last one sounds like he has influence too. As well as an unusual name."

"Marsh Wycherley," Izzy said. "I did a quick search on him. Big in the area. Stinking rich. Originally from south of Shrewsbury, where there are several Wycherleys."

"Influence again, then," said Jack.

Except when they arrived at his home, a large house with gabled roofs sitting on a low ridge to the north of Clitheroe, with a view across the descending countryside, they discovered he might have influence, but was also handsome. His wife was on her way out when they arrived, which made everything more convenient. She was also a handsome woman, with strong features and a good figure.

"Please, come through to the lounge," said Wycherley, leading the way. "Can I get you anything? Tea?

Coffee? Something stronger? Or is it true you cannot drink while on duty?"

"Nothing, thank you," said Jack.

The lounge, when they reached it, was huge, with tall bifold windows looking west. Izzy imagined the sunsets would be amazing, but not today. The rain had set in for the duration.

Wycherley took a wooden round-backed chair and waved vaguely at a collection of others. As before, Jack sat slightly out of his eye line as Izzy started the questions.

"Have you been informed of the reason for our visit, Mr Wycherley?"

"Something about Rosie Wilson, I was told. Terrible about what happened. Do you have any leads?"

"I can't say anything at the moment, but there will be a press release as soon as we know more. Can I ask you how well you knew Rosie?"

"Knew them both, Rosie and Mike. And Grace, of course. Sweet little thing. I hear she's missing."

"You appear to know a lot about the case, sir."

"I take an interest, and I know a lot of people."

Izzy wondered if some of those people worked for the police. She had already formed an impression of the man, but was willing to have her mind changed. He was of average height, but had a forceful presence. He dressed casually but well. His brown hair was cut a little long and curled over his ears, and he wore a narrow goatee. His eyes were green, and studied Izzy in turn.

"Can I ask when your affair with Rosie started?" she asked.

He showed no surprise, and a tiny smile briefly touched his lips.

"So that's what this is about, is it?"

"We are questioning several people who know the Wilsons, so we can get a better picture of them. Their place in the countryside. Who they knew."

"And you heard about what happened between me and Rosie. Who told you?"

"I am not at liberty to say, sir."

"No, I expect you're not. Not that it was any great secret."

"Even from your wife?" Izzy asked.

"Oh, Jenny and I share an understanding. We have a good life. A wonderful life. And many, many friends." His eyes looked into Izzy's, and she knew exactly what he was saying.

"And did Mike Wilson also have an understanding?"

Wycherley shrugged. "He knew what Rosie was like, but whether he knew about her and me, that I don't know. Ask him if you want, though I expect that might be a little awkward at the moment."

"When did your affair start?"

"It wasn't an affair. It was an arrangement. One we both enjoyed, but also one we knew was temporary. Rosie took lovers like other women shopped."

"You didn't tell me when your arrangement started, sir."

He examined a corner of the room.

"Two years ago now. May time, I'd say. She made it clear what she wanted at a dinner party we attended.

214

They're big on entertaining around here. It was in Liverpool. All the great and good of Lancashire, Merseyside, Manchester and Cheshire were there. As well as Mike and Rosie."

To Izzy, it felt like a put-down.

"And how long did the affair last?"

"Until mid-summer. Almost exactly. She dumped me on the solstice. We drove out to a small hotel in The Lakes and spent the afternoon there. Afterwards, she told me she thought it best if we broke things off."

"How did you feel about that?"

Another shrug. "To be honest, I was grateful. She was an enthusiastic, skilled and adventurous lover, but these things have a sell-by date to them, don't they? We both knew ours had arrived."

Izzy's dislike of the man increased with every answer he made, but knew she had to mask it.

"I take it Rosie was not your first liaison, sir?"

Wycherley said nothing, only smiled.

"Do you know if Rosie took lovers often?"

"Word is she's had over a hundred men since she was a schoolgirl. I expect you're going to have to interview a lot of those lovers before you find who killed her, mind." He leaned forward, his expression serious. "But it wasn't me. Jen and I were in Paris for five days; we got back late, two days ago. Our wedding anniversary. I can find the tickets for our flights if you want to see them."

"You are under no suspicion, sir. We are merely attempting to get a deeper understanding of Rosie

Wilson. Would you be willing to offer a DNA sample, Mr Wycherley? It will only take a second."

"Why?"

"We are requesting all men we interview to offer one voluntarily, sir. So we can rule them out from visiting the Wilson's house recently. When was the last time you were there, Mr Wycherley?"

"Never. We always met at hotels. Nice ones, mind, nothing seedy. Country hotels. I deal with many of them, so it made our meetings easier. Do I have to give a sample?"

"It is entirely voluntary, sir."

"In that case, I think I'd rather not." He rose to his feet. "Are we finished here? I need to be somewhere else."

"On his way to another meet-up, do you reckon?" asked Jack as they drove west. A thin line of lighter sky showed in the distance, promising an end to the rain.

"Perhaps, but everything I read about him says he's a good businessman, with fingers in a lot of pies. Maybe he has many meetings that don't involve the removal of his trousers." Izzy saw Jack smile.

"Are you hungry?" he asked.

"Starving."

"There's a friendly pub on the way back to your place. Fancy calling in? We can compare notes and write them up, but I don't think those men had anything to do with what happened to Rosie, do you?"

Izzy shook her head. "No, but we had to talk to them."

Forty minutes later, she picked at the remains of a burger, and sipped at a pint of Hen Harrier now they were off duty and Jack had offered to drive her home. She held her hand out.

"What?"

"Can I see the notes you made?"

Jack pulled his notebook out and handed it across. "Do you want another pint?"

"Shouldn't we be getting back to base to report in?"

"We should, but it can wait until tomorrow. There's nothing incriminating here, and nothing we don't already know. I'll drop you off at your place and go home."

Izzy watched Jack as he walked to the bar. He might prefer a companion of his own sex, but nothing he did hinted at the fact.

She opened his notebook and scanned through Jack's writing. Like him, it was precise, and almost painfully legible.

She sipped at the new pint when he set it down and tapped an entry.

"You've circled the colour of their eyes," she said. "Ethan Walton's and Marsh Wycherley's. Why?"

"Genetics," said Jack.

Izzy stared at him. "Genetics?"

"The gene for blue eyes is recessive." Jack smiled. "I know, it's a long word, but try to keep up. A child will usually have blue eyes if one parent does, and the other has either blue or green eyes. Like two of the men we spoke with today. It's not guaranteed, because some-times you have to go back to grandparents, but it might be useful."

Izzy tried to recall what colour Mike Wilson's eyes were. Brown, she thought.

"Are you saying Grace isn't his child?"

"I'm saying it may be that way. Someone who knows more about it than me needs to find out. But it's a damn shame Wycherley didn't let us take a DNA swab. It could tell us for sure. The timing is pretty close, if he was with her May until mid-summer the year before last."

"Would it make any difference if he was? We got a sample from Ethan Walton, and he could just as well be the father if what you say is true. From what we've heard, Rosie had enough lovers it could be just about anyone. And even then, we *know* who killed her, and it was neither of them."

"We think we know, Iz. But we've been wrong before. Until we find our suspect and a motive, we can never be one hundred per cent sure he killed her. And don't forget, the PM said she was pregnant again. Three months. So if we're interested in men she'd screwed, that's how far back we should be looking. Of course, this one could be Mike's."

When Izzy's phone rang, she picked it up and looked at the caller ID. It said number withheld.

"This might be work," she said, answering.

She listened, nodded, then cut the call.

"It was Harrington, wanting to know if we're on our way back." Izzy pushed the almost untouched second pint away from herself. "They've been trying to contact Mike Wilson, but he's not picking up. They released his house today, and he was told he could return. Harrington says if we're on our way back to my place, can we call in and find out if he's there."

"What do they want him for?"

Izzy shook her head. "No idea, but Harrington's been in touch with the NCA, and they're working out what help they can offer. In the meantime, Harrington wants Mike Wilson taken into custody. He's seen the video footage of him losing his temper with Rosie, and Carys has found some intel on him that might be significant."

"What intel?"

"Harrington didn't say." She stood. "Let's go see Mike. I'll call Harrington back and ask if he wants us to bring him in. I'm sure between us we can manage, even if he is a big fella."

TWENTY-SEVEN

It surprised Izzy when she experienced a moment of anxiety as Jack turned into the long drive that led alongside the river to Caxton Farm. She didn't know where it came from, or why. The farmhouse nestled peacefully in the valley. If it held memories of the brutality that took place there, it did not speak of them.

"I'll do the talking," said Jack.

"And if he objects to being taken back to the station?"

"I don't think he will, but if he does, we'll deal with it."

"Harrington told me they found the dogs," Izzy said. "They had meat in their stomachs, which tested positive for both arsenic and rat poison. They stood no chance."

"Poor buggers. Do you think he'll replace them eventually?"

"Not sure his head's in the right place at the moment."

Jack pulled up in the yard, and they both got out of

the car, then checked each other's bodycams were operational. The front door stood open as they approached, and once again, Izzy experienced an unfamiliar scratch of fear. She ignored it as Jack knocked on the doorjamb.

"Mr Wilson, are you home? It's DS Ward and DC Wilde. Can we come in?"

Silence greeted them.

Jack glanced at Izzy. "Do we go in or not?"

"There's no tractor in the yard. Perhaps he's out working somewhere."

"And left his front door wide open?"

"People sometimes do things like that in the countryside."

"Well, they shouldn't."

When Jack stepped through the door, Izzy followed. The house carried an abandoned air. It felt reduced. Izzy had sensed the same in other buildings after a crime had taken place. As if the bricks themselves held fast to a violation they had been a silent witness to.

Jack pointed to the stairs. "You check upstairs. I'll do down here. Yell if you find him."

Izzy climbed the steps two at a time. At the top, she recognised the layout from the first time she came here, but since then, the carpets and walls had been deep cleaned. She could smell a faint lemon scent from whatever had been used.

She quickly checked the nursery, but it was empty. Even the cot had been taken out. Faint marks showed on the carpet where it had stood. When Izzy checked the master bedroom, she saw the cot had been moved in there. It stood to one side of the king-sized bed, close enough so that whoever slept there could reach out and touch it in the night. Clothes lay on the bed, all of them Rosie's. Dresses, blouses, underwear, tights. Pictures sat on all the furniture. Pictures of Rosie, photos of Grace. There was only one of Mike. It looked to have been taken on holiday somewhere, perhaps in Spain or Portugal. It showed Mike and Rosie arm in arm in bright sunshine, with the sea behind them. They were laughing. Rosie was heavily pregnant, voluptuous, tanned and beautiful; a woman who would turn heads.

Izzy checked the other bedrooms, but Mike wasn't in any of them. She went downstairs and found Jack in the kitchen.

"Anything?" he asked.

"He's turned his bedroom into a shrine. Pictures everywhere. Rosie's clothes are laid out on one side of the bed. Her side, I imagine."

"Do I need to see it?"

"Don't think so. It's weird, but not significant. He's not here, is he. Maybe he's done a runner."

"Why would he do that?"

"Because he's not stupid. He's a person of interest."

"He's got no previous. If he had, Carys would have found it." Jack turned away and walked out through the hallway.

Izzy took a last look around. Everything was immaculate. The cleaners had been called in after CSI finished. She went to catch Jack up where he stood outside the door.

"We should check in the barn," he said. The wide double doors stood open.

"If he was in there, he'd have come out when we arrived, wouldn't he?"

"Like you said, not if he knows we're here to take him in," said Jack. "Best check it now we're here."

When they entered, they discovered where Mike Wilson was, and what he had been up to. He swayed at the end of a rope, his face a dark puce colour. The rope was thrown over a solid beam, one end tied to a hook set in the wall. A stepladder lay on its side beneath the man. As Izzy stared, she saw Mike Wilson's left foot kick.

"He's still alive, Jack. Get him down."

She ran to the ladder and righted it, then held it while Jack climbed. He tried to lift Mike, but he was too heavy, and the ladder too precarious. But he lessened the tightness of the noose around his neck.

"Cut the fucking rope!" Jack's voice was a grunt of effort.

Izzy looked around in panic, then ran through the wide doors and into the house. She grabbed a knife from the wooden block in the kitchen and ran back. She sawed at the rope, panic telling her she was too late.

When the rope finally parted, Mike Wilson's total weight fell on Jack, making the ladder tip sideways, and they both fell to the dirt floor. Izzy ran across and knelt beside them.

"Are you okay, Jack?"

He sat up. "I'm fine. Check on him, Iz."

Mike Wilson lay on his front. Izzy rolled him over,

then pulled at the noose around his neck until it gave enough to slide over his head. She touched his neck, seeking a pulse and finding none. Then Jack was there as well.

He put his head sideways on Mike's chest.

"I think I hear a heartbeat. I'll start CPR while you call for an ambulance. You'll need to use the house phone."

Except when Izzy went inside, the phone wasn't in its usual place in the hallway. She checked the entire house because she knew there should be three phones, but saw none.

Back in the barn, she said, "He's ripped them all out. I need to take your car and drive to the top road. Give me your keys. Are you getting anywhere?"

"Don't know." Jack's voice shook as he pushed against Mike Wilson's chest. Fast movements, solid movements. If Mike lived, he'd probably have a couple of cracked ribs. "Keys are in my pocket." He shifted so Izzy could reach.

It was a strangely intimate moment as she burrowed her fingers into his pocket before pulling out the keys. She ran to the car and drove fast until she got a signal on her phone. She called for an ambulance first, then contacted the MIT at Hutton and told them what had happened.

"I'll tell Harrington as soon as he gets out of his meeting," said Ailsa, who had picked up. "He'll have to call the IOPC and warn them they may need to take over the scene if Mike Wilson dies. Try to keep him alive, but touch nothing you don't need to."

"I'm not sure Mike Wilson is going to live, but either way, it's a suicide attempt, not a crime. I'm going back down. I'll call again once we know the state of play. Tell Harrington as soon as he's free."

Izzy spun the car around and returned to the barn. Jack was still pumping Mike Wilson's chest, alternating with breathing for him.

"Let me take over," Izzy said, and Jack moved aside.

She knelt close to Mike Wilson and started compressions, having to put more effort into them than Jack. They were still alternating fifteen minutes later when they heard the distant wailing of a siren that grew rapidly closer. The paramedics took over. They wired Mike up and confirmed his heart was still beating, but almost certainly only because of what Jack and Izzy had done.

"How long was he strung up?" One asked as another injected something into Mike's arm.

"Can't have been much more than three or four minutes, or he'd be dead," said Jack. "We were lucky he didn't jump off the stepladder, or he'd have snapped his neck. He was a good eight feet off the ground when we found him. Is he going to live?"

"Most likely. Whether he'll suffer brain damage is another matter. We'll know more when we get him back to Preston." The man looked at his female companion. "Are we ready to move him?"

"As ready as we're going to be."

When the ambulance had gone, Jack said, "We'd best get back to the office and tell them what happened here. But first, I want us to see if he left a note."

"Not that I saw, but then I wasn't looking for one. Besides, who would he leave a note for?"

"He's got a sister who runs a smallholding south of Warrington, and Rosie has a sister and two brothers. He might've wanted to explain himself."

"Ailsa warned me the IOPC is going to investigate us if he dies." Izzy had never had contact with the Independent Office for Police Conduct, but had heard tales from those who had. Even those who were acquitted said it was a bruising encounter.

"Then let's hope he doesn't."

"Do you reckon he meant to kill himself, or was this a cry for help?" Izzy asked. "He must have been in there all the time we were inside the house."

"I don't know, Iz. We were in there long enough for him to be dead if he'd jumped off that ladder when we arrived. Maybe he wanted us to find him."

They spent ten minutes looking, but there was no note. They opened every drawer and went into every room, but other than the strange shrine to his wife and daughter in the bedroom, everything appeared normal. The sky was darkening by the time they pulled the front door shut. Izzy locked it with the key that had been inside, then slipped it under a pot on the side of the house. If Mike Wilson lived, and if he ever wanted to return to the place where his wife had died, he'd need it to get in. As Jack drove back to the road, Izzy thought about loss and how it diminished everything and everyone it touched.

TWENTY-EIGHT

They were halfway back to Hutton when Harrington called Izzy's mobile. She listened, said, "All right, boss," and put her phone down.

"What does he want now?"

"To save a bit on overtime, I suspect. You can drop me at my place. He says nothing will happen until they get an update on Mike Wilson, so we have the rest of the evening to ourselves." Izzy grinned. "Oh joy."

When she invited Jack in, he surprised her by saying yes. He surprised her even more when he accepted the offered beer.

They sat at the scarred kitchen table and drank from their bottles.

"Are you shocked at what he did?" asked Jack.

Izzy shook her head. "Not much, no. He's lost his wife and kid. Life must seem pretty bleak to him right now. Did you know farmers are more susceptible to suicide than most professions? Something to do with the isolation, I expect. In the old days, it used to be brucellosis."

Jack frowned. "What?"

"You can catch it from cows. Or at least you used to; there's less of it about these days. It can cause depression in humans."

"Christ, you know some random shit, Iz." Jack shook his head. "What about the cattle?"

"I expect most of them are pretty depressed already. Why did he hang himself, Jack? Most farmers who do it use a shotgun. He'll have at least one at the farm."

"I didn't see any cabinet. Did you?"

Izzy took a moment to think before shaking her head. "No, but he'd be an unusual farmer if he didn't own one. Maybe it's in an outbuilding or, more likely, the cellar. There'll be a record of it somewhere if he does. We can check in the morning."

"Not much point, is there. He didn't shoot himself."

"It wasn't a cry for help, though, was it? Us turning up at the right time was a fluke."

It was Jack's turn to think. Izzy watched him, aware it was the first time he'd entered her house. She wondered what he thought of it. Then wondered if she cared. She liked Jack. They made a good team, and Jack was a good boss who allowed Izzy to make her own decisions. But after work, they went their separate ways.

"He'd have heard us arrive, and waited," said Jack. "I reckon he wanted to be found."

"I don't see it. He meant it."

"Maybe." Jack took another sip of his beer.

"I wonder if he knew about Rosie and her lovers? That could be another reason. Not the fact she took them, but the humiliation when people found out. And it would come out. Bound to."

"We found out about them easily enough," said Jack. "It seems to be common knowledge among the farming community, so I'd be amazed if he hadn't heard the rumours. But is it relevant if it was a stranger who killed her?"

"What happened to Rosie wasn't random, Jack, I'm sure. It was planned. Coming all the way out here from London. Staying in that B&B the night before. He came prepared to drug the girl. The only thing we don't know, is whether Rosie was the random element in this, or deliberately chosen. What if the killer was one of her lovers? Someone she dumped who took it badly?"

"Why would she have someone in London? We have a half-decent image of the bloke, and you must admit, going by that sketch, he's no looker."

"All three we interviewed today were handsome men, weren't they?"

"Handsome enough."

Izzy laughed. "Well, I thought so."

Jack returned the laugh. "Go on then. Which ones? See if we agree."

"Walton and Wycherley. Baines is good-looking but too old. And way too strait-laced."

Jack smiled. "You're only saying that because you'll never do anything about it. And none of them would be interested in me. Marsh Wycherley came across as very much a macho man, so he's not my type in any case. But there was something I sensed. He'd do nothing with another man alone, but maybe if his wife was involved, he might. He fancied you though, I could tell."

Izzy made a noise through her nose. "I saw that too. Same with Walton." When she reached for her beer, she discovered the bottle was empty.

"Do you want another?"

"I won't finish this one. I need to go home, and how would it look if I got breathalysed?"

"It happens. We both know it does. Sometimes, a fellow cop gets a pass. It's not like it used to be, but everyone knows it happens." Izzy got up and fetched another beer for herself. She thought briefly about her words, and how she recognised the attraction in the men, without being attracted to them in turn. There were times when her self-imposed chastity felt more like a straitjacket than a shield. But she was too afraid to loosen the ties, fearing what freedom might bring.

Once Jack had left, she finished her beer, then drank another, glad they had eaten so she didn't have to cook. She thought about opening another bottle, then decided against it. Instead, she brought her book down from beside the bed and sat in the comfortable old armchair next to the unlit fire. She tried to lose herself in a fictional world, but her mind kept circling back to the case, pulling at threads, building theories, only for them to come crashing down like a tower of wooden blocks.

TWENTY-NINE

When Izzy arrived at work the following morning, Sarah was waiting for her.

"Mike Wilson has been sent over from the hospital. They kept him in overnight for observation, but word is he's one lucky man, thanks to you and Jack."

"Unless he'd rather he hadn't woken up," Izzy said. "Where is he?"

"Interview room one. I'd like you with me when we talk to him."

When they got there, Mike Wilson sat on the far side of the interview table, a scarf around his neck to hide what would be significant abrasions and bruising. Sarah sat across from him, while Izzy sat as far away as she could. She was there to listen to what he had to say, nothing more. Izzy knew Sarah was the right person for the interview.

"How are you feeling, Mike?" Sarah asked, her voice soft and full of compassion. "I understand it might be difficult to speak at the moment, so you can keep your answers short.

"How do you think I feel? I was a fuckin' idiot."

"What you did was wrong, but understandable. Your life's been turned upside down, but ending it would be a mistake. My colleagues are working hard to get Grace back, and when they do, she will need her dad."

"I expect her's dead too by now," said Mike.

"Grace needs you to be strong."

Mike gripped his head in his hands. "I can't stand the thought she's been taken by the bastard who killed Rosie. If you ever find him, keep him a mile away from me, or I swear I'll rip his fuckin' head off."

"That might not be such a good idea, but at least it's a reason not to try anything foolish again."

"I got an appointment with a shrink later," said Mike.

Izzy glanced down at her open notebook, where she had listed the questions she wanted Sarah to ask. As sorry as she felt for him, there were things she believed he still held back. Whether they were relevant to the case was another matter, but one they could decide only when they knew what they were.

Sarah asked about the dogs. She started slow, getting dates and times, then homed in on the important parts.

"We have analysed the stomach contents of your dogs, Mike, and can confirm they were poisoned. Do you have any suspicion who might be behind that?"

Mike shook his head. He was pale and seemed to have zoned out.

"Have you annoyed anyone recently?"

"No one in particular, no."

"Was there any food lying around where you found them? Where was that, exactly?"

"In the barn, weren't it. They slept in the barn in the day when they weren't workin'. Had a big crate they used to share. Good dogs, they were. The best. And no, no food around. I double-checked in case I'd left summat out, but I hadn't. Someone must've tossed them poisoned meat and done a runner."

"Wouldn't the dogs have barked if a stranger came into the barn?" asked Sarah.

"They always have. Sounded vicious, but they were as soft as pap underneath."

"And you heard nothing?"

"Nowt."

"Did you ask Rosie if she had?" It was a hard question to ask, but Mike seemed to accept it.

"'Course I did. She said she heard nowt either."

"Might it have been someone the dogs knew?"

"If it weren't me or Rosie, they'd've barked their heads off, whoever it were. Mebbe whoever did it came when we were out somewhere."

"Did you intend to replace them?"

"We talked about it, but I said to wait and see how things went. Don't have so many sheep now. No money in it anymore. Same as most farming these days. Missed them dogs, mind. Missed 'em to buggery."

"Do you have many visitors at the farm?"

"Not so you'd notice. The usual, though the post is left at the top of the drive now. They didn't want to bring it all the way down anymore." Mike offered a tiny smile. "Said the dogs were dangerous. Talking bollocks, of course, but it were a new man. Don't think he liked them."

Sarah said, "Do you know the name of the postman who said that?"

Mike shook his head. "New, weren't he."

Izzy made a note to follow up on the postman. She expected nothing to come of it, but knew that every little thing had to be covered. It would be easy enough to find out the name. She supposed there was an outside chance the new postman had poisoned the dogs, but she didn't think so. She believed she knew who had done it, but also knew not to make a judgement without evidence.

"Did your wife have visitors of her own?" Sarah asked. "Perhaps when you were working?"

Mike stared across the table at her.

"Visitors? What do you mean by that?"

He looked barely under control, and Izzy tensed. She saw he knew about Rosie's lovers. But knowing and admitting it were two different things.

"Did you ever hear any rumours?"

"There are always rumours about one thing or another."

"About Rosie and other men."

Mike stared into space, his head moving from side to side, then he nodded.

"Mebbe," he said.

"Did you talk with her about these rumours?"

"No point. She'd've denied everything, but I knew

better. She was always flighty, even as a girl. Liked to play the field, if you know what I mean. Had plenty of boys in school. Why she chose me is a mystery to this day, but we had a good marriage. We understood each other. I knew she needed space and ... well, distractions. As long as she was home every night, I could pretend, couldn't I?"

"Did it anger you she might have lovers?"

"'Course it did, but what could I do? I never raised a hand to that girl and never would. We loved each other. Loved Grace." A tear tracked down his cheek. "Rosie meant nothing by it. It were just summat she had to do."

"Except you did lift your hand to her," said Sarah. She, like everyone else, would have seen the still image Priya had uploaded, as well as the section of CCTV recording where he stood over his wife.

"Don't know what you mean."

Sarah opened an envelope and slid a colour photograph across so he could see it. Mike stared down at it.

"Do you deny you hit your wife?" asked Sarah.

"It were a slap. A light one at that. Nowt more than a slap."

"Which knocked her off her feet. Why did you slap her, Mr Wilson?"

The atmosphere in the room changed at her use of formality.

"I heard about summat and asked her if it were true. She denied it, so I – yes – I slapped her."

"What did you hear?"

"Someone told me she was up the duff again. A friend

of hers. A woman friend, not a man. Asked me if I was pleased, expectin' I'd know all about it."

"Most men would be pleased. A sister or brother for little Grace."

"Except her weren't mine either," said Mike. "We both wanted kids even before we were married, but nothing happened, not for years, so Rosie went for tests. Doc found nowt, so she nagged me until I went. Low sperm count, they said. Very low. It's why she couldn't get pregnant. But she still wanted kids. So … well, I don't need to spell it out, do I?"

"Do you know who Grace's father is?"

Mike shook his head. "Don't want to know. Someone I might meet, and I don't know what I'd do if I stood before a man who'd shagged my wife. So, I never asked. But with Grace, we'd both agreed to it. This other one came out of the blue. That's why I slapped her."

"But you knew she took lovers, didn't you?" Sarah's voice remained soft.

"I already said, we never talked about it. She knew I knew, but we said nowt to each other. Best not to, we both thought. Let sleeping dogs lie." He shook his head at his own words. "Only a sayin', mind."

It took another ten minutes, during which Sarah expertly guided Mike Wilson slowly back from the place of anger her questioning had put him.

When they were done, the interview room door opened, and a uniformed Angela Pugh entered the room. Her face was expressionless. She glanced at Izzy and Sarah before turning to Mike Wilson.

"Mr Wilson, I am arresting you on suspicion of conspiring to murder your wife, Rosie Wilson, and your daughter, Grace Wilson. You do not have to say anything, but it may harm your defence if you do not mention when questioned something which you later rely on in court. Anything you do say may be given in evidence."

Mike surged to his feet, his face beet red. "What the fuck!"

Izzy stood, but Angela showed no hesitation as she grasped Mike's arm.

"If you would come with me, Mr Wilson, I will take you for processing."

"I never touched 'em," Mike said. "I loved Rosie, loved Grace. I tell you, I done nothing. Nothing at all."

"Mr Wilson..." Angela waited, and eventually, Mike's shoulders lost their tension, and he left the room with her.

When Izzy looked at Sarah, she shook her head. "Harrington must have a reason for the charge. Poor bastard. As if everything else isn't already enough, he gets this. We'd best go upstairs and find out what the hell's going on."

THIRTY

"Izzy, come here." Ed Harrington called out as soon as she entered the incident room.

She was aware of eyes on her as she crossed the room, but did not see Jack.

"Boss?" Izzy stood in front of Harrington. She wanted to ask why Mike Wilson had been arrested, but knew she couldn't.

"I know you think Mike Wilson is innocent, Izzy, but I have my reasons for arresting him." Harrington raised his voice so everyone in the room could hear. "You interviewed Ethan Walton yesterday, didn't you?"

"We did."

"He came into the station earlier today, and said he had something to tell us. Rosie Wilson said she was going to divorce Mike. She wanted to marry Ethan."

"Why didn't he mention this when we were with him yesterday?"

"Told me he wanted to, but needed time to think about it. Overnight must have been long enough."

"Did he say Rosie told Mike about any of this?"

"He claims she did. Said both of them told him to his face at their house. Ethan said Mike punched him."

"Any sign of bruising?"

"He said it was a month back. Mike also said he'd kill Rosie before he'd watch her walk away with another man and take his daughter from him. Except Ethan claims Grace is his."

"Mike told Sarah he knew Grace wasn't his but didn't want to know who the father was. Do you believe Ethan?"

"He's a credible witness. You took a DNA swab from him, and we have Grace and Rosie Wilson's on record. It should be simple enough to determine if he's telling the truth." Harrington scanned the room. "His statement is on the system for you all to look at. Do that and see what you think. However, the main thing you all need to know is what Carys discovered last night. It's the reason I requested the arrest warrant. Tell them, Carys."

Carys rose from her chair. "HOLMES threw up Mike Wilson's name concerning an old case. He was arrested twenty years ago on a charge of GBH. He had just turned sixteen. It looks like a playground argument that got out of hand. Mike was waiting for the kid when he left the school premises. Only one witness – Rosie Clayton, as she was then. The case against Wilson was solid, until the lad he beat up dropped the charges, and Rosie claimed she wasn't there. Even if she was, nothing happened. I've added details to the case file, so you can all take a look."

"Does this change how we regard Mike now, boss?" Izzy's belief in Mike's innocence was looking less sure.

"We have to go with the evidence we have today. The accusation from Ethan Walton, and Wilson's history of serious violence, means I had to act. He will be processed and kept in a cell. We're probably doing him a favour, since he tried to kill himself. I'll also get a shrink to speak to him again. Maybe he'll save us all a bunch of work and confess."

"Only if he did it, boss."

Harrington shook his head. "I'd like it if we all sang off the same hymn sheet on this, Izzy. Sarah's been talking with Social Services. Abigail has been placed with a foster carer until we contact her father in Brighton. I've requested an officer in that force to inform him. We should hear back within a couple of hours. I made sure they knew it was a priority. Also, there's a call booked with someone at the NCA as soon as I'm finished here. It will be recorded, of course, but I'd like someone else to be present. Can you be with me, Izzy?"

"Why me and not Jack, or one of the others, boss? I'm not a full member of the team."

Harrington lowered his voice so the others couldn't hear. "Maybe that's why. And you push the envelope. I don't always agree with you, but I welcome a different take, despite what you might believe. And Jack called in to say he'd be late, his car broke down, and he's waiting for the rescue service."

"Do you want me to go and pick him up?" Izzy asked.

"There's no time. An NCA officer is waiting for my call as soon as this briefing is over."

It took fifteen minutes before Izzy followed Harrington into his office.

"If I want you to contribute anything, I'll ask," he said.

Izzy pulled a chair up, wondering why she was there, not someone else. Ailsa was the obvious choice.

When Harrington put the call through, it was answered at once, and he put it on speaker.

"Superintendent Harrington?" The voice was female, the accent southern.

"Yes, and I have DC Izzy Wilde with me. Who am I speaking to?"

"This is DI Paula Raven, Superintendent. I've read up on your case, and it has, as I believe you already know, similarities with those in other force areas over several years. The National Crime Agency does not get directly involved in active cases, but we do advise and liaise between forces. Which is why I am talking to you now."

"Who will take this from us?" asked Harrington.

"The case remains with you, of course, as the most recent incident occurred in your force's jurisdiction. I'll send you contact details for those involved in the other investigations, and you can get in touch."

"I take it the cases are linked?"

"A similar MO, and DNA trace, matches some of what you have. I believe you have the girl with you who was taken from the first murder our man can be linked with?"

"Abigail's in a temporary foster home at the moment," Harrington said.

"It was assumed she had been taken and killed," Raven said, "Or murdered at the scene, and her body disposed of. However, as you know, her DNA was found at another scene in Cambridgeshire. It was initially missed, or dismissed, because her grandparents and aunt live nearby. Someone assumed it had been left there when she visited as a baby. But you know what they say about assumptions."

"I do," said Harrington. "How many other cases match our killer's profile?"

"Other than Jessica McFadden, we have identified at least five more over the last eight years, including yours. All in separate police force areas. They are all officially linked now, and Lancashire will be the lead force on this."

Izzy watched Harrington's expression change. There was concern, yes, but also pride. Izzy knew it was standard operating procedure.

"I'll brief my team," Harrington said, "and see if I can call in extra officers and civilian staff."

"Remember, you can call on officers in the other divisions, Superintendent. Their Chief Constables have been briefed, and are appointing a liaison contact. Their details will be with you before midday. And if you need to visit any of the locations, they will help your people. All right, do you have anything you want from me?"

Harrington glanced at Izzy and raised an eyebrow in a question.

"DC Izzy Wilde, here," she said. "The boss asked me to sit in."

"Do you have a question, Izzy?"

"One, initially. It's about the girl. She's in the system now, and placed in a foster home. I assume she will be returned to her father. When will that be? His wife's murder was a long time ago, but it might be useful if someone from here spoke with him."

"That would be a matter for you up there, not me. But I can check on progress for you. Sometimes, a call from the NCA often expedites matters. I also know Charles McFadden remarried and has had kids since his first wife's death. Returning his daughter will need careful handling."

"We have an excellent Child Protection Officer at Preston, who has been seconded to my team for the duration," said Harrington. "I'll speak with her and see what can be arranged. Thank you."

"You're welcome. All right, we'll end this now, and I'll get all the details sent over to you ASAP."

Raven broke the call.

Harrington sat back in his chair. "I expect Charles McFadden will want to come up here to meet Abigail. I'll assign Sarah to him when he does, but I'd like you and Jack to tag along. Don't swamp him with questions, but if you get the opportunity, ask him about what happened when his wife was killed. But tread carefully."

"We'll do our best, boss."

"I'm sure you will. In the meantime, enter your notes from yesterday's interviews."

"What if Charles McFadden doesn't come here? Izzy asked.

"I consider that unlikely. He's learned the daughter he believed dead is alive. Any father would be on his way already."

An hour later, Izzy was sitting with Jack in the canteen, bringing him up to speed on what was happening, when Sarah found them.

"I need one of you." She looked between them. "Izzy, your car's running, so come with me."

Izzy gave Jack an apologetic look before she followed Sarah.

"Where are we going?"

"To Social Services."

Izzy drove her car onto the A59 and turned north. "I take it we're going to City Hall?"

"We are."

"Is Abi all right?"

"As far as I know. We heard back from Brighton. The officer who went to tell her father she was with us, informed Harrington that he was unwilling to travel up here. Too far, he said."

"Too far to visit the daughter he believed dead?" Izzy wondered what kind of father Charles McFadden was. She hoped he treated his new children with more compassion. "Too far north, I expect he means. Maybe he thinks we still walk around in furs."

"That's a bit harsh," said Sarah. "It will take time for him to come to terms with the news. In any case, he's asked if we can take her down to Brighton. I need to go as the child protection officer, but Harrington wants detectives to accompany me. He told me he'd like you and Jack to come too, if I have no objection. Which I don't. He prefers people from his team are there, rather than local officers unfamiliar with the case."

"Then why isn't Jack with us now?"

"I don't want to swamp Abi or Flis, her case worker, with too many people. Now we know other cases are linked to ours. Harrington wants you to talk to Abi's father about what happened seven years ago. Abi knows you, and Jack gets on with everyone. Better than sending strangers."

"You mentioned this Flis before. What's she like?"

"Felicity Roberts is empathetic, and kids like her. I think you'll like her as well. She asked to be assigned as the case worker for Abi. Flis will have to be with us in Brighton, of course. She told me we can't just turn up and dump Abi on his doorstep. There's a process." Sarah smiled. "I'm hoping you might drive; it's a long way to Brighton. Just remember, Abi's a kid, so don't drive as fast as you are now."

THIRTY-ONE

Frank sat on the sofa, watching the lunchtime news. When Preston was mentioned, he leaned closer to the screen, then slumped back when an artist's impression appeared. He tilted his head to one side. Was that meant to be him?

"Police have today issued a sketch of a person of interest to the Lancashire Police. The man is the prime suspect in the murder of Rosie Wilson, and the kidnapping of her eleven-month-old daughter, Grace. CCTV images show someone believed to be the same man leaving Preston station for London at 6:18 PM on Saturday, the 13th of May. He was carrying a child. If you have seen or recognise this man, do not approach him, but contact the police on the number shown on screen, or dial 101."

A photograph of Grace Wilson filled the screen. Her blonde curls and bright blue eyes made her easily recognisable.

The piece ended, and Frank turned off the television. He stared at it for a while before cursing. There had been no mention of his name, which was good. Keeping his surname from Cally for all these years had been challenging at times, but it was bearing fruit now.

There was no mention of other killings, which disappointed Frank. He wanted people to know what he had done. Not who he was, but *what* he was. He wanted a name like the Yorkshire Ripper. He'd already thought of one that fit. The Footpath Killer. The idea of writing to the press and suggesting it crossed his mind. He yearned to hear people utter that name. But he suspected the voice would advise against it.

Walking to the small second bedroom, he gazed down at the girl. Grace. He knew her name now, but did he want to keep it? He had changed Cally's name to sound similar to his own girls'. Not that he wanted to use *their* names. That would only remind him of their mother, which he didn't want. It had been easy enough to give Cally a new name, because she had been a similar age to Grace. But now he knew her name and liked it, he considered letting her keep it.

He watched as she slept, hair framing her face, blue eyes hidden behind pink lids. Her eyes moved beneath them, and he wondered what she was dreaming about. Mummy and daddy? He recalled Cally at the same age. How sweet she had been, and how quickly she accepted him as her new daddy. He recalled his own girls. Like this one, sweet girls before their mother turned them against him. Frank knew he had rights but had never been able to exercise them. He hadn't seen the girls in over fifteen years. They'd be teenagers now, getting into trouble, going out with boys. He knew they had another man they called Daddy now, but it wasn't the same as blood. The pain of their loss had eroded Frank's sanity, he knew. He'd never been clever, but now the world confused him even more. Only the voice at the other end of the mobile phones, which arrived in plain envelopes postmarked from various locations throughout the UK, brought him solace. Offered him a means of redemption and justice. Women were trouble. Some more than others. The voice confirmed that. It was calming, almost hypnotic, planting ideas in Frank's mind, like the footpaths. "Stumble across them," it whispered. "You will find a weapon when you need one." And he always had. The voice promised he would never be caught. And if the police ever did get close, there was only one way out. Frank sometimes dreamed of sacrificing himself for the only entity that understood him, ensuring he left no trail to the man behind the voice.

And then, standing over the cot, Frank smiled as he returned to himself. No more mummy, Grace, he thought. I'm your new daddy now. The girl was so sweet. He knew he'd have no trouble approaching houses with her in his arms. And soon, she would be walking. In a year or two, he'd get one of those backpacks to carry her in. Take her with him along new paths. Except he didn't think he could wait that long. He wanted the voice to call him with a new target. He wanted it very badly.

Grace would wake in half an hour. He would play

with her for a while, maybe read a story with her curled on his lap. It might calm him, and she liked it. She cried a lot, which he understood, but time heals, is what people say. Except it hadn't healed his hatred of women. Particularly those who betrayed their husbands.

Frank rubbed his face, feeling the stubble where he hadn't yet shaved. He thought he might let it grow into a beard so he looked different. Change his hair colour. The girl's too.

Frank went out the front door, locking it behind him, then walked fast to the chemists two streets away, where he bought hair dye. There were scissors at home. Next time Grace fell asleep, he'd cut her hair and dye it brown. No more pretty little blonde girl who might be recognised. And Frank thought he might go for the grey, distinguished look. Not that he feared the sketch shown on the news report. Frank knew he looked nothing like *that* loser, whoever he was.

THIRTY-TWO

Ominous clouds loomed over the English Channel as Izzy pulled the unmarked Mondeo estate to the side of the road in Hove. The drive to Brighton had taken over five hours, and they had stopped twice to use the services and get coffee, water and juice. Abi, Flis Roberts and Sarah sat in the back. They stuck to easy topics like the weather, sports and holidays. Izzy had dropped the three at a small hotel along the seafront, before she and Jack drove to Charles McFadden's house to brief him on what would happen. DS Harrington had already cleared their presence with the Sussex police.

"It can't be fun living around here," said Jack. "The parking's a nightmare."

"But look at the houses. Got to be well over a million, every one of them." Izzy scanned the white-painted frontages. Most had off-road parking, but often enough, another car blocked the driveway. Facing south, she could see the dancing glimmer of the sea at the end of the road.

She opened her notebook. "Charles McFadden. Thirty-nine, so thirty-two seven and a half years ago when his wife Jessica was murdered and his daughter taken. The case is still open but inactive, and Charles McFadden has always believed his daughter was killed and her body never found. He married again six months later, which raised some eyebrows." She glanced at Jack. "Does that surprise you?"

Jack shrugged. "You can never tell, can you? Maybe he wanted to move on, put it all behind him. I couldn't do that, but then I'm not the marrying kind either."

"I noticed."

Jack smiled. "You're a detective, Iz. You're meant to notice things."

"I'm interested in meeting this Charles McFadden. What kind of father doesn't immediately rush to meet a daughter he believed dead?"

"We shouldn't pre-judge. He might have married fairly soon after his wife died, but the pain will still be with him. He might surprise us, and want Abi back in his family immediately. If he does, we can return first thing in the morning. There's still plenty of work to do on the case."

"Flis told me if he does, she'll need to stay down until she's sure Abi is settled."

"He's got other kids now, hasn't he?" asked Jack.

"Boy and a girl, she's..." – Izzy opened her notebook and checked – "...four and the boy is five. The new wife's name is Sylvia. She's five years younger than him."

"What does he do? If he lives here, it must pay well."

"Dentist. Owns his own private practice and employs four others. So yes, I expect it does pay well. His wife works for a local estate agency. All right, shall we do this?"

Jack unbuckled his seat belt. "Do you want me to do the talking?"

"You're better at the soft stuff than me."

"You always say that, but it's not true. You could be just as good if you wanted. If you stopped showing your hard face to the world."

Izzy wondered about his comment as they walked up a steep driveway to the house. Was Jack right? He saw into people in a way she didn't, she knew that. Had he seen into her, and recognised something she hadn't in herself? As always, she pushed such thoughts aside for another time, knowing that another time would never come.

When she knocked on the front door, it was opened by a tall, blonde woman. She cocked her head to one side, her eyes moving between them.

Jack drew his warrant card and showed it. Izzy did the same.

"I am Detective Sergeant Jack Ward. My companion is Detective Constable Isabella Wilde. Are you Mrs McFadden?"

She half turned and called into the house, "Charlie, the police are here!"

A man of medium height came to stand beside the woman, the two of them forming a barrier to entry. He was two inches shorter than her, his feet unshod in bright red socks.

"Is this about Abi?" His accent was broad lowland Scots, as if he'd only moved south a few weeks before. He carried a casual confidence that came only with the assurance of money and a trophy wife. He looked past them. "Is she in the car?"

"Abigail is nearby, but we would like to talk to you first," said Jack."Can we come in, sir?"

"When can we see Abi?" asked Sylvia McFadden.

"You may prefer it if we talk inside, rather than out here on the street."

Jack waited. So did Izzy.

Sylvia said, "Come in, then." She turned and walked away. After a moment, so did her husband.

Jack went inside, with Izzy following. The hallway opened up into a living room that spanned the entire width of the house. Through an arch lay a gleaming kitchen, beyond it a small garden. Two children sat on a wide sofa, watching a cartoon on television. They were good-looking kids who took after their mother.

"We let them watch for half an hour before bath time," said Sylvia, as if she was being judged.

"What can you tell us about Abi?" asked Charles McFadden. His manner was awkward, and Izzy wondered if he was the same at work. Perhaps his patients took it as an indication of efficiency.

Izzy saw Jack struggle to frame his first words. Then he lowered his voice and said, "I believe the Brighton police have already contacted you with information regarding your daughter."

Charles McFadden stared at Jack without expression. "Are you sure it's really her? It was so long ago–" He broke off. "Take the kids upstairs, Silv. It's almost time."

She turned off the television, which triggered groans of complaint, then herded the two children into the hallway and upstairs. When they had gone, Charles McFadden said, "You have really found Abi?"

"Yes, sir."

"I didn't believe the police officer when she came around. But if you're here as well ... Where?"

"She was found in Lancashire, sir, but is now in Brighton. I can ask someone to bring her here if you are ready to see her."

"I can't ... I don't ... yes, of course. But let me talk to Silv first. And the kids. We need to tell them ... fuck, I thought she was dead. I thought Abi was dead. I can't..." He waved a hand. "Sorry, you'll have to give me a few minutes."

"Of course, sir. Would it help if we left you and your family some time to come to terms with the news?" Jack pulled a card from his pocket and held it out. "Call me on this number when you are ready for us to return."

"Did you find the bastard who killed Jess? Is that where Abi was, with him?"

"We cannot comment on an ongoing investigation, sir."

"Ongoing...? Are you telling me he's still out there? Is he

still..." His eyes widened. "Still killing? Did you say Lancashire? There was something on the news at lunchtime about a murder there. Near Preston, it said. A farmer's wife, was it? And there was a sketch of a man. We have the telly on at the office while we eat our lunch. Didn't pay much attention, to be honest. What was Abi doing there? Was she with the farmer and his wife? Did they buy her? You hear about things like that, but you don't dream it might come so close to home. Don't think—" He shut his mouth with a snap, perhaps aware he was talking too much.

Izzy hadn't known about the news item, because they had been packing and then on the road. Someone must have briefed the press. She could picture the scrum outside Preston police station, and force HQ in Hutton. Or perhaps not. It was Lancashire, and as far as crime went, Merseyside trumped them every time. But it was also murder, and the media loved a good murder almost as much as a natural disaster or disgraced politician.

"Your daughter was found at the scene, fast asleep on a sofa. She had been drugged, most likely so she couldn't see or hear what was happening."

"He took another kid, didn't he? From the farm-house." Charles McFadden ran fingers through his dark hair. "Like he took Abi. He took another kid. A young one, wasn't it? About the same age Abi was when she went missing. Christ, has he had her all this time? The fucking bastard. I'll kill him."

Get in line behind Mike Wilson, Izzy thought.

From upstairs, the faint sound of splashing water and

children's laughter reached them, bringing home the dilemma facing the man.

"You need to discuss this with your wife, Mr McFadden," said Jack. "Call me on that number when you're ready to talk again. Let me know when you want to see Abigail."

"What's she like?"

"Normal. Ordinary. Pretty."

"That's good, isn't it? Normal is good. How normal can she be?" He looked at the card held in his fingers. "Yes, I'll call you. Me and Silv will talk once the kids are down. Are you staying in Brighton?"

"We are, sir."

"Good." He waved the card. "I'll call. Can you see yourselves out?"

When they reached the car, Jack said, "What do you think, Iz?"

"About him? He seemed shocked, but not shocked enough. You?"

"The same. But it didn't feel like an act. I suspect it's just the way he is."

"Not your sort of person," Izzy said, "nor mine. But it takes all sorts."

Jack laughed as he fastened his seat belt. "Us two are prime examples of that, aren't we?"

Izzy returned the laugh. "Well, one of us is. Let's go tell Flis and Sarah what's happening."

It was growing dark when they returned, this time with Flis, Sarah and Abi. As they approached the door, it opened before they could knock. Both the McFaddens had changed their outfits. She wore an expensive perfume, and an even more expensive-looking dress that showed off her figure. He wore slacks and a jumper hanging across his shoulders. They had both showered.

Flis stood closest to them, Abi's hand in hers. They had briefed the girl on the way, telling her she would see her father. Flis had been good. So had Sarah. But it was clear Abi didn't really understand. At one point she asked, "Do I have two daddies?"

Now Abi looked up at Charles McFadden without expression.

Then she tried to pull away, but Flis had her gripped tight.

"No," sobbed Abi. "I want my *real* daddy."

Flis went to one knee, so her face was level with Abi's. "This *is* your real daddy, sweetheart. The other one took you away from him when you were little. Do you want to come in and say hello?"

"I don't have to stay, do I?"

"Not tonight if you don't want to. But one day soon, you might change your mind."

"I want to stay with you, and Izzy and Jack." Abi glanced at the couple, who remained in the doorway as if rooted to the spot.

"Come on, five minutes," said Flis, rising.

When she took a step forward, Sylvia McFadden

turned and went inside. Her husband remained where he was, so everyone had to turn sideways to pass him.

In the big lounge, Sylvia said, "Does anyone want a drink? What about you, sweetie? Squash? Coke?"

"Can I have a coke zero, please? What's your name?"

"Sylvia. Do you want to come and help me pour the drinks?" She held her hand out, and after a moment, Abi released her hold on Flis's and took it.

"You're very pretty," she said.

"So are you." Sylvia glanced at the others. "Wine, beer, spirits?"

"Nothing for us," said Jack.

"I wouldn't mind a coffee," Izzy said.

Flis nodded. "Me too."

"Three coffees, then. Whisky, Charlie?"

"A big one." He went to sit on the sofa, and waved a hand to indicate they could sit where they liked.

It felt strange, but Izzy was sure nowhere near as strange as it must be for Charles McFadden. She was impressed by the way Sylvia took control. Impressed at how she had made Abigail like her. Maybe it would work out after all.

Except it didn't.

THIRTY-THREE

When they returned to the hotel, Flis put Abi to bed, and said she would stay with her until she fell asleep. Izzy, Jack and Sarah sat downstairs in the empty bar and drank bottled beer. They had stayed at the McFadden's house for forty minutes, at the end of which Charles hadn't said a word to his daughter. Sylvia had done all the parenting. She even took the girl to peek in on her brother and sister. They had left when Abi went to her father and tried to sit beside him. He had stood and gone upstairs, which is when Abi began to cry. On the way back in the car, she had been silent, staring out at the street lamps as they splashed light across her face, which still showed the tracks of tears.

"I don't think it's going to work," said Jack. He was on his second beer, the first having gone down in a couple of swallows. "How could he do that to his daughter?"

"He's coming to terms with things," said Sarah. "Until today, he has always assumed she was dead. Now, she appears as a nine-year-old, and according to Sylvia, Abi looks like his dead wife. Too many memories."

"Will he come around?" Jack asked.

"He might, with time. And Sylvia was so good with her."

"But not him."

"It's a shock, Jack, that's all."

"We can't sit on our arses waiting for him to make his mind up."

"We're going to have to," said Sarah, who had changed out of her uniform and now wore a summer dress. "What happened tonight is a shame, but it could take a while before Abi gets used to a new family, and they to her. The poor thing has had her life turned upside down. Dragging her down here wasn't my choice, but I accept it had to be done."

"I got the distinct impression Charles McFadden isn't too keen to take her back," Izzy said.

"He doesn't have to," said Sarah. "He might be her biological father, but he's started a new family since. I've made enquiries, and Jessica McFadden's parents live in Cambridgeshire. Her sister too. If things don't work out here, I'll ask Flis about us going there, to see if they might want to adopt Abi."

"That's allowed?" asked Jack.

"Of course. Social Services always prefer to place a child with family if they can. They'll have to run DBS checks on all three of them, but I expect them to come back clean. There'll be paperwork, and Flis is used to handling all that. But it's still early days yet."

Jack finished his second bottle and stood up. "I'm going to take a walk to clear my head. Anyone coming?"

Sarah nodded. "I could murder a real ale." She glanced at Izzy. "How about you?"

Izzy shook her head. "I might get an early night. I don't seem to have had more than a couple of snatched hours since this case started. Try not to get up to any mischief, you two."

Izzy took another beer from the bar, writing it down in the honesty book, then went upstairs to her small room where a single bed awaited. Only the best for the Lancashire constabulary.

She undressed and slipped under the covers, then stared at the sliver of view between two houses down to the sea. Streetlights cast long, wavering rays of light across the uneasy water, matching her mood. The tide was high, rattling against the pebble beach. Investigations were going on back in Lancashire, and she felt out of the loop. If she was paranoid, she might think they had been sent down here to get them out of the way. But she knew Harrington respected both her skills and Jack's, which worsened the enforced absence from MIT.

Izzy wished she had gone out with Jack and Sarah. It wasn't too late, but she was afraid of getting drunk. Pressure was building inside her, demanding she confess her fears. But who to? Jack, maybe. Sarah was another possibility. A shrink made sense, but she couldn't go that far, afraid of what else might be uncovered.

She thought of Charles McFadden. He was a lousy father, but compared to her own, an angel. Was that what unsettled her? A need to live up to him? Chief Superintendent Blackwood now. Her mother hadn't told Izzy that in their weekly phone calls. And her father hadn't communicated with Izzy in over five years.

She reached for her book, seeking escape, letting herself fall into the fictional world on its pages. She was still awake when she heard Jack and Sarah return, whispering and giggling like teenagers. For some reason, hearing them flipped a switch, and Izzy's demons fled to whatever dark place they lurked.

She thought about Abi, and what knowledge she held in her head. Considering what her life had been like, she seemed remarkably normal. And she might be helpful. Izzy decided she would ask Flis in the morning if she and Jack could take Abi to London, to see if they could identify where she had lived. Where she and Frank, whatever his last name was, lived. And if they were lucky, he would still be there.

Izzy smiled, turned off the light and rolled over, sleep washing over her like the incoming tide.

THIRTY-FOUR

"You must be batshit crazy even *thinking* I'd let you do something like that!" Flis glared at Izzy. "That poor kid was abandoned by the man she believed was her father, and now she's trying to come to terms with discovering her real one. A man who has a new wife and a new family. Abi needs time to adjust, not dragged around like some fucking parcel. Sarah and I are going to stay here until we know whether the McFaddens will take her into their family or not. You two can do whatever the fuck you want, but Abi stays in *my* care."

Izzy held back her own anger as she stared at Flis. She knew she was right, but the thought Abi could break this case gnawed at her. Izzy knew people thought she lacked compassion. She didn't know if she did or not. But she knew she should allow more of herself to show, instead of keeping her emotions wrapped tight inside. Priya was a friend, but would never understand her reluctance to submit to any man. Jack might be easier to approach, except he was on the job, and as if by some unwritten rule, they spoke little about their personal lives.

When Izzy glanced at Sarah, who sat in an armchair in the hotel lounge, she was watching the conversation but saying nothing. There would be no help from her.

"You're talking about a man who got up and walked away when Abi tried to sit next to him," Izzy said. "She was ready to reach out, to close the gap. He wasn't. And what will Jack and I do while you two play nursemaids?"

"Whatever you like. We're going to try again with Abi and her new family."

"How long will it take before you're sure she can be left with them?"

"A week, two most likely. Can you look after Abi while we go to the McFadden's house and talk to them without her around? Sylvia said they'd be at home all weekend. We'll be gone a couple of hours, is all."

"What am I going to do with a kid?"

Sarah laughed, the tension in the room broken. "Were you never a child yourself, Iz?" She held a hand up before she got a reply. "No, of course you weren't. I can see it now. You emerged from the womb a fully-fledged adult. Take her shopping. Buy her some nice clothes. She's got nothing to wear other than what we found her in. Jack will help. He understands people."

Izzy thought she understood people too, just not the soft side of them. Izzy saw the deception in people. The bad. She saw through the lies. It was, she thought, what made her a good cop, a good interviewer.

"Do you think I can use the debit card Harrington gave us?" Izzy asked Jack as they left the hotel.

"Try it. Just make sure you keep all the receipts; he'll want to see them."

They walked with Abi between them, her hand in Jack's. Izzy noticed a few people look at them with 'Aw, what a lovely family' expressions on their faces.

"Can I go to any shop I want?" asked Abi.

"Of course you can, sweetie," said Jack. "Just name it."

"Can we go to Primark? Daddy..." Her voice trailed away, and she took six steps before starting again, "...my old daddy, used to take me to Primark. It's my favourite."

"Don't you want to look at some of the other shops?" Izzie asked. "There are some fabulous clothes shops in the centre of town. You can get something lovely."

"Daddy says Primark is good for clothes. He doesn't want me to stand out."

"Is that where he took you in London?"

Abi nodded. "On my birthday, and at Christmas."

"When is your birthday?" asked Jack.

"June the 22nd. So soon." She offered a shy smile, and Izzy thought she might be coming out of herself a little. She also knew Abi's birthday was not June 22nd.

"Was this Primark you went to close to your house?"

"Oh no, it was right in the middle of London. We took a bus, and sometimes those trains that run through tunnels, but mostly the bus. Daddy likes to sit up top so he can see everything. So do I. They have buses in this place, too. I've seen them, but most aren't so tall."

Izzy opened her phone and searched. She found a

Primark near the town centre, and set it to guide them there. At least it wouldn't be much of a strain on the bank card. But she also determined they'd take Abi to some of the boutique places, to see if they could find something to make her stand out. She was a pretty girl but had been convinced she was ordinary. No doubt it had been safer that way. The man she believed was her father wouldn't want her to be noticed, just as he appeared to pass through life without raising a single ripple. Other than murder, of course. No waves, but one giant tsunami now and again.

"Once daddy took me to the big Tesco near our house because I needed new pyjamas and..." – she lowered her voice – "...underwear." Her face flushed at the shared intimacy.

"You were lucky to have a big Tesco close to you. Is that where you did your shopping?"

"Daddy does the shopping. He almost always leaves me at home. I watch TV until he comes back. He brings me chocolate as a treat."

Izzy thought it interesting Abi still spoke of her life with the man in the present tense. She knew she'd have to find a quiet space and record all of this before she forgot it. She glanced across at Jack, who met her gaze and nodded briefly. *Keep it up; this is good stuff.*

In Primark, Abi soon discovered that Jack offered far better advice on what suited her than Izzy, which allowed her to open her phone and search for large Tesco stores along the A40 into London. She found a whole bunch of the smaller shops but only two big ones. The first was near Northolt, the second close to Shepherd's Bush. She tried to recall what Abi had said about where they lived, whether a house or a flat, but failed. Another question to follow up on. She also needed Abi to describe the street she lived on. Housing or mixed? Semi-detached or detached? She knew the girl was unlikely to be a great help, but any information would be valuable. Izzy also knew she couldn't push Abi any harder. She suspected she was already pushing more than she should, but Abi had given them helpful intel.

Jack and Abi approached with a collection of clothes, and they went to pay. Izzy wondered if spending at Primark would flag a message on some computer screen back in Hutton.

Once outside, Izzy persuaded Abi to look at some offerings in the smaller shops. Eventually, Abi chose a carpet jacket in red and yellow, which changed her appearance entirely.

By the time they returned to the hotel, Flis and Sarah were back. Both looked at Abi's purchases and commented on each, before telling her she would be meeting her family for lunch.

"Do you need us for anything else today?" Izzy asked Flis.

"Sarah and I can look after Abi, so go do whatever you want."

When they were alone, Jack said, "We're not going to London, Iz."

"I know."

"So what will we do, roll our trousers up and paddle?"

271

"Better than that," Izzy said. "I called Ailsa to ask about progress, but she said there wasn't much to report. However, she put me through to Harrington, who wanted to speak to me. I thought he'd heard about my plan to go to London, but fortunately, it wasn't that. He contacted a DI in Brighton to let him know we were down here. The man offered him the name of the SIO who worked the case seven years ago, and he wants to meet us. He's retired now and lives inland. So, do you fancy a trip to the country, Jack?

* * *

Upper Beeding appeared like a town locked in the 1950s, but ex-DI Martin Goss was more 1970s. His hair fell to his chin, and he sported a neat goatee. He wore blue jeans, a linen shirt, and sandals on his feet. He opened the door of his small house and looked at both of them before offering his hand.

"You must be the detectives from up north." His voice was soft, with a Suffolk accent. "Come on through, we can sit in the garden out back to talk. I take it you do want to talk?

They followed him through a neat living room with guitars on the wall, and vinyl record covers in frames. Bands from the 70s, most obscure enough that Izzy recognised none of the faces or names.

"I take it you're enjoying retirement," Jack said.

"Too bloody right. I liked the job, but you know what it's like as well as me. It can be hard sometimes. Particularly death. That's why you're here, isn't it? The murder of Jessica McFadden and her daughter, Abigail. It was one of my last cases, and it still nags me today." He opened a door from the kitchen into a small, walled garden.

They sat at a metal table, in surprisingly comfortable chairs.

"You can't have heard yet," Izzy said. "We're here to bring Charles McFadden's daughter back to him. Abi's having lunch in his house right now."

Martin Goss stared at Izzy. "Abigail's alive? Your skipper didn't tell me that."

"Yes, she's alive."

"She must be eight or nine years old by now. I was always convinced she'd been taken and killed, and we never found her body. Alive." He shook his head. "Miracles do happen then. Where was she?"

"Living with the man we believed killed her mother. Our case is linked, as are several others. But at the moment, we believe Jessica McFadden was probably his first victim, which is why it's good of you to speak to us. Can you recall the details of the case, Mr Goss?"

"Call me Marty, and I'll call you Isabella and Jack, if I can."

"I prefer Izzy."

"Done. And every part of that case is etched in my memory. Is there anything in particular you want to know about?"

"Are there any footpaths near the house where the crime occurred?"

"Footpaths?"

"We have–" Izzy stopped, started again, "I have a theory our killer follows footpaths to each scene. He took

Abi from the McFadden's house, and we believe she has been with him ever since. He takes her with him when he kills."

"Then he's a fucking monster," said Goss.

"Of course he is," said Jack."

"How do you have Abigail now if you haven't arrested the man?"

"He abandoned her in the farmhouse," Izzy said. "We think he was interrupted and had to flee the scene. This time, he took the Wilson's child. Eleven-month-old Grace."

"Christ, this gets even worse. Ask me anything you want. Whatever I can do to help, I will."

"The footpaths," Izzy reminded him.

"Two pass close to the McFadden's house, as was. One within fifty yards. The house is in the Patcham district, which is the commuter belt, hard up against the A27, but also on the doorstep of the Downs. So it's prime footpath country."

"We have the case record," said Jack, "but it would be useful to hear your thoughts on it, Marty. We all have them, ideas we don't write down, hunches and theories."

Goss stared into space for so long Izzy didn't think he would answer. Then he rose and went into the house.

She looked at Jack. "Do you think we've upset him?"

Jack shrugged.

Goss returned after a few minutes with a red notebook. He set it on the table, but didn't open it.

"Have you seen Charles McFadden?" he asked.

"Twice. As I said, Abi, a social worker, and our FLO

are having lunch with him, his wife and their children. Why? What do you know about him?"

"Did you like the man?"

"There are many people I don't like," Izzy said, "but that doesn't mean they're guilty of something."

Goss patted the cover of the notebook. "These are my thoughts, some of the things I couldn't put in the official record. I wanted to, but my DCI stopped me."

"What kind of things?" asked Jack.

"Most of it's a load of bollocks, but not all of it. My main concerns were about Charles McFadden. I think…" He took a breath, his eyes tracking between them. "I'm not saying I was right, but I believed McFadden might have had his wife killed. He didn't do it himself, though he was initially in the frame. Husbands often are. But what I think is, he paid someone else to do it."

"How sure are you?" asked Jack.

"Not enough to get anyone to believe me. Not enough to charge him. I wanted to look at his bank records, but was told I couldn't."

"Are you suggesting a cover-up?" Izzy asked.

Goss shook his head. "Not a cover-up, just lazy policing. We pulled in several local men but had nothing on them. In the end, it was put down to a passing stranger. And yes, maybe a walker. We looked into that as well, but found nothing worth pursuing."

"Why McFadden, then?" asked Jack.

He rubbed his belly. "Gut, nothing more. I'm sure both of you have the same thing happen sometimes. He wasn't upset enough. Some of the others put that down to shock, but he never showed anything of loss. Loss of his wife and kid both. And then ... less than half a year later, he married the daughter of one of the neighbours. I wondered at the time if they'd been having an affair before his wife was killed."

"Can we tell our DCI about your theory, Marty?" Jack asked.

"If you think it might help. All I've ever wanted is a resolution to this case. It's bugged me ever since. So yes, tell them."

THIRTY-FIVE

Lunch was tense, but Sarah was grateful none of the children appeared to notice. Abi sat between four-year-old Kate and five-year-old Ben, her half-sister and -brother. She talked with them, and they asked questions in return, but they were shallow, which was to be expected.

"Can we take Abi to the playroom?" asked Ben once they finished their chocolate chip ice cream, the container still on the table, its contents slowly melting.

Charlie McFadden looked at Sarah rather than his wife, but she responded.

"Of course you can, darlings. Do you like dolls, Abi?" She smiled at the girl, more accepting of her than her husband.

Memories, Sarah thought. Abi came with memories he almost certainly didn't want to revisit.

When the children had gone into the playroom with Flis, Sylvia rose to clear the table.

"Leave it," said Charlie. He turned his gaze on Sarah. "I'm not sure this is going to work. Sorry."

"It must be difficult, but you should give it time. We can stay in Brighton for as long as you need us. Or I can return to Preston, and come back when you want me."

"What I want is my life back. This is..." his hands moved, trying to express something words couldn't. He had to delve deep for something, anything. "It's crazy. I don't know her. I don't even recognise her."

"Abi was only eleven months old when she was taken," said Sylvia. "It's not a surprise you don't recognise her. Nor will she recognise you. But she is your daughter."

"But not yours." Charlie's voice was cold.

Sylvia looked as if she had been slapped.

Sarah watched the couple, recognising the deep pain held by Charlie, but also the compassion shown by Sylvia. If it were up to her, Abi would already be a part of their family.

"It's a matter of blood, isn't it?" Charlie's face tightened when he realised what he had said.

Charlie pushed on through. "You feel sorry for her now, Silv, but give it three months, or a year. How will you feel when she's thirteen and acting up?"

"What if she doesn't? Besides, I don't think she will. She's already mature for her age. And look how well she gets on with Ben and Kate."

"They were eating fucking ice cream. That doesn't tell you anything."

Sarah waited, unsure if now was the time to intervene

or not. She wasn't sure the couple realised she was still at the table. They'd gone into their own world. A family world. She wondered how solid their relationship was. Not that she blamed Charlie. Bringing his long-lost daughter to his door was a lot to take in. Then there were the memories. Sarah had already seen how they flooded through him. Those moments would return every time he looked at the daughter he believed dead.

Sarah stood. "I'll let you talk between yourselves while I look in on the children."

She didn't wait for a response, but followed the sound of laughter. Two female voices, one male. Two much younger than the other.

When she reached the playroom, bigger than her living room, she stayed in the doorway and watched them together. Flis stood across the room, her eyes on the children. Sarah thought Abi might want the toys for herself. She was the eldest, so Sarah would expect her to be dominant. Instead, she helped Ben and Kate build an ornate tower with plastic Lego bricks. Rather than place them herself, she directed the other two until the multi-coloured tower was almost two feet high. Then, all three of them pushed it over, laughing wildly.

When Abi looked towards the doorway, her laughter died when she saw Sarah.

"It's all right, carry on. I just came to see how you're all getting along together."

"Are mummy and daddy arguing again?" asked Ben.

Again?

"Of course not. They're doing the washing up."

"We have a machine for that."

Ben started picking up the bricks and tossing them into a large wooden box. There were other wooden boxes set around the edges of the room, some three layers high. They held soft toys, board games, jigsaws, more Lego, CDs and DVDs ready to slot into either a stereo system or the smart TV bolted to the wall. Sarah wondered if the toy overkill was a displacement for lack of attention. Except she had learned that Sylvia only worked three days a week, and those days were short and covered by school hours. Lack of attention from their father, then? Who had wanted these two children – him or her? Would children remind him of the one he had lost? The wife he had lost? Sarah was used to dealing with the abused, the damaged, the grief-stricken, those in cold shock. She saw into people and tried to help, but sometimes they didn't want to be helped. Was Charlie McFadden one of those? And if he was, what did it mean for Abi?

"Is it time to leave?" asked Abi, rising to her feet.

Sarah smiled. "Not yet."

Abi turned away. "What shall we play next?" she asked Ben.

Sarah tried not to analyse why she had asked him and not Katie. Ben was the older of the two, and would probably make most of the decisions. Once his sister was older, that might change.

"Do you like Lion King?" asked Ben. "It's Mummy's favourite, and now it's ours too."

"What's Lion King?" said Abi.

"It's a film, silly. Everyone knows about Lion King."

"Not me. But I like films. It's not too grown-up, is it? Daddy doesn't like me watching grown-up films."

"He never said that to us," said Ben.

"My other daddy," said Abi, making Ben frown.

"You have two daddies?"

"I didn't know I did, but now I do. Except … I don't know what happened to my other one. I went to sleep, and when I woke up, he was gone." A tear tracked Abi's cheek. "I might never see him again."

Sarah wanted to go to her but held back. When she glanced at Flis, she saw she wanted the children to work this out between them. She was pleased when Katie stood and went to hug Abi. Then Ben hugged them both.

"You have a new daddy now," said Ben. "And a new brother and sister."

Abi kissed the top of his head, then Katie's, and all three hugged even tighter.

Sarah turned away and went back into the dining room, which was empty. She found Sylvia in the kitchen, bent over as she loaded the dishwasher.

"Where's Charlie?"

"Went out. We fought." Sylvia straightened up. "I want Abi to live with us, but I don't think he does." She brushed blonde hair from her face. "What happens to her if he gets his way? Flis is Social Services, isn't she? Will it be some shitty home for kids?"

"Not if we have anything to do with it," said Sarah. "Abi has been placed with a local foster couple, but we will seek a permanent placement. Charlie's parents are still around, aren't they?"

"Yes, alive and kicking." Sylvia smiled. "They live near Cambridge. So does his sister. You must have looked this all up."

"Can I ask you an awkward question?"

"Sure. Is it to do with Jess?"

Sylvia's use of the shortened name told her Charlie must have spoken about her.

"I was wondering if she made a will. Often, they name guardians for their children in case of the worst-case scenario of both parents dying."

"Oh, I know they did. They each had one."

"Charlie told you?"

"No, Jess did. We were friends. My family lived near their house. I was younger than her, twenty-one when she died. For some reason, we hit it off straight away. It's probably why Charlie came to me after, though I didn't fight him off. I'd always fancied him." Sylvia slapped her palm across her mouth. "Oh God, listen to me. I must sound like a heartless bitch."

"Not at all. You would have been shaken up if you and Jessica were friends."

"She named her mum and dad and sister in her will. To look after Abi if anything happened to the two of them."

"You knew Abi as well then, I suppose?"

Sylvia laughed, her good humour restored. "I used to babysit for her all the time. She was such a cutie. Now, she's beautiful. They liked to go out, Charlie and Jess. She liked a good time."

Sarah looked at Sylvia. Tall. Lissom. Beautiful.

"And did Charlie enjoy a good time, too?"

"He loved her. Charlie did whatever Jess wanted. Always. He was lost when she was taken from him. We all were, but Charlie more than most. I think he's struggling now because Abi looks like her mum, and will do so even more as she grows up. It brings back all those memories."

"Does Charlie ever visit Jessica's parents?"

"Never. We argued about it once, and he told me the kids were ours, not theirs. He wants nothing to do with them. I think the Bowmans remind him of Jess. But I've got their addresses if you want it."

"No need, we have them both."

Sylvia smiled. "Of course, I forget you're police dressed in ordinary clothes. You probably know everything, don't you?"

"I wish I did."

Sarah wasn't sure if they would need to contact Jessica's parents, but she was sure they would want to meet their granddaughter at least. They were also a potential backup if Charlie couldn't be convinced to accept Abi. She hoped it wouldn't be needed. If it was, Abi's grandparents might provide a suitable home for her, and a much better option than a foster family. Unless her grandparents treated her the same way her father did. Somehow, Sarah didn't think that would be the case.

THIRTY-SIX

"Where's Abi?" Izzy asked, when she and Jack returned to the hotel.

Sarah and Flis sat downstairs, as if waiting for them. Sarah had some news.

"Upstairs, watching TV," she said. "She's upset, and with good reason. Everything went to bollocks."

"What happened?" asked Jack.

"It was all going pretty well. Abi was playing with her stepbrother and sister. Sylvia liked her. Even Charlie seemed to be coming around to the idea. Not today, but maybe in a week or two. Then Ben took a doll from Abi, and he says she hit him."

"Slapped?"

"Punched. Made his nose bleed. Shit, Iz, this is not what any of us need right now. Flis was with them, but left the room to use the loo when it happened."

"What are you going to do?"

"I don't know yet. But I'll tell you one thing – we are

not letting that poor girl enter the system. But if she loses her temper this way, she'll be hard to place."

"Do you think she'll strike out again?" Izzy asked.

"I don't know. It might have been a one-off. It might be because she's not been socialised like most kids. Maybe it's been her and the man she thinks is her daddy, and nobody else. It's no way to bring up a child."

"He's a killer, Sar," Izzy said. "For all we know, he's been abusing her."

"If he has, he's been bloody careful. The hospital checked her out pretty well. Flis and I have seen a whole bunch of abused kids, and we both agree Abi shows none of the signs."

"Have you reported the incident to Social Services in Preston?" Jack asked Flis.

"Not yet. Once I do, I'll have to make an official report and tell them what she did. It'll always be a black mark against her." Flis sighed and leaned forward. "She's a good kid, I'm convinced of it. But she's been through a lot of shit, and it looks like sometimes it comes out."

"What are you going to do?"

"I called Jessica McFadden's parents and told them we have their granddaughter with us. They want us to go up there in the morning. You and Jack are not required to come with us, but I wondered if you wanted to talk to them. I spent half an hour on the phone, and they're excited to see Abi. A granddaughter they thought they'd lost for good."

"We'd like to come," Izzy said. "And we have some news of our own. Better than yours, we hope, though it does complicate the situation. We went to meet a guy by the name of Marty Goss, an ex-DI involved in the murder of Jessica McFadden. He's retired now, but it's a case that still haunts him. The kicker is, he's convinced Charlie McFadden hired someone to kill his wife."

Flis winced. Sarah stared at Izzy.

"Holy shit, Iz, do you believe him?"

"Not yet, but I'm sure we can make some enquiries. Marty said the rest of the team had already made their mind up, that some passing perv did for her. He wanted to dig into it more but was told to leave it. Jack says he'll contact Harrington and brief him, see if we can get access to bank records around that time."

"I had a conversation with Sylvia at the house," said Sarah. "She used to babysit Abi. She told me Charlie and Jessica's marriage was turbulent. As his new one might be. Ben let slip an interesting comment. He asked if mummy and daddy were arguing again."

"I've seen that situation more than I want," said Flis. "There are no bad marriages, only bad people. I've watched a family tear itself apart, only to get married to new partners and start the cycle all over again."

"Might Sylvia be in danger?" asked Jack.

Sarah shrugged. "I'd say not. Charlie's a grumpy sod, but he worships her. Let's see if Harrington can come up with any evidence. This man you met might be wrong about this."

"It might be better if he is," said Jack. "One marriage torn apart is surely more than enough. I agree with Iz, we'll come with you and talk to Abi's grandparents.

They're bound to have questions about the ongoing investigation."

"There's Jessica's sister as well. She lives near her parents in Cambridgeshire. I gave her a call after I'd spoken to the grandparents. Ellie Bowman is four years younger than Jessica McFadden would be, and single. She volunteered the information that some people just aren't cut out for marriage, even though I never asked."

"I'm not averse to the idea," said Jack, "but I'm still looking for the right guy. Maybe a cross between George Clooney and Antonio Banderas."

Flis laughed. "In Preston?"

"I may even be willing to go as far as Liverpool or Manchester. I hear there are a lot of actors around those parts."

"Dream on," Izzy said. "You'll have to fight a thousand women to get to the dreamboats."

"Oh, a man can dream."

Izzy turned back to Flis. "Are you saying the grandparents might take her? Will Social Services allow that?"

"We would always prefer to place a child with family if possible, provided they're willing to take them. So Abi could go to her grandparents, or even the sister, though that might be trickier because she's single. We won't know until we get there."

"Have you run this past Abi?"

"Not yet. We can raise it with her when we go out to eat. Sarah's found a nice-looking Italian place. Abi's bound to like pizza. Is that okay for both of you?"

"As long as they have gelato," said Jack.

Abi was quiet at the restaurant after Sarah raised the idea with her. Flis thought it better she did it, as she might be leaving their small band in the morning if Cambridgeshire Social Services took Abi's case over.

"How would you like to meet your grandpa and grandma, Abi?" Sarah asked.

"I don't have one," she said.

"Your new grandpa and grandma. Your mummy's mum and dad."

"Do you mean Silvia?"

Izzy saw Sarah's mouth purse. There was an answer to Abi's question, but it wasn't easy.

"I mean, your real mummy. She ... well, she died."

"Daddy never said anything about that."

"Charlie's first wife," said Sarah, attempting the near impossible. But Abi seemed to grasp the concept.

"Ah, I see now. Do I have to live with them? With Charlie and Sylvia and Ben and Katie?"

"Not if you don't want to."

"Why did you punch Ben?" Izzy asked. She saw Flis and Sarah scowl at her, but the question was out there now. Another tough one.

Abi was quiet for so long that Izzy thought she wouldn't answer, then she said in a voice almost too soft to hear, "I didn't."

"You made his nose bleed."

Abi looked into Izzy's eyes, something stubborn in her own.

"He grabbed the doll I was playing with. I didn't want him to have it, but he pulled so hard it hit him. *He* made his nose bleed, Izzy, not me. But he told everyone I did it. It's not fair." Tears showed in her eyes. "They don't want me to be their sister. Ben said so. He called me ugly and stupid."

Izzy turned to Flis, whose eyes were wide.

"Is that really what happened?" asked Flis.

"I don't tell lies. Daddy taught me never to tell lies."

Fucking paragon of virtue that he is, Izzy thought.

"Would you like to see your grandpa, grandma, and aunt tomorrow?"

"Don't know," said Abi. Her eyes were on the scant remains of the pizza in front of her. "I like Silvia, but I don't like the others."

"Not even your real daddy?" asked Flis.

Abi shook her head.

"If you see your grandpa and grandma tomorrow, you might like them."

Izzy was unsure Flis could make such a promise, but remained silent. The pizza had been good. So was the ice cream. Now, it was getting late, and she could see Abi was exhausted from the stress of the day. Too many new things, and names and faces to come to terms with. Too much conflict. She believed her when she said Ben hit himself with the toy. Maybe moving her around again so soon after what happened wasn't a good idea, but she was content for Flis and Sarah to take the lead.

———

Early the following morning, Izzy sat in the passenger seat as Jack drove north on the A23 away from Brighton. Abi had said scarcely a word since they left the hotel. Izzy was unsure where they would end up but suspected it wouldn't involve a return to Brighton. Traffic was heavy, and grew heavier as they came closer to London. Jack was a slower, more careful driver than Izzy, who tried to tamp down her impatience at him when he didn't take a gap in traffic where she would have. They were all quiet. All tired.

Traffic on the M25 moved, but it moved at its own glacial pace. They crossed the Thames at Dartford, and eventually swung north on the A11.

"How old are they?" asked Abi, who sat in the back between Sarah and Flis, who was sleeping.

"How old are who, sweetie?" said Sarah.

"My grandma and grandpa. How old are they?"

"In their sixties. It's not so old these days."

"Older than daddy was," said Abi.

Izzy turned in her seat to look back at her. "How old was he, your old daddy?"

Abi frowned. "I don't know."

"Did he have birthdays?"

Abi's frown deepened, and Sarah cast a warning glance at Izzy. *Drop it, before she has a meltdown.* But it was Abi who spoke next.

"He always got a card on his birthday," she said.

"From you?" Sarah took over. Izzy was grateful, aware trying to question Abi now would be unlawful if she did it. Sarah was more of a grey area. And if Abi revealed something, it might be possible to confirm it another way.

"I wanted to buy him one, but he was always with me when we went shopping. They have to be a surprise, don't they? The ones he got were from his friend."

Izzy felt excitement, but held her tongue despite a dozen questions ready to spill out. She had to trust Sarah.

"What friend? Did you ever meet him, or her?"

"Don't know if it was him or her," said Abi. "All Daddy got was a card on his birthday every year. He kept them in a drawer in his desk, which was always locked."

"So you never saw the cards."

"I did once. Daddy left one on the kitchen table when he went to answer the door. It was the postman with a parcel. I sneaked a look."

"Do you remember what was written in it?"

"A bit. Something about congratulations. And another one bites the dust." She offered a shy smile. "I remember that bit because it comes from a song, right?"

"Queen," said Sarah, and smiled back.

"It came on the first day of June. I remember that as well."

The first of June, Izzy thought. Is that date significant, or not? Does it tell us anything? She didn't think so. But if they arrested a suspect, it might help corroborate he was the man they sought. However, there was plenty of other evidence: DNA, fibres, fingerprints. It wouldn't be hard to place him at any of the scenes once they found him. The information about the birthday cards was interesting. Did it imply Abi's pretend daddy had an accomplice?

Someone who helped him? Or even someone who ordered him to kill? Izzy knew they didn't have enough information to make such a leap, but something about the idea made sense to her. Either the man was a genius who had never been caught, or he had help.

Ahead of them, the traffic came to a complete halt.

"Did you get presents on your birthday?" asked Sarah.

Abi nodded. "Daddy always bought me something, every year. Clothes usually, but a bunny one year."

"A real one?"

Abi laughed and shook her head. "No, silly. A stuffed bunny. I called it Hoppy. Daddy thought I said Poppy, but I said no, it's Hoppy." She laughed again, then leaned against Sarah and closed her eyes. "I might have a sleep, if it's a long way to go yet."

Sarah put an arm around Abi and made her comfortable. "That's a good idea, sweetie. I'll wake you up when we get close."

The traffic started to move again, taking them nearer to what Izzy hoped might be a solution for Abi. One that offered her a better future than her past. The man she called daddy appeared to have treated her well. But that didn't make him any less of a monster.

THIRTY-SEVEN

Jessica McFadden's parents lived in an elegant, detached house a few miles south of Cambridge. It looked like a shrunken Elizabethan manor house, with leaded windows, steep rooflines, and tall chimneys. Three cars were pulled up on a circular gravel driveway. A BMW SUV, a Tesla, and a Mini Clubman. Two carried recent number plates, the BMW a personal plate, which told Izzy it belonged to Abi's aunt. Jack drew up and turned the engine off. Izzy opened the door and got out to stretch. She glanced in to see Sarah gently shaking Abi awake. Flis pulled out her phone and called Cambridgeshire Social Services to tell them they arrived. She had explained the evening before that she would inform them as a courtesy, but Abi remained her responsibility until she was placed.

The front door opened, and a tall man emerged. He had a full head of grey hair cut a little long, combed back from a high forehead. He wore tweed trousers and a waistcoat over an open-necked shirt.

Izzy approached and held her hand out. "Mr Bowman? I'm Detective Constable Wilde. My companion is Detective Sergeant Ward. Abi's social worker, Felicity Roberts, and Child Protection Officer Sarah Anderson are in the car with your granddaughter."

"How is Abi?" Thomas Bowman continued to grip Izzy's hand, his grasp firm. The kind of man who tested others.

Izzy knew he had been a consultant surgeon at Papworth Hospital in Cambridge. He had a reputation for taking on cases others considered hopeless. According to their available records, his success rate was slightly more than fifty per cent. It might not sound so good, but had he not operated on them, every patient would have died. Not such bad odds when you looked at it that way.

Thomas Bowman released Izzy's hand and shook Jack's.

Izzy decided she liked the man. He had no side. What you saw was what you got.

"Yes, we'd like to see Abigail, if that's all right."

"It's why we are here, Mr Bowman," said Jack.

"Please, call me Tom. My wife, who you will meet soon, is Betty. And my daughter is Ellie. But I expect you know all that, don't you."

"We do, sir," said Jack, not yet ready to take the man up on his offer of first-name terms.

Izzy turned and nodded to Sarah and Flis, who led Abi

out. When Izzy turned back, she was surprised to see Thomas Bowman's eyes bright with unshed tears.

He shook his head, opened his mouth to speak, then coughed into his fist. "She's the spitting image of her mother. Of Jess. I'm sorry, but … well, we never thought we'd see our granddaughter again." He half-turned towards the house. "Come out, both of you. Come and meet Abi."

A tall, willowy blonde in her thirties emerged first. Ellie Cartwright. She came and stood by her father, watching as Flis brought Abi forward. The girl shuffled her feet through the gravel, eyes downcast.

Betty Bowman came out to join the others. She was more than half a foot shorter than her husband, with short, well-cut hair, white with a faint blue tint some older women affected. She was lean and fit-looking, and Izzy tried not to add 'for her age' to the judgement.

She stepped forward, went to one knee and held her arms out. Abi hesitated and glanced up at Flis, who nodded.

"Go give your grandma a great big hug, Abi."

Still, she stood rooted to the spot, until Ellie Bowman came to join her mother. Abi looked between them, then ran to Ellie and threw herself into her arms. If Betty Bowman was upset her granddaughter had not chosen her, she didn't show it. Instead, Ellie held out an arm to welcome her into the hug.

"Please, come inside," said Thomas Bowman. "Have you eaten lunch?"

"We were going to find somewhere once you had met Abi," said Izzy.

"Then eat here. We have plenty, and we can talk. About everything." He glanced at the small, huddled group. "They'll come in when they're ready. We have some toys, but they might be too young for Abi. She's … well, older than I imagined, even after you told me she is almost nine years of age. Of course, I should have known, but sometimes you don't think." He held his arm out. "Please, come in."

Izzy discovered the inside of the house was as elegant as the outside, with subtle, expensive furniture.

Once Abi had gone deeper into the house with the others, Thomas Bowman turned to Izzy and Jack.

"Does finding Abigail mean you have made some progress in the case of my daughter?"

Izzy saw Jack hesitate, so she stepped in. The man deserved honesty. As much as she could offer, anyway. Some protocols and rules needed to be followed.

"The death of your daughter has been linked to several other cases. Jack and I are investigating a recent death in Lancashire."

"Is that the one I saw on the news? Farmer's wife?"

"I was the first officer on the scene, and found Abi asleep on a sofa in the kitchen."

Thomas Bowman frowned. "What was she doing there? Did these farmers, I don't know, abduct her, adopt her?" It was the same question Charles McFadden had asked. Izzy supposed it was an easy assumption to make rather than what the truth was.

"We believe she was abandoned there, Mr Bowman."

"Abandoned?"

Izzy was uncomfortable. There was more she could tell the man, but did he want to hear it?

As if he could read her mind, he said, "Look, I've held hearts and livers in my hands, Detective. I've cut chunks out of people's brains. If you're afraid you might upset my composure, then think again. Tell me what happened."

Izzy took a breath. She glanced at Jack, who seemed perfectly happy to let her continue without him. She hoped he would step in if it looked like she was revealing too much.

"At the moment, sir, we believe Abi was taken when your daughter was killed. She has been living with the man ever since, until recently."

"Why did he leave her at the farmhouse?"

"The Wilson's daughter is missing."

Thomas Bowman stared at Izzy. She tried to meet his gaze without looking away. She could almost see him working through what she had told him.

"The same man?" he said.

"That is our working hypothesis for the moment. It's one reason we came to see you. Mainly to bring Abi here, but also to ask you some questions."

"Can we keep her?" He paused and waved his hand. "Sorry, that could have come out better. Are we able to have our granddaughter stay here with us? Adoption? Or is that even necessary?"

Izzy thought it interesting he made no mention of Charlie McFadden.

"Flis is better able to answer questions like that," Izzy said. "If possible, Jack and I would like to speak with each of you separately to see if you can offer anything to help our investigation."

"Jess died over seven years ago. We were interviewed by the police then. What use can we be now?"

"We won't know until we've spoken to you," Izzy said. She wished Jack would help out, but knew he would note everything. Thomas Bowman's words, his manner, his body language. "How about we start with you, Mr Bowman?"

THIRTY-EIGHT

Izzy drew Jack aside and asked if he would stay with the others, while she spoke to Thomas Bowman.

"Can't it wait? We should let them have some time together," he said. "Let them get to know their granddaughter before dragging them away for questioning. You need to chill. They're not going anywhere, and neither are we. Besides, they're not suspects."

"What if they know something?"

"Still full speed ahead, Iz?"

"For fuck's sake, Jack, he's out there somewhere! What if he's planning another kill?"

"He won't be, not this soon. You're good at your job, but remember it's a team effort."

"Sarah and Flis can look after the girl."

"Her name's Abi." Jack cocked his head, examining Izzy. "What's the matter with you?"

She shrugged, a tension in her shoulders. "I've got a bad feeling, is all. It's like everything's drifting away from us. What if he is a killer for hire? We won't know how long before he finds another customer. We've got new information, but it's not enough. He's out there, and we don't know who he is, or where he lives."

"We've got the sketch," said Jack. "It's a good likeness. We can show it to them, and ask if they've seen him before."

"Slim chance, that is."

"I know, but we take what we can get. We'll drink tea with them, and let them get to know us so that it won't feel like an interrogation when we do talk."

Izzy didn't like it, but knew she couldn't go against Jack. Technically, he was her supervisor, which meant she was supposed to do what he said.

The tea was excellent, served from a china teapot in porcelain cups, a milk jug on the table, and an assortment of cakes and biscuits. It looked like someone had gone to the local deli because the croissants were crisp, fresh, and slightly warm. Izzy ate two, and tried to tamp down her impatience. It helped that she watched Betty Bowman and her daughter playing with Abi, who seemed to have relaxed in their company. Thomas Bowman sat in a leather armchair, with a smile on his face. He glanced at Izzy and nodded, as if offering thanks, then stood.

"If you want to talk to me, now might be a good time while Abi gets to know her family. You're all welcome to stay for lunch afterwards, if you can."

Izzy glanced at her phone for the time, out of habit, even though two clocks were in the room. "That would be nice. Is there somewhere we can talk?" She glanced at

Jack to see if he wanted to join her, but he was on his knees playing with Abi. He looked up and gave a slight shake of his head. *You do it.*

Izzy followed Thomas Bowman into a well-appointed study. Bookshelves lined almost every inch of wall space. A set of French doors led out to an immaculate garden.

"Please, sit." Thomas Bowman went behind his desk. Izzy sat in one of the two chairs facing it and took out her notebook.

She held it up. "Do you mind? This isn't a formal interview, but it might be useful to record anything you say that is relevant."

"Go ahead. What is it you want to know?"

Izzy drew out a large writing pad and slipped a copy of the sketch Jeff Harding had done. She laid it on the desk.

"Do you recognise this man?" she asked.

Thomas Bowman looked down at it.

"Is this him? The man who killed our Jess?"

"It's an artist's impression of someone seen near the location who is a subject of interest."

Thomas Bowman smiled as he looked up to meet her eyes. "You can say whatever you want to me, Detective Wilde. I've had a long and distinguished career in the health service, and have a reputation as a hard man. There's no need to hide anything from me. What was the most recent victim's name? Oh, and just for the record, I don't believe I have ever seen this man. I might be approaching my seventieth year, but still have all my marbles."

Izzy tried to decide if he was being confrontational. Perhaps he was always this way. To the point. Precise. And he said people thought him a hard case. She could see how that might be a valuable skill for a surgeon.

"Did they tell you how your daughter died?" It was a harsh question, but she thought he could take it.

"They did not. I identified her body, but all that showed was her face, which was untouched. I asked to attend the PM."

"They let you?"

"No, which was probably for the best." Thomas Bowman's expression was set. "I've seen every corner of the human body, but it's different when it's your own child. Do you have children, Izzy?"

"I'm single, and no kids, Tom." She decided she could respond in kind if they were on first-name terms.

"Then you can never understand the pain I felt at the death of Jess. It unmanned me. And as for Betty … I'm not sure she's fully recovered even now. Despite what people claim, time does not always heal. She throws herself into her committees. Plays tennis, swims, and does yoga and tai chi, but the sadness remains. If you catch the bastard, it might help, but I doubt it. I hope you do, though. It could save someone else from going through what we have."

Izzy was gentler when it was Betty Bowman's turn, but she saw the truth of what her husband had said. Something had broken inside her, and not yet healed. Perhaps Abi could help her do that.

Betty knew nothing about the sketch either, but her daughter was different.

She came into the study with a long stride and straight back.

When Izzy slid the sketch across the desk, Ellie picked it up and studied it with sharp hazel eyes for almost a minute before looking up.

"Yes, I've seen him before. But he was younger then."

Izzy leaned forward. "When would that be?"

"About six weeks before Jess was murdered. I saw him twice, a week apart. The first time I was staying down with Jess. They wanted a babysitter while they went to a work dinner, and their usual one was on holiday. Besides, it was never a hardship to look after Abi. She was such a sweet baby." She met Izzy's gaze. "It's difficult for me to match that baby up with the girl sitting out there reading a story. The hair is the same, but it was much finer back then. You're sure it's Abi?"

"We are. Tell me about the man."

"I was in the park with Abi in her pram. He rode past on a push-bike, hit an obstacle and fell off. I went to check if he was all right."

Izzy wondered if it had been an accident, or if he had been checking out Jessica McFadden and her family.

"And you're sure it was him? It was a long time ago and sounds like a short encounter."

"Yes, I'm sure. And yes, it was a long time ago, but I'm one of those people they call super recognisers. I can see a face for less than a minute and remember it if I meet that person ten years later. It's a useful skill to have in my line of work." She glanced at the sketch still in her hand. "Yes, it was him. He's good-looking, in a bland way, if you don't think about him being a killer."

"What was your impression of him at the time? Or did you not have one?"

Ellie looked off into a corner. "I'm trying to remember. You're a woman, so you know how we can pick up a vibe from some men, but I don't think I did with him. He seemed … harmless." She scowled. "That wasn't the case, but I'm trying to be honest with you."

"But you do remember him."

"Mostly because he fell off his bike, and I went to help him. It was a small thing, but it stuck with me."

"You said you saw him twice. Tell me about the other time."

"It was near here. I run. Seriously. Marathons, triathlons, and I'm good. I was out training, following one of the footpaths near where I live."

"Which is close to your parents, I understand."

"A short distance away in Little Shelford. Which is why I was running on the Icknield Way. It's a long-distance path and makes for easy running. He was walking towards me, and…" Ellie's face went slack, her eyes blank. Then she blinked. "Fuck. He had a girl with him. She wasn't very old, maybe two or three. Was that Abi?"

"If it was him, then it's possible, yes," Izzy said. "Did he recognise you from your previous meeting? And when was this?"

"About two years after Jess died. It would be the

summer of 2018. He was carrying the girl in one of those papoose things on his back, and she had a wide-brimmed hat almost obscuring her face. If I'd recognised Abi, I could have stopped all this back then."

"You had no reason to recognise her, Ellie. She was a baby the last time you saw her. Children change a lot at that age. You're doing well to remember. Did he know who you were?"

"I don't know. He smiled and nodded before walking on." Ellie shivered. "What if he'd killed me?"

"He wouldn't. He goes after married women in their homes." Izzy hoped she wasn't giving too much away. The timescale made her wonder if the man had been checking out his next victim. She knew there was a linked case in Cambridgeshire, but needed an OS map. Had he been following another footpath, just as he did before killing Rosie Wilson? The name of the woman came to her. Gillian Blanchard had lived in an old farmhouse near where they now sat. Izzy noted to check the date, knowing this could be significant. It was years ago, but any evidence gathered then would still be available. She knew this information had to be passed over to Cambridgeshire Police, and they might send someone out to interview Ellie. "Did you think it was strange when you saw him again?"

"I don't think I did. Now … well, knowing what I do…"

It seemed almost too much of a coincidence that the man should pass as Ellie was running the other way. Was that what he did? Connect the dots between one killing and another? Had he remembered Ellie and followed her?

It wouldn't be hard. Her name would have been in the papers, in the church records of those who had attended her sister's funeral. These days, on the internet, it was possible to track people down easily enough. But if he had, either he was extraordinarily bold, or not very clever. Izzy wished she knew which.

She made another note and circled it.

Check out the other victims. Linked in some way?

"It's weird," said Ellie. "I told you I got no bad vibe from the guy. Neither then, nor the first time. He seemed ... well, all right. Harmless. Unexceptional. Except if what you say is true, he wasn't."

"Isn't," Izzy said. "He's still out there."

"I have something that might help," said Ellie. "I'd almost forgotten about it, but talking has brought it to mind. After the man had gone, I went on with my run and found a wallet lying on the side of the path. Brown leather. I picked it up and looked inside. There were two fivers, a receipt from a shop in Cambridge for a map, and an old paper driving licence. It's one of those that don't show your picture. So I turned around and tried to catch up with him."

"What made you think it belonged to him?" Izzy asked.

"I don't know for sure. A hunch. I'd not passed many people, so I must have assumed he'd dropped it. And if not, then he'd say so, and I could hand it in to the police. But it did give his name, Chris Symonds, and an address in London. I even thought about posting it back to him."

Izzy leaned forward. "Did you catch up with him?"

"No, I didn't. I should have, because I'm fast, but he was nowhere on that path. And yes, I still have the wallet. I had a plane to catch to Chicago, so I threw it in a drawer. I intended to call the police when I returned, which was ten days later."

"Did you call them?" Izzie asked.

"Of course." As if to do anything else was unthinkable. "I rang, and they said as some time had passed, and nobody had reported it missing, maybe I should just post it on to him. Which I also did."

"Except you say you still have it."

Ellie nodded. "It came back a week later with 'unknown at this address' stamped across it. I didn't know what else to do, so I stuffed it back in the drawer. I expect it's still there. I'll drive over and get it before we eat. There may be fingerprints on it."

"If there were, they'll almost certainly have degraded by now, but yes, if you could get it for me, that would be useful."

After she had gone, Izzy glanced through her notes, adding one or two things. Ellie's story made a difference. So did the wallet, especially if it showed a name and address. Did the man Abi called Daddy have multiple aliases? Was Chris Symonds one, or was it his real name? Izzy suspected not, if the address was fake. Ellie meeting him again made Izzy wonder if she might have been a target as well as, or instead of, her sister. But without catching their killer, they would never know.

She was about to get up when the door opened, and Thomas Bowman entered. He did a double take to see her behind his desk. He seemed to have something on his mind.

"Can I see that sketch again?"

Izzy drew it from inside the journal and passed it to him. He studied it for some time, then said, "I told you I'd never seen this man before, but I think I was wrong. I saw him about six weeks before we lost Jess." He continued to stare at the sketch.

"Where?" Izzy asked. "Brighton or here? Did Ellie tell you she saw him twice?"

He glanced up. "Yes, she did, which made me re-evaluate my earlier response. It was here. Or rather not here, but at some function we were attending. It was the wedding of one of Jess and Ellie's friends, and we were all there."

"He was a guest?" An excitement ran through Izzy.

"No, not a guest. I met him outside when I went for some fresh air and a cigar. I still used to smoke then. He was working on the hotel grounds, clearing dead wood where a tree had blown down. He asked me for a light, and we got to talking." Thomas Bowman shook his head. "He was so ... ordinary. But I'm sure it was the same man. He told me he tidied up after people. The way he said it seemed strange to me at the time. If it hadn't, I don't think I'd have recalled him now." He shrugged. "But I don't suppose it will help you catch him, will it?

THIRTY-NINE

Izzy found Jack playing with Abi. She stood until he noticed her, then indicated they needed to talk. She walked outside so the others couldn't hear their conversation.

"What is it?" asked Jack. "Has Harrington rung you?" He pulled his phone out to check he had missed no calls.

"Ellie claims she has our suspect's wallet from several years ago. She's gone to fetch it. His old-style paper driving licence is in it, with his address and, presumably, his signature and date of birth, together with a name: Chris Symonds."

Jack stared at Izzy, taking in what she had said.

"How did she get hold of it?"

Izzy told Jack about how Ellie claimed to have seen the man twice. Once, just before her sister was killed, the second time, a couple of years later, before one of the other murders took place.

"There'll be some follow-up needed," Izzy said. "Dates checking and so on, but it gives us a lead, doesn't it?"

"More than a lead, I'd say. We need to call HQ and tell them about it, and the name. It's the best chance we've had so far."

"As soon as Ellie returns."

When Izzy returned to the house, Flis indicated she wanted to talk, and led the way to the now-empty study.

"I contacted the local Social Services in Cambridge, and put the wheels in motion to evaluate the Bowmans. They'll perform the background checks, but I don't think there'll be any problem. I need to sort out a Residence or Special Guardianship Order for Abi. That won't happen today, but Abi can stay here with them if she wants to. It is, after all, a family visit. I'll find a hotel nearby and stay until things are sorted. Will you be going back to Preston?"

"I need to see what Jack and Sarah think, but I expect so. Is there anything we can do in the meantime?"

"You can give me a lift when I find a hotel, but nothing else. Thanks, Izzy. It's been a pleasure working with you."

"Yeah, well, let's hope it's the only time." Izzy smiled. "But don't be a stranger. Is there likely to be any issue getting this order Abi needs?"

Flis tilted her head. "I don't think so. I've been watching them together, and it's clear the grandparents, as is the sister, are besotted with her."

"And Abi?"

"She's had it tough. Abandoned at that farmhouse. Coming around in hospital. Taken to Brighton to meet a father she doesn't know. Falsely accused of hitting her half-brother. And now this. She's in shock. It would surprise me if she weren't."

"She'll be better off here, won't she?" Izzy said. "Her father doesn't want her back. If she doesn't come here, where will she end up? God knows what happens to her then. Abi's what, eight and a bit years old? She should stay here, where she's wanted."

"I raised the idea with Ellie Bowman, and she told me that, between her mother and father, they know pretty much everyone in the Council. A process has to be followed, which will take a week at least, even if it's fast-tracked. And Social Services hate to rush anything, with justification. But if the Bowmans have contacts, and pull a few strings, it can be done in that time. I'll get flak from my bosses when I tell them I intend to stay until it happens."

"Forget the flak. You did say you cleared this with Sarah?"

"Of course, and she agrees. Abi should stay. She's young enough to adapt. She'll start to feel more comfortable in a month, and by then, we'll have the Residence Order. In six months, she'll think of this as her home."

"What do we do now?" Izzy asked.

"We eat the pleasant lunch Betty and Ellie have prepared. Then I suppose you go home and get on with the case. I expect you've got more information to add to what they've no doubt found out while you've been away."

"More than a little," Izzy said with a smile.

She went to find Sarah, who was with Ellie Bowman and Abi. When Sarah saw Izzy, she rose and came across to her, and they went into the hallway.

"How's Abi doing?"

"Good. Well, okay. Sometimes, you can feel when something is right, and this is. I think Abi knows it, too. I've watched her change, even in our short time here."

"We've got a good lead on the man she calls daddy," Izzy said. "Ellie should be back soon with his wallet."

"His what?"

So Izzy had to retell how Ellie came to have it.

"Wow," said Sarah. "This could break the case wide open."

"Depends. Ellie's had the wallet for five years, and she thinks the address might be false, but it's our best information on him yet. With his driving licence, we might be able to dig out other information about him." Izzy felt a buzz of excitement, of progress. "We'll be heading back to Preston after lunch. I want to go as soon as Ellie returns, but I appreciate we can't just dump Abi here."

"No, you can't."

"Are you staying?" Izzy asked.

"Abi's no longer my responsibility. Her care has been passed over to Social Services now. I'll cadge a lift back with you and Jack, if you can hang fire until around five or six. Abi needs the extra time with her family before we rush off."

Izzy didn't want to wait, but knew Sarah made sense, and a few extra hours wouldn't make a big difference. When she heard the crunch of tyres on gravel, she turned to see Ellie's BMW pull up. She got out and came across with the wallet in a plastic zip-lock bag.

Izzy snapped on a pair of latex gloves and took it from her with two fingers, pleased that Ellie had taken basic precautions. It was unlikely they would get anything from the wallet, other than confirmation that any DNA on it matched that found at Caxton Farm, and the other locations, but protocol had to be followed.

Before lunch, Jack stood beside Izzy as she carefully opened the plastic bag and emptied the wallet's contents onto Tom Bowman's desk. She photographed everything, turning the notes and driving licence over to record both sides, then sent the images in a secure message to both Priya and Carys, who she asked to inform Harrington. She also said she'd call him when they were on the way back.

In a lull after lunch, Flis came to Izzy.

"Have you thought of something else?" Izzy asked her.

"Not me, but I wanted to ask if you'd like to come for a drink with me when we're back in Preston."

"Like in be friends?"

Flis laughed. "I'm not sure I'd go that far."

"Why?" Izzy was suspicious when people wanted to get close to her. She knew it was her fault, but that didn't help. Maybe this was an opportunity to start changing things.

"Because I think you might need a friend," said Flis.

"Jack's my friend. So is Priya."

"Who's Priya?"

"A friend," Izzy said, though she suspected that might be an exaggeration. "You'd like her."

Flis took a breath. "Look, this might be a bad idea. It's just..." She took another breath, which she held before letting it out slowly. "Okay, I'll just say it. I work with kids. Some are damaged. Some are fucked up. Izzy, you're not like them, but I see some signs in you. Signs of an abused past. If you think it might help, I hear all kinds of things all the time. I'd happily listen to anything you want to tell me."

Izzy stared at Flis. It was almost tempting, but she knew she could never open up. What she had experienced wasn't abuse. She held the knowledge she possessed locked inside, because letting the world's light reach it would mean facing her torment. Her responsibility for the death of her sister. This week had shown her a shadow of what her life had been. A controlling husband. An alienated child. Izzy's father had been a selfish man, who always had to be the centre of attention. Despite that, she had loved him. Unsure if she still loved him.

"I'll think about it," she said.

Flis looked into her eyes. "Yeah, sure. Do that." She turned away.

Izzy wondered why she'd dismissed her. She suspected it was a mistake.

They were later leaving than Izzy had hoped, but they couldn't be seen to rush off, and their plans had changed with the information in the wallet. As Izzy drove away,

Abi stood with a hand in those of her grandfather and grandmother. She seemed happier in their house than she had ever been in Brighton. Izzy glimpsed Flis, standing in the hallway behind them. She would remain nearby, until Abi's status was finalised.

FORTY

Just over two hours later, Izzy stared at heavy traffic after dropping Sarah at Euston station. She had called Harrington earlier and spoken at length. She thought it made sense that she and Jack follow up on what they had discovered from the contents of the wallet, and he had agreed. Izzy had already emailed a photograph of both sides of the driving licence, so the details could be checked. The original was with Sarah and would be delivered to MIT in the morning.

After an awkward conversation earlier with Sarah, the plan had changed. They would all three drive into London, but Sarah would catch a train back to Preston, while Izzy and Jack searched for Chris Symonds' trail. She had fed the address from the driving licence into her phone. The house hadn't come up, which wasn't unexpected, so she went by the street name.

Izzy accelerated hard to slot into a non-existent gap. When the car behind used its horn, she lowered her window and offered a middle finger. Traffic was dense, stop-start, and Izzy bullied the car from lane to lane. She cut across traffic until they reached narrow side streets, where the GPS led them towards their destination. When she pulled up on a double-yellow, she swore.

A tall office block stood on one side of the street, an empty plot on the other, where construction machinery skulked behind a high metal fence.

"Is this the right place?" asked Jack.

"It's the right street. According to the driving licence, the house address is number thirteen. I see why GPS didn't give me a better location now. I wonder how long since the house was torn down? It would explain why Ellie had her letter bounced back." She started the engine and drove, until she found somewhere to park, then walked back.

There was a pub on the corner of the street, but it might not be for much longer, based on the development around it. They went inside and ordered soft drinks. The bar was crowded with office workers drinking away the day's stress, but the barmaid looked like she might have been standing behind the bar since the blitz.

"How long has that office block been up?" Izzy asked when a brief lull in trade came. The conversation volume was intense and made it hard to hear what the barmaid said, but she managed to catch it despite the strong accent.

"Couple'a years, love. Good for trade, but it's not like the old days. I knew every bastard came in here at one time. Hard cases, too, most of 'em. Not like this bunch of softies." She looked Izzy up and down, then did the same with Jack. "You Old Bill?"

"Guilty as charged."

"Lucky you weren't here when this was a proper boozer. We used to get the Krays pop in now and again. Nice enough fellas, both of 'em, but they only liked coppers if they were bent."

"I'll take your word for it. I'm looking for someone who used to live around here, when there were real houses."

"Oh yes?"

Izzy saw the barmaid close down. She had been amused until now, but they had stepped over a line, and they'd get nothing more from her. Even so, Izzy pulled out the sketch and showed it to her.

"He's probably changed from what he used to look like, but did you ever see him in here?"

The barmaid didn't even look before shaking her head. "Never seen 'im, petal."

"What about the name Chris Symonds?"

"Never heard of him either. Now you can both fuck off. No offence intended."

"None taken."

Outside, Jack said, "This is a waste of time, Iz. We should follow Sarah and get back home. This whole area's changed completely since Symonds lived here. They have all the resources at MIT to track him down. We're just wasting our time here."

"The barmaid knew him, I'm sure."

"She didn't even look at the sketch."

"Made out she didn't, but she did."

"It won't do us any good though, will it?"

"If she knew him, then someone else might. Let's go on a pub crawl."

"Around here? Are you looking for trouble?"

Izzy grinned. "Always, Jack. Come on, I'll keep you safe, promise."

Jack shook his head. "An hour, Iz, then we leave for home."

She laughed. "I'm not sure expenses will cover another hour's parking, anyway."

In the fourth pub, with ten minutes of Jack's deadline remaining, they struck a narrow seam of gold. An old man nursed a glass of stout at a corner table. His table, it seemed. Izzy imagined him sitting there for eighteen hours a day. Coming in for his breakfast, the makings of which were chalked up on a blackboard ready for the following morning, and not leaving until chucking out time.

When Izzy sat across from him, he looked at her with eyes clouded by cataracts, but not enough that he couldn't take them both in.

"You're a fancy tart, ain't ya?" he said. He nudged his almost empty glass, and Jack took it for a refill.

"How much you charge, darlin'? I might even get it up for you."

"More than you can afford, old man."

His laugh was thick with phlegm before turning into a cough.

"So more'n a tenner. That's rich for around here. Or used to be. So, what do you want if it ain't my body?"

Izzy showed him the sketch.

"What's the pillock done now?"

"You know him?"

"Lived around here all my life, darlin'. I know everybody. At least, I used to. They're a bunch of wankers these days in their suits and fancy shoes and ties. Used to be only girls wore ponytails. World's gone to fuck."

"What's his name?" Izzy needed confirmation the man wasn't stringing them along.

"You're a tough one, ain't ya? What's in it for me?"

"A pony," Izzy said, and the man laughed.

"You got to be kiddin', love. I'll give you his name for a bullseye."

Izzy would have to find a cash machine, or maybe Jack had £50 she could borrow. She knew they'd never get it reimbursed.

"I already know his name," she said. "Chris Symonds. All I want is confirmation, and that isn't worth fifty quid."

"You're right, darlin'. If you were right, that is. His name ain't Symonds."

Izzy sighed, sure she was being taken for a ride. "Okay. A bullseye."

He held his hand out. "Money first, darlin'."

Jack returned with a pint, and Izzy asked him if he had any cash. He did.

She handed two twenties and a ten across, which disappeared faster than a magician's trick.

"Frank Davis," he said.

Izzy stared at him, using the expression she used on suspects when she knew they were lying. Which, she had to admit, was pretty much all the time.

"Are you sure?"

"Of course I'm fuckin' sure, darlin'. And I can tell you, whatever he's done, you don't want to find him. He's a tosser of the first degree. Not the sharpest tool in the box, and nasty with it. Not that you'd know if you met him. Used to come in now and again. Seems all right at first, but he's dead behind the eyes, like a shark. Been that way since his missus fucked off with their kids. Can't say I blame her."

Izzy tried to get her head around the new name. It fitted with what Abi had said the suspect's name was. Frank. Now, they had the second part. Frank Davis. She glanced at Jack, but he showed nothing.

"Is that when he moved away, after he broke up with his wife?"

The man looked up at a ceiling yellow from the days smoking was allowed.

"Fifteen years since, I reckon. And good riddance to both of 'em. I hear she went abroad when she got herself a new man. She was a foxy tart, so it didn't take long. America or Australia, somewhere like that. Starts with an A, anyway."

Izzy was disappointed. A conversation with the man's wife might have proved enlightening. It might be possible to track her down and get local police to question her, but it was a long shot.

"Do you know where he went after he left the area?"

A shake of the head. "And never want to. What's the dipshit done, anyway?"

"I'm afraid I can't say."

"Wouldn't surprise me if he killed someone. A woman most like. He took against all women after Tracy left him. Loved those girls of his to bits. Fair broke him, it did."

"What's your name?" Izzy asked.

"Why?"

"You know this man. We might need to talk to you again."

"What man?"

Izzy showed him the sketch again. "This man. Frank Davis."

"Never seen 'im. Never heard the name before, either. Understand me, darlin'?"

"Fifty quid for that?" said Jack, when they were outside.

"He thinks he's clever, but we know where he drinks. We can send the local cops around to question him if we need to. And we know our suspect's name now."

"Do you believe he gave us the real name?"

"I can't see why he'd lie about it."

"Because he's a cantankerous old git, fifty pounds richer for leading us along."

Izzy smiled. "There is that. I'd better ring Harrington and tell him the driving licence is a false lead."

"It's not entirely, Iz," said Jack. "The address must have been right, or close enough anyway. That old guy knew him from the sketch, meaning he must have lived around here. So the name might have been fake, but the address wasn't. Priya can search the local records and find out who lived there."

"Did he use a false name on purpose?" Izzy asked.

"More than likely. And did he deliberately drop that wallet so Ellie would find it?"

"That's some long shot, isn't it?"

"Planning," said Jack. "If he showed himself to her deliberately, it's not much of a jump to think he left something behind, to lead the police away from who he is."

"Maybe. But we have a first name for his wife, even if we don't know where she lives. Marriage records are online these days, and go back to the 1800s. Another job for Priya. And we have confirmation that Davis, if that is his name, might be capable of killing. Except the old guy made out he wasn't that bright, and whoever planned these killings is clever. Has to be, or we'd be closer to him by now."

"How many men are there called Frank Davis, Iz? It's got to be a pretty common name."

"We've got some of the best tech anywhere. Put Carys and Priya on the case, and they'll sift through them all. Abi told us they lived in west London, so that'll narrow it down. Come on, let's get back to the car and go home." Izzy felt a new enthusiasm rise in her. "This is progress, Jack. This is real fucking progress."

FORTY-ONE

Izzy dropped Jack off at his house at a little after three in the morning, then drove to Goosnargh, undressed and fell into bed. She set no alarm but woke to the sound of birdsong. When she looked at her phone, she discovered it was ten minutes before seven. Not even four hours of sleep, but she didn't want or need more. She got up, showered, and ate a slice of toast. Then, she called Priya and asked her to meet at Hutton HQ.

The incident room was quiet. Only three people were working, but one was Ailsa, and Izzy went directly to her and pulled up a chair.

"Where is everybody?"

"Harrington's allocated some tasks to the other force areas where previous murders were committed. He's giving them a couple of days to check their files, and then we'll pull together anything they send back. He thinks it might give us more chance of discovering who our offender is. Harrington's cock-a-hoop over the info you sent back from the ex-DI in Brighton. He's convinced himself we're looking for a killer for hire. Shame about that fake driving licence, but finding it was good work." Ailsa offered a sympathetic smile. "But it sounds like you have our man's real name, which is even better work."

"Finding the licence was a fluke rather than good work," Izzy said. "Did it tell us anything?"

"Fake name, fake licence and address. Nothing but office blocks there now, but even back in the day, the address shown didn't exist, but there were terraced houses all along the street. I fed the name you got into the system."

Izzy leaned forward. "And?"

"There are thousands of men called Frank Davis in the country. I filtered by age, give or take five years each way, but that still leaves several hundred. Harrington's trying to decide whether it's worth asking local forces to interview each of them. He thinks if he asks, he'll get pushback, and he's probably right."

"Is that it, then? We sit and wait for something new to come in?" Izzy's positive mood was ebbing away.

"Look, you did well. You got us a name. How sure are you it's right?"

"Seventy per cent."

"Better than we had before," said Ailsa. "If this guy is a serial, and everyone thinks he is, Caxton Farm is just one of several crime locations. The NCA sent Harrington contacts for all the other forces where similar deaths have occurred, and he's been in touch. If anything comes back, it will be a long slog. We have to work hard and look for connections. As I said, Harrington likes that he might be a killer for hire. If he's right, it means the investigation will change direction. Everything becomes slower now other forces are in the loop. More admin. More discussion. He might change his mind, but I doubt it. He seems pretty set on the idea."

"What happens to Jack and me in this new setup?"

"I guess you return to normal duties." Ailsa offered an apologetic smile. "Sorry, Izzy, but you knew it would happen eventually. Now let me show you what we discovered after Sarah dropped the wallet into us. I've been here since five, working the data. The name on the driving licence might be fake, but there's still information we didn't have before."

Ailsa reached into a drawer and removed the wallet encased in a clear evidence wrapper. The contents had been removed and lay inside the large envelope, including something Izzy had missed. She put her finger on it, a pale red business card visible through the plastic.

"What's this?"

"Interesting, isn't it?" Ailsa said. "It was tucked inside one of the seams. Whether deliberately, or by accident, we don't know. He might have been trying to hide it, or accidentally pushed it in. The wallet's old and some of the stitching has come loose."

Izzy leaned closer to read what was on the card. Ambrose Cartwright Recycling.

"I've already searched Companies House," Ailsa said, "and Ambrose Cartwright Recycling is registered and has an HMRC record. According to that, it's still trading."

Ailsa switched browsers and went into the Companies House database. "Turnover is forty-mill, net profit twelve point five." Ailsa switched again. "Tyler Cartwright, the MD, paid himself over a million in dividends last tax year, so they're doing well. I rang the number on the other side of the card – you can see it if you turn the envelope over – and got a message. Their reception is open between eight and six. Which is about now."

"Where are they based?"

"Business is registered in London, but then most are. His home address is in Folkestone. Hang on." Ailsa opened a map and zoomed in before selecting street view. "A nice detached five-bed outside town on the edge of the Downs. Triple garage. All set back from a B road." She switched views. "Good-sized garden surrounded by open countryside."

"We can get a local cop to pay a visit if we need to talk to him, yes?" Izzy asked.

"It'll save you swanning off again, so yes. I'll enter it as an action and assign it to someone to liaise with the local force there. I tried to cross-reference the name Frank Davis to Cartwright, but came up with nothing. I'd have expected some trace if he ever worked for the company."

"The old guy in the pub said Davis used that name fifteen years ago when he moved out of the area. I'll enter what we found out so everyone can read it."

Ailsa nodded as her fingers flew. Izzy watched her for a while before growing bored. She stood and stretched. The exhaustion she had expected before was creeping up on her. When the door opened and Priya entered, followed by Ed Harrington, Izzy went towards her friend first but was intercepted.

"I need to speak with you," said Harrington. "In the office. Now."

"Be there in a sec, boss."

"Now."

"That's what I meant." Izzy handed Priya her notebook. "I've circled what's important. See what you can find out. Talk to Ailsa; she's onto something."

Izzy turned and followed Harrington into the small, enclosed office.

"I hope your jolly to Brighton was worth the time and expense. Social Services informed me we have to cover the costs incurred by Felicity Roberts. What the fuck were the four of you thinking when you left the girl with the Bowmans?"

"Flis cleared it with Social Services in Cambridge, and she's staying down there – at her own expense – while she tries to expedite a Residence Order."

"Except her father doesn't live in Cambridge, and he's made a complaint. Claims you took Abigail against his direct wishes. He wants her back."

"He didn't when we were there, boss. Flis says she saw him about to slap her when he thought Abi'd hit her son. She's not normal, and we understand why they might not want her in their life, but slapping a kid is out of bounds. McFadden has a new trophy wife, and two cute kids. Abi's a reminder of the past. Of what he lost. Of the blood he witnessed. He's making trouble, is all."

"He's still her father, and if he says he wants her back,

then that's what will happen. But not until we get clarification on this information you sent back. If he did pay to have his wife killed, we can hardly return the girl to him."

"Ailsa told me you think it's a possibility."

"She might have exaggerated," said Harrington. "A possibility, but does that mean the other cases were the same? That's a lot of reviewing what each force knows, and interviewing people again. One of the husbands has died. Others have moved, one to Germany, I think. I'll contact Felicity Roberts later today to appraise her of the situation."

"Are you going to tell her to put the adoption process on hold?"

"How long is it going to take?" asked Harrington.

"Flis said ten days to a fortnight."

"Then she can continue with that. We should know more before then."

"Can I call Flis, boss? She might want to forewarn the Bowmans. I'm sure they'll happily take Abi if she has to return to Brighton. They have no intention of kidnapping the girl. All they want is what's best for their granddaughter."

"Okay, but make sure she knows if McFadden is cleared and still wants the girl back, she'll have to go. I've asked Brighton to pull him in for an interview, and to go in hard. They've told me that will happen today. Now tell me what else you found out."

Izzy told him about Frank Davis, the breakup of his marriage to Tracy, and his link to Ambrose Cartwright

Recycling. They stood facing each other, and as her story continued, she saw Harrington start to relax.

"Ailsa and Priya are working the data right now. You might like to pass this info on to the other forces involved."

"Ailsa can do that directly. She has all the contact details. And there's one other thing. Clem McDermott wants Priya back working with him in Preston. He says he needs her."

"Then he's lying."

"He's the senior technical officer. If he says he needs her, I have to accommodate his request. But maybe not until tomorrow, or the day after. Ailsa says Priya's good. One of the best she's ever seen." He glanced past Izzy to where the other team members gathered as Ailsa wrote new information on the whiteboard. "It looks like you might have done okay after all. But so that you know, I'd have preferred you checked with me first before swanning off to Cambridgeshire."

"Yes, boss, I'll try harder."

"Good. I want you and Jack to be our feet on the ground in case something comes up. You're still part of MIT, until we catch this bastard, but remember, I want a team player. Are you okay with that?"

Izzy knew she had no choice. Refuse, and she'd be off the case altogether.

"Yes, we're okay with that."

Harrington smiled. "I thought Jack was your sergeant. Does he get no say?"

"Of course he does, boss, but I know he wants to follow this as much as I do."

"If the trail goes cold, you'll have to return to your old duties, but that's a way off for now. We'll issue you new actions every day, of which there are still plenty to complete. You and Jack divide them between yourselves and report back what you discover. The first one is revisiting Caxton Farm. If all the cases are the same, then Mike Wilson has to be interviewed again. You and Jack have dealt with him, so I want you to push him, and see how he acts. If what we've heard is correct, his wife had been shagging half the men in the district. In my eyes, that's motive enough to have her killed. I've issued an authority for someone to look into his bank account, but while we're doing that, I want you and Jack to have a word with him. Have a nosey around, and see if anything seems out of place."

Harrington turned away, Izzy dismissed.

She went to find Jack.

FORTY-TWO

Jack drove, but Izzy couldn't help pointing out sharp bends and hidden dips.

"Do you want me to pull over so you can drive?" he asked after she warned him of a farm track that emerged onto the road immediately after a sharp right-hand bend.

"No, you're doing fine. I'm just trying to help."

"You're a skilful driver, Iz," said Jack, "but a fucking awful passenger. Look at the scenery."

She smiled sweetly at him and did as asked. The Forest of Bowland had never lost its charm for her, even after eight years of seeing it every day since she moved to the area to attend university. After a couple of minutes, when she bit back an urge to ask him to drive faster, she reached out and turned the radio on.

Jack changed the station from Radio 1 to 2.

"Jeez, you're an old man already."

"I guess I am. Is this trip a chance to escape the team,

or do we expect to learn something? I'm not altogether easy with the idea Mike had Rosie killed."

"Neither am I, but it's an action that needs ticking off."

"Won't he be embarrassed at how we found him last time?"

"We saved his life, Jack, so he might even be glad to see us."

Izzy thought Mike would be in the fields, but was in the yard when they arrived. He looked rough. His hair was uncombed, and three days of stubble showed on his cheeks. His pale green shirt had a stain that looked like blood, but was hopefully ketchup.

"Have you got some news?" He stood in the doorway, blocking it.

"Nothing new, I'm afraid, Mr Wilson," said Jack. "But we'd like to review some of your answers you gave when questioned at the station."

"I already told them others I didn't kill Rosie, so you can fuck off."

"We have to check everything, however insignificant," said Jack. "I know it might seem we keep asking the same questions repeatedly, but that's the nature of police work. Shall we stay out here, or do you prefer us to come inside?"

Mike Wilson turned away, and they followed him.

"I'll make some tea, shall I?" said Mike.

His voice was dead, as if all enthusiasm had been ground out of him. Izzy understood why he might feel that way. He had lost almost everything, and each time he stood in the hallway, he would remember how he had found his wife.

Izzy was about to follow him into the kitchen, but the phone rang as she took the first step.

"Can one of you get that?" said Mike. "Arseholes from the press, and nosy buggers ringing all the time. Gets on my tits."

Izzy lifted the phone and said, "Mr Wilson is unavailable."

"Izzy, it's Ailsa. I tried your mobile but couldn't get you, then remembered you've got no signal down there. Is Mike Wilson around?"

"Making us tea."

"I want you to make some excuse and go outside."

"Jack, too?"

"That would be best."

"What's wrong?"

"I'll tell you once you're outside."

"You might need to wait a couple of minutes. We need to drive up the hill."

Izzy looked at Jack, still standing in the hallway, watching her with a raised eyebrow. She put a finger to her lips and gestured for him to follow her.

Outside, she told him Ailsa wanted them to call back. When Izzy got a bar on her phone, she rang HQ.

"You still there?"

"Still here. Is Jack with you?"

"He is. I'll put you on speaker."

"Hi, Jack," said Ailsa. "It might be a good idea for you both to drive away from the farm."

"We'd better tell Mike Wilson we're going first," said Jack.

"Under no circumstances return to the house. Ryan just got back from Wilson's bank, and there's something fishy going on. He drew out ten grand three weeks before his wife was killed. Harrington is even more convinced it's proof we're dealing with a killer for hire. We checked gunshot licences, and Wilson has two, stored at the farm. Harrington's on the phone now, trying to assemble an armed team to come out there and arrest him, but it looks like it might take at least two hours."

Izzy stared at Jack, seeing the same shock on his face as she felt.

"We can't just leave," Izzy said, knowing that's exactly what they were meant to do.

"Drive away. Call me back when you're a mile away."

"What the fuck?"

"Do as I say, Iz. Do it now. Call me when you're away from there. I've got some info on that business card from the wallet, but it'll take some time to explain."

Izzy glanced back towards the distant house. The front door remained open, but of Mike Wilson, there was no sign. She pictured him sitting in the kitchen, the kettle boiling and ignored, his eyes vacant.

A chill ran through her as she broke the connection.

Jack drove fast up the track, the tyres protesting as he turned onto the narrow road at the top. He went half a mile, then pulled into some woods. Neither of them had spoken.

"I'll call Ailsa back," Izzy said.

It took a minute before they were connected.

"How far away are you?" asked Ailsa.

"A mile," Izzy lied. "Any word on the flying squad? Is that what you wanted to tell us?"

"Nothing yet. Harrington's getting pushback from upstairs. We contacted Ambrose Cartwright, and asked if they employed a Frank Davis. The admin woman looked up his details, then put me straight through to the owner, Tyler Cartwright. He said they used to employ him, but not anymore. Davis worked for his father, who died five years ago. Tyler took over the business three years before that and brought it into the twenty-first century. I'd explain everything, but it would take too long, so I'll cut to the chase. Frank Davis was sacked for being too hands-on with the female staff. He blew hot and cold, and nobody knew which he'd be on any day. Ignored the women working there most of the time. Treated them like dirt. Then he'd touch them up. Tits, bums, thighs, faces. He was rough with it, too, so he was sacked. Didn't take it well. Anyway, we have his National Insurance number, except it comes up as not being allocated anymore, which is weird." Ailsa's voice went distant, as if she had turned her head away. "In a minute. I'm telling Izzy and Jack now." She came back. "Sorry, Harrington wants me. Look, I'll give you the headlines. Harrington is even more convinced Frank Davis kills to order, and Mike Wilson employed him to get rid of his wife. He believes that's what the ten grand was for. This is why Harrington's still trying to get hold of armed officers, but it's more likely they won't come out. Okay, I need to—"

"Wait," Izzy said, stopping Ailsa before she cut her off. "Look, I can't talk now."

"A quick question. I'm sure you must have raised it. Did Ambrose Cartwright have an address for Davis, and details of next of kin? If we can trace his ex-wife it might help."

"I asked, and they said there's no next of kin recorded. Same with his address. He gave one, but it's another dead-end. All right, that's all I know right now. I have to go. Good luck, both of you. I'll be in touch if I have anything more."

Izzy stared at her phone without saying anything. She tossed it onto the dash, turned to Jack, and cocked her head in a silent question.

"I'm still processing all that, Iz."

"Do you think Harrington is right?"

"Could be, but it's a stretch. It was a stretch when Marty Goss told us his suspicions. I'm not saying Davis isn't a contract killer, but based on what that old guy in London told us, he doesn't seem bright enough for that kind of work. Murder, yes, because he's punishing married women for what his wife did to him. But killing to order is another level altogether."

"Suppose Harrington is right?" Jack held a hand up. "I know, I agree with you he's probably not, but stranger things have happened in police work. But suppose he is. That could mean the other deaths were also contracted out to Davis. Again, I'm not saying I believe it, but I agree with you what little we know about him indicates he's the wrong kind of guy. He hates women; that's why he kills. He's trying to kill his ex-wife, over and over again. And he'll keep doing it if we don't stop him, because it will never be her. This will mean a shit-load of new actions, which will not be easy to carry out this long after the events."

Izzy was impressed at Jack's reasoning. What he said made sense.

"I don't believe Mike paid to have his wife killed, even if she had all those affairs. He might have lost his rag now and again. We witnessed that on the CCTV, but he'd never harm her. What was it Ethan Walton said? Mike always took her back." Izzy stared into Jack's eyes, seeing his intelligence and sympathy. "I want to go back and ask him why he took that money out," she said. "Record the reason and drive away. Leave the poor bugger to nurse his pain. Maybe he'll have healed enough to try again in a year or two. And when we catch Davis, we'll get our hands on little Grace."

"You heard what Ailsa said. We're not going back there. I'm pulling rank on this one, Iz. We follow orders and return to base."

"I'm concerned for him, Jack. Mike's already tried to kill himself. What if he tries again, but with something more guaranteed to do the job, like a shotgun? Ailsa said he's got two of them registered."

"You like to push things, don't you?" said Jack.

"I don't enjoy sitting on my backside, while other people take their time getting their shit together."

"I'm still going to say no, and you kn–" Jack broke off as his phone rang. He answered and listened. The call was short, and when it was done, he turned to Izzy with a frown. "That was Harrington. The higher-ups have squashed his plan for an assault on the farmhouse, thank God. But he wants us to go back there and confiscate any weapons Mike has on the premises, and then bring him in for formal questioning."

"Does he want us to arrest him?"

"Not yet, but we don't give him the option of saying no."

Jack drove back the way they had come at a more leisurely pace. Izzy wondered if it meant he didn't want to get there.

FORTY-THREE

The door remained open from when they had left. Izzy entered the hallway first. She glanced at Jack, and he pointed to the camera strapped against his chest. She nodded and turned hers on.

"Mr Wilson?" Izzy called out, not expecting any answer, but he replied from the kitchen.

"Have you come back for tea? I made a big pot, but it might have gone cold by now."

When Izzy went through, Mike Wilson sat at the kitchen table, his face slack. She wondered if he was still drugged after his attempt on his life. She knew he'd talked with psychiatrists, and had heard they considered he was unlikely to try again.

"Tea would be good," she said, pulling a chair out.

Jack sat several feet away from her, a deliberate move to distance them in case Mike struck out. He would only get one of them before the other reacted. Except Izzy didn't think he would. All she saw was a broken man.

Sunlight fell through the tall windows, but didn't reach the table. The pale wooden cabinets shone from where the post-incident team had recently cleaned.

She glanced at Jack, but he showed no sign of raising anything. It was the way they worked. He knew Izzy was better at asking questions, and him at organisation and people skills. They would be a good team, if they continued as one.

"What do you know about Frank Davis, Mike?" Izzy softened her voice and tried for sympathy. She knew how it was meant to sound, and believed she'd done a reasonable job.

"Who?"

"Did you pay Frank Davis ten thousand pounds?"

His eyes rose from the table. "Do what?"

"You withdrew ten thousand in cash from your bank in Preston. They had to clear it with headquarters because it was cash. What was it for?"

"Farm stuff."

"What farm stuff?"

Mike seemed to think for a moment before saying, "Second-hand bailer."

"Why cash?"

"That's what the guy wanted."

"Isn't it unusual to pay in cash?"

"We're out in the sticks here," he said. "It's not like the city. Not even a city as small as Preston. Folks trust cash out here."

"I take it you have a receipt?"

"Would have, if we'd done the deal, but all this shit happened, didn't it."

"What is the name of this farmer, Mike? Do you have his phone number so we can check it out?"

For a moment, Izzy tensed as he put his hands on the table, the muscles standing out in his arms. Then he slowly stood.

"I don't know why the fuck you need to check it out, but I expect I got it written down somewhere. Help yourself to tea. There're biscuits somewhere in one of the cupboards."

"Who cleans for you?" Izzy asked before Mike could leave the room.

"Cleans?"

"The kitchen's immaculate. Did you do that?"

"Your fucking people did that. But Katie comes twice a week. Always has. She was due to come yesterday, but I forgot to tell her there was no need, so I let her clean anyway." He leaned closer. "Paid her in fuckin' cash. Is that all right?"

"I'm not the taxman," Izzy said. "Katie who?"

"Katie Richards. Comes out from Chipping on Tuesdays and Fridays. Mind, not so much for her to do anymore."

"Thank you. If you could find that information for me."

He shuffled from the room.

"What was that about the cleaner?" asked Jack.

"I was curious. It's another thing to check on, though. She might have sensed something, or even seen something, in the weeks before Rosie was killed. Cleaners are invisible and pick up all the crap lying around – the emotional crap as well as the physical."

"Not mine," said Jack.

Izzy laughed. "You've got a cleaner? I thought all gay men loved to clean."

Jack shook his head. "You are a vessel full of lazy assumptions, Detective Constable Isabella Wilde." He smiled to let her know he was teasing. "Do you want a biscuit?"

"What kind?"

"Do I look psychic?"

"Sometimes, yes. See if he's got any chocolate chip cookies."

Jack rose, walked to the cupboards, and started opening them randomly. He was still doing so when Mike Wilson returned, but instead of bringing a name and phone number, he carried a loaded shotgun.

He pointed the gun at Izzy, then frowned. She wondered if he didn't want to shoot a woman. But he seemed to have no qualms about men as he turned towards Jack.

Izzy picked up the still half-full teapot and threw it at Mike. It sprayed warm tea as it turned through the air, then hit him square on the chest.

Not good enough, Izzy thought, so she got to her feet and picked up her kitchen chair. It was stupid, she knew, because it offered no protection, and Mike was too far away to hit with it.

Jack moved fast. He grabbed the recently boiled kettle. This time, it hit Mike square in the face.

The shotgun went off. Jack yelled and fell sideways.

Izzy didn't look at him. Didn't want to see what had been done to him. She ran at Mike Wilson, but when he raised the gun again, she threw herself sideways moments before it fired.

She got to her feet, ears ringing, ready to lunge because the shotgun was empty now. She saw Jack clutching his leg. There was blood, and Mike Wilson had disappeared.

"Get the fucker," said Jack through gritted teeth. "He ran through there."

Izzy picked up a kitchen knife, and went in search of Mike. Her mind was cold, her body loose, ready to do battle.

She found him in the big living room, as he snapped the shotgun closed again, showing her he'd reloaded. So be it. They were close, and she believed she could reach him before he aimed the barrel her way.

But he didn't want to kill her anymore. If he ever had.

Before Izzy could react, before she could do anything to stop him, Mike Wilson spun the gun around, put the barrel in his mouth and pulled both triggers.

Izzy's only thought was, *Well, we can't save him from that.*

She was cold and emotionless when she turned away, knowing she had to leave the body where it was. Knowing questions were going to be asked. At least they'd had the foresight to start their cameras recording.

She went back to the kitchen and used the knife to slice along Jack's trousers, to reveal a scatter of holes in his shin. There was only a little blood.

"That's got to sting," she said.

Jack shook his head. "Not as much as the bollocking we're going to get."

"Then they should have sent the fucking response team. Fuck 'em, Jack." She held an arm out to help him to his feet. "Come on, let's clean you up. There'll be something around here to bind it until we get you to Preston."

"Not yet," said Jack. "Call it in first. I can wait until someone gets here."

Izzy went to the phone in the hall. She lifted the handset and dialled. The ringtone echoed through her head as she waited for someone to pick up.

FORTY-FOUR

It was almost two hours before Izzy and Jack stood outside DCI Ed Harrington's office, neither of them speaking. All their talking had been done in the car on the way back to Hutton. Izzy had washed Jack's wound, used antiseptic from the bathroom cabinet, then bound it with gauze. Jack had been shot, but that wasn't what was on their minds. There had been a death following police contact, so Izzy and Jack waited in the car until someone from the Independent Office for Police Conduct arrived at Caxton Farm. They would interview them both and not release the scene for CSI until they had finished. What had happened should have been pretty obvious, Izzy thought.

When they were released, Izzy drove Jack's car and helped him hobble into Preston Royal Hospital. After a brief examination in A&E, he was told his injuries were minor. More blood than damage, and after the odd shotgun pellet had been picked out and his leg bandaged, they had reluctantly climbed to the second floor at Hutton HQ. They had been called in front of Harrington, and both knew a bollocking of the first order was about to come their way.

Nobody in the open-plan office looked at them as they crossed the room. It was an unwritten rule. Everyone knew why they were there, but pretended they didn't exist.

"I'll take the blame," Izzy said. "I was with him when he did it. You were injured."

Jack shook his head. "We were both there, Iz. I could have stopped you."

"No, you couldn't. He had a gun. He'd already fired at you and injured your leg." She glanced down. "How is it, by the way?"

"Stings a bit. I was fortunate it was only birdshot. Which means he meant to scare us, not kill us.

"It wasn't birdshot he used on himself." An image of Mike Wilson with the shotgun barrel in his mouth, the wet explosion of sound as he pulled both triggers, came to her with a sudden shock. Yes, she thought, I am in shock. But I'm still alive.

A change in the office's atmosphere caused Izzy to turn to see what the difference was.

"Look out," she whispered.

Assistant Chief Constable Andrews strode through the room, looking neither left nor right. His tie was snugged tight at his throat, his uniform immaculate, and his black shoes perfectly shined. He glanced at Izzy and

Jack but said nothing before entering the office without knocking and closing the door behind him.

The blinds to the open-plan area had been pulled down, which wasn't a good sign.

It was five minutes before the door opened, and Harrington ushered them inside. He went to stand behind his desk. ACC Andrews stood to one side, arms behind his back.

"I won't ask you to sit," said Harrington, "because this won't take long. The matter is now with the IOPC, so you'll speak only with them about what happened at Caxton Farm. However, as you both had your cameras operating while you were there, the sequence of events should be obvious. You will return to normal duties for now, but I don't need to remind you to discuss what happened only with me, officers from the IOPC, or your staff associate if you decide to ask for one. Understood?"

"Yes, boss," said Jack.

Harrington waited.

"Izzy?"

"Yes, boss."

"Good. IOPC has requested you both be checked for gunshot residue. Then, you will be interviewed separately. Once that's finished, we need your clothes – I'm sure we've got something in stores that will fit you both – then you can go home. Do you understand all that?"

Both of them nodded.

"I need you to say it."

"Yes, boss," said Jack.

"Yes," Izzy said.

Harry briefly glanced at the ACC, who gave nothing away.

"I expect nothing to come from the IOPC investigation, but we have to go through the process. They've finished with the scene and released it to CSI. Based on her scene analysis, Babs has already reported back to me to confirm that what you say happened is accurate. Blood patterns and gunshot residue all show it was suicide, as do your body cams. But we need to know what led him to do it. IOPC will want to speak to you about that, to ensure you applied no undue pressure on the man."

"He's lost his wife and kid," Izzy said, knowing as she spoke she should keep her mouth shut.

"Yes, he has. This will all come out in your interviews. I take some responsibility because I asked you to return to the farmhouse. Did you put any undue pressure on Mike Wilson?"

"We asked him about the cash he took out of the bank," said Jack, speaking before Izzy had the chance. She knew he had done it intentionally, allowing her to calm herself. "And as you know, we are partly responsible for this new theory about a killer for hire."

"Explain." It was the first time ACC Andrews had spoken.

"It started with a wallet, and a visit to an ex-DI from the Brighton police," Jack said. "Ellie Bowman gave us a wallet she found, which we discovered belonged to Frank Davis, our chief suspect. At the time, neither of us knew it, but a business card inside told us where he once worked. The Human Resources department there confirmed the name, and that he had been dismissed eight years ago for inappropriate behaviour against female staff. Before that, we spoke with ex-DI Marty Goss, who worked the first case we can link our suspect with. Mr Goss has always been convinced the victim's husband paid to have her killed."

ACC Andrews looked at Harrington. "This is all documented, Ed?"

"Yes, sir. Izzy and Jack entered their notes into the system when they returned."

The ACC looked at Jack. "How is your wound, Sergeant?"

"Graze more than a wound, sir. I'll be fine."

"You have your interviews with IOPC once you leave here," said Harrington. "When they're concluded, I suggest you both go home. Take a couple of days to recover."

"I'd rather keep going, boss," Izzy said.

"Doing what?"

Before Izzy could reply, ACC Andrews said, "I don't think I'm needed here anymore, am I, Ed?"

Harrington rose to his feet. "Thank you for coming, sir. I'm sure both Izzy and Jack appreciate it."

Once the ACC had gone, Harrington sat and stared at them across his desk.

"I know everything went wrong, but did you get any feel for whether Mike Wilson might have hired someone to kill his wife?"

Izzy glanced at Jack. As her DS, she would expect him to answer the question.

"Izzy did most of the talking, boss, and after I was shot, she took command of the situation."

Harrington looked at her. "DC Wilde?"

She tried to gather her thoughts. Tried to decide whether to answer truthfully, or diplomatically. As always, she chose the former. Not necessarily the right choice, but she could make no other.

"We were not there long, boss, but in the short time we were, I'd have to say he didn't. Sorry."

"Why are you sorry?"

"I know you think it might be why this guy is killing."

"I'm head of MIT-1, Izzy. I thought the idea was worth pursuing, but would not be in my position if I didn't follow the evidence and trust my officers. So I'd rather have the truth from you than any pandering. Okay?"

"Yes, boss. I don't think Mike Wilson paid to have his wife killed. I've not known him long, but I regarded him as sound. Troubled, yes, suicidal, clearly, but those things are not surprising. Do we have any feedback from the other cases regarding the theory?"

"Nothing yet, and I'm starting to have my doubts. I contacted someone I know in the Brighton force and asked him about this Matt Goss. He told me Goss is the only one who believes his theory. Said the man was obsessed with the idea. It must be confirmed or ruled out, but we'll keep it on the table until that happens. So how does our man choose his victims?"

"You're asking me, boss?"

"I am. You've been involved in this case longer than

anyone else, and in contact with Mike Wilson all that time. So yes, I'm asking you."

"Based on what we heard in London, I believe we're dealing not with a killer for hire, but with a sad, conflicted man who harbours a deep fear of, and hatred for, women. Married women with kids, specifically."

"And how does he choose his victims? At random?"

"I think it almost is. He follows footpaths until he finds a suitable target. I suspect he may do this frequently, several times a year, but only occasionally finds the right subject."

"So you *are* saying it's random. Jesus, Izzy, this is all pretty far-fetched."

"I know, sir, but we have some idea where this Frank Davis currently lives. Abi told us their house is close to the A40 going into London. I think it's worth getting some feet on the ground and showing his picture around. Someone there might know him. Might know where he lives."

"It's not a bad idea," said Harrington, "but it's a job for the Met, not us. Have you raised this idea with anyone else?"

"Not yet, sir."

"Then don't. I'll pass it on. It will come better from me. Now, both of you go and get interviewed, then take some time off until you're cleared."

"Why did you throw me to the wolves there, Jack?" Izzy asked as they walked through the office, where everyone's eyes once again deliberately avoided their progress.

"It wasn't deliberate. Harrington was right; you're more involved than anyone, and I trust your judgement. Now we follow orders, get interviewed, and put our feet up for a few days."

"Fuck orders," Izzy spat out. "We're on the trail of something here. You want to know what I think?"

"Do I have to?"

Izzy grinned. "Go on, I know you do."

"Why do I feel even if I *do not* want to, you're going to tell me anyway?"

"Ah, you love me really." Izzy's mood changed in an instant. "I told the truth back there. Mike didn't pay anyone to kill his wife. Harrington asked me if I thought it was random, and I do. Don't ask me why because I'm not even sure myself."

"I agree with you, but we're off the case. Not our job anymore, Iz."

"I can't just turn my mind off. Have you read the reports on the previous deaths, the ones the NCA think are linked to this Frank Davis?"

"Of course I have. So what?"

"You haven't, have you?"

They reached the top of the stairs. They had to descend to an interview room, report, and spend an hour explaining themselves. Izzy hoped she could manage it without striking out. She knew Jack would leave before her, but didn't want him to. She wanted to convince him.

"I read them, Iz. Scanned them, anyway."

"I read them all. Look, we need to go. Will you wait for me outside? I want to talk to you."

"Why should I?"

"Because I think he hadn't finished with Rosie. He was interrupted when Mike returned. I suspect Frank Davis is out there somewhere right now, looking for someone else to kill."

Jack stared at Izzy. "Have you told anyone else about this?"

"No one but you."

"Why not?"

"I'll tell you when we get coffee."

"You'll be at least a half hour longer than me. And there I thought I might get time to do something in my evenings off, like go fishing."

"Then go buy yourself a fishing rod, and some bait or flies. Whatever you sad bastards do."

FORTY-FIVE

Jack was waiting for Izzy when she left the building.

"The coffee places will be shut by now," he said as they approached his car. "How about we grab something to eat and drink? There's that place near the river. It's a cocktail bar, but it does food, and if we're lucky at this time of day, we'll get a table looking over the river."

"I don't want to get bladdered," Izzy said.

"I do. You can always take Priya up on her offer to stay over."

"You make it sound so tempting."

"What do you want to talk about, Iz?"

"I told you. Him. Frank Davis."

"Let's wait until we get there. Find a nice, quiet corner. We don't want to scare the locals."

"In a cocktail bar?"

"Have you ever been?"

"Not that one, no. You?"

"A few times."

Izzy laughed. "Are you taking me to a gay bar, Jack?"

"It's not a gay bar. Well, not exclusively. But it is a cocktail bar, so yeah, maybe. But the food is good, and they serve beer."

They found a parking spot several streets away, and walked towards the river. Inside, Jack was greeted by the barman, who knew him, so they managed to get a table next to the window. The view out was of the stone-arched railway bridge, and the wide Ribble. Izzy glanced at the menu, already knowing what she wanted. Then she picked up a second one that listed drinks and cocktails. When the waiter arrived, she ordered a burger and a beer. She was tempted to try something more exotic, but the night was still young. Except they were in Preston, and both knew they couldn't be seen legless in the city.

As Jack studied his menu, her eyes scanned his face. She rarely studied him this way, and she recognised, not for the first time, how handsome he was. She wondered why he was still single, but suspected it was his choice, like hers. She only hoped it wasn't because he had his own demons tucked away somewhere, but she doubted it. Jack was always the eye of the storm. The calming influence in any situation, and Izzy was glad they were teamed together.

Jack ordered pulled pork, fries, and a Mai Tai. His fingers brushed the waiter's as he returned the menu, and Izzy smiled.

"Really?" she said.

"Really what?"

She nodded towards the retreating waiter. "You and him?"

Jack laughed. "A man can't help but dream, can he?" Jack's face changed. "Now, tell me what you're planning before the food comes. I don't want to spoil our meal with work."

"What are we going to talk about if not work?"

"Our hopes and aspirations," said Jack.

"Jeez, Jack, is this us bonding?"

"Oh God, I hope not. I'm just trying not to think about what you plan on talking me into."

"You know we can't sit on our arses, don't you?"

"I told you, I'm going to stand on a riverbank and wave my rod about."

Izzy laughed so hard that several people turned to look at them. She reached across and took Jack's hand.

It was time to tell him, while it felt as if they were close.

"I have no intention of sitting on my arse. I have a lot of leave I can take, so I intend to revisit the Bowmans. Specifically Ellie. If she and Jessica were close, it's possible she'd know if her sister had affairs. And if she did, whether Frank Davis wanted to punish her for her infidelity."

Jack stared at her. He shook his head and withdrew his hand from hers.

"You're kidding, aren't you?"

"No. I've got more leave due than I can shake a stick at. I'll request four or five days in the morning. The DCI did tell us to take some time off."

"In my case, because I've got a bad leg."

"Aw, diddums," Izzy said, making Jack laugh.

"Have you not learned your lesson yet, Iz?"

"What lesson? I hit it off with Ellie. I want to be her friend. Friends meet up, don't they? See, even you and me are sitting in this nice cocktail bar talking like grown-ups."

Jack snorted another laugh. "Except there's only one grown-up here, Iz."

"Don't worry, you'll get the hang of it one day. I promise not to do anything I shouldn't. Me and Ellie will be a couple of girls chatting over a pint in a nice Cambridgeshire pub. Log fire. Brasses on the walls. All that stuff."

"You're crazy."

"Maybe." Izzy leaned to one side as the waiter returned with their food and drinks. Once he had gone, she said, "I take it that means you're not coming with me? You don't have to. I'm aware of the risk I'll be taking."

She took a long pull of her beer. As she did, she realised she wanted to get drunk tonight after all. Which meant either a hotel, or risk sleeping in Priya's spare room. Or, she thought, a taxi. It was only a few miles to Goosnargh.

"I've got leave due as well," said Jack. "Harry Gray might be happy if neither of us are around until we get cleared. Which we will be, of course."

"Of course. So you'll come?"

Jack sighed. "God knows why, but yes, I'll come.

Besides, I like the Bowmans, and it will be good to see Abi again. Have you spoken with Flis?"

"Before we left the station. She was having dinner with Ellie Bowman, and told me Charlie McFadden had seen sense and withdrawn his demand for the return of Abi. Whether his being interviewed about his wife's death factored into it, I don't know. Flis believes he was only trying it on. He didn't want her back, but didn't want Ellie's parents to have her either. Flis says it means she can probably get the adoption process moving."

Izzy drained her beer and held the glass up for another.

"I thought you were only having the one," said Jack.

"Sometimes girls lie. I'll get a taxi. Are you sure you want to come to Cambridge with me?"

"Want might be putting it a bit strong, but I can't let you run off alone. I need to keep you out of trouble."

"Tomorrow?"

"If we can persuade someone to grant us leave," said Jack.

"I don't intend to stop now we have a lead. If we have to wait another couple of days, then that's what we'll do."

"That lead will have been passed on to the other police areas by now. Maybe it will let them start their investigations up again." Jack met Izzy's gaze. "If your claim is true, you do realise the implications?"

"That Frankie boy might have killed even more than we've linked him to so far. It always seemed odd that the time intervals were irregular. That's not the way serial killers work. But maybe I'm wrong."

"There's always a first time."

Izzy laughed. "Can you sound a bit more enthusiastic, Jack? We're police. We're meant to send bad people to jail."

Jack ate his food. Izzy ate hers. They drank too much, and when they left the bar, Izzy slid her arm through Jack's as they walked to the taxi rank.

FORTY-SIX

It was the end of the next day before Jack and Izzy's requests for five days' leave was approved. Both were due more, but five days would be sufficient. Harry Gray was happy to sign off on it, perhaps relieved they would be out of the way for a while. Izzy picked Jack up the following morning at his small semi-detached house on the edge of Broughton. It was 07:00, and he invited her inside. He'd made breakfast for them, knowing she wouldn't have eaten.

An hour later, Izzy drove fast, her hands at ten to two on the wheel, the speedometer hovering ten mph above the limit on the motorway as they went south. On secondary roads, and in towns and villages, she observed the limit. They took the M6 south, the traffic stop-go as they approached Birmingham. Izzy pulled off to follow the A5, then cut across country. It was slower, but the scenery more than made up for the loss of time.

Izzy had called Ellie Bowman the evening before, to

check she would be at home, pleased when she answered and said, "Hi, Izzy," with enthusiasm.

"How did you know it was me?"

Ellie laughed. "I put your number into my contacts, of course. Same as you did me, I expect."

She told Izzy she would be in all weekend, and when asked if Abi was with her grandparents, she said, "No, she's here with me for the day. I thought I'd give them a break."

"How is she?"

"Confused, which is natural, but she's a sweetie and should settle soon. I think she'll be pleased to see you. She called you Aunt Izzy yesterday."

Izzy wasn't sure how she felt about being called that.

"How's the adoption going?"

"Good. We have permission to keep Abi with us while it's being finalised. It means Flis left for home earlier yesterday. She cursed the work she knew would be piled on her desk when she returned."

"See you tomorrow." Izzy had cut the call. She wondered if Abi called Jack uncle. He might be more pleased than she was.

Now, she drove slowly along the high street of Great Shelford, before following roads through estates, and pulling up in front of a pleasant detached house. Open fields were visible behind, and a sign for a footpath pointed along the side of the house.

"She must be doing well for herself," said Jack.

"I asked her what she did when we were last here. She works for one of the big consultancy firms. I expect she's pulling down six figures a year at least. And I don't suppose her parents are short of a bob or two. Not that any of that makes up for losing your sister and daughter to a maniac."

"No, it doesn't."

Izzy was about to get out of the car when the front door opened. Ellie Bowman stood there, tall, willowy, casually but well dressed. Abi stood at her side with her hand in hers, and when she moved forward, Ellie let her go.

Abi ran to the car and put her hands on the window.

"Are you coming to visit, Aunt Izzy?" A grin split her face.

Izzy nodded, opened the door and got out. Abi hugged her arms around Izzy's waist as soon as she could.

"Aunt Ellie made chocolate cake. It looks lush, but I can't try it until you arrive." She took Izzy's hand and tugged her to follow. Behind them, Jack exited the car with a smile on his face.

At the door, Ellie hugged Izzy before doing the same with Jack. She whispered into Izzy's ear, "If you need to talk to me, maybe Jack can take her out back."

Which half an hour later, is what happened. Izzy stood beside Ellie, watching Jack push Abi on a sturdy wooden swing.

"You have a swing?" Izzy asked.

Ellie laughed. "It was here when I bought the house. I meant to take it down, but fortunately, I didn't get around to it." She looked at Izzy. "I always thought we might get Abi back one day. I don't think Mum and Dad did, but I couldn't let myself believe she was dead as well as my sister."

Izzy hugged her again, seeing the glitter of tears in Ellie's eyes.

"Have you come with news?" Ellie asked as they moved apart.

"Maybe. But I've also come with questions."

"Then we'd best sit down."

Ellie turned and walked through to a smaller room at the front of the house. Sunlight fell bright through a window that looked across the street, beyond which lay a park with a lake surrounded by trees. An open fire was laid with paper and kindling. The furniture was simple but expensive. Ellie sat in an armchair. Izzy took the sofa.

"You were here less than a week ago, so what's new?"

Izzy took a breath. She didn't want to mention Mike Wilson, but she did want to raise a question related to why he killed himself.

"The primary team has a new line of enquiry, so some of the work is being spread across the other force areas. It's still being worked on in Preston, but not as hard. It's always the way. It turns into a slog if we don't make a breakthrough at the start. Jack and I are following up on one or two loose ends. Can I ask you about your sister?"

"Jess?"

Izzy nodded, wondering why Ellie had to even ask.

"What do you want to know?"

"I'm sure these questions will have been covered at the time, but it was a while ago now–"

"Eight years, five months and..." – Ellie stopped to think – "...thirteen days."

"As I said, this will have been covered, but we have more information now."

"What information?"

"I'm not at liberty to reveal that at the moment."

"Then why should I answer your questions?" Ellie wasn't being aggressive. Her voice remained level, her expression neutral. Izzy imagined her at work, speaking with heads of industry worldwide, and knew she would be excellent at her job.

"Because it may help us, and it may help you as well. If we catch this bastard, then you might achieve some closure."

"I never will. But," Ellie shrugged, "it could help Mum and Dad, so ask away. I don't promise to answer everything if I don't want to. Just so you know."

Izzy liked her even more.

"This one is awkward. Did Jessica and Charlie have a good marriage?"

Ellie gave another little shrug. "I'm hardly one to ask. I don't do relationships. I work. It's my escape."

"From what?"

"Oh, we all have something we want to escape from, don't we?" Ellie's eyes met Izzy's, asking a question she was unwilling to answer even if she knew what it was. To her, Ellie's life appeared idyllic. Except she, too, had lost a sister.

"Did Jessica ever say anything to you about their marriage?"

Ellie leaned forward, her hands draped across her knees. "We were close as girls. She was older than me by three years, and I always looked up to her. She was my big sister, and I loved her. I still love her, even though she's gone." Ellie took a deep breath, and Izzy knew this was the moment. She would either open up or close down.

She opened up.

"She changed when she was around fifteen or sixteen. Turned wild. Mum and Dad didn't see it because she was still their perfect daughter at home. But I saw it. In school. Outside school. She liked boys too much. She liked boys way too much."

"She slept around?"

"And some. She even got a nickname. Jessy no knickers."

"She was like that when she met Charlie?"

"That was at university. I visited her once or twice, but that was all. I didn't like who she had turned into." Ellie cocked her head to one side. "Sometimes, I wonder if she's why I don't do relationships. It might be, and I'm grateful to her if it is. You want to know if she slept around after they were married, right?"

Izzy nodded, and waited.

"Of course she did. Jess could no more stop shagging men than she could stop breathing." A tear ran down Ellie's cheek. "Fuck, I didn't mean it that way. Sorry."

"Don't be. I intend to catch the man who killed her, and whatever you tell me is going to help. Did Charlie know about her affairs?"

"I don't see how he couldn't. Mind you, he wasn't any better himself. Jess told me they had an open marriage. Slept around, invited other couples over and ... well, you know."

"Not personally, but I think I understand what you mean. Tell me about Charlie. Was he the jealous type?"

Ellie's eyes narrowed. "Exactly what are you asking me, Izzy? He had nothing to do with what happened to Jess. Or are you saying he might have?"

"I'm trying to dig deeper, is all. To look for gaps I can squirm through for more evidence. I don't know what's important until I find it. If this makes you uncomfortable, say so, and we can stop."

"Not uncomfortable. Sitting in front of the CEO of a multinational while he tries to look down your dress makes you uncomfortable. This, not so much. Charlie made a pass at me once."

"I take it you rebuffed him?"

"Too fucking right I did. And do you know what he said after?"

Izzy waited.

"He said it was a shame, because he'd always wondered what it would be like to fuck two sisters together. I almost punched him."

Izzy thought back to her time in the man's company. She didn't like him, but she met many people in her line of work she didn't like. He hadn't given her any weird vibes, though. But then she was the police, and she knew people acted differently around her because of it. Ellie's response added weight to Izzy's theory that Frank Davis targeted women who slept around, even if their marriages seemed perfect from the outside. She knew each of the other force areas where killings had occurred were interviewing the surviving husbands. She also knew the police mindset gravitated towards suspicion. Questions would have been asked. Marriages examined. Ellie had provided her with relevant information about her sister's marriage. It was enough, for the moment.

"How is Abi?" Izzy asked.

Ellie smiled. "Screwed up, of course, but if she stays here for a while, I'm hoping she'll get used to us. She will stay with Mum and Dad during the week, then come to me for the weekends. That's the plan, anyway. She looks just like Jess did at the same age. I expect she'll look more like her as she grows. I want to be with her to see that happen."

"I heard Charlie McFadden dropped his claim he wanted her back. That was a quick turnaround."

"We got a letter from a lawyer Dad instructed, informing us of the same thing." Ellie smiled. "Charlie likes to make trouble. That's what he did here. He didn't want Abi back. I think it will work out, her being here with us."

"That's good. Abi needs a home that wants her."

"I dread to think what her life must have been like living with a killer."

"As far as I can tell, he treated her well. She even called him daddy. And it seems he made sure she witnessed nothing he did."

"Flis said to keep an eye on her all the same. She

thinks living the way she did might have left some psychological damage. She's given me the name of a woman locally we can take Abi to. She's meant to be the best." Ellie smiled. "It's one of the advantages of living near Cambridge. The hospitals and medical staff are great." Ellie looked out through the window rather than at Izzy when she said, "Abi might be able to help you find this man, though, couldn't she?"

Izzy stared at Ellie. She had raised the idea first, but did she know what she meant? Time to see how far she was willing to go to catch her sister's killer.

"Abi spoke about where she lived with him, but she couldn't pinpoint the exact location. All we have is a vague area to look in. I had thought about driving her around to see if she recognised anywhere, but..." Izzy raised a shoulder as if dismissing the idea.

"I could raise it with her. Maybe ask if she wants to take a shopping trip. She told me she lived in London before she came here. Is that right?"

"West London."

"Where are you staying tonight? I don't want to push her too hard, but tomorrow maybe?"

"We'll find a hotel nearby. And if we go, you'll have to come with us," Izzy said.

"Of course. I'm not going to abandon Abi now. Come over first thing, and we'll see how she feels." Ellie rose. "I think she already loves Jack. He's a good man, isn't he?"

"The best kind."

Ellie smiled. "Are you and he...?"

Izzy laughed as she shook her head.

FORTY-SEVEN

Izzy knew what they were about to do pushed the boundaries, but she also knew she would do it anyway. She and Jack found a pub with rooms for the night. Over dinner, both agreed they should report what they intended to do back to MIT in Hutton. Jack wanted to tell them before they left in the morning, but Izzy persuaded him otherwise. If they didn't find Frank Davis, no one need ever know. If they did, they would be the heroes. She hoped.

Izzy had offered to drive, but Ellie said her car was more comfortable. They wafted along the motorway in the top-of-the-range BMW, then around the M25, before taking the A40 towards central London. To their right, giant aeroplanes seemed to hang motionless as they stacked to land at Heathrow. Houses lined the road, too close to the streaming traffic. They made Izzy picture her cottage in rural Lancashire and realise how fortunate she was.

Abi stared through the window on the left-hand side, Jack seated in the back beside her. She showed no expression, no particular interest. She was excited when Ellie told her they were shopping in London. And they would, eventually.

"Thanks for this," Izzy said to Ellie. She had watched her behind the wheel and was impressed. She drove as she did all things, with confidence and ease. It was not flashy or aggressive, but did the job as efficiently as possible.

"I could hardly let you take Abi off without a responsible adult, could I?"

"Thanks all the same."

"Aunt Ellie!" Abi's voice came from the back, excited.

Izzy turned in her seat. "Aunt Ellie's driving right now, sweetheart. Did you want something?"

Abi pointed to her left. "I saw a place I know. That is what you want, isn't it?"

"Turn off where you can," Izzy said to Ellie, before turning back to Abi. "What did you see?"

"A shop daddy used to take me to when we needed food. There's a café around the corner we sometimes go to on Sunday for breakfast. They do good breakfasts."

Izzy opened her phone and loaded a map. She searched for the shop and found it half a mile behind them. It was one of those express places that popped up everywhere there was space. She zoomed in, then set a pin and watched as the app tried to work out how to get back to it.

"There's a sharp turn coming up soon."

Ellie had already eased through the traffic to the inside lane and nodded. Her eyes scanned ahead, watching for the turn.

"In a quarter mile, go left, then left again. I'll talk you in."

Izzy glanced back to see Jack's reaction, but he whispered to Abi, asking her how close the shop was to where they lived. She was trying her hardest, but clearly didn't know the answer. Hopefully, as they got closer, memories might come to her.

"Is this going to be dangerous?" Ellie asked quietly, while they drove along a street lined with rundown houses. All the small front gardens had been concreted over for parking.

"No," Izzy said, unsure if she spoke the truth.

"I'm not asking for me," said Ellie.

"Understood. We'll stay in the car as long as we can. If Abi shows us where Frank Davis lives, I'll call it in."

Ellie drove under the 20-mph speed limit, but Abi showed no recognition as she stared through the side window. Izzy pinched her screen and found the convenience store Abi had pointed out from the A40.

"Right, then left," she said.

They pulled into an empty parking space outside the shop five minutes later. Slightly the worse for wear, it fitted perfectly into its surroundings. The roar of the nearby six-lane roadway was relentless.

Izzy got out and opened the back door. She held her hand out, and Abi looked nervously across at Jack.

"It's all right. I'm coming as well," he said.

Abi took Izzy's hand. A sign on the wall told them they could park for five minutes.

Izzy leaned into the car. "Stay here, we won't be long. If you have to leave, I've got your number, and I'll call you."

She and Jack walked into the store with Abi between them.

"Do you recognise this place?" Izzy asked.

"It looks different. There used to be newspapers over there, but they're gone. And there were magazines. Sometimes, Daddy bought me one when he bought his. I read good."

Izzy walked with her to the counter, where a man of Asian descent stood as if the weight of the world lay on his shoulders. She drew her warrant card out and flashed it.

"About bloody time," said the man in a broad cockney accent. "I've called for police a thousand times about the bloody shoplifters."

"I'm not here for that, but I'll file a report. Do you recognise this girl?"

The man glanced at Abi and shook his head.

"We get all kinds of kids in here. How am I supposed to tell one from another?"

"Do you keep records of your customers, for delivery perhaps?"

He laughed. "We're not fuckin' Amazon, love."

Izzy turned away, pulling Abi along after her. The shop was a waste of time.

"That man said a bad word," said Abi.

"Yes, he did. Do you recognise him?"

Abi shook her head. "Different man."

"You said you sometimes went for breakfast on Sundays after coming here. Do you remember where the café is?"

"Not exactly, but it was close."

Izzy left Abi on the pavement beside Jack and walked to Ellie's car.

"Drive around and find somewhere to park. We're going to walk around a bit and see what Abi remembers."

"Not without me, you're not. She's in my care now. Get in, and I'll come with you after we park."

Finding somewhere was easier said than done. Almost every street was resident-only parking. Finally, they found a metered space half a mile from the shop, paid for two hours and walked back.

They had covered half the distance to the shop when Abi, who now held Ellie's hand, said, "There." She pointed. "That's the café daddy brings me to. Over there."

Set on the corner was a small place, with windows on two sides and a few small tables and chairs outside. A plastic sign in one window told them they could have the best all-day breakfast in London. When they entered, a bell rang over the door, and a white man appeared from the back. He stood behind the counter and waited, his face expressionless.

Izzy took Abi's hand and led her forward. She took her warrant card from her jeans pocket and showed it to the man, who barely glanced at it.

"What you want? We do breakfast." His accent was Eastern European, his English stilted.

"Do you recognise this girl?"

The man glanced at Abi before shaking his head.

"You want food?"

"What I want is information."

The man's gaze moved beyond Izzy, taking in Jack and Ellie.

"I already tell you. I don't know girl."

"What about the name Frank Davis?"

"What about it?"

"Do you recognise it?"

Another shake of the head.

"Let's have something to eat," said Jack. "I'm starving, and I expect everyone else is too." He stepped past Izzy. "Four breakfasts, mate, one of them a child's. Three teas," he added and looked at the others, "unless anyone wants coffee?"

"Tea's fine," said Ellie.

Izzy didn't bother to reply because she didn't care.

"And a squash for the girl."

The man went into the back without a word.

Jack pulled two small tables together, arranged the chairs, and sat so they had a view of the street.

"Is this the place you came to?" Izzy asked.

Abi nodded. "I know that man. Daddy called him a bad word, but his breakfast is good."

"I expect you must have lived close to here then. How long did it take to walk here?"

Abi shrugged. "A bit. But not too long. We came across the canal and through the park."

"What park?"

Abi shrugged again. "The park. I don't think it has a name."

A thin woman came with a tray, and put three mugs of strong tea and a glass of squash on the table, then knives and forks. She left without speaking, but Abi's eyes followed her.

"Do you know her as well?" Izzy asked.

Abi nodded. "Daddy used to call her Fay. He said she was a bit of all right."

"Is she married to the man?"

"I think so. They argue a lot, and Daddy told me that's what married people do. Are you married?"

Izzy saw Ellie smile.

"I'm not, and neither is Jack."

"Aunt Ellie isn't married, either. I think I might want to get married when I'm big. How old do you have to be?"

Izzy was about to say sixteen, then remembered the law had changed.

"Eighteen."

"I have to wait almost ten years?"

Izzy smiled. "Afraid so, darling."

When the food came, Izzy demolished hers, only growing aware of her hunger when she put the first piece of bacon in her mouth.

"Once we're finished here, we can walk around for a bit," she said. "You can tell us if you recognise anywhere."

"All right." Abi drained her juice and pushed her half-eaten small breakfast away. "I need a wee."

"I'll take her," said Ellie.

"It's all right, I know where it is." Abi rose and walked to a narrow corridor. Over the entrance, there was a small sign that read: TOILETS. Izzy expected it should probably be in the singular.

"Is this going to get us anywhere, Iz?" asked Jack.

"I don't know, but tell me if you've got a better idea."

"I haven't, but we should call this in and leave it up to the Met. If this Frank Davis lives nearby, it ought to be simple enough to track him down from Council records. If Abi knows this couple, they almost certainly know Frank Davis. I take it you smelled the dope when you came in?"

"Of course."

"The local cops can use it to pressure them."

Izzy gave the suggestion some thought. Jack was right; this wasn't their jurisdiction. Handing it over to someone better able to track the man down made sense. Except she hated the idea of handing the task over to someone else. She knew she lacked trust in the ability of others. Suddenly, she was no longer hungry and put her knife and fork down. The excitement she had felt drained away.

"Do you want to wait here while I fetch the car?" asked Ellie.

"I'd still like to walk around for a bit. You go to the car if you want. I'll send you a pin when we finish so you can pick us up." She glanced at her phone for the time. Eleven-fifteen. "Jack's right. One more look around, and then we call in what we know." She glanced at him. "I'll leave that up to you, as the more rational of us."

"Less excitable is all," said Jack with a grin. He looked around. "One of you ought to go check on Abi. She's been in the toilet a long time."

"Maybe she needed more than a wee," Izzy said as she rose.

She went along the corridor, where the smell of marijuana was more pungent, and found the single small room, which held a stained toilet and tiny hand basin. Crumpled paper towels littered the floor. There was no sign of Abi.

Izzy saw an open doorway at the end of the corridor. When she went through it, the woman who had brought their food was outside smoking a cigarette, which she immediately dropped and stepped on.

"Did you see a young girl come out this way?" Izzy asked.

"The one was with you? Yeah, she went off with Frank."

"Frank Davis?"

"I only know him as Frank. He's a good tipper but a bit free with his hands, if you know what I mean. One minute he won't meet your eyes, the next, he's got his hand on your arse."

"Where did they go?"

"Out on the street. After that, I got no idea."

"Where's the other guy gone? Is he your husband?"

The woman laughed. "We fuck, but he ain't my husband, love."

Izzy went back inside. The coincidence of Frank Davis turning up was too thin to accept. She suspected they'd been lied to. She was also unsure how to break the news to Jack. But she was more worried about Ellie's reaction.

FORTY-EIGHT

"She did what?" Jack surged to his feet. "Abi went off with him?"

"Or he took her," Izzy said. "I didn't see it, so I'm only reporting what I heard."

Ellie sat rigid, her face stiff with shock and suppressed anger.

"What the hell have you done?" said Jack.

Izzy wanted to say, "What have *we* done?" But even she knew this was all her fault. Jack had agreed to come with her because they were a team. Ellie had humoured them both. And now they had lost the daughter of her dead sister. Not just lost. They had brought her back to where Frank Davis lived, and he had taken her. How had he known they were here? Had he come deliberately to fetch her? It didn't seem possible, but it must have happened that way.

Izzy believed Frank Davis must have known Abi was

at the café. He would be afraid of what Abi might reveal about him, what she could tell people. Davis had abducted the Wilson's daughter and abandoned Abi because, as she grew older, she would ask too many questions.

Izzy didn't think Frank Davis could allow Abi to live.

"We have to call this in," said Jack. "Get more feet on the ground."

"Davis was here only minutes ago. Call it in, but God knows where he'll go if we wait for reinforcements. They can't have gone far. Let's split up and look for them. Ellie, you go back to the car. Jack and I will do the searching."

"Fuck that. I'm looking for her, too."

Izzy knew there was no time to argue, so she nodded and dropped two £20 notes on the table before leading them to the street. Then she turned back into the café and went to the counter.

"Hey, are you still there?" she called out.

Nothing happened for a while, and then the waitress appeared.

"Where's the boss?" Izzy demanded. "Get him."

"He went out. Said he needed to go to the market."

"Was it you called Frank Davis, or him?"

"I didn't call no one."

"So it was him." Izzy pulled out her warrant card and waved it before the woman. "Do you want me to take you in for questioning?"

The woman shook her head.

"Did he call Frank Davis, or not?"

"They're friends," the woman said. "Kind of, anyway. So he might have. I don't know ... maybe."

"Do you know where Davis lives?"

Another shake of the head.

Izzy pushed past the woman into the back, where a single gas range needed a deep clean.

"Hey, you can't come in here without a warrant," the woman said.

"You know about warrants, do you?" Izzy saw her eyes skitter towards a stained cabinet. "If I think a crime is being committed, I don't need a warrant. Love."

Izzy stepped across to the cabinet and tried to open it, but it was locked.

"Where are the keys?"

"Lost 'em."

Izzy shook her head. She knelt and felt around the back of the cabinet, touched something metal and found a single key hanging from a nail. When she slid it into the lock, it turned.

"It's him who deals the stuff, "said the woman, backing away.

"Try to run, and we'll get you," Izzy said. "If you don't deal, that might look bad for you."

When Izzy looked inside, she saw bags of weed, others with tablets, and in one corner, a stack of bottles labelled up with marker pen: GLB, and GBH.

"Did Frank Davis buy this stuff from you?"

"I told you, it weren't me."

"Then your fella. Did he?"

"Might've done."

Izzy considered following through on her threat to take her in for questioning, but knew Davis had to be close. She turned and walked out to where Jack and Ellie waited.

"Davis bought his GLB off the guy, who's done a runner. He has to be close, so we split up. Ignore South because he lives on this side of the A40. Call if you see either of them." Izzy turned away and strode off in a direction she thought was North.

In the distance, she saw trees. Abi had mentioned a park they crossed on their way to the café. Izzy pulled her phone out, scowling when she saw the battery held less than fifty per cent. She checked the map, changed to satellite view, and saw a green space a quarter mile away. She started to run along the street, swerving around people, eyes scanning the road for any sign of Abi. Izzy wondered what she would do if she saw them. Could she take Frank Davis on her own? Or was it better to follow, and then call the others in? No, not the others. Only Jack, until they were sure. And then call the MIT and tell them they'd found their killer, and to contact the Met. Maybe even ask for armed officers. Except if Abi was with him, Izzy didn't want any shooting. She dismissed the thought as too cataclysmic that she might not find them.

She caught her foot on a broken paving slab and almost went flying, but found her balance in time. Closer now. She glimpsed grass at the end of the street. She sprinted across a road, car horns blaring, then ran along high railings until she found an entrance.

The park ran a hundred yards ahead, perhaps half that from side to side. Kids played football and sat on swings in a playground. Two older men used fitness equipment that used their weight for resistance, their faces red from the effort.

Izzy walked, scanning left, right, ahead, as a growing sense of panic flooded her. This was the end of her career. She'd be lucky to find work stacking shelves in a supermarket.

Then she saw them on the far side of the park. Not running, but walking fast. Frank Davis held Abi's hand, and appeared to be dragging her along.

Izzy slowed, keeping them in sight. If Davis looked back, she knew she was safe. If Abi did, she would recognise her. If so, would she say anything? But neither turned. They reached the far side of the park and went left. Izzy held back, watching until they entered a side street, then sprinted to the corner. When she risked a glance into the street, she thought she'd lost them. Then she saw the top of Frank Davis's head from behind another set of railings. Izzy set a pin on her phone and texted her location to Jack with a message telling him she'd found them. She didn't contact Ellie. Didn't want her involved until they arrested Davis.

When the man disappeared, Izzy ran again and found herself at a gate that gave onto a canal towpath. Another quick look, and she saw the canal curve gently around, but no one was in sight. She followed, walking fast until she caught sight of them again. Abi's hand was still in Davis's, but she seemed reluctant to go with him.

Izzy wondered how much further Davis's house lay, assuming that was where they were headed. She risked getting closer, knowing she was more than fast enough to catch them, but worried what would happen to Abi if she did. She believed she could take Davis, but feared what he might do if he saw her coming. And then she had no choice.

Brick steps led up to a bridge that spanned the canal. As the couple reached it, Davis glanced back and saw Izzy. He leaned down and spoke to Abi, who also turned. She said something and then tried to pull away, but he held her fast.

As Davis dragged Abi up the steps onto the bridge, Izzy sprinted as fast as she could. Her feet barely seemed to touch the ground. It was like flying.

Then Davis lifted Abi and tossed her over the parapet of the bridge. She hit the water off the canal headfirst and disappeared. By the time Izzy reached the bridge, Davis was running along a narrow passageway, and Abi still hadn't appeared. Izzy climbed onto the parapet, took a breath and let herself fall.

The water surprised her with its warmth, but her feet touched a piece of metal, and she feared Abi might have been injured on something similar. The canal was ten feet deep, its water murky. Izzy broke the surface, took another breath and dived. She could hardly see anything, going by touch, hands reaching out to encounter an old shopping trolley, a discarded steel car wheel, more metal and bricks. She tried not to think about what else might be down there.

Then she saw a pale shape. It lay wedged between the edge of the canal and a waterlogged tree trunk. Izzy swam towards Abi, and pulled her free. On the bank, she turned her on her side, but she lay motionless.

Izzy rolled her onto her back. She opened her phone, wiped the screen on her jeans, dialled 999, set it to speaker, and put it on the ground. She started chest compressions on Abi. When her call was answered, she gave her name and number, and asked for an ambulance and the police. She continued to pump Abi's thin chest, then breathed into her mouth, knowing it might do no good if her lungs were full of water. She lifted the girl, bent her double and slapped her hard five times on the back.

Abi coughed and threw up what looked like a gallon of filthy water. Then she began to cry.

Izzy sat down hard, holding Abi against her as she tried to soothe the girl. She reached out with a free hand and called Jack to tell him what had happened, and to inform Ellie. Then she sent a new pin so they could find her. Only when that was done did the guilt blaze through her. This was all down to her. What if Abi had drowned?

But Abi started to calm down and clung to Izzy. She raised herself and whispered into her ear as the sirens reached them.

The ambulance came first, then the police. Jack and Ellie were last on the scene, arriving together.

"What the fuck, Iz?" said Jack.

"Abi's going to be all right," Izzy said. "She told me

Davis and the man at the café dragged her out. And she knows where he lives."

"No!" said Ellie. "You are not using this poor girl anymore. She's going in the ambulance with me to get checked out, and I never want to see either of you again."

FORTY-NINE

Izzy stood in an interview room at Wembley Police Station. She wore clothes someone had brought in for her before taking her soaking ones away. The price labels were still on them, and she wondered if she'd be sent a bill. The way her luck was going, almost certainly.

She tried the door, but it was locked, which was no surprise. There was a laminate-topped table set in the centre of the floor, the legs bolted down. A recorder sat on the table, three wrapped cassettes beside it. Two chairs were placed on one side of the table, two on the other. A camera sat in the corner of the room, high up on the wall. She imagined Jack sitting in a similar space, perhaps next to hers.

They were in trouble. How much she didn't know, but she suspected it would be bad. She regretted bringing Jack with her. This was none of his doing. She would tell whoever came to interview her the same: Jack is innocent. He's a good colleague who wanted to help me out, that's all. Everything was my idea.

She didn't think they'd believe her.

Izzy thought about what Abi had whispered to her, in the final moments before the world went crazy.

"I remember where I live," she had said. "Down there and turn left. Daddy's house is number seven. I don't love him anymore."

Izzy paced. She stared at the camera and stuck her tongue out, then paced some more. It was fifteen minutes before the door opened, and a detective walked in.

"Sit," he said, in a voice that brooked no argument. "Tell me, DC Wilde, exactly what the fuck were you thinking of?"

She glanced at the recorder. "Are we off the record?"

"For the moment, yes."

"Am I free to go?"

"No. I'm still waiting for you to sit."

Izzy sat.

"I'm sorry, you are?"

"DCI Sam Mallick of the Met." He remained standing. "Can you explain what you are doing on our patch without clearing it first?"

Izzy believed it was a good sign a DCI came to talk to her. If this were a formal interview, someone of his rank would never attend. Still, she wanted to defend herself. Get her objection in early.

"We didn't think we had anything to clear. The girl has been adopted–"

Mallick interrupted. "Is in the *process* of being adopted. Did you think I wouldn't check?"

"Where is she now?"

"Abigail and Ellie Bowman have done nothing wrong. The girl's been checked over at Northwick Park and discharged. They are both sitting in reception, waiting for you. God knows why. If it were me, I'd abandon you here."

Izzy was surprised, after the last thing Ellie had said to her. but tried not to show it.

"And Jack? He has nothing to do with this. He told me it was a bad idea."

"He claims otherwise." Mallick pushed fingers through his dark hair and sighed. "Look, I'm meant to be giving you a bollocking, but the way I see it, you did what you thought was right. Bringing the girl here, maybe not so much, but Ellie Bowman told us she thought it was a good idea. I doubt she did, but that's the story she's sticking to."

"It was all my idea," Izzy said.

"See, why did you have to say that? I called your skip, DI Gray. He told me you are a good officer, but can be hot-headed. I suspect he chose his words with care."

Izzy started to get the feeling things might work out.

"What's happening with Frank Davis? Did you get him?"

"Officers were sent to the house at 7 Jarrow Terrace, which you told us about, within fifteen minutes. It's a two up, two down, door straight onto the street, tiny back garden. Entry was made, but there was no one in the house. I've called in CSI to sweep the place."

"I'd like to see inside it myself," Izzy said.

"Why do you think I'd let you do that, after what you've already done?"

"Because without me, you would never have found him. Frank Davis isn't an unusual name, and London is a big place. I assume you've looked up what he's accused of?"

"Your skip told me. Multiple murders over several years. None in our patch, which somewhat goes in your favour. There was talk of having you arrested for the kidnap of Abigail McFadden, but Ellie Bowman cleared that up."

"Will what I've done mess up her adoption?"

"I don't believe so. It looks as if there will be no issue with the Bowmans adopting her. After all, they are her closest relatives, other than her father, and word is he doesn't want her." Mallick shook his head, as if he couldn't understand a father not wanting his long-lost daughter. It made Izzy like him better. "I've been informed a Residence Order is due to be issued soon, possibly even today."

"Frank Davis took her," Izzy said. "She didn't want to go, but the guy at the café helped drag her out. Oh, and he's dealing drugs from the kitchen. All the usual, including GBH and GLB. Which Davis has been using to knock Abi out while he does his work."

"I'll get someone sent around to take a look. How much is there?"

"I don't know what it's like in London, but it would be enough to put him away for a few years in Preston. I'm starting to think Frank Davis might have tried to kill Abi in the farmhouse, where he committed the most recent murder."

"But we don't know that," said Mallick. "I skimmed the case summary, and it's his MO. He knocks her out before he does anything. If he weren't a monster, I'd say that shows some trace of compassion. But he is, so I guess it doesn't."

Izzy was aware the conversation was going on too long. It had drifted away from the subject of her guilt, which told her she might not be in as much trouble as she feared.

"What's going to happen to me now?" she asked.

"Nothing. Some people think you're a bit of a hero. Not me, but others. You and DS Ward can fuck off back to Preston. I'd recommend you have no more contact with Abi or the Bowmans, but I suspect that's unlikely to happen."

"Ellie told me she never wanted to see me again."

"She must have changed her mind." He shook his head. "Why is beyond me."

"Can I at least look inside Davis's house before we go?"

"Why would I agree to that?"

"Because, as you say, I'm a bit of a hero. And I won't get in the way. I've worked enough crime scenes."

"God knows why, but I'm minded to say yes. You only. Your DS stays here, or outside, or wherever he wants. I hear this is as much your case as anyone else's, despite you being a DC. Maybe being closer to the case, you'll see something we might miss." Mallick pushed his fists into his back as if it ached. "DS Ward is waiting outside for you. I'll arrange for a car to take you to Jarrow Crescent."

Izzy stood. "Thank you, sir."

"This chat might have been more formal, DC Wilde, but your skipper told us he authorised you to come here. Should have told us about it first, of course, only polite. I think he was covering his arse more than he was yours. Anyway, it's done now."

Outside, after Izzy had hugged Jack, she wondered why DI Harry Gray would have done such a thing. Was it no more than the northern bumpkins sticking together? She doubted he was pleased with what she had done.

"Where's Ellie?" Izzy asked. "Mallick told me she was waiting for us."

"She was, but I told her to take Abi home. Ellie told me she's changed her mind about never seeing you again." Jack smiled. "And I thought she was clever. No accounting, is there? Can we please go home now?"

"Soon. But you're aware my car is still sitting outside Ellie's house? If she really has gone, we'll need to catch a train there. But before that, Mallick's allowing me to take a peek inside Davis's house. There's a car outside waiting to drive us to Jarrow Crescent."

When they went out, a score of police stood around, some dressed in bulky bulletproof vests, pistols in holsters at their waists, others with rifles. All wore hard helmets and had cameras attached to their chests, their bodies bulky with all the kit.

"Aren't you curious about where he lived?" Izzy asked Jack.

"Not particularly. We should catch the Tube to Euston and try to find a train to Cambridge. We still have a few days' leave due."

"I suspect that's been rescinded. You can go if you like, but I want to see his lair." Izzy smiled.

"Do you honestly think I dare leave you to your own devices?" said Jack.

The house was small, squeezed in between two others that were no bigger. The front door hung open, police tape across the entrance, and a constable outside with an access log.

Izzy opened the door of the police car that had brought them and got out.

"No," said Jack.

She ignored him and walked towards the ruined door.

"DCI Mallick told me I could take a look inside. I'm job, so know not to touch anything. Just a look. I'm DC Isabella Wilde."

The constable checked his log for her name, then put a tick against it together with the time. Then he studied her. One of their own. Still. Just.

"Someone was here not long since. The kettle's still warm. Dirty plates in the sink. Looks like he had lasagne for his lunch."

"There should be a baby with him. Any sign of her?"

"I heard there's a cot, and a pack of nappies and other

stuff, but if she was here, he took her. The place is a mess, but that's nothing to do with us. CSI are inside. I don't need to tell you not to get in their way. With luck, he'll have left something behind that might tell us where he's gone." He looked her up and down again, not attempting to hide his interest.

Izzy assumed he was stupid, or desperate. Her new clothes were cheap, scratchy, and hid any figure she possessed.

He smiled. "I hear you did good. Are you going back to, where is it, Liverpool? Or maybe we can get a bite to eat later."

"Me and Jack are going home to Preston, yes. It's quieter than Liverpool, but we lack the famous bands."

"Who's Jack?"

"My sergeant, DS Jack Ward." She walked past him, despairing of men.

The CSIs ignored her. They would assume she was meant to be there if she was granted access. Izzy entered each room but soon experienced a sense of disappointment. It was a house with furniture, a bed, and a cot. Nappies. Clothes. The man who had lived here was gone, and she felt no sense of him.

"Has anyone found a rucksack?" Izzy asked one of the CSIs.

The woman looked up and shook her head. "Not that I heard, and as you can see, there's nowhere to hide anything."

Izzy went outside. She wanted to stay in London because Frank Davis was here, hiding in plain sight among the thronged millions. But she also knew there was no point. He'd leave the city. Go somewhere far away. Scotland, maybe. They had walking trails up there, too. Open access as well, so he could go wherever he wanted. He'd lie low, and then the pressure to kill would start to build again, and he'd look for his next victim. He might never get caught. They had been told Frank wasn't any Einstein, but he seemed to have done a pretty good job of things so far. Even if they knew his name, and what he looked like.

Izzy knew she'd never stop looking.

When she returned to Jack, she said, "Come on, let's get my car and go home."

FIFTY

Izzy had been back at work for a week, but was no longer part of MIT. She might have suffered a worse punishment that a return to normal duties, but she had saved Abi's life and almost, but not quite, captured Frank Davis. DI Harry Gray had given her the job of tracking down stolen quad bikes from farms in the area. There had been a spate of thefts over the last three weeks, and both he, Izzy and Jack suspected a new gang were targeting the Forest of Bowland. No doubt he was trying to ease her into things, but the mundanity of the task, after briefly being a member of MIT, made her want to punch someone. The theft of farm equipment was a real problem, and the value of stolen machinery could run into hundreds of thousands of pounds for just one farm. It still failed to excite her. Insurance companies paid out, but Izzy suspected some replacements would have been stolen from another area of the country. Though the word was, most were stripped down, and the parts shipped abroad where fewer questions were asked.

The work felt makeweight, but she did it to the best of her ability. Which, she believed, was more than good enough. At 8 a.m. on a Wednesday, she pulled her car into a side track and sat with the windows down, listening to birdsong in the surrounding treetops. The land ahead descended to the broad flatlands, where the Ribble meandered and glittered in the late May sunshine. Izzy tried to still her mind. Tried not to think of Gabi, her dead sister, who at times like this, seemed to sit on her shoulder and whisper a plea for retribution. Except Izzy knew there was no retribution. Sometimes, that was the trouble with the police. Justice and the law were not always in people's best interests.

She thought of Frank Davis. Did he hear voices in his head? Did they urge him to kill again? Or was it too soon after Rosie to lose himself in fresh bloodlust? Next time, would he take eleven-month-old Grace as cover? Walk another footpath until he came across his next victim. Izzy wondered how many women Frank Davis had seen that way and not approached. How many women had escaped, oblivious to how close they had come to death? How close, perhaps, she had come to death herself. She suspected if cornered, Frank Davis would lash out. He appeared to have no sympathy for his victims. The killings were all cold-blooded, almost as if he felt nothing, not even hatred. Reading the case notes on each death attributed to him, he carried no weapon to the scene. Instead, he found an object at the site and used that. The older, the better. The more unsuitable, the better. For Rosie Wilson, it was assumed this was a rusted hand sickle taken from the shed in her yard.

It felt too random for a contract killer, but that was still the angle the Murder Investigation Team followed. Charlie McFadden had been questioned under caution and released. He claimed to have an alibi, which the Brighton Force were checking. Izzy expected it would exonerate him. She didn't like the man, but wouldn't wish this on him. It irked her that Harrington was still unwilling to let go of this idea, because it meant they were not following other avenues of investigation. It was one more thought. One more fly buzzing inside her head.

Izzy knew the voices she heard were not like those in Frank's head. They were not even voices because they spoke in her own voice. Most concerned her father, of course. A bullying narcissist who had controlled her mother and tried to control Izzy, too. A man she detested and worshipped in equal parts. He was the reason she had joined the police force. At first, to escape him, only to discover she was emulating him.

Gabi's death made it hard for Izzy to trust any man. Which, perhaps, was why she trusted Jack as much as she did. He walked a different path and was, therefore, safe. She wished she was less tightly strung, but didn't know how to change.

Perhaps it was time to consider getting professional help. Flis had offered to find someone if Izzy asked. But that would mean confession, and that she could not offer. Perhaps it was finally time to try to forge a more normal relationship with someone. Except she didn't know anyone outside of work. And everyone inside felt off-limits.

Izzy knew she needed someone, and wondered if she might have met him when, thirty minutes later, she arrived at a farm where CCTV showed three men in balaclavas trying to start a tractor worth £150,000. They had fled when the farmer came out with a shotgun, and his three dogs ran at the men. They drove off in a dark SUV, which had almost certainly been stolen earlier that night.

Izzy was still talking with the farmer, sipping tea made too strong and too sweet, when a vehicle bumped down the farm track. A beat-up Skoda Yeti she didn't recognise. However, she did recognise Rob Peters when he climbed out. And he her. He offered a warm smile and then went to shake the hand of the farmer before coming back to Izzy.

"I take it you'll have seen the recent CCTV, but might the history be useful for you?" he asked.

"Possibly. Can you send a link to Priya like last time?"

"Will do."

"Did you need to come out here?" Izzy asked. "I thought everything you wanted was all in this amorphous cloud."

"It is, but I like to tread the ground and check the memory sticks in each camera. Call it customer support. Haddon likes me to be hands-on. It's good for business."

"You came all the way out from Preston?"

"I live in Longridge," he said. "I handle the clients in

The Forest of Bowland, and even over into Yorkshire, though they give me stick about my accent."

"That's Yorkshire for you."

Rob laughed. "We ought to go out for a drink sometime, Izzy. You live in Goosnargh, don't you? That makes us practically neighbours."

Izzy wondered how he knew, but suspected he had wormed the information out of Priya. She said nothing for a while as she stared at the surrounding hills of The Forest of Bowland, wondering why she didn't say yes to Rob. Her strange mood that day made her think it might be time to loosen the shackles she had wrapped too tightly around her emotions.

Before she could speak, he said, "No worries. I'm sure we'll run into each other again. Let me know if you change your mind." He offered her a card, but she didn't take it. And then he was gone, driving up the farm track in the battered Skoda, the sides scraped where it had squeezed down hedge-lined lanes.

Izzy wondered if her standards were too high, then laughed into the warm summer air. What standards? Rob Peters was a good-looking man and, from what she knew of him, a good one. And she was an idiot. She set her half-full cup of sweet tea on the bench and followed him along the lane in her equally scarred Golf. She didn't have standards because she'd always tried to ignore any feelings she might have had about men. She thought about Frank Davis, and what she knew of him. About the real man. Had he rejected love because of the pain it might bring? *Is that what I'm doing?* Izzy thought. *Am I afraid of getting close to anyone, in case I get hurt?* Mentally hurt, she knew, because she feared no man physically.

When her phone rang, she glanced at the screen to see Priya's number, grateful to be distracted from her thoughts.

"Did you tell Rob Peters where I lived?"

"You are always such a joy to hear from."

"Well, did you?"

"I might have. We were talking about his work, and he asked where you lived. Then he asked me out on a date. I told him I didn't like being second best. When I told him the real reason, he laughed and said, 'Shame'."

"I assume you called me for some reason?" Izzy asked.

"I think I might have found something."

"Is it to do with a missing Massey Ferguson tractor, by any chance?"

"What? No, of course not. It's about Frank Davis. You need to come to my place so I can show you."

"I take it this isn't official?"

"I did a little digging in my own time."

Izzy shook her head. "I don't want to get into trouble. I came too close to that last time."

"You won't. If anyone does, it'll be me. Or are you too busy chatting up strapping farm hands to come see your best friend in the entire world?"

"You are? Since when?"

"Since I'm your only friend, Iz."

Izzy cut the connection and tossed her phone onto the passenger seat. She stayed where she was for a while, watching the sunlight dance across the undergrowth as treetops swayed in the breeze. The light danced like she wanted to dance, without thought or plan. To simply be. A force of nature.

Izzy laughed, wondering why she was thinking this way. It wasn't like her. Perhaps having too much time on her hands wasn't good for her. Or had Rob Peters turned some hidden lock inside? If so, did she want to examine what had been exposed?

She started the engine and backed onto the road, then drove to Preston as fast as she could. Not because she wanted to get there, but for the sheer joy of it.

Priya welcomed her with a hug, enveloping her in her scent. Pure Chanel.

"What have you got for me?" Izzy asked.

Priya sat in a chair that had cost a month's wages, and moved a mouse to light up the three monitors that had cost even more.

Izzy pulled up an ordinary chair and sat.

"Show me."

Priya brought up a spreadsheet on the central screen. On the left was access to Companies' House, on the right a map of London, where several red pins glowed.

"I started digging into the data for 7 Jarrow Crescent. Out of curiosity, really, but then out of intrigue. I might link him to a bank account, credit card, or something. We could track him that way."

Izzy leaned closer. "And?"

"I found nothing, which is interesting enough in itself. So I did more digging. I went into the systems for the local councils and Land Registry."

"You hacked them?"

Priya laughed and pushed against Izzy with her shoulder. "No, though I could have. Most of it's freely available, particularly if you have police authorisation. The name Frank Davis is in none of them. Not the Frank Davis we're looking for, in any case."

"Then he rented, or used a different name. There'll be a record of it somewhere, won't there?"

"That's what I thought, but no, there isn't. Frank Davis doesn't appear to exist anywhere. Not our Frank Davis. There are many others elsewhere, but none where you found him. There was no driving licence record, meaning what was in his wallet was a fake. There is no record he even passed his test. No passport. No National Insurance number or Tax code. The NI number we got from Cartwright is fake. The guy is a ghost. He doesn't exist. But..."

Izzy waited.

Priya smiled. "What's it worth?"

Izzy laughed. "In your dreams. Now tell me what you know."

"The house in Jarrow Crescent is owned by a blind trust called Glover Holdings, which was registered in 2007. There's an address for it, but it's one of those places where five hundred companies share the same address. When I went in search of a bank account, I found nothing. If this company is paying for property, or renting it, they must use cash. Which, in this day and age, I would classify as a miracle."

"You can't buy a house for cash, can you?"

"I assumed the same, but you can, in a round about way. In particular, it's even easier if you buy at auction. The Money Laundering Regulation passed into law in January 2010, but it's been updated several times since. It covers most of the areas related to house purchase, but only if it's handled through solicitors. Interestingly, local councils are exempt. And there's nothing to stop someone knocking on your door with a suitcase of twenties, and asking if they can buy your house. That must be what this trust does. I went back to look at 7 Jarrow Crescent, and it was purchased in exactly that way in 2008. Before MLR came into effect."

"There must be something online about this trust," Izzy said.

"The Land Registry shows Glover Holdings as the owner." Priya smiled. "It might think it flies under the radar, but nothing can disappear these days. I did more digging and found five other addresses owned by Glover Holdings. Three in London. One in Bristol. Another in Inverness."

Izzy recalled her idle thoughts about Frank Davis escaping to Scotland. Now, it felt like more of a possibility.

"How do they pay for services and rates?"

"Cash," said Priya. "It's still possible to walk into a post office and hand over a bunch of twenties and your details. Maybe not for much longer, but at the moment, yes. Cash might no longer be king, but it still possesses a heartbeat."

Izzy glanced at the monitor displaying the map of London.

"I take it those red dots are the other houses in the city?"

"They are."

"And I assume you have all their details for me?"

"I do. I emailed them to you, but you haven't opened them yet."

"You need to pass this information to MIT. I assume everything you discovered was found the legitimate way?"

"I didn't look anywhere I wasn't meant to. Well, I might have, but everything I gave you is in the public record. If Frank Davis has moved out of his old house, he will likely live in one of these other places. The best bet would be the London houses."

Izzy stared at the map.

"Can you print it out for me?"

Priya stared at her. "Print it? Really?"

"So that I can show it to people."

Priya hit a key, and her printer, which she rarely used, hummed into life.

"This holding trust," Izzy said. "Can you send me everything you know about it? It must have trustees."

"It does, but they don't exist either. Did you think I wouldn't check?"

"You said you left no trail."

Priya nodded.

"Good. Whoever's behind this, you don't want them seeing your fingerprints on their data."

Izzy picked up the printout of the locations, checked her phone to see the email Priya had sent, and then left to tell Harry Gray what she had found. He would know it wasn't Izzy who had dug it out, but that didn't matter. He would pass it on to Ed Harrington, and Izzy wanted him to know where it had come from. What really mattered was they had a one in three chance of Frank Davis opening the door to a knock. Provided he was still in London. And this time, she knew they'd do things the right way, and inform the Met first.

Izzy wanted to be there when they went in.

FIFTY-ONE

Izzy was back in London. She, Jack and Priya had taken an early train. The Glasgow to London express left at 06:05 from Preston, and got them into Euston at 08:00. The day had come to life as they sped through green countryside, towns and cities. Then, the outer suburbs of London spread their tendrils, driving out the peace and beauty with noise, fumes and people. DI Harrington had sent Priya because she had been the one to mine the data, and the Met had requested her presence. In Hutton HQ, Carys had spent days trying to find out more about Frank Davis and failing. She wanted to know how Priya had succeeded. On the train, Priya told Izzy and Jack she might have a lapse of memory over how she had got all the information.

They took the tube to Westminster, then walked along the Embankment to New Scotland Yard. It took a moment for them to be issued security passes, and then a young female DC came to escort them in. She took them to the second floor, where DCI Sam Mallick waited.

He looked the three over before going to Priya and holding his hand out. "I assume we need to thank you for these locations?"

Priya took the hand. "We all contributed, sir."

"No need to call me sir. And you did good work." Mallick released Priya's hand. "We should talk."

"I look forward to it. But you do know I'm a civilian?"

"Of course. We're like all police forces. Everyone employs civilians. And I don't think there's much you can't find out based on what you've discovered so far."

"When do we knock on doors?" Izzy asked, impatient.

"Others will fill you in on the details. I'll introduce you to DS Magda Winter shortly. She's in charge of the house searches."

"Are we allowed to ride along?"

"Ask her, not me."

Priya remained with Mallick while a uniformed officer took Izzy and Jack to a basement garage where cars were parked, and several armed officers stood around. A female detective came towards them.

"I take it you're DC Wilde and DS Ward?" she asked. "My name is Magda Winter, and I've been informed you want to accompany my officers when they go into these addresses you provided." No handshake was offered.

"If we're allowed," said Jack.

"Your Super told me you were good cops, so you're allowed. But I don't need to tell you to stay out of our way. We're offering you a ride-along as a matter of courtesy. It doesn't mean you can get your hands dirty. Understood?"

Jack nodded, and after a moment, so did Izzy.

"You need to come up to speed on what we've learned due to what your colleague uncovered, so I'll give you a quick briefing later. We go in at 03:00 tomorrow, so you'll need a hotel. They're expensive around here, but this is London, so they're expensive everywhere. I assume your skipper is happy to pay for your rooms, because we won't."

"We'll sort something out," said Jack.

Winter looked at Izzy and tilted her head in a question.

"I do speak," Izzy said, "but Jack does it so much better than me. And our colleague's name is Priya Devi." She was relieved when Magda Winter gave a brief shrug as if to say 'whatever,' then smiled. "What do we need to know?"

"You already have the locations of the houses of interest, as you provided us with them. I want you to familiarise yourself with their locations, then you'll need an early night this evening. I'll let you decide which team you want to ride with, or you can split your forces across three."

Jack looked at Izzy. "What do you think?"

"Let's decide later." She looked at Winter. "I'd like to study the locations a bit more before making my mind up."

"I already said you can choose whichever you want, but don't leave it too late to tell anyone, and do not get in the way. Be back here by 02:00, and we can sort a seat out for each of you. Take it as payback for what you provided. It would have taken us much longer to find out what your colleague did, even if we knew where to look. DCI Mallick wants to talk to her over the next few days. There might be an opening for her here, if she wants it." She looked between Izzy and Jack. "Might be an opening for both of you as well. You would need to go through the same process as everyone else who applies to the Met, but I can tell you any application you make will be favourably looked upon."

Izzy didn't know if that was what she wanted or not. Or what Jack wanted. They would need to talk tonight once they found somewhere to stay. And then an early night. Except Izzy felt excitement filling her and didn't know if she could sleep. It wouldn't be the first time she'd pulled an all-nighter.

Fifteen minutes later, Jack sat across a small table from her in the corner of a room as they flicked through page after page of intelligence. Some had come through the NCA, but various boroughs and the Met police had collated the majority. There was no smoking gun, but there was a promise there might be one if they dug deeper.

At 2 pm, they met up with Priya, asked where was good to eat and walked across Westminster Bridge to an Italian restaurant. Izzy had bought a tasteless sandwich on the train, but had eaten nothing since. Her head buzzed with both possibilities and exhaustion.

"I take it you were offered a job?" Izzy asked Priya as they waited for their food.

"Kind of."

"And?"

Priya shrugged. "I'm thinking it over. The Met, London, is where things happen, but even my brief acquaintance with them makes me uncomfortable. Oh, they talk the talk, but I also saw the looks. I'm female, Asian, and gay. Great for ticking all the right HR boxes, but will they accept me?"

"Sam Mallick's Asian as well," said Jack.

"He is. He's also a little too hands-on, if you know what I mean. But I will consider it because, like I said, it's where everything happens. Preston is a backwater compared to here. He also said he would talk to the two of you."

"Policing is the same everywhere." Izzy was annoyed at what Priya had said. She liked Preston, liked where she worked, most of the time in clear country air.

The food came, and Izzy cut a slice from her pizza and chewed on it, as an excuse to allow herself time to think. In the end, she swallowed and told the truth.

"He hasn't spoken with us yet, but his DS mentioned the idea. If Mallick asks, I don't know what I'd say." She looked a question at Jack.

"Maybe. I've always liked the idea of London, but not the Met so much. Too macho. Too many homophobes, like Priya said. If it's mentioned, I'll think about it. You?"

"I'm leaning the other way. I don't want London. I enjoy living where I do."

"It's small-time, Iz," said Jack.

"Murder's not small time," she said. "And if most of what I do is small time, then perhaps that's why I like it." She looked back at Priya. "You want it, don't you?"

"I might say yes. Or rather, fill in an application. I'm unsure whether that would be for the Met or the NCA. This is the heart of things, Iz. This is where all the data lives. I like the idea of making connections and linking disparate ideas into a whole. So maybe, yes. But I'll miss you."

Izzy laughed. "No, you won't. You'll be run off your feet down here at work, and then in the pubs at night."

It was Priya's turn to laugh.

"Will you get a raise?" Izzy asked.

"London weighting, and a couple of grades advance, but it won't be enough to live somewhere like my place. But that's paid for, so I can rent it and use the income to help me here." Priya pushed her plate away, half the pasta uneaten. Izzy reached out and stole a piece.

"We'd better get back," said Jack. He reached into his jacket and pulled out his wallet. He was old-fashioned and never used his phone. "I'll get this. One of you can pay for dinner."

"I think that might be on the firm," Izzy said. "Not the booze, mind."

"Early night, remember?" said Jack.

"I really will miss you, you know," said Priya.

"Don't worry, I'll visit now and again."

"No, you won't."

"I'll try."

"No, you won't," repeated Priya. "But it's okay. I'll be in London and getting more than is good for me. You should try it, Iz. It might loosen some of those bolts holding you so tight."

Later, back at the hotel they'd booked, taking two rooms rather than three to save money, when Priya walked naked into the room after her shower, Izzy rose and said, "I'm going out to clear my head. Don't wait up."

Izzy walked to Waterloo tube station and took a train north across the Thames towards the first address she had memorised. There was a quarter-mile walk from there once she left the train. It was gone eleven, and the streets were quiet until she passed a pub on the other side. A poor excuse for a fight was going on outside, where three men were pushing at a fourth. Izzy stopped to watch, ready to intervene if necessary, but she saw it wouldn't come to anything.

"You touch my wife again, and you're fucking dead!" shouted one man, before all three turned away and re-entered the pub.

Izzy walked on. By the time she had gone twenty paces, she had forgotten about them. It was a skill she had learned on the beat in Preston when she was in uniform. She supposed there were often fights at this hour, as there were pretty much everywhere. Over her two years in uniform, she had learned to weigh events in the balance before getting involved. She would step in if she thought serious injury was likely and, most times, she could control the situation. She was tall but slim, and many men considered her an easy target. They only tried such a thing once. Over time, Izzy had gained a reputation, and could usually stop trouble just by walking towards it. Then, she applied for the role of Detective Constable and found such a skill to be less in demand. But it still lay there, ready to emerge if needed. Which is why she felt no unease at walking dark, lonely streets, or passing groups of youths lurking in the doorways of late-opening off-licences.

Magda Winter had told them to familiarise themselves with the locations of the houses. This is what Izzy was doing. She found the first of them and crossed the road, merging into a shadowed doorway to study it. The curtains were open, but no light showed inside. Izzy waited ten minutes, then moved on. Even if whoever lived there had gone to bed, there would be some residual light.

She returned to the tube station and took a train to the next location, where she had more luck. The house was set on a smart terrace, in a classier area, less than half a mile from Westminster Bridge. Izzy thought of what Priya had said about moving to London, and knew she could never afford a house here. Light and noise spilled out from a pub on the corner two hundred paces away. The narrow tables outside were packed. Izzy ignored the exuberance drifting from the pub and sank back into a doorway.

She waited.

As before, the curtains remained undrawn, but this time the room was lit.

A narrow balcony stood in front of sliding doors on the second floor. At street level, an upmarket café sat in darkness. A rolled-up awning spanned the width of the windows. She imagined that come daylight, the pavement would have tiny tables and chairs set out, and locals would sip at their expensive macchiatos while pedestrians had to step into the road.

A shadow passed across a cream-painted wall in the apartment above the café, and Izzy tensed.

The shadow returned, and then a figure stood at the window. Izzy couldn't make out his face because most of the light lay behind him. A man, not tall but well-built. The light behind caught his brown hair, just as Frank Davis's had been described.

The man slid the doors open and stepped out onto the narrow balcony.

Izzy saw him in a spill of light from the street lamps, and knew it was him.

Her eyes locked on her prey. He was less than a hundred feet away, and she felt she could reach out and touch him. She took her phone out, intending to call Magda Winter.

As soon as she did, she knew she'd made a mistake.

On the balcony, Frank Davis caught the movement. His eyes met Izzy's for a second, and he smiled, then stepped back into the apartment and closed the doors.

Izzy called Magda anyway.

It took a while for her to pick up, and then she said,

"What? I've just got to bed. We've all got an early start in the morning. Or have you forgotten?"

"I've got eyes on him." She read off her location. "He's in a second-floor apartment."

"Did he see you?"

"It's possible." Izzy didn't want to admit her stupidity.

"Is he still there?"

"Lights are still on. Should I check the back, in case there's another way out?"

"No. Stay where you are. I'll have people sent. Fuck, but they won't be ready yet. Stay exactly where you are. If he comes out, I want you to ... no, if he comes out, do *not* confront him. If you can follow, do so, but don't get seen again. I'll get someone there as soon as."

Izzy thought Magda had rung off, but then she said, "And what the fuck are you doing watching the house at this time of night?"

"Clearing my head, sarge, nothing more."

"I see."

This time, she cut the connection.

Izzy waited for the reinforcements, her eyes locked on the still-lit window, but she saw no more movement. She had to hold herself in check because, in her mind, she saw Davis sneaking out through some back door, never to be seen again. But she feared if she moved from where she was, he would somehow know and escape through the front. So she stayed.

It was a mistake.

FIFTY-TWO

It was an hour before they admitted Izzy into the second-floor apartment, dressed in a forensic suit with only her eyes visible. When they did, she found two CSIs setting numbered plastic markers on the floor, the tables, in the kitchen. Izzy was sure they would do the same in the bedrooms, of which there were two leading off a short hallway ending in a fire door. It moved in a light breeze, making a metallic knocking as it swung back and refused to latch. Metal plates were laid along the floor, and Izzy used them as she went to look through the door. She saw an open staircase that led to a small garden. At the end of it lay a gate which offered access to the next street. It stood open.

Izzy went back to the living room. One of the CSIs looked up at her, a black woman with short hair. Her eyes were attractive, the rest of her face covered.

"Anything?" Izzy asked.

"A ton of trace, fingerprints, DNA, but I heard you

already have those. But their presence confirms your guy lives here." Her eyes tracked what she could see of Izzy. "I've not seen you before. Are you new?"

"Visiting from out of town."

The woman's eyes creased as she smiled. "Welcome to London."

Izzy laughed. "Have you seen a rucksack anywhere?"

"Not me, but Graham's doing the bedrooms and bathroom. He might have." She returned to her work, moving carefully, meticulously. As she always did when she saw CSIs doing their job, Izzy considered the work of the police would be much harder without their professionalism and skill.

In the master bedroom, she found a white man who was the opposite of the woman outside. He was tall, stick thin, his skin even paler than it should be. Izzy imagined him hiding from the sun.

"You are?" he asked without looking up from where he painted fingerprint powder on the bedhead with a fine brush.

"DC Izzy Wilde. I wondered if you'd found a rucksack, or if he had time to take it with him."

"This your case?" He didn't look up at Izzy.

"I'm working on it, but not my case as such. I called it in when I saw him at the window. By the time anyone got here, he was well gone."

"Why a rucksack?"

"I imagine he's a bit of a prepper. Has one to hand with everything he might need. I was curious to see what was in it."

Now, the man turned and looked at Izzy, his eyes tracking her from head to toe.

"I've not looked in the wardrobes yet." He glanced at Izzy's gloved hands. "You can take a peek if you want, but don't touch it if you find what you're looking for."

Izzy nodded and started to turn away.

"Before you do, I found something that might be significant. How much do you know about this case and others? I understand the suspect might be a serial."

"We're pretty sure he is. Why?"

"Take a look in the dressing table over there. Top drawer. I don't make judgement, but it might be significant."

Izzy went to the dressing table. When she pulled the drawer open, the air left her lungs. She glanced back at the CSI. "Yes, it's significant."

Laid out on a length of velvet were rings. Wedding rings. Engagement rings. Eternity rings. Her gaze ran across them, but if one had once belonged to Rosie Wilson, she did not know which one it was. Analysis might be able to tell, but even if it did, there was no one left to return it to.

"I'll bag each one up separately," said the CSI. "But I thought you might want to see them first."

"Thanks." Izzy tried to recall if rings were missing from Frank Davis's other victims but had no recollection. Viewing the contents of the drawer, she suspected they had.

Izzy stepped along the plates and then opened the first wardrobe. Clothes hung inside. Shirts. Trousers. A shelved area held underwear, vests, and socks. A small rack on the floor contained shoes. Two pairs of walking boots were set on the floor beside it, too big to fit on the shelf. One pair were adult-sized and new. The other would fit a child. Izzy wondered if Frank Davis had the same equipment in each house, or had he brought these with him. In which case, the child-sized boots would take a while before they were of any use to Grace, but she was sure they would fit Abi. It seemed strange to her Davis had kept them. It would have been safer to dump everything of Abi's.

Izzy stepped back. She opened the other wardrobe and saw the rucksack. She glanced at the CSI. "Thanks, this is what I'm looking for."

The man rose to his full height from where he had been kneeling. "Why is it so important?"

"I don't know if it is, but if it's the one he used in Lancashire, it will be worth examining. If I can, I'd like to take a peek inside. I'm curious what he loads it with."

"Maybe it's empty." The man came to stand beside Izzy.

"Doesn't look empty."

"No, it doesn't. Look, you know how this works. I have to tag everything, but there's a lot of stuff in this flat. Put it on the bed – I'm finished there now – and empty it. There are plastic sheets over there. Put one down, and lay everything on it one by one. There's a camera on the sideboard. Record each item as you place it, then tag it. He went to a bag in the corner and pulled out a set of plastic evidence bags. He handed them to Izzy. "Do you know how to do all that?"

"I've seen it done often enough." She pulled on a pair of neoprene gloves and set the rucksack at the foot of the bed. Slowly, she unzipped the top and peered inside. An excitement sparked through her when she saw the contents.

"Are you sure I'm okay to take the stuff out of this?" she asked the CSI.

"No, but go ahead. I heard they've already got a ton of trace on the guy and the kid he took, so we're going through the motions here. I don't suppose we'll find anything new."

The mention of Grace made Izzy ask, "And the kid? No sign, I take it?"

"There's a single bed and a cot in the other bedroom. Take a look if you want. We're finished in there now."

Izzy looked into the rucksack, then left it on the bed. She wanted to explore the contents, but was curious about where Grace had slept.

The second bedroom was less than half the size of that used by Frank Davis. As the CSI had said, there was a single bed, neatly made, and a cot with a pale mattress. Izzy did not know how long an infant could remain in a cot before moving to a bed, but guessed eleven months was too young, unless Frank Davis didn't care. She wondered how he treated her, how he had treated Abi when he had her.

Izzy knew they needed to catch him before he decided Grace was surplus to requirements.

She looked around the room and then inside the single wardrobe. There was nothing in it other than an opened bag of disposable nappies. No clothes. Frank Davis had turned his back on Abi, and Grace wasn't old enough to need many outfits yet. Izzy recalled the stack of baby clothes at Caxton Farm, but parents and relatives had bought those. Now, both parents were dead.

Izzy went back to the main bedroom. The CSI was still working, but there wasn't much more to do.

Izzy crossed to the bed and took the items from the rucksack one by one. As the CSI had said, she knew the drill. She examined each item, photographed it, then slid it into one of the plastic ziplock bags. She wrote the date, time, location, and her name and number on the front. Then she took a second photograph for the chain of evidence.

Socks, walking trousers, a small bathroom bag with a toothbrush and toothpaste, a comb, a pair of nail scissors, both of which would confirm the DNA they already had; underwear, more socks, energy bars, bottles of water, six of those ready meals that all tasted the same whatever they claimed to be. More nappies and a tub of cream. It gave Izzy a moment's thought. Looking at them, they gave the impression Frank Davis cared for the girl he had abducted. That didn't fit with his other actions, but Izzy knew she was the wrong person to devise a reason why.

When the main compartment was empty, Izzy unzipped the top pocket. She drew out an Ordnance

Survey map. She expected more, and checked all the other pockets, but only one map existed.

She turned it over. The front cover read *OS Explorer Map 209: Cambridge, Royston, Duxford & Linton*.

Not what she expected. She wondered if Frank Davis had left it there after checking out Ellie's house. Except that made no sense, because years had passed since then, and this map looked almost new.

She opened it to see a circle drawn in highlighter around Great Shelford, where the Bowman's house lay. She folded the map to show the area of interest, before sliding it into another evidence bag, sealed it and wrote on it.

When Izzy glanced across, she saw the tall CSI finishing up, and she waved the map at him. "I found this in the rucksack, and I think it might be important. Can I take it to show Magda and Sam Mallick?"

The CSI came across and held his hand out. Izzy passed the map over and then pointed to where the location had been highlighted. He looked up at Izzy.

"I put it in the evidence bag folded this way. I want to show it to someone else."

"Sorry, can't be done."

Izzy understood the reason. She couldn't break the chain of evidence. Instead, she took several photos on her phone and placed the envelope containing the map on the plastic sheet. She knew she could buy another map.

Out on the street, Izzy called Magda.

"Where are you?" she asked.

"Just leaving Davis's house. I think I know where he's headed."

"Good, because nobody here's got a Scooby. Tell me."

"The Bowmans. Davis left too fast to take everything. I found an OS map in his rucksack, and the Bowman's house is highlighted."

"Why would he go there?"

"He feels cornered. He does a runner, and we never see him or the girl again, or he lashes out. Makes a statement."

"You're telling me he intends to do the latter?"

"I believe he knows Abi is with them. Finding out *how* he knows might be interesting, but I'll leave that up to Priya."

"Why Abi?"

"They've taken her from him. She knows too much about him. He might believe Davis made a mistake when he panicked and left her behind at the farmhouse. I don't know, sarge. I can't see into his mind, and I don't want to. But that's where he's going. I'm sure of it."

"Get back here. I'll call the team together. They'll curse you to blue heaven because they've only just been sent home to get some sleep."

"Sorry."

"Don't be. This might be our chance to catch the slippery bastard."

By the time Izzy returned to New Scotland Yard, the others were starting to arrive. Jack and Priya were already there, the hotel only across the river.

"I called the Cambridgeshire Police," said DCI Mallick. "They're sending people out to keep eyes on the Bowman house. No need to wake them at this hour. The morning will be time enough." He looked at Izzy. "You and Jack are closest to this guy. What do you think?"

"Izzy's closer to him than me," said Jack.

"Which is why I'm looking at her."

"We should have caught him by now," Izzy said. "We had our chance in Preston, the same at the first house. Again, at this one."

"So why didn't we?"

"In Preston, we didn't know enough. At the first house, he was too quick. He got out of there before we had a chance to track him. Here, it's my fault because I let him see me. I should have followed procedure."

"It's what we do," said Mallick. "Without procedure, everything turns to shit. So we're going to do the same again now. Except this time, he's coming to us. We're not chasing him down. We can get in place and collar him."

"We need to be careful of the kid," said Jack, "and the Bowmans. It would be an idea to get them out of there. Ellie, as well. If Davis knows where they live, he'll almost certainly know where Ellie lives, too."

"All right, I'll get it done. We'll take them to a safe house by train. We'll use half a dozen locals to assist. You two and–"

"I'd like to ride along as well," said Priya.

"All right, you three, but I don't need to tell you that as a civilian, you must keep out of our way. I'm sending Magda to liaise with the local force to provide most of the officers. I'll also get an armed squad out there, just in case."

Thirty minutes later, Izzy sat in the passenger seat of an unmarked BMW, with blue lights flashing and Magda Winter behind the wheel.

From the back, Jack said, "Christ, I hope to fuck they don't end up shooting him. I want to see him in court."

"So do I." Izzy glanced in the rear-view mirror to see that Priya had gone to sleep. She knew she should feel tired too, but sleep was the last thing on her mind. She wanted vengeance. For some reason, the case felt personal, and she didn't know why. Perhaps the cavalier fashion in which Davis had abandoned Abi. Izzy wasn't one for introspection, but she suspected this case hit her because of how her father behaved. There had been little affection, and even less love. After Izzy left, it took only two years before her mother did the same. She never spoke of her reasons, but Izzy believed her mother had gleaned the truth about Vick Blackwood. He was a bully, who cared only for himself. Izzy suspected he had married and had kids because it looked good on his CV.

She had driven to Cheshire to meet her mother in a hotel, where she was staying while looking for a house to buy. She tried to discuss her reasons for leaving, but her mother resisted. And then her father had turned up, tracking his wife through police contacts. He was a big, strong man, but when Izzy walked in on him slapping her mother to her knees, she stood between them. When he raised his hand to her, she kicked him hard, where it hurt a man the most, then kicked him again. She had to fight the urge to keep on hitting him. Why he didn't retaliate, she didn't know. If it was any other man, she might say it was compassion, or love. With her father. she knew that was not the case.

Now, she pushed the memory away, as she always did. It was not the worst thing she knew about him. A psychiatrist would tell her she needed to examine her feelings, but Izzy would tell them to fuck off and examine their own. She coped.

And in the morning, she would cope the shit out of Frank Davis. She didn't care whether he walked away from this or not. All she cared about were those kids, the Bowmans, and justice for Rosie and Mike Wilson, and all the other families the man had ruined.

FIFTY-THREE

"Has anyone told the Bowmans what to expect?" Izzy stood before Sam Mallick, with Magda Winter nearby. Almost all the officers at the scene were from the Cambridgeshire force, but Mallick was in overall command. There had been talk of getting Superintendent Harrington to come across, but he declined, saying he trusted the officers there.

They stood in a small group, two hundred yards from the house, hidden among light woodland that backed onto a park and, beyond that, the town centre. It was two days since Davis's house had been identified, and the hour was five in the morning. The sun had recently risen, but beneath the tree cover, shade remained.

"I called them and asked if they wanted to stay or go," said Mallick. "He was all for staying, but his wife persuaded him she wanted her husband around a while longer. They left ten minutes ago with Abi in an unmarked car for the station. They are heading for a safe house twenty miles away. I'd have preferred they were driven there, but Cambridgeshire told me I've already used up too much of their resources."

Izzy glanced around. "If Davis is coming, he's likely to approach through those trees. They provide cover until he's 50 metres from the house."

"Agreed, but a footpath comes in over there." Mallick pointed, but there was nothing to see. "I think he'll come that way. It's his modus operandi. To follow a trail. You taught us that."

"It's what he's always done, but we've shaken him up."

"You've shaken him up," said Mallick. "Besides, we have people watching the park, which is the direction we expect him to come from. It's the easiest way from the station. If he doesn't take the footpath, they'll let us know. And when this is over, I want to talk to you."

"You've already offered me a job, and I said no."

"I want to see if I can change your mind."

"You can try. My answer will be the same."

Mallick smiled and turned away.

The woods were a cacophony of birdsong. Dew clung to the grass underfoot, and a thin mist drifted between the trees.

"I'm going to look around the other side," Izzy said.

"I don't need to tell you to be careful, do I?"

"Probably not, boss."

Izzy found Jack on her way through the woods, then a

little later reached Priya, who had stayed in the car to catch up on her sleep.

"This doesn't feel right," Izzy said.

"Jeez, Iz, this is all your idea," said Jack.

"I know, but I've been thinking."

"Is that a good idea?"

Izzy poked her tongue out. "The Bowmans are too old. None of the women he killed were older than their mid-thirties. Most were younger. The Bowmans don't fit that profile."

"Except you said this is all about Abi," said Priya, stretching as she exited the back of the car.

"It is, but who was she living with when we took her to London?"

"For the weekend," said Jack. "The rest of the time, she stays with her grandparents. Everyone's staked this place out, Iz. It was circled on that map you found. You can't drag everyone off to Ellie's house."

"I know. But Davis knew we were on to him after the raid on his house in west London. What if he purposely left the rucksack behind, knowing we'd find the map, and see the Bowman's house highlighted?"

"You're making him out to be some kind of genius," said Jack. "But everything we know says he's not."

"I agree. But someone else is. Abi gave us the clue when she said her daddy got messages. I believe Davis is a tool manipulated by someone else."

Jack laughed. "Now you have gone too far. You've been reading too much fantasy, Iz."

"Maybe. I'm tired, and my head is too full of thoughts. But I still think it's worth checking on Ellie."

"Clear it with Mallick first."

Izzy returned within ten minutes.

"He said they have enough people here to watch the Bowmans and told us we could go. I think he was glad to see the back of us. We do the same there and watch. If he comes here, there are more than enough to arrest him. If he goes to Ellie's, we call the others in to do the heavy lifting."

———

Priya stayed in the back of the car with her laptop, studying the CCTV feed from King's Cross station. Jack went to the far side of Ellie's house, where a footpath led through a field from where he could keep a lookout. As Priya's fingers worked, she explained she was looking for Frank Davis and Grace, but had so far seen nothing. She had started the clock at midnight. The station was almost deserted at that time. Now, she had rolled forward to 8 a.m. She had already looked at trains from the station to Cambridge and identified several possibilities.

"What if you don't see him?" Izzy asked.

Priya pointed at the screen. "Look how many people there are at this time of day. It's likely I will miss him, but there's a slim chance I won't. If I see him, it will tell us when to expect him here."

"And if you don't?"

"We wait," Priya said. "If you're right he's coming to us."

"What about CCTV at the station here?"

"I checked. It has it, but it's not connected to the cloud, so I can't access the feed unless I go there, which I'm not going to do."

Izzy went to sit in the driver's seat, an impatience running through her she tried to ignore. They were parked two hundred metres from Ellie Bowman's house. Close enough to see it, far enough away not to put Frank Davis off if he came here. Izzy thought he would.

Izzy glanced at her phone to get the time. Nine-fifteen.

She thumbed a number and waited.

"What?" Mallick's voice was short.

"Anything there?" Izzy asked.

"I'll call you when there is." He cut the call.

Izzy knew she shouldn't have called. Mallick would have his phone on silent, but even a slight movement might tip Frank Davis off; like she had. She'd done it because she was impatient. She knew it was a failing in her character, but it had also come in useful at times. Sometimes, the early bird did get the worm, rather than a nasty bite from a feral cat.

"Davis was in King's Cross at 6:55 this morning." Priya spoke from behind, and Izzy turned to look at her. "The closest train was the 7:10 to Cambridge, but it was almost straight through. The 9:14 followed it out, and stops at almost every town, village and hamlet on the way. I think he'll have taken the slower train. He seems to be forensically aware, so probably knows those stations have less cameras than Cambridge station. If I'm right, he gets into Shelford at 8:24. Which is 10 minutes from now, give or take. You need to tell Mallick. He might want eyes on when the train arrives."

"Thanks." Izzy turned away, her phone already ringing.

"What did I say to you?" Mallick's impatience was palpable.

"Priya thinks he's on the slow train from King's Cross that gets into Shelford at 8:24."

"Is what she does legit?"

"I believe so, though I consider it best not to ask her directly. But she gets results." Izzy glanced at her screen. "Eight minutes from now, boss. We're closer than you to the station, but I'd like to stay here."

"It's not much further to the Bowman's house," said Mallick. "I'll send a couple of plain clothes officers to the station to get eyes on him. You stay where you are. Is Jack still with you?"

"He's covering the far side of the house."

"Good."

When the call ended, Izzy smiled. Mallick thought Jack was a voice of reason for her, but he didn't understand their relationship. True, Jack was more careful, but he knew Izzy got results where his slower approach might fail. Of course, there were times he was right not to jump in with both feet.

Thinking of him, Izzy got out of the car and walked down the path between houses to the field where Jack told her he would be, but she couldn't see him. The map she had studied showed the footpath running along the rear of the houses, from the town centre towards more woodland, and then following the river Cam to Whittlesford. Izzy spent a couple of minutes looking for Jack and not finding him. She started back along the path as her phone rang.

It was Mallick.

"Miracle of miracles, the train got in four minutes early. We have eyes on him now. He's heading into town. If he starts to come this way, we'll pull him."

"Let him come, boss. Unless he shows you, you won't know which house he's heading for."

"And by then, it might be too late. We've got enough on him to pull him now without risking anyone else."

"How's Grace doing? Can they see her?"

"Hang on."

Mallick put her on hold and came back in less than a minute.

"She's not with him."

"He left King's Cross with her in tow." Izzy broke into a run, heading back to the car. "I want to check with Priya. I'll call you back."

At the car, Priya showed her the video. It was brief, and showed Davis from behind, but Grace was in his arms.

"She was with him when he left London," Izzy said, when Mallick answered. "Priya has it on video."

"I'll get someone to check at the next station along

the line, see if he left her on the train. It's possible he doesn't want her as a distraction."

"I think he brought her because that's his MO, boss. Except this time, we know he's coming, so he can't use her as a distraction. Maybe he knows we're waiting for him."

"Then why bring her to King's Cross at all? It makes no sense."

"Are you sure it's Davis your people are shadowing?"

"They have that sketch your guy did in Preston. They say he looks similar enough."

"Similar *enough*?" Izzy said. "Can we go on similar enough? Go ahead and pull him, boss. Pull him now. If it's Davis, you have him. If it's not, it means he's here, and we've no eyes on him."

But Izzy was talking into a dead phone.

"Can you track where Jack is from his phone?" Izzy asked Priya.

"Hang on." She worked the keyboard and trackpad, then turned the screen to show a map with a flashing green dot.

Izzy tilted her head, orienting the image.

"What the fuck is he doing over there?"

"Why not call and ask him?" Priya let her frustration show. "No, that's too logical for you. I'll do it."

She put the call through on her laptop. It rang, and continued to ring. Too long.

Priya cut the connection.

"Try again," Izzy said.

"He's probably got no signal. The coverage here is iffy, to say the least."

"Try again," Izzy insisted.

Priya scowled, but put the call through. This time, she let it ring longer. Half a minute. A minute. Izzy was about to tell her to break the connection when the call was picked up, but it wasn't Jack who answered.

"Who is this?" said a voice she didn't recognise.

"Who am I? Who the fuck are you? And what are you doing answering my partner's phone?"

"Ah, I assume I'm speaking to Detective Constable Isabella Wilde. I am answering Detective Sergeant Jack Ward's phone because he is otherwise tied up." The man giggled. "Quite literally. But it's all right, because he has company."

The screen changed to show an image.

Jack was tied with rope to the thick trunk of an oak. His eyes were closed, and a bruise showed on his forehead. Abi was tied to the left of him, the baby Grace crying on the ground with the rope around her throat.

"Cut it," Izzy snapped, and Priya broke the connection.

"You still got his location?" Izzy asked.

"Same place. Hang on, I'll send it to your phone."

When Izzy's phone pinged, she opened the message. The screen showed an OS Map with Jack's location, and a route on foot from where they were. It showed a distance of a kilometre and a time on foot of fifteen minutes.

Izzy was sure she could beat that.

"Call Mallick. Tell him Davis is here, and he has Jack

and the two girls. How the fuck he got hold of Abi, I've no idea, but got her he has. Get the troops over here now. All of them. And get him to check on the Bowmans. Abi's meant to be with them."

Izzy didn't wait to see if Priya followed her orders.

She turned and ran as fast as she could.

FIFTY-FOUR

Izzy's lungs burned, and her heart felt as if it was about to explode through her ribcage. She ignored the footpath and took a direct line, pushing through the undergrowth and weaving between trees. Then she saw Jack and the girls. There was no sign of Frank Davis, other than his handiwork.

Izzy went to her knees beside Jack, reached to her ankle and drew out a knife.

"Police issue, I assume?" said Jack, who had come around.

"Where is he?" Izzy looked around as the rope parted, the knife quicker than working on the intricate knots.

"He went that way." Jack nodded to the north. "Give me the knife. I'll cut the girls free and take them to Priya. He's gone to Ellie's house. Go after him, Iz. Call Mallick and tell him."

"Only when I know what happened here."

"I didn't see him. There was a trail through the grass.

Two sets of footprints, and I followed them. When I found Grace and Abi, they were already tied to the tree. I went to untie them, instead of calling you first. That was a mistake. He hit me from behind, knocked me cold. When I came round, we were all tied together. Now go."

"Take them to Priya and get her to drive them away from here. We'll have the cavalry coming as soon as I call. I'll do nothing but observe, unless Ellie's in danger. She should have gone with her parents, except now we don't know what happened to them."

Izzy looked at the girls. Little Grace seemed to be asleep, and she feared Davis had used his drugs on her, but Abi looked fine. She offered a shy smile.

"How did you get here?" Izzy asked her.

"Daddy found me on the train when I went to get a drink. He told me I had to go with him. I didn't want to, but he made me. I'm sorry, Aunt Izzy."

Izzy reached out and touched the girl's head. "You're safe now, sweetie. Go with Jack." She hoped she spoke the truth, but Davis was a slippery devil, who'd outflanked them more than once.

This time, she followed the footpath as she ran, until she emerged from the woods at the rear of the houses. There was still no sign of Davis. She called Mallick to update him and check what was happening. She told him to check on the Bowmans, because Abi was meant to be with them. When she broke the call, she stood behind Ellie's house and studied the windows. She could see through those at ground level but not above. A narrow balcony projected out from a set of French doors from, she assumed, the master bedroom. Below it, a wide patio took up a third of the rear garden. It was half-filled with pots holding olives, box bushes, lavender and rosemary. The swing Izzy had watched Jack pushing Abi on was set in the far corner. That day seemed a lifetime ago.

If Davis had come this way, there was no sign of him. Izzy turned away and ran down the footpath between the houses until she reached the car. The back door was open, and there was no sign of Priya. Izzy leaned in and saw her laptop in the footwell. She also saw blood. What appeared to be a great deal of blood.

Izzy stood back and examined the ground.

The trail of blood led to Ellie's house.

Izzy reached for her ankle before remembering she'd given her knife to Jack. As she straightened, she checked her body cam was recording, then walked directly to the front door, making no effort to hide. It failed to open when she tried the handle.

There was blood on the tiles in front of the door.

She moved left, put her back to the wall, and risked a quick look into the room. Two sofas, a big TV, no people.

She did it on the other side with the same result.

She banged on the door.

"I know you're in there, Frank. Come out now, and it will go easier for you. You can't escape. You're surrounded."

Nothing.

Izzy cursed.

She phoned Mallick.

"Where are you?" She spoke before he could.

449

"Still at the Bowman's house. We've got trouble at this end. They failed to turn up at the station where people are waiting for them."

"That's because Davis duped us. There's trouble here, too. Big trouble. I don't know how, but Davis attacked Priya. He's got her and Ellie Bowman locked in her house. Get your arses over here now, sir."

"Are you sure it's him? If we leave here and you're mistaken, we could miss him again."

"Of course it's fucking him! Jack was knocked out and tied up. He's with the kids. They're both safe, but Priya and Ellie aren't. And someone's been injured. There's blood. How long to get here?"

There was a moment of hesitation. Izzy pictured Mallick opening an app on his phone and plotting the route.

"Ten minutes, maybe fifteen. We're on our way. But if you're wrong, this is your career down the drain."

"I'm not wrong." But Izzy was talking to a dead phone.

Far in the distance, she heard sirens.

Ten minutes was too long.

Ten *seconds* was too long!

She went down the path to the rear of the house and boosted herself over the high fence. On the far side, she saw a shed she had missed before. When she tried the door, it opened, and she glanced inside, but nobody was hiding there. She was about to turn away when something caught her attention.

Hooks along the wall held garden implements. A

spade. A fork. A lopper for branches. Two saws. A lawn-mower on the floor. There was a gap between the fork and the branch-lopper. She stared at the space, but couldn't work out what had been there.

She was wasting time, so she grabbed the fork and turned to the house. She ran, holding the fork in front of her. When she slammed the tines against the kitchen door window, it shattered. Izzy reached in, turned the lock, and went inside.

She stood, trying to calm her breathing so she could hear. Nothing.

"Frank, come downstairs before this ends badly for you."

"Too late for that." The voice came from the hallway beyond the kitchen, and Izzy paced softly to the door.

The sirens had been louder outside, but she couldn't hear them in the house.

"The children are safe. That will work in your favour, Frank."

"I'd never hurt my girls, but I know this is the end for me. Might as well take another pair of bitches with me." His voice was calm, and rational.

Izzy stepped into the hallway. She knew Tom and Betty Bowman were the wrong age group to interest Davis, but Ellie and Priya were smack in the middle of it.

Davis stood at the top of the stairs. He had a curved blade in one hand. His other gripped Ellie around the waist.

"Where's Priya?"

"She's having a little lie down on the bed. I don't think she's feeling very well."

"Last warning, Frank." Izzy could hear the sirens, louder now. "The big guns are about to arrive. And I mean guns. Armed officers."

"They won't shoot. They're just as likely to blow the bitch's head off as mine."

"No, Frank; these guys are good. I think you're buggered."

"Maybe, but dead's better than locked up." He barked a laugh. "But just in case..." He turned away, dragging Ellie after him.

Izzy went up the stairs slowly, hesitating on each tread before taking the next.

Frank Davis had left the bedroom door open. Izzy could see Ellie's foot through it and tried to devise the best approach.

There was blood on the carpet.

Davis did something, and Ellie screamed.

Izzy went into the room.

Priya lay on her side on the bed, blood staining the sheet. Davis held the curved blade against Ellie's throat, and Izzy realised it was the same type of implement he had used to kill Rosie Wilson, but this one was almost brand new, and not rusted. The shining blade was red with Priya's blood. A white wire snaked from Davis's shirt pocket to an earbud, and he seemed to be listening to something, or someone.

Izzy held the fork in front of herself as a weapon,

wondering if she could get to Davis before he opened Ellie's throat.

Maybe. Maybe not.

She tried to calculate the odds and failed. Ninety per cent wasn't good enough.

The sirens were loud now.

Davis could hear them as well as Izzy.

"They're almost here."

"Yes, they are, so let Ellie go."

Izzy saw Davis smile, his arm holding the weapon tense. She ran at him. The distance was short, and he panicked, jerking backwards. The curved blade slid across Ellie's throat. She screamed and fell sideways, but there was space between them now, and Izzy attempted to close the gap.

Davis backed fast through the open doors onto the balcony. He raised one leg over the railings before looking back at Izzy.

"She's here," he said, causing Izzy to frown. "What do I do?" He cocked his head to one side, then nodded, raised his arm and flung the curved blade at her. It twisted through the air, but his aim was off, and it fell harmlessly to the floor.

"Do it then, if you can." He smiled, his expression beatific as he lifted his other leg over the rails. He stared at Izzy, then glanced down and leapt back into open space. Izzy heard a loud crash from below but ignored it. The noise of sirens filled the air now, then suddenly died. The troops had arrived. They would take care of Davis.

Izzy went to Ellie and held her chin. She turned her

head. There was a long, livid scratch across her neck, but it bled hardly at all.

"You'll live. Go downstairs and let them in."

She went to the bed and turned Priya onto her back.

"Where?" she asked.

Priya shook her head. "Side. I didn't see him, and he didn't hesitate."

Izzy gripped Priya's T-shirt and tore it down the front. She saw the gash in her side and felt faint.

Izzy ripped the bedsheets and wrapped them around Priya's waist. She tore more and covered those over the others. She was still doing it when Sam Mallick entered the room with what seemed like a dozen armed offices.

"He went out that way." Izzy nodded at the balcony. "I think he might have escaped us again. Did you bring medics?"

Mallick turned to one of the armed men, and told him to fetch the paramedics. He glanced at Priya, then stepped out onto the balcony.

Izzy wanted to go and look, but she couldn't leave Priya.

They had to drag Izzy away from her.

She stood in a corner of the room as chaos surrounded her. She watched the paramedics work. They checked Priya's stats, putting in drips, one with saline and another with blood.

That was a good sign, wasn't it? Priya must be alive for them to do that ... mustn't she?

Someone called for an air ambulance.

Another good sign, Izzy thought.

Mallick came into the room and took Izzy by the arm. She resisted.

"You can't do anything for her. Let them work, Izzy. Come with me."

"He jumped. He's getting away."

"No, he's not. He's lying in a bunch of broken pots down below."

"Is he dead?"

"I'm going to find out. You might want to come and see."

They went out through the damaged kitchen door. Two more paramedics knelt beside Frank Davis, but as Izzy and Mallick approached, one rose to his feet and shook his head.

"Looks like he broke his neck when he hit one of the pots. Bad fracture of the skull, as well."

Mallick put his arm around Izzy.

"It's done. You did a good job. Of course, there'll be an enquiry, and the OPC will get involved."

"I'm already under investigation for Mike Wilson's death. They'll think I make a habit of this kind of thing."

"I heard you're cleared of any involvement in the farmer shooting himself. Suicide, plain and simple. Or as simple as it ever gets. I can't prejudge anything, but it looks like Davis jumped. Your camera recording should confirm that. As far as I can tell, you saved lives today."

"If Priya lives."

"She's getting the best help."

Izzy heard a helicopter approach. It hovered over the field beyond the houses before landing.

Paramedics carried Priya down on a stretcher and out through the back gate. Izzy stood where she was, alone now apart from the body of Frank Davis, and watched as the helicopter rose into the air and banked away north.

Izzy glanced down at Davis. She saw the earbud had come loose. It lay on the ground, but was still attached to the phone in his shirt pocket. She pulled on neoprene gloves and knelt, worked the phone loose. If Priya hadn't been injured, she could have found out where the call Davis had been listening to came from. Izzy laid the phone on Davis's still chest, then realised the call was still live. She picked the phone up, pulled out the headphones and put the call on speaker.

"Who is this?"

"Ah, Detective Constable Isabella Wilde. I would say it is a pleasure to hear your voice again, but I would be lying. I take it your presence indicates Mr Davis is indisposed?"

"What is he to you?" Izzy didn't recognise the voice, but it had a strange blandness to it, and she suspected whoever was at the other end was using software to disguise who they were.

"He was a friend. I expect I will have to find another one now. Ah well. Do not sleep too deeply, Izzy, in case I send them for you." The speaker cut the call, which is when Jack came through the gate.

Jack looked down at Davis and nodded.

"Was someone on his phone?" he asked.

"It sounded like Davis was being told what to do. We

need someone to analyse the phone and see if they can work out where the call came from."

Jack put his hand on Izzy's shoulder. "Later, Iz. Come on, Mallick's waiting for us."

Izzy reached out to put her palm on the bruise on Jack's face, and he winced.

FIFTY-FIVE

Izzy sat with Priya's hand in hers; small, delicate, warm. Thank God it was warm.

Machines glowed. Traces traced. Priya slept, drugged.

Her injuries were severe, but not as serious as Izzy had feared back at Ellie Bowman's house.

Mallick had wanted her debriefed, and so did the OPC, but she told them they would have to wait, or come and drag her out.

DI Harry Gray had called from Preston and told her she needed to come home. Some questions had to be asked about her behaviour. Izzy was unsurprised.

Beyond the window-blind, the sun set in a blaze of incandescence. Izzy needed sleep but wouldn't submit until Priya woke. The doctor told her she had been fortunate. The blade of the hand sickle had missed everything vital, passing her liver by four centimetres, and her kidney by a little more. There had been blood, a lot of blood, but the paramedics had stemmed the worst, and the air ambulance had taken her to Addenbrooke's Hospital within ten minutes. The doctor said Priya would survive.

Frank Davis, of course, had not. Izzy hadn't thought of him. He was old business. She knew she had questions to answer, but her body cam footage would show exactly what had happened. This should feel like the end, but it didn't because of the voice she had heard at the other end of Davis's phone. And the threat it made. An empty threat, she was sure. Even now, the phone was on its way to a specialist unit in Cambridge, and they would squeeze every last drop of data they could from it.

But all that could wait. What mattered now was the woman who lay in this room.

Izzy rose and adjusted the blinds, so the growing light didn't play across Priya's face, but when she turned back, her eyes were open.

She went and sat beside the bed.

"Do you hurt?"

Priya moved her head in what might have been negation. "The drugs are wonderful. You should try them." Priya closed her eyes. "How did he get past everyone, Iz?"

"Mallick told me Davis was a clever bastard, but he wasn't. He was being guided the whole way."

"Guided? Who by?"

"Don't know yet, but we will. His phone is being analysed now."

"I'd love to get my hands on it," said Priya, her eyes still closed.

"You don't have to do everything yourself."

"Says you."

"Do you remember seeing him at King's Cross?"

Priya offered the faintest nod, and said, "He took the express, didn't he?"

"Straight into Cambridge, then a local train south. The same one the Bowmans were on."

"Did he kill them?" Priya asked.

"Knocked them out, together with their police protection officer. Abi was away from them at the time, but he found her and took her. Nobody saw anything because they were in a carriage on their own, as a precaution. Some precaution. Davis got out at the next station and walked back to Ellie's house. I suspect that was his destination all along. Another footpath, another trail. Poor kid. Mallick wants to examine how he knew where the Bowmans were being moved to. It smacks of insider information. At least they're both still alive. So are Abi and Grace."

"There's stuff about Frank Davis you need to know once I'm up and about," said Priya. "I did some digging and didn't like what I found. It might be connected to what you told me, but I need to search deeper to see if it is."

Izzy wanted to ask her what she meant, but the effort of talking had exhausted Priya, and after a minute, her breathing softened, and her grip went slack.

Izzy stared at the machines, checking her vital signs. As far as she could tell, they looked good.

She waited. An hour passed. Then another. Izzy didn't mind. Each hour meant Priya would grow stronger.

A trolley clattered along the corridor outside, and a nurse opened the door.

"Oh, I didn't know she had a visitor. Is she awake?"

"She was. Went back to sleep."

"Do you want some tea? Or coffee?"

"Coffee, please. And leave one for Priya, for when she wakes again."

The coffee was awful. Izzy suspected if she had asked for tea, it would have tasted the same. She poured hers and Priya's down the sink in the corner of the room, then went out and down to the café on the ground floor, and bought two flat whites. When she returned to the room, Priya was awake, half sitting up.

Izzy handed her one of the cardboard cups, and sat on the side of the bed.

"What did you mean about Frank Davis?"

Priya sipped her coffee, but it was too hot. She shifted on the bed.

"Hurts a bit now, but I don't want any more morphine. I hope they let me leave in a day or two."

"They'll let you leave when you're mended. Don't argue with them."

"Me? Argue?"

"Do you want me to help you sit up?"

"Would that mean putting your arm around me?"

"Probably."

"Then yes."

Izzy smiled. She slid an arm beneath Priya and eased her up. When she had finished, Priya's breath came shorter.

"Use it if you have to," Izzy said.

"It'll pass." Priya wriggled, seeking comfort and failing to find it. "Davis doesn't add up. I backtracked from the apartment he was in, and discovered he doesn't pay for anything himself. It's all handled through that blind trust, but I can't get any further. It's locked up tighter than Fort Knox. I can usually get into most systems, but not this one."

"When did you find this out?"

"While you were being superwoman and freeing Jack."

"What happened? Did he come for you?"

"It was my fault," said Priya. "I had my head down, digging through the data."

"The doctor said you were lucky he missed anything vital. You lost a lot of blood, but they put more into you in time."

"I was stupid letting him get close to me."

"What do you think about Davis? Is this trust something he set up to hide his real identity?"

"It hides *an* identity, Iz, but I don't think it's his. I will track him down as soon as I get out of here. He must have a record somewhere. A birth certificate. An employment record. It wouldn't surprise me if he doesn't have a police record, too. Thanks to you, we know his wife's name. She might have left the country, but data knows no boundaries. Once I track her down, there'll be a marriage certificate with his real name on it."

"Once you're up and fit, I want you to look at the phone he had on him. There was someone else on the other end. I think he was directing Davis. The local techs are good, but they're not you."

"Don't wait for me, Iz."

"If they find anything, it won't be our responsibility. Davis lived down south. The Met, not us, will handle this. I think I'm relieved. I'm looking forward to getting stuck in the mud, and looking for stolen tractors and red diesel again."

"You say that now, but I know you better," said Priya. "Lancashire is still the force in charge of the investigation, so MIT Hutton will be informed." Priya closed her eyes. "You can go now. I'm not dying, and need to sleep."

In the corridor, Izzy glanced at her phone. It showed a dozen missed calls and messages. From Sam Mallick, and Magda Winter. From Harry Gray, and Ed Harrington. Several from a number she didn't recognise. She knew she'd have to respond to them before long, but not tonight.

Outside, Izzy clicked on the unknown number, curious, and waited as she walked towards a bus stop beyond the hospital entrance.

When the call was finally answered, Izzy said, "Who is this, and what do you want?"

The response was a laugh she recognised.

"This isn't your number, Mama."

"I lost my old phone, darling, so I had to buy a new one. How are you?"

"Busy."

"You're always busy, but not too busy for me, I hope."

Izzy tried not to sigh. "No, never too busy for you, Mama. What do you want?"

"Well..."

Izzy reached the bus stop, where nurses and doctors, some still dressed in scrubs, were going off duty. She waited for her mother to say something else, a scratch of unease rising when the silence continued.

"Is it papa?" Izzy asked.

"I thought I saw him when I was out shopping."

"Did he come near you?"

"No, but I'm sure it was him."

"Was he looking at you?"

"No, but..."

This time, Izzy let the sigh loose. Her mother could be delicate at times, hard as granite at others.

"It would be lovely to see you, darling."

"Let me see what the next couple of days brings, Mama. I might be tied up for a while."

"Oh, there's no rush. Whenever you can, my sweet. But it would be nice to get together, yes?"

"Yes. I'll call you in the morning."

In the distance, she saw a bus approaching and swiped the screen to open her payment app. All the while, her mother was still talking, happy now, telling Izzy about the mundanity of her week.

Izzy got on the bus, tapped her phone to pay and sat. She realised she didn't know where the bus was going, but assumed it would arrive at the nearest station at some point. A man in front looked back at her, and Izzy switched the call from speaker and held the phone to her ear.

"Look, Mama, you can tell me all your news when I come to see you. I'm about to catch a train. I'll call you tomorrow. Love you."

She broke the call before her mother could reply, and slid the phone into her pocket. All the chatter had been camouflage. The real reason was her father. A man who could never take no for an answer. Especially from his own family. There had been a clause in the divorce agreement requesting he avoid all contact with his ex-wife. It seemed it wasn't enough for Vick Blackwood. Despite being a senior police officer, Izzy knew her father considered himself above the law. Or followed a law of his own. It might be nothing and could wait a few days.

Izzy put her head against the seat and closed her eyes.

FIFTY-SIX

Izzy sat in her small back garden, a glass of chilled wine on a tiny wooden table, and chicken salad on a plate. The space was dense with flowers, all of which she had planted. When she had moved into the small house, the garden had been wildly overgrown, full of rampant brambles and nettles. It had taken her half a year to dig it all out. Another three months to choose and plant what she wanted. Now, it was her safe space, a haven from the memories in her head.

She heard a car approach along the lane, turn into the small drive beside the house, then heard footsteps on the gravel, followed by a knock at her door.

Izzy rose and went to the side of the house, where she found Harry Gray standing there.

"I only made dinner for one, boss, but you can have a glass of wine if you like."

Gray smiled, but there was a tension behind it.

"I don't suppose you've got a beer, have you? Only one, mind. I've got to drive back."

She opened the side gate to let him through, then fetched a cold Brewdog from the fridge. She didn't offer a glass, and he didn't ask for one.

"Are you here to have *that* conversation with me, boss?"

"I expect I am, but we don't have to do it right this second. Finish your dinner. Drink some wine. I'll drink this beer, and we can enjoy the evening. Have you heard how Priya's doing?

Izzy thought Harry would already know, but perhaps not under the circumstances.

"She's still recovering, of course. Gone to stay with her sister in London. You know the Met are after her?"

"I heard a rumour. It would be a shame to lose her."

Izzy smiled. Ate some salad. Drank more wine. She got up and brought the half-empty bottle out. She thought she might need it.

Behind them, the sun sank closer to the horizon, its rays painting the rounded slopes of the Forest of Bowland. She thought of all the footpaths running across this landscape, linking villages, hamlets and towns. Izzy could think of a dozen that passed close to where she sat. Frank Davis was dead, but if what Priya said was true, someone else could be giving more orders, right now.

"Have you heard anything about Frank Davis's phone?"

"Nothing." Gray held a hand up. "Sorry, not that I heard

nothing, but they got nothing from it. It was a burner, registered only that morning. One outbound call was made to another burner number, also bought at Euston station, but three days earlier. And then that call you heard the end of. The boffins analysed the voice, but said it was artificial."

"He put it through some software?"

"More than that. You can speak, and AI replaces your voice with someone else's. So it's a dead end."

"And me? Am I in trouble?"

"The IOPC has concluded their investigation into Davis's death and recorded it as self-inflicted. Same for Mike Wilson. You're cleared on both. I heard someone say you seemed to make a habit of getting too close to dead people, but I shut them down. You did well, Izzy."

"So I'm in the clear?"

"You are, but keep your head down for a while. Do your job. You're hot-headed sometimes, and think you know better than anyone else, but a good cop all the same."

"Would someone else have stopped Frank Davis?"

"Twenty police were headed to that house. You should have waited."

"By which time Priya would have bled out, and Ellie Bowman had her throat slashed open. I did what had to be done."

"You're arguing again," said Harry. "I'm not saying you were wrong, but not everyone agrees with me. We all have to take orders, Iz. From the Chief Constable down." He looked into her eyes. "Maybe the police isn't the right place for you if you can't accept that. You might want to think about your career choices."

"I don't need to," Izzy said. "I did good police work today, boss. Do you remember Harrington had this theory about Davis being a killer for hire?"

"Vaguely, but that's old news now."

"I was up on the fells this morning, talking with a guy who had a spreader stolen overnight. I gave him a report for the insurance, and we got to talking. He laughed because he'd be getting more than if he'd sold it to Mike Wilson. It seems Mike's story about the money he took out for farm machinery was true."

"Maybe keep that to yourself. I hear Harrington's been putting out feelers to Jack about joining MIT in Hutton. Word is he wants you as well."

"How would you feel about that, boss? Losing both of us?"

"If it's what either of you want, I'd be pleased for you."

"What does Jack say?"

"I think he wants to talk to you first."

"He knows where I am." Izzy poured more wine into her glass. "Sure you don't want another beer, boss?"

"I do, but I'll wait until I get home. Do you recall Ethan Walton claiming Grace was his kid?"

"Of course. It annoyed the hell out of me he kept it to himself during our interview. Did he think we wouldn't find out from his DNA swab?"

"Well, that's the thing, Iz. We got the results back, and he isn't Grace's father, nor of the child Rosie was carrying when she died. We still don't know whose they are."

"Except it wasn't Mike."

"No, it wasn't Mike."

"What about the other names Ethan gave us? I take it they've also been eliminated?"

"We got voluntary DNA samples from 90 per cent of them, none of which threw up a match. Nobody's looking any longer. There's not much point with both of the Wilsons dead and the case closed."

"What about other DNA samples?" Izzy asked. "I take it Davis's presence at the B&B was confirmed?"

"From samples taken out of the shower drain, for both of them."

"And the other cases – are they all closed?"

"In the process of being shut down. There was some discussion about the theory of a killer for hire, but someone from the Brighton force got in touch to tell us this Marty Goss is considered a flake by everyone down there. Claims the man went off the rails when he retired. Too much dope. The surviving husbands in the other cases were re-interviewed, of course, but none are under suspicion. It had to be done, but it feels wrong to bring everything up again after so long."

"So that's it?" Izzy said. "The killer's dead, and even if we know nothing about him, he won't take any more footpaths looking for someone to cut up."

"Yes, that's it," said Harry Gray. "You've been through a lot, Izzy. I checked, and you still have over five weeks of unclaimed leave. I'd suggest you take some of it."

"Maybe I will. I want to put in for five days if I can. I want to visit my mum. She called the other day and sounded upset on the phone."

"I don't see that being an issue. The investigation is over, and now it's just a case of ensuring everything is tied up tight." Harry drained his bottle and set it down. "Enjoy your dinner. You can request the leave online, and I'll get it approved. Did you know Jack asked for a week as well? He's going fishing in Scotland."

Izzy laughed. "I thought he was joking about the fishing."

"See, even you can get it wrong sometimes. Have a good time with your mum, Izzy. Where does she live, down south?"

"Cheshire. New build in a small town, where the footballers haven't yet pushed prices out of reach."

Harry Gray smiled and stood. He held his hand out, and Izzy shook it.

"Take care, Izzy. See you in a couple of weeks."

When he was gone, Izzy sat again and looked at the garden, the food in front of her forgotten. She thought about her mother, and wondered what she wanted to see her about.

She wanted to talk to Jack about Harrington's approach when he returned from his leave. Jack was always the voice of reason.

Abi had been returned to the Bowmans, and her adoption was finalised. She had even heard that Grace might be adopted by Rosie Wilson's sister, who had three kids of her own. She was farming stock, like Rosie, and talk was she would be taking over Caxton Farm.

Izzy thought about Frank Davis, or whoever he was, and what lay behind his actions.

Once she returned from Cheshire, she'd talk with Priya to find out what she had uncovered, and maybe discuss what else could be unearthed.

Izzy sat until the stars appeared, then went inside and brought a shawl out, so she could watch them wheel across the sky. A shooting star cut the dark. She smiled and made a wish, knowing she could never tell anyone what it was.

AUTHOR NOTE

I would like to thank a number of people who have greatly assisted me in making the writing of *The Murder Trail* as authentic as possible. I won't name them, as several still currently work in the police, the forensic service, and social services. They will know who they are, and I cannot thank them enough.

The next book in the Izzy Wilde series, *A Lethal Kinship*, will appear in 2024.

For those of my readers who follow the Thomas Berrington Historical Mysteries, book 4 of the Tudor series, *The Beasts of the City*, will also appear in 2024.

ALSO BY DAVID PENNY

The Izzy Packer Crime Thrillers

The Murder Trail

———

The Thomas Berrington Historical Mysteries

The Red Hill

Breaker of Bones

The Sin Eater

The Incubus

The Inquisitor

The Fortunate Dead

The Promise of Pain

The Message of Blood

A Tear for the Dead

———

The Thomas Berrington Tudor Mysteries

Men of Bone

A Death of Promise

The Hidden Dead

———

The Thomas Berrington Prequels

A Death of Innocence

———

The Thomas Berrington Bundles

Purchase 3 full-length novels for less than the price of two.

Thomas Berrington Books 1-3

The Red Hill

Breaker of Bones

The Incubus

Thomas Berrington Books 4-6

The Incubus

The Inquisitor

The Fortunate Dead

Thomas Berrington Books 7-9

The Promise of Pain

The Message of Blood

A Tear for the Dead

Unit-13: WWII Paranormal Spy Thrillers

An Imperfect Future

Printed in Great Britain
by Amazon

34115973R00280